Fourteen years ago, Storm Tera failed to save the world. Born a prophecy child, foretold to save magic, he went into war untrained, unprepared and lost everything. Ever since, he's been in self-exile, turning his back on magic as it grows and festers inside of him, unused and unwanted.

Then a young witch makes an offer he can't refuse: to go back in time and undo the mistakes that led to his failure. They have one chance to rewrite the past, to save everyone he lost, and ultimately...to save magic.

Storm is about to play a game of cat and mouse with time and the Fates. Necromancy is in his blood, but if he can't find a way to prevent the death of Rowan Copry, he can say goodbye to magic, and life as he knows it, forever.

THE DEATH OF

ROWAN COPRY

Elaine White

A NineStar Press Publication
www.ninestarpress.com

The Death of Rowan Copry

First Edition, October 2024

ISBN: 978-1-64890-806-4

Also available in eBook, ISBN: 978-1-64890-805-7

CONTENT WARNING:

This book contains graphic violence, mentions of parental death, death by magic, mentions of off-page child neglect, cursed secondary character, mentions of dementia/Alzheimer's, mentions of magically assisted death, resurrection, mentions of secondary character's forced marriage.

To all those who dream of rewriting the past.

Chapter One

August 1, 2040

WAKING IN A bed of tangled sheets, coated in sweat, was nothing new for Storm. Every night of the last fourteen years had been predictable, from the racing heartbeat and the slow-fading memories, to the shaking of his right hand every time he reached for a cigarette. He took his first puff, raked a hand through his hair, and swung his legs out from under the thin sheet.

Storm walked into the bathroom and started the shower. Eyeing the mirror, the inevitable awaited: black smoke as dark as his magic swirled in his eyes, tempting him to delve into the darkest of powers, a birthright no one had bothered to teach him. If he'd known how to wield forbidden magic, he wouldn't have spent his adult life having night sweats and nightmares, all because the

Fates were bickering bitches.

The thin line along his top lip suggested he was dehydrated. His tawny skin showed paler than usual, meaning he could add anaemia or vitamin deficiencies to his worries. That was all part of living in the West of Scotland, he supposed: sea air and lack of sunshine. Pushing aside the long fringe of his raven hair, he wondered if the time had come to move somewhere new, less conducive to invisibility. If he wasn't careful, he'd fade for real.

Ignoring the temptation to test his untapped abilities, Storm showered to wash off the shakes, sweat, and lingering memories of the worst night of his life. He dressed in the invisibility of a white T-shirt, black jeans, and a black leather jacket, the same thing everyone else wore in this neck of the woods who came here to disappear. There was a reason he lived above a biker bar, miles from the nearest town, deep in the heart of the woodlands. The storms were turbulent here by the sea, and most witches knew better than to settle where magic was at its wildest.

Storm was safer living far from other magic users, friends and enemies alike. He'd come here to escape the world of magic, laws and backstabbing, and the politics of guardians, gods, and elements. Running didn't exorcise his demons. He took them everywhere he went. If anyone was desperate enough to seek him out, they knew where to find him. The wind could tell them if they had the sense to listen.

He didn't bother with keys or a wallet as he left the apartment and descended the steps. Wards carved into the wooden door frame kept everyone out. His bar tab was paid at the end of every month, when he got his pathetic human salary from the docks, and Storm kept strict control of his vices and exit strategies.

Magic coursed through his veins like a torrent of the most volatile cyclone. Nothing calmed the raging heat and hate beneath his skin like working on the docks, unloading the fishing boats. The movement, the lack of a routine, and never knowing what tomorrow would bring was the unpredictability his soul craved, the freedom and life of a drifter, with no job, boss, or family to tie him down.

On solid ground, with nothing but compacted earth and weeds beneath his black boots, he stopped. Storm tipped his head to the sky and basked in what the world could tell him. Rain was coming; not an unfamiliar warning in this area, promising not to be heavy or dangerous. He mentally pushed the warning aside and moved on to the next. The wind wanted him to know magic was in the air, someone powerful approaching from the west. He'd suspect someone was passing through, coming for his help, but the wind seemed unsure. When Storm stuck his tongue out, the first drop of rain brought little clarity. *Something* was coming. A deeply buried instinct screamed *Beware! Nosy. Too curious.* Whoever was on their way, the rain thought they should mind their own business.

Around Halloween, curious kids would drift through town in hopes of seeing the crackpot Storm Tera: prophesied Chosen One, mage of the elements and earth. Too early in the year for that, he wondered what was hunting him and why they made the wind nervous.

Storm mused over what was coming, wondering if they would be brave enough to approach or if he'd get to keep his peace for another day. Hopefully, the latter.

He went into the bar beneath his apartment, ignoring the stale air and sticky floor to focus on the familiar hints of hops and cigar smoke. The latter came from the old man in the corner, a permanent fixture since Storm moved here three years ago.

He smiled, remembering the first time the man had spoken to an invisible companion. Storm had tapped into his powers, wondering if a spirit, demon or creature was toying with the man, but there had been nothing.

Storm caught the bartender's eye. He gave a nod of greeting and took the centre stool at the bar like always. No one spoke to him; they never did. The bartender tended to flirt late at night when Storm was leaving. He'd get that look in his big blue eyes, tip his head in curiosity and wait for Storm to make the first move. He never did, never would.

How could he explain the nightmares that plagued him each night? No ordinary person, those who lacked even the simplest magical gifts, would understand the black mist clouding his eyes whenever he felt too strongly, all because he didn't know how to suppress the darkness in his veins.

Settled in his stool, Storm tapped out a cigarette and used Ithen's old lighter for his second smoke of the night. At barely after midnight, he'd only left the bar a few hours ago but no one would remark on his return. They never did.

A glass of scotch appeared along with a tentative smile. When he didn't react, except to lift his glass and take a drink, the bartender moved on, knowing better than to hover.

A lesson he wished the rest of the world would learn.

*

TWO SCOTCHES LATER, Storm glanced at his watch as the hairs on his arm rose in warning. He'd been here for thirty minutes, impatient for someone to make an appearance.

"Why don't you start talking?" Storm said aloud, refusing to give the mysterious presence the recognition of turning. If they planned to hover behind him, they better get to the point.

Three seconds, three staccato heartbeats, and the click-clack of shoes brought them to his right side. A young girl leaned her forearms against the bar as she clasped her hands and heaved a sigh. "I can't believe I found you."

Storm rolled his eyes. He should have known better than to hope the entity the elements warned him of would be passing by. He glared at the girl who stood by his stool. She had black hair, a single electric blue strand on one side, tucked behind an ear that was pierced along the top ridge. Her nose ring glinted in the light reflecting off the bar bottles, and her face turned ashen white at his stare. "Whoever sent you, go home and tell them to piss off. I'm not interested."

The girl reached into the pocket of her cropped leather jacket and slammed a ring onto the counter: the ring he'd ripped off his finger as he'd walked away from the massacre fourteen years ago, thrown into the flames to forever be forgotten; the ring that symbolised everything that made him the Chosen One.

"You need to return to your coven and fix this." The girl held onto her anger until the door squeaked open and a single crow's caw made her flinch.

Storm smiled at the message that resonated loud and clear. "Fix what?" he asked, taking another puff of his cigarette as he rolled the crow's words over in his mind.

Leave. Run. Ithen.

The last word stung, but he wondered how one caw had translated into three individual, separate commands that the crow thought Storm needed to acknowledge. Why would those words make the girl flinch?

"You're the Chosen One. You could have prevented this," she said with obvious desperation, laying the blame at his feet.

He wouldn't deny things had changed the night of the massacre. Storm had committed his first and last murder, and the covens had fallen apart. No longer with a founding family to follow or protect them, they'd splintered across the globe, putting entire countries between the few families left who cherished the old ways.

"Be specific. By 'this' do you mean magic?" Storm asked, taking a punt at the reason she'd come here. He'd sacrificed the Copry coven and refused the request by the mages and witches left after the war to form a new coven. Without him, they lacked a leader. "The world is better off without magic. Makes life a fairer playing field," he said, wishing he'd known that before one of his closest friends died because he was human and had no ability to meet the Coprys in a fair fight.

"We have the power to send you back," the girl whispered, leaning closer and darting her gaze around the bar, as if afraid someone might hear. Even if they did, Storm doubted they'd care or understand. The bartender had a touch of magic, an empath, and the old man in the corner stank of rotten magic never tamed. Everyone else was too drunk to notice.

Storm was the last of his line, the last Tera—the earth coven—after everyone in his family had died due to the complications of dark magic. The joke was that they'd been hated by the other covens since they first discovered their talent for the forbidden arts. If magic hadn't wiped them out, Storm didn't doubt the other covens would have. Yet they expected him to lead them?

"Tell us when the prophecy fell apart, and we can change everything! We can stop this from happening," she said, the heat in her voice suggesting a personal stake beyond reclaiming magic.

Storm evaluated her out of the corner of his eye. He hadn't eradicated magic, only levelled the playing fields by taking out the most powerful coven, the Coprys. Four other covens remained, and they kept out of his way. Tapping out a new cigarette, Storm imagined the impossible and wondered when the tide had turned against them. When Denver died? When Cesa Copry found the amulet to boost his coven's powers? When the bastard accidentally killed his son with a curse meant for Storm? When Ithen died?

Storm could bring Ithen back, stop Cesa from getting the amulet, and stop Denver, Foley, and even Rowan from dying. He'd have to go far back, to before he botched his training, before he came into his powers. He'd need to have his memories to make this mean something. Without them, he wouldn't know what to do differently.

Could he change anything? The Fates had all the power. If this was how they'd determined his life should go, there was no fighting, no changing his destiny, or denying them their pound of flesh. The Fates were the queens of magical power. Beyond the elements, and light and dark magic, there was no other more powerful...not even the Chosen One. Not wanting to miss a golden opportunity to stick it to the hags who had given him this shitty life, Storm gave in. He led the girl to a table in a quieter corner of the bar. If she had a way to send him back to where this prophecy shit started, he'd hear her out. Once he was seated in the wooden chair and placed his scotch on the table, Storm gave her the signal to talk.

Sliding into the booth opposite and brushing her long fringe over the top of her head, she introduced herself: "I'm Grace. Grace Glade."

"Ah." Bloody-minded and stubborn as hell, Grandma Glade

had taken Storm in when his parents died. She said the Fates were foolhardy to let him walk the world without guidance, so she took him home and taught him what she knew. A white witch, one of light and goodness, she never knew the dark magic he needed to win the war, but few knew the dark arts like his family.

Her name was a blast from a past he'd rather forget. Gladys Glade—Seer, Woman of the Waters—her power was second only to his, as far as Storm was aware. She'd been out of the country the night Cesa Copry used the amulet to boost his power. They'd been thrust into a world of uncertainty and chaos, forcing Storm to step into a position he wasn't ready for. If she'd been there, Gladys would have stood by his side and helped him hold the tide of cursed Coprys. Storm bet ten to one she had the same regrets he did. He could see her now, rushing to the woods outside his little shack where he lived alone, hoping she'd arrived in time, terrified by the wave of power and the tipping of the balance.

Averting his gaze to the slow-filling bar, Storm wondered what Gladys thought after she walked through the massacre he'd left behind. Was she ashamed? Did she understand what he'd done and his reasons?

By the looks of the waif, Grace was Gladys's granddaughter. She had the same stubborn look in her eyes that swore she wouldn't leave unless Storm went with her, the same force of nature batting at his magic. She must be an untrained seer if the trickle of contact meant what he thought.

Good luck to her. Gladys was the only one who had ever read

his mind, his cards and his future. No other seer or reader, no matter how talented, could bear the burden. A girl in his high school had read his tarot cards once, but her hand kept shaking when she tried to turn his future card. Storm had taken pity on her and done it himself. He'd never told anyone what the card was, not even Gladys.

The Ten of Swords marked the lowest point of his life with nowhere to go but up; the Three of Swords signified rejection and betrayal; and the Tower meant disaster and groundbreaking change in circumstances. They should have been a foreboding three-card spread for the girl, but they'd soon found that two cards had been stuck together. Trapped beside the Tower was one further card that had the poor girl's hand shaking. Storm turned over a reversed Ten of Wands and knew there was no hiding from his fate. Signifying a failure to delegate and a breakdown, the card only added to the reading that blatantly warned of a life-changing event likely to end in regret and failure. None of that could be a coincidence when he was yet to face the final war that changed his life.

Storm wondered if he could go back in time far enough to undo that reading, but that had been two years before the war and there was only so much he was willing to risk.

"Grandma Gladys said you would remember her," Grace said with a glimmer of hope.

She must be a novice witch because Storm had learned before the age of ten that Gladys was *always* right. "She never was any good at staying out of other people's business," Storm remarked.

Grace huffed and tossed her hair over her shoulder. "Grandma says she was practically your mother so it *is* her business to poke around in yours."

That was exactly what Gladys would say, though she'd give less attitude and a slap to the back of his head. Unable to resist, Storm levelled her with a hard stare and set his glass on the table. "What exactly is wrong with this world?" he asked, needing to hear her stake in this. "I eradicated the crooks: the guys using their power to make everyone else look like kids playing games, the guys on a path to destruction. I did what I had to do and fulfilled the prophecy—saving the world from power-hungry madmen with magic."

"You disrupted the balance," Grace replied, the words rolling off her tongue with the weight of truth. "You left witches without the balance to safely practice their magic. The elementals are literally losing their minds without contact with magic, and my brother has been chosen to fix your mistake!"

Normally he'd have smart words for her, a warning that payback was a bitch, that karma was kicking the Glades in the ass for not dragging themselves away from their cushy life to help him, but the thought of anyone else being chosen made him bristle.

"Excuse me?"

"Grandma read his cards. The Fates are putting him on the same path they sent you, hoping he'll succeed where you failed,"

Grace revealed, her tone laden with sadness and regret, and a flash of an image Storm was sure she didn't intentionally share.

She was strong, potentially the next matriarch, though currently only fifteen or sixteen. The image came through loud and clear and set Storm's teeth on edge. Her brother was fourteen at a push and far younger than Storm had been when he faced that hellish day.

"I don't know who your brother is but he's not my family, and he's not a necromancer. He *can't* fulfil the prophecy," Storm argued, because there were only two ways to fulfil the prophecy: being a Tera and being a necromancer. Storm was the last of both.

"Exactly. He's destined to repeat your failure," Grace shouted, her voice loud enough to attract attention. The moment her control snapped, Storm raised his hand in a dismissive wave, and a quick silencing charm surrounded their table. "He'll fail and lose everything, maybe even his life, all because you're too scared to fix what you broke!"

Now he knew her reasons and why Gladys had sent her. They were breaking the rules, stomping on the covenant between witches, mages, and the Fates.

One lesson he'd learned from Gladys was that time belonged to the Fates. No one messed with time without their permission, and to ask required a necromancer. Death was the bargain made while resurrection would allow them to perform the spell if the Fates approved, and if they didn't...well, the necromancer wouldn't be needed.

"How?" Storm wondered, reminding the girl she'd told him to *fix* the past.

Her breathing calmed and she lifted her gaze, blazing with anger. "Stop resisting who you are. Become the dark power you were always meant to be."

Yeah, the same old shit. She needed to be more specific, but after the bombshell she'd dropped, he wasn't ready to get snarky. He needed to think clearly. "How do you know that going back will change anything?"

Grace reached with her right hand, hesitating with a jingle of multi-coloured bangles before touching his hand. The image she sent was intentional and clear, showing Storm a vision of himself at Adam's Grove, his favourite place to think and clear his mind. Sitting on the grass, Denver and Foley were nearby laughing, I then sat by his side with a hand on his thigh, and Rowan lounged in the grass, though he'd never been a part of their friendship circle. Storm had been afraid to make friends with him, being a Copry son and a forbidden crush, and it remained one of his biggest regrets.

The vision was everything he'd wanted when the war was over: peace in place of death.

He didn't need to ask, nor did he need to know where she'd taken those images from, since all his nightmares started as dreams and ended in blood, death, and blame.

She was a seer: Grace Glade, the next matriarch, the Girl of the Gales. Her talent was more forced than Gladys's but strong, powerful. and unshakable. Whatever Grace set her mind to would fall into her lap because she was a bulldozer, a true believer in the Fates and their powers, a girl hell-bent on wielding her power to get what she wanted.

Instead of questioning him, Grace set her jaw and gave a brief nod. "Grandma has found a spell to send you back, under the blood moon. Tomorrow—" She paused and shook her head, her eyes closing in pain. "—tomorrow our matriarch will pass on to her next existence, and we'll have lost our chance. Without her, we don't have the power, and I wasted months trying to find you after your last disappearing trick. Don't waste this last chance to change your life...and save the world."

Chapter Two

STORM HAD BECOME good at walking away, damned proficient, but not this time. He had the chance to change everything, to undo every regret, to get one night's sleep without nightmares, to make sure those nightmares never had to exist.

Storm paid his bar tab in full, dug his truck out of the garage beside the bar, packed everything he owned into a single duffel bag, and left a note at the bar for any of the guys from the docks who might want to hire him come Monday.

He wouldn't be back.

He couldn't face returning to this place. If Gladys's spell failed, if he ended up in the same situation with the same nightmare behind him, he'd find somewhere else to live. Somewhere with crashing waves, inaccessible for 80 percent of the year, where no one would find him.

Storm didn't mind the long drive ahead, despite facing hours on the road. He needed the time to think about Denver and Foley, about Ithen and how the war started, and how his life as the Chosen One had ended. He could think about the life he could have, erasing his past and building a new future, if he managed to change his fate.

The coincidental timing of Grace finding him on the last night before their time ran out to perform the spell meant something. When Grace said Gladys was dying, he almost shivered at the intense war of emotions that swelled inside him: anger that she wouldn't be around anymore, guilt for walking away, mortification at what she must have thought of his final actions on the night of the war, and an unfathomable sense of relief that only compounded his shame. He couldn't understand why he would be glad to see the back of the woman who had raised him for more years than his parents ever had.

The prophecy had been clear about his fate, about the weight of free will, and the importance of his powers. Magic had never lied, but Storm knew something was hidden amongst the words that could change the course of the war if only interpreted differently this time.

While Grace slept in the passenger seat, a backpack at her feet, Storm drove north to the rolling hills of the Highlands and the clear waters of Loch Lomond. He cracked the driver's window open to let the salt air fill his lungs and the sounds of nature provide a soundtrack for their journey.

Fate awaited him. Whether he succeeded or failed a second time, he had a chance to make things go his way, the opportunity to save the people he loved and reverse the tidal wave of death that had transformed his life.

One damned prophecy—some scroll the Fates had woven into existence the night he was born to bind him to a task he had never been prepared for—was all that stood between Storm and a new, better life.

With blood of shadow and a heart of light, one shall be born under a storm of earth and wind. Master of elements, friend to the darkness and commander of demons, he shall bring forth a new era of magic. The Chosen One will face a Great Battle where success will bring about a Golden Age of magic, but his failure will make him a harbinger of doom to all who possess the gift. The world of magic will prosper or fall by his hand. For he is the one who is the sum of all powers and without him, magic cannot survive.

Every word was seared into his brain, branded by time, pain, and grief. Whatever the words meant, Storm only had a few short hours to find new meaning in the prophecy that governed his fate.

*

STORM FELT THE tension in the air the moment he pulled the car into Gladys's driveway; the warning he wasn't wanted, the trees whispering the return of *the Dark One*.

Grace was still asleep when he put the vehicle in park and stepped out. They'd been on the road for three hours, from Stranraer to Loch Lomond, stopping only so Storm could sit in a lay-by, gripping the wheel as he talked himself out of turning around.

The door opened as he walked up the front path, and Gladys stood in the doorway. The woman was eighty and hadn't changed much in the intervening years, still tall enough to reach his shoulder. "Why does it always take the end of the world to get you to behave?"

He rolled his eyes, put a hand on her arm and guided her into the house. "It's five in the morning. You shouldn't be out in the chill air," he admitted, not sure he liked how unsure the wind had become since Grace arrived on his doorstep.

Gladys folded her arms, stubbornly refusing to sit. "What has the wind been telling you?"

"Not much. You know better than anyone how connected I am to the elements, especially when they're in turmoil. Something has stirred them up and they're scared."

The witches and mages thought he was a freak for how close he'd become to the elements, more than any elemental witch could manage. They'd never understood why the wind *chose* to talk to him. Why did the rain nourish and calm him when it was torrential and angry? Why could *he* walk through a tornado and feel nothing but a gentle breeze and a light mist of rain?

Storm still didn't fully understand but both sides respected the bond they'd made. He didn't need to know why to cherish the gift.

"You look dead on your feet. Go to your old room to sleep," Gladys said, rubbing his arm in reassurance before turning and walking away.

The house felt strange and smelled of cardamom, and the walls whispered secrets in a voice too faint and historic to make out. If Storm had mastered necromancy as the rest of his family had, he could tap into that magic, but the thought of speaking to the dead, of *raising* the dead had always frightened him.

He'd been born on the Day of the Dead—the holiday of his ancestors—and had an unnatural affinity for voices no one else could hear. The thought of encouraging that gift was more than he was ready for at eighteen. He'd shunned most of the traditional lessons, planning to learn when he was older, when he knew more about how to give and take equally.

Now he'd never know enough. Ithen had been the last to understand the intricacies of necromancy, an academic who had studied the dark texts but never physically practised. If he'd known how, he could have stopped everyone from dying.

Storm straightened the knitted blanket along the back of the sofa. He couldn't count how often he'd walked into this room and felt overwhelmed. The living area had always been the safest place in the house, where he could sleep in peace without the unseen whispering in his ear. To the left: a place for boots, coats, and the most conflicted area of the house, the most possessed, the darkest and most foul place he'd ever been.

Gladys never noticed. Storm wished he hadn't, but this house was old and full of *things*. Some ancient ancestor built the house when the country was new and young, putting his blood, sweat, and tears into every log, wall, and window. Storm could *feel* the history, the violence of the day, the danger, lingering in every inch.

A shiver racked his spine as he pushed the thought away. The path along the back of the sofa toward the kitchen, the wooden staircase on the left, and the garden beyond the kitchen that used to be his refuge were all familiar, yet not right. Maybe after he'd had some sleep, he'd go out to clear his mind, to get rid of the ghosts haunting this house.

Nothing in the old cabin-designed house had changed. Every stair continued to creak, and he walked into his old bedroom to find the only difference was one extra single bed on the wall by the door.

It was a tiny space for a growing boy, barely eight feet by eight, a box room with a single bed beneath the long window straight ahead. The old crate bedside table was how he'd left it, a single alarm clock and a paperback on top, his books still inside. Storm raised an eyebrow and crossed to his old bed, the sheets fresh but the same he'd last slept under. Gladys had been taking care of his room long after he moved out when he was fourteen. He'd told Gladys he was never coming back, so why the time capsule?

Although disturbing, there was a sense of comfort in finding everything as he'd left it. If everything was about to change, if he went back in time to change *everything* about his adult life, it was fitting to be surrounded by childhood familiarity first.

The kid lying in the other bed was asleep. He had the complete opposite colouring as Grace, albino white hair and a weaker jawline. Storm figured this was the brother, DJ, that she'd mentioned during the drive, the one cursed to a prophecy he could never fulfil, named after Gladys's son who had died young.

What the hell were the Fates thinking? DJ was small and fragile in a way Storm had never been.

Sighing his displeasure, he ditched his bag by the side of the bed and flopped onto the duvet to close his eyes. Knowing what needed to be done was one thing, but knowing DJ would face the consequences of his failure if he walked away was another.

He wasn't aware of when he fell asleep, he only knew something had changed. The dark things lurking in the house crept closer, the whispers giving way to screams, pleas, crying and bargaining, the same as with most other nights in this house long ago. He'd been better at blocking the sounds out then but was too tired to manage tonight.

The ghosts gave way to memories which morphed into a different cacophony of sights and sounds. The thought *of dying and finally being free,* when Cesa tossed a curse his way...seeing the horror on Rowan's face as he raced toward Cesa...the way the world held its breath as Rowan stepped in front of Storm and the curse hit. The rush of wind against his ears screamed a warning, telling him this was wrong, this wasn't right, and Storm caught Rowan's body as he fell in slow motion, while Cesa shouted his shock somewhere in the distance.

Magic made a vicious weapon, working through the human body and attacking the vital functions to ensure death. Even as Rowan lay in his arms, blood trickling from his mouth, muttering words he couldn't hear, Storm turned toward a scream that spoke of more pain than he'd ever experienced. Foley stood over Denver's prostrate body, shock written across his face as he fell to his knees and Storm realised Denver was dead.

Piecing together the facts as his mind and heart fled into panic, pain and confusion, he realised Cesa had thrown a death curse. The spell had hit Rowan, passed through him and hit Denver, both standing in a perfect line of motion, running to save his life.

One white witch, one human: both dead because Storm had failed.

Consciousness returned in a flash, without the sweating and the fight or flight response. Storm raked a hand through his hair as he fought the memories. A cough made him turn instinctively toward the door.

DJ sat up in bed, the duvet draped protectively across his lap, his eyes sad and face pale. "Does the house haunt your dreams too?"

Storm swore internally, wondering why Gladys kept him here if he was sensitive enough to hear the voices. Most seers couldn't connect to the abyss—the world between the living and dead, where spirits, demons, and magic lingered until called upon—but if DJ knew the house was haunted, he was at risk of more than bad dreams, as Storm had once been.

"No. My demons are personal." Storm sat up against the headboard, the familiar creak of the wooden base and the squeak of the mattress reminding him he was in the one place he swore he'd never come back to. Instead of lingering in his thoughts, he flashed DJ a smile. "The house is old and speaks to those who listen, hoping you'll help heal the pain," he explained, in case he hadn't reached that less than reassuring part of the deal. As though seeing and hearing ghosts wasn't bad enough, they thought anyone who could communicate with them should be responsible for their problems.

If DJ wasn't in the room, he'd give them the finger to remind them of the deal he'd made years ago: if they left him alone, he wouldn't blast them into the darkest parts of the abyss.

"Because the house has seen death," DJ whispered in understanding.

"The hazard of being old, I guess. How deeply do you feel the spirits?"

"What do you mean?"

Scratching the stubble he'd have to shave before he faced Gladys, Storm thought about how to phrase his concerns. "When you dream about the house, do you see the spirit world like a movie in your head? Are they distant, like a normal dream? Do you start to forget the minute you wake up?" The way DJ squinted thoughtfully, hand shaking as he toyed with a loose thread on his duvet, said he wasn't prepared to admit his dreams were different. "Or do you feel their presence in your bones, when you're dreaming? The pain, the fear that danger is lurking around the corner, waiting for you?"

DJ's green eyes widened, different to Grace's dark gaze, enough to suggest the translucence of the colour was due to a gift no one but Gladys knew of.

A faint creak drew their gaze to the doorway, where Gladys stood with an arched eyebrow, her arms folded over her chest. She'd changed into a black floor-length dress with a sweetheart collar and added the onyx jewellery passed from one matriarch to another. "Don't frighten the boy," she scolded, stepping into the room to brush a motherly hand over DJ's white hair.

Storm swung his legs over the edge of the bed and offered a placating smile. "Your house is freaking him out." Rising from the bed, he grabbed his bag and headed for the door, planning to wash in the bathroom at the end of the hall. "At least I'm willing to tell him the truth."

Gladys glared but didn't stop DJ from catching Storm's hand as he passed. Those big eyes stared and barely glanced in Gladys's direction. "I feel them in my bones. The house is in pain. If I don't help, the spirits will hurt me."

"DJ!" Gladys said the word, but her tone was undecided between panic and scolding. Did she think he was making this up, or was she afraid of who he was speaking to? The one who was willing to be honest and let him know this shit was normal.

Storm ignored her protests and eased DJ's hand off his. "The house will never hurt you. I feel them in my bones, too," he said because DJ needed to hear the words. "If you're not careful, the spirits *can* make you hurt yourself. You'll prick your finger on invisible splinters, trip or fall down the stairs for no reason." He'd done that more times than he could count, moving out at a young age to get away from the chaos and pain. "Be careful, be smart, and don't touch anything that freaks you out. Do *not* invite them in."

DJ nodded, so solemn and afraid his heart hurt. "How do I stop them?"

"Build a wall in your head and put the dark things behind it. When you go to sleep, build more of your wall to help you sleep in peace." Storm paused and glanced at Gladys, deciding to say the words aloud. He wished he'd been smart enough to maintain his wall over the years, but he hadn't needed one in so long. "If tonight goes to plan, you won't go to sleep tonight. You won't exist. You won't even be a thought in your mum's head yet and this house will haunt me instead."

DJ looked at Gladys with suspicion. "Okay."

Storm turned to leave, but DJ stopped him after only a step. "You can't let Rowan die."

"What did you say, sweetie?" Gladys asked, her sugary-sweet voice suggesting she was freaking out, and she'd never seen this side of DJ.

"Huh?" DJ rubbed his eye and blinked, his mouth opening to speak.

Storm raised his hand and twisted his wrist, sending the kid toward a sleep without dreams. When he flopped onto the bed, Gladys frowned, knowing who to blame for his unnatural sleep. He nodded toward the corner of the room where the shadows were the deepest. "Something is hovering. It's been watching my dreams...and his." What did the creature see in DJ's dreams to warn him that Rowan wasn't meant to die? "It's figured out what we're doing and trying to help."

"Why are *my* ghosts helping *you*?" Gladys asked, returning to the same grouchy woman who'd raised him but never coddled or doted on him the way she had with DJ. He wondered if that was enough of an explanation for DJ's obvious mistrust of the woman.

Storm spared her a glance as he walked toward the bathroom, pausing at the door to offer an honest answer. "Because you're dying and you're such an old bag you never told me?"

She had the grace to blush. "It was my business."

"Hmm, what did you say to Grace? You're basically my mother, so my business is your business? Doesn't that work the other way?" he asked, knowing she wouldn't agree. Storm shut the door on her silence, ran the shower, and prepared to freshen up. DJ's words clung to his bruised heart, troubling him. He didn't like how Gladys treated his gifts, dismissing his abilities and knew that if the past couldn't be changed DJ's only hope was for Storm to fix the problem before he left. Just in case.

*

STORM STEPPED OUT onto the porch to tip-tapping knitting needles. He leaned against the support post, opposite the swing chair Gladys occupied. He gazed at the garden, the colours more vivid in the early morning light.

Two hours of sleep would have to be enough; they needed to spend the rest of the day finalising the spell to perform at midnight, under the blood moon. "Why does DJ possess the sight? He's a white witch, a seer by birth, and shouldn't have that ability."

Gladys paused her knitting, avoiding him to gaze at her overgrown garden of white flowers. "He's a strong empath. I presume the spirits opened a previously unknown doorway," she theorised, unconcerned by what that was doing to DJ. She met his gaze and raised an eyebrow. "Curious that they'd tell you to save Rowan Copry, no?"

"No." The Gladys he used to know would understand, but he was beginning to realise he *didn't* know her as well as he thought. "Of everyone killed during the war, Rowan was the only one Cesa didn't hate or target. He'd give everything to save his son." He remembered the bargaining and pleading Cesa had done with the universe when Rowan died and would bet his life that Cesa regretted ever starting the war. If he'd known Rowan would sacrifice himself to save Storm's life, he may never have sent that killing spell. Storm dug cigarettes from his jeans pocket and lit one.

Grace emerged from the house and scrunched her nose. "Those things will kill you."

"Promise?" He flashed a grin, to remind her who she was dealing with: the necromancer, untrained though he was; the Dark One, the one who held the fate of magic in his hands. He wasn't afraid of death. Storm's biggest regret after losing the war and everyone he cared about was living on without them, each day meaning less without the people he loved most by his side.

Grace stomped into the house, leaving him to face Gladys's glare. "You can't spend the rest of your life grieving for silly boys who never loved you. Do this and you will discover your true fate."

He couldn't decide what irritated him more: the years he'd spent away from home, making his own decisions and guiding his own fate or the thought of being lectured by an old woman who was dying and pinning all her hopes on him.

He savoured his smoke—the last he was likely to enjoy in this timeline—and decided to prod. Everyone was being secretive about this spell Gladys had found, and he needed to know more before he let anyone screw with his past or present. "When I go back, will I have my memories? I need to make different choices to change the outcome of the war, so will I know what needs to be changed?"

"No." Gladys didn't mince her words, resting an appraising eye on him. "Your memories will be with you in your dreams. Whether you trust and learn from them will show us what your true fate is."

"Meaning?"

"If you trust them, your fate was always yours to decide. If you do not—"

"My fate was sealed from the start, and the Fates are royal bitches." He nodded his understanding. Even now, he was at the mercy of the bloody Fates.

Gladys nodded and continued the annoying click-clacking knitting needles. "I've imprinted words into the spell to ground you to the time, allowing your mind to focus on choosing your destination. The words will remain in your head, cementing your memories of the past until you return to the moment you choose. Whenever you hear the words, you'll get flashes of memories from the past."

"The future."

The clicking stopped for a blessed moment as Gladys raised an eyebrow. "Excuse me?"

"If I'm *in* the past, any memories will be from my future. *If* you want to be technical." He wasn't being an infuriating shit, but he wanted to be correct and precise because all spells required focused intention. If they made a mistake, he'd go nowhere or get lost in the In-Between—the place where lost spirits dwelt and no witch ever wanted to go. Unlike the abyss, which was a neutral place, anyone who ventured into the In-Between by accident was stuck there. No one could find their way out without help, and that usually required someone being aware they were trapped there which seldom happened.

"I don't."

Storm ignored her pissy attitude for now. He'd say something later if needed, when the rest of the Glade coven had gathered to offer their strength to the ceremony. "What are the words?"

"Denver. Foley. Ithen. Storm."

"How original." The names haunted him enough in this life, that he figured karma was making sure he'd take them back to his past. "I better not get a flash of memories every time I hear those words. At least take out my name," he insisted, refusing to explain to everyone in his past why he was acting weird and had persistent headaches.

"No making changes!" Gladys snapped, more of a cranky bitch now than she'd ever been. This whole dying thing hadn't mellowed the old grouch. "Though I wonder if I should have included Rowan." She tutted and returned to the knitting she was making a mess of. "No matter. You'll figure it out or you won't."

"Awfully reassuring. It's not like the fate of magic, four lives, and my future rely on this going well or anything."

Gladys rose from her seat, smacked him on the head and headed into the house, silently refusing to admit she was cold, while tugging her shawl around her neck.

Storm knew better than to follow. Gladys hated anyone smoking in her house, and he could deal with the cold long enough to wait. He'd finish his smoke, think about what she'd said, and gather the guts to challenge her inaccuracies in front of her entire coven.

If he intended to mess with time and the Fates, he wouldn't

go by half measures or garbled spells. This had to be done right or not at all, and someone of Gladys's age and power should know better.

So why was she the one making all the mistakes?

Chapter Three

STORM WHILED AWAY the hours pretending to play chess with DJ. For every move, he offered advice about how to block out the voices, how to placate them when the ghosts wouldn't leave and techniques on how to help friendly spirits pass on, if he was brave enough to try. Since no one else was teaching DJ about his unusual ability, Storm figured he should.

Grace avoided him, convinced her ability would help during the ceremony, but Storm guessed Gladys would bear the real weight of the spell. If Grace did anything, she'd be learning from her matriarch, and Storm was selfishly relieved that he would either be in the past or unconscious whenever Gladys kicked the bucket and was gone from his life forever.

Storm savoured the final taste of his last cigarette. In a few minutes, when the moon hit the right spot in the sky, they'd perform the ceremony, and he would be eighteen. When the cigarette was done, he ground it into the ashtray on the porch wall and pushed away from his perch.

Gladys was doing something with salt, muttering to Grace about the proper etiquette of the spell. DJ had asked to be excused, preferring to sit in the field of white flowers with his back to the ceremony. With the whole Glade coven gathered—three families of grandparents, parents and their children—power lingered in the area. Whatever the outcome, Storm would face it like a Tera. He was done running from the past. This time, he would dive in head-first.

Stepping over the threshold of mason jars full of Christmas lights, Storm offered Gladys a raised eyebrow for the theatrics. He was surprised they weren't candles or other Hollywood shit.

"These eyes aren't what they used to be," she said, glancing around to make sure no one else was listening. Gladys grabbed his arm and urged him into the centre of the circle the jars had created.

Storm stepped into the perfect central position as Gladys stepped away to accept a book from Grace.

"Keep your mind focused on what point of time you want to return to," Gladys called out as the rest of the coven took their place, one to each of the mason jars. "The coven will speak the spell, and I will repeat your focus words. If I falter, Grace will continue without me. You need to focus on the timeline. Repeat the time and date to yourself," she advised, despite having been through the plan a dozen times during the day.

The waiting had been the worst part, knowing what needed to be done but having to wait for the coven to arrive, for the moon to rise and everything to come into place.

Storm stood in place and focused his mind. "Take me to the night of my eighteenth birthday." That was when this started, when he came into his power, decided what magic to learn and began his training. If they had any chance of making this work and changing fate, he had to undo everything that followed that night: the fighting, the training, the lack of dedication he'd put into his magic. He had to relearn everything and hope to hell it worked.

Gladys walked the circle, weaving magic in her wrinkled hands with every step. "The gods who gave us the Fates...the gods who created this dark being...lend us your hand, your power, your will and send him to the night of his ascension. Send him back in time. Break the laws of the Fates and help us save those who come after us," she said, her voice strong and unwavering for the first time during his short visit.

A crackle of white light appeared between the hands that twisted and formed the spell with light. "Allow him to fulfil the prophecy that will save us...you...and magic. Give us one chance to right this grievous wrong, and pray he can make a change worthy of your sacrifice."

Storm's words faltered as dark clouds swept in from the west, the wind rushing to his ears with whispers of "*magic*" *and* "*gods*" and a suggestion of the Fates' anger. A drop of rain splashed onto his forehead, offering peace and replenishment, promising to wipe the slate clean and start anew. Storm managed his first smile in hours. The rain had come to cleanse this place, to accompany Gladys home when the spell was over, to wash away the dark magic woven in his palms. He hadn't tapped into his magic consciously, but as always, the black mist in his veins responded to the storm and Gladys's words.

"Keep going," Gladys shouted, until her coven chanted Latin words asking for all she'd spoken, in a language the gods understood. While they took over—looking ridiculously un-witch-like in their jeans, cable sweaters and work clothes—Gladys gave Grace a nod and the two began the last part of the spell.

"Denver. Foley. Ithen. Storm."

Closing his eyes, he cemented them into his brain, drawing a mental image of each boy as their name was spoken, focusing on what time and place he wanted to appear. If the spell went to plan, he'd come out the abyss during November second at ten o'clock at night, just as the ceremony of his ascension was starting. The worst case was that he'd step from the abyss just as his past self was leaving the same hallowed place after gaining his full powers, marking the end of the ascension ceremony rather than the beginning.

Either way, Storm had a chance to make things right. If he arrived at any time other than an hour previous or post his ascension, he was screwed.

"Denver. Foley. Ithen. Storm."

The power beneath his skin prickled with heat in an unspoken demand to be used or released. The storm brewed above, violent and angry as the rain poured, soaking them from head to toe. When Storm would normally be exempt from the effects of the rain that had always been a friend, he was drenched in seconds along with everyone else.

Gladys blinked the water from her eyes as calmly as he did, ignoring the weather to focus on her words. Around her, the coven faltered, their voices growing weak with cold or fear. If they weren't careful, they would add an unexpected layer of fear to the spell that could ruin their intention.

The thunder rumbled loud enough to drown them out and a flash of lightning split the moon in the sky. Grace squealed and rushed to cower behind a woman who must have been her mother. Lacking her voice, her power, Gladys faltered.

Storm curled his hands into fists and closed his eyes tight. "Denver. Foley. Ithen. Storm." A breath, a beat, a roll of thunder and the chanting began again. "Take me to the day of my ascension," he said, adapting his previous chant due to the time constraint. He couldn't do both chants and be precise; they didn't have the time. Half an hour would see the end of the moon's peak and the close of the magical window.

Their voices blended in the night, Storm's strong and insistent, while Gladys sounded weak and tired. The words became a mantra, spoken over and over again until they were perfectly in sync.

Storm could feel the spell weakening. If they didn't get another boost of power soon, this would end with nothing more to show for their efforts than a raging thunderstorm. Storm didn't realise how badly he wanted this to work until a quiet voice repeated the chant; a sweeping voice with not an ounce of demand or violence, yet the entire world responded. The storm sucked in a breath, paused for a split second and broke abruptly, leaving DJ standing beside Gladys, taking her hand with a warm smile. His words grew in strength and power as his voice joined theirs.

"Denver. Foley. Ithen. Storm."

Storm nodded to the brave kid, though DJ seemed embarrassed by the recognition. Bolstered by the tangible effect of his added power, all three voices grew louder, stronger, until they were shouting into a now calm sky: "Denver. Foley. Ithen. Storm."

"Take me to the day of my ascension," he added, needing the specific command to get him to the place he was needed.

The words rolled through his mind, in thought, in voice; Gladys's voice pleading due to her weakened state; DJ shouting the words with a command the sky would gladly obey.

Storm held his breath, hoping and praying they'd done this right. This was his last chance to be the Chosen One, not the screw-up he'd become.

*

STORM WAS ENVELOPED in darkness, the strength of DJ's will sending him into the abyss: the dark place, the home of necromancy. There was no better confirmation that phase one had worked than standing here, surrounded by endless night.

A sharp-tipped talon dragged along his shoulder blade, and Storm shivered, closing his eyes to avoid seeing what creature was approaching. The touch brought a memory unbidden to the forefront of his mind, of being twelve years old and watching talon-tipped fingers creep over the edge of his bed in the middle of the night. Untrained as he was, he hadn't understood what they were asking, knowing only that they wanted to latch onto him. He had some vague sense that the demon needed to feed on his strength and would give him everything his heart desired.

Thank the gods he'd been too terrified to agree.

Those nights still haunted him but not as badly as the night he lost the war. Storm pushed the image aside, not knowing whether he'd conjured the demon with his thoughts and fears or if they'd been waiting until he was weak enough to offer anything for their power.

Another scrape of the talon flicked against his hand by his side. He instinctively looked to see if the contact had left a mark and saw the door he needed, a shimmer of magic in the nothingness of the dark. He almost thanked the demon for the guidance, but prudence made him bite his tongue. Nothing good ever came from being grateful to a demon, and he wasn't interested in getting involved in a pact or trade.

Storm kept his mouth shut and looked around, searching for a path to the doorway. More shapes moved in the darkness, indecipherable one minute, a bloody scar, withered hand or a sneer barely visible the next. The doorway seemed far away and close, the distance indistinct in the darkness. Storm crouched to touch the surface he stood on, solid and secure but invisible to the eye. He traced his fingertips across the platform, using both hands to find an edge to guide him. Two side steps and he may have fallen off the ledge by accident. Bloody demon.

Scrunching his nose against the deep-seated fear of heights he'd never confided to anyone, Storm closed his eyes and slipped his right leg over the edge.

He didn't want to do this, but he wasn't staying here in limbo. Shuffling around, he held on to the ledge with both hands and swung his legs over the edge. He maintained a death grip, wondering what would happen if he fell into the nothingness; would he disappear and cease to exist, or would he fall for an endless eternity, never to find ground again?

This was too important to fail now.

"One," he counted, shaking his head at the thought of what he was about to do. "Two." He eased his grip on the ledge and took one final breath to calm his nerves. "Thr—" Storm let go before he'd finished the word, knowing if he got to the end of three, there would be a four and a ten and a never-ending cycle of doubt. He let go mentally and physically, falling through the depths of the abyss, hopefully heading toward the door leading to his past.

Chapter Four

Fourteen Years Ago
November 2, 2026

A HEADACHE THE size of Texas beat at his skull. Realising he was lying on grass, Storm pushed against the ground and attempted to sit up, confused and disorientated. The last he remembered he'd been sitting on a blanket in the field at his little shack, preparing for the ceremony to ascend to his true powers. He lifted his right wrist to glance at his watch, relieved the date and time showed it hadn't been long since he last looked.

A strange swirling churned his gut, a hungry, desperate feeling that clawed at his insides. His magic had woken, demanding something he couldn't interpret. Storm needed to get somewhere safe, familiar, then visit Gladys and figure out what had happened to make him feel unsettled in his own skin.

For now, he focused on trying not to vomit.

"What in the Mother happened to you?"

Startled by the low, deep voice, he looked up to find Rowan standing over him. Without conscious thought, words fell from his mouth in utter panic: "I can't let them kill you."

Rowan's smirk morphed into a scrunch of eyebrows, then descended into a chuckle. He tipped his head to the sky and muttered to the elemental gods. The unfortunate tip of his head when he glanced at Storm gave a crystal clear view of startling cornflower blue eyes. Damn him. Storm had always had a thing about eyes, the supposed window to the soul. If that were true, Rowan needed to be scrubbed in vinegar because Storm had only ever been captivated and confused by the swirling depth of Rowan's eyes that kept so many secrets.

"Good to know. Who is trying to kill me?" Rowan asked, folding his arms over his chest. That look grated against the barrier Storm had long ago erected against Rowan's power to spellbind him with a glance.

Storm pushed those thoughts aside, as he always did, to focus on the question. "I don't know. I don't think—" Why couldn't he find the words or the thoughts to make sense of what he'd said? He had no choice but to ignore the warning, refusing to give any Copry—no matter how pretty—the knowledge that pieces of his memory were missing. "What are you doing here?"

Squinting in concern, Rowan unfolded his arms and

crouched to get within a comfortable eye level, apparently aware Storm wasn't capable of standing. "Do you know where *here* is?" he asked, reaching for Storm's forehead.

He'd normally swat the hand away, but the warmth was soothing and comforting against his skin. "Nope." Those blue eyes evaluated him while Rowan absently nibbled on his lower lip, drawing Storm's distracted mind straight to his mouth.

Storm let his gaze rake over Rowan for a different reason, surprised the son of his arch-nemesis didn't appear to be in his usual mood. Something sad and deeply buried held him at a distance from his magic, and he was dressed differently: in black trousers, an off-white shirt and black suspenders. Gods be damned, the man looked like he'd stepped from a 1920s Hollywood movie, a vision he'd never expected to see, never mind anticipated could make his heart race. Rowan's hair was perfectly placed but no matter how good he looked or how much the style suited his tall, lithe frame, accentuating the muscles of his broad chest and strong shoulders, sadness permeated his aura.

"You're on our land. What are *you* doing here?" Rowan asked, a faint flush to his cheeks that said he didn't know what to make of Storm's appraising look.

Rowan was a year older, not exactly out of bounds romantically, but on his No-Go list for many more reasons than age. Storm cleared his throat and wondered why he couldn't catch a break. He'd lost parts of his memory of the day, let Rowan see his attraction—something he'd sworn *never* to do—and couldn't seem to get his head into shape.

"Honestly...I have no idea," he confessed, hating saying the words to a Copry. "I think I had a vision."

"Not a dream? Or a hallucination?" Rowan checked, without being condescending, unlike his father.

"No. This was vivid, about the covens and...the future." Rowan shouldn't be the one he was talking to about this. Storm shifted onto his hip, waited for the dizziness to pass and moved onto his hands and knees in an attempt to gradually get to his feet. He could only hope a defensive spell over the Copry land had confused and disorientated him; otherwise he was in trouble.

"Come on. I'll help you sneak out before my father sees you," Rowan said, moving closer to help Storm stand. "Damn. You have a bump the size of a watermelon and it's bleeding." He shifted his weight to support most of Storm's, and together they managed to get him to two feet. Rowan held him by the shoulders and shook his head. "You were probably sleepwalking, having weird dreams about magic and fell and banged your head. Simple. I'll get you presentable and you can get on your way." Rowan clearly wasn't convinced by his theory but the quaver in his voice said he didn't want to know what else could have caused the wound, and Storm couldn't disagree.

"I think I was going somewhere," Storm said, eyeing the field he'd never been in, to figure out *where* he'd been going. He must have wavered off track or hit his head before drifting onto Copry land.

"Sleepwalking."

Ignoring the truth was pointless, with such a strong feeling of wrong in the pit of his stomach. "No. I was going somewhere important. I have to...do something," he admitted, allowing Rowan to slip his arm over a strong shoulder to steady him. When Rowan took a first step, Storm matched him. They tested three, with Storm pausing to shake off the dizziness after each step, before he was able to match Rowan's pace.

The field backed onto Tera land, six acres occupying the house he'd never lived in and the shack he'd taken over when he was fourteen. He loved living in the shack, being away from the chaos of the covens, with only Gladys capable of breaking through the magical protections Storm had set around his home. How the hell had he walked three or four acres in his sleep, to bang his head and drift onto Copry land? Cesa had erected a six-foot electrical fence between their land the moment Storm's parents moved in and he discovered they were of the dark arts. How did Storm get past the fence? Why would he bother?

Rowan heaved a sigh when they turned a corner at a row of tall bushes that hid a summer house that looked dilapidated, probably abandoned since Rowan's mother died when he was a child. Storm didn't want to go inside. He was afraid that in the state he was in he'd see something he couldn't avoid. He didn't want to insult Rowan by mentioning what may haunt the inside. He doubted he'd want to know if his mother's ghost remained in her favourite part of the grounds.

Shoving open the glass-paned door, Rowan helped him shuffle over to a nearby chaise, old and well worn. "You're disorientated by the head wound and because your magic goes screwy on the day of your ceremony. Once you've bonded with your full abilities, things will be better," Rowan said, grabbing a footstool to drag in front of the chaise.

Storm wasn't sure why he cared or what he was afraid to say, but he needed to rest and not have to think. Rowan fetched a first aid kit from a cupboard, returned, and started treating his head wound. While he worked, Storm looked closely and discovered the summer house wasn't abandoned. The original furniture remained: the chaise, the footstool and a coffee table. Rowan had claimed the space with a stereo on a desk in the corner, a few cushions, blankets stuffed into an armchair and books piled high beside the desk.

This looked a lot like his shack, like a sanctuary, an escape, a private place others shouldn't have been invited to share. Why had Rowan brought him here?

*

ROWAN INSISTED STORM stay for an hour to make sure his wound had healed and he wouldn't fall asleep. Due to witches and mages healing at an accelerated rate, his head wound was almost closed by the time he left with more questions than answers.

When Rowan had asked how he felt, how his magic had responded, what he'd been doing before he lost his memory, Storm didn't have answers. His magic had swirled in his gut, but he hadn't connected to anything willing to give him information. The wind had been silent, there had been no rain, the trees hadn't whispered, and that all amounted to an answer that made Rowan more nervous than the sleepwalking story. Whatever he suspected, he wasn't sharing. He simply told Storm to be careful and set his watch alarm to beep every five minutes so he didn't fall asleep and walked him home.

As weird as it had been to sit and talk to Rowan like a real person and not think of him as a Copry, Storm was confused. As an elemental, Rowan was unlikely to have any hint of seer abilities. He didn't have the sight dark magic gave Storm, and he shouldn't have *any* psychic ability. Rowan's talent revolved around the elements, and he could read the tarot better than anyone Storm had ever met. Yet, Rowan hadn't offered to read him, hadn't glanced at the black bag sitting on the desk they both knew held his personal deck.

At home, seen safely to the door by the sole Copry son, Storm was so on edge by what Rowan *wouldn't* say that sleep was impossible. He'd set his watch in front of Rowan, but sitting in his shack—three tiny rooms that held everything he owned—was claustrophobic. He wouldn't feel better sitting there doing nothing. The space felt too small, as though the walls were bearing down on him.

The living area was bare, a tattered sofa he'd salvaged from the skip, a square wooden table and a single dining chair, with only the tablet Gladys had given him for his sixteenth birthday providing entertainment, filled with e-books and C-dramas. A few potted plants on the side window and each side of the door, both black-leafed plants to promote spiritual awakening, cleansed the air. He'd carved runes into the door frame to ward off the ghosts haunting Gladys's house, to make sure they never followed him home and no demons could get in while he slept. The single door opposite the front door led to his bedroom, housing a mattress on the ground, a few wooden crates lined against the wall and at the end of the bed to hold his clothes, and a door leading to a fully plumbed bathroom. The shack was a few renovations away from the cabin his dad had intended, but Storm had everything he needed in life. What he needed *now* was fresh air and open spaces.

Grabbing his satchel from the dining chair, he tucked his tablet inside, added paracetamol from his medicine stash in the bathroom and left, shutting the door tight behind him. The minute he stepped outside his head felt lighter, unburdened.

Storm walked in the direction of the field he'd been studying in, hoping to find his books where he'd left them. People didn't normally drift onto Tera land, but as he'd proven today, anything could happen.

"Foley, come back!"

A few feet from the poppy field a mile from his study area, Denver's familiar voice made him pause. Straining to listen while wondering what he was doing here, Storm inched closer. He wavered as the wind slashed his mind, filling his head with a snapshot of confusing images: Foley standing beside Denver's prone body, screaming and crying; Denver lying on the ground, in the mud and the rain, unseeing eyes staring at the sky; a young boy's voice in his head, saying words that made no sense: *Denver. Foley. Ithen. Storm. Take him to his ascension. Save us!*

Shaking off the memory...dream?...nightmare? Storm waited until his knees stopped shaking and took another step. He reached the hulking great tree of Adam's Grove, a tree his dad's great-great-grandfather had planted when the Tera first claimed this land. From his vantage point, hidden from view by the three-foot-wide trunk and his friends not expecting him, Storm could observe but remain unseen.

Denver stood by the den they'd made when they were kids, eyes downcast, his whole demeanour radiating disappointment and sadness. Instinct told Storm to go to his friend but something deeper said *not now*. The wind whispered, *"See...look...watch."* He couldn't trust his mind, but he could always trust the wind.

His friends were arguing about their parents, not an uncommon occurrence but something he thought they'd settled years ago, when Foley first became their friend. As elitist witches, his parents thought Foley shouldn't befriend a human and a necromancer. Foley had never cared but Denver's parents hadn't known magic existed until Foley accidentally created a magical fire in their living room, four years ago. Gladys had been forced to explain that witches, mages, and demons existed, and that their son had befriended the Chosen One, someone destined to raise the dead.

Storm couldn't blame them for not being welcoming. Ever since, Foley and Denver joked about tattling to their parents whenever the other acted out. Why had they resurrected the argument?

"We can't *ever* tell them. I thought you would understand that," Foley insisted, sounding pained but resigned, as though they'd had this argument before.

"Why would I understand being kept a secret?" Denver shot back, making it clear they'd been keeping secrets from more than just Foley's parents.

Storm's stomach plummeted, realising they must be in a relationship that Foley didn't want to tell his parents about. Back when Storm accidentally revealed his crush, Foley had said he wasn't ready to date. When Storm asked Denver if he fancied anyone, he insisted he was focusing on his schoolwork rather than dating. They'd been clever never to give outright lies, knowing Storm would sense them. The wind would have ratted them out without hesitation, without thinking about the consequences.

Betrayers, the wind whispered.

Storm swatted the word away, using the physical motion to distract his thoughts while dragging his gaze from his two best friends. Not wanting to get caught eavesdropping, he walked to the left, around the other side of Adam's Grove. He'd go the long way to the field, collect his books and go to his shack until the ceremony.

What a birthday! He'd suffered a mysterious head injury,

Rowan was keeping secrets, there were ominous portents around every corner, and now his best friends had revealed their secret relationship.

This did reaffirm something Gladys had told him, that he'd thought nothing more than an old woman's worrying for her non-biological son. *Love isn't all it's cracked up to be,* she'd said the day he came home from school when he'd confessed his crush to Foley and faced his first rejection. *Sometimes people stab you in the back. Sometimes they lie to your face. All you can do is endure, survive and become stronger.*

Love is the harshest lesson in the world because we only learn its true power after we've had our hearts cut out, Gladys had warned. Necromancer or not, that had been scary to hear. *Protect your heart and be cautious. You can't afford to give your heart freely. You are stronger and more powerful than all of us. Don't let anyone use your power.*

Storm smiled as he walked, remembering how snarky he'd been, how he'd flashed Gladys a big smile. *I promise. I just wish there was someone who* wanted *to use me for my power.*

Gladys had smacked him over the head in her way of showing affection.

Gods, he would miss her.

Faltering in his next step, Storm frowned and wondered where that thought came from. Gladys was about sixty, but she was far from dying. She was as sprightly as she'd been ten years ago, yet the sense of impending loss was strong. He rubbed his chest and focused on the feeling, recalling a distant memory of Gladys knocking him on the head when he was older. Except...that was impossible. The image was clear in his mind, something about...teasing him? About...magic?

"Awfully reassuring." Storm frowned and curled his hand into a fist. He was sick of these fleeting thoughts and impossible memories since he'd hit his head, of feeling like he was an imposter in his mind. Rowan knew something, his *brain* knew something, and both were trying not to tell him what that was.

Once this ascension ceremony was over, he would camp out in Rowan's summer house until he told Storm what was happening and why. Storm wasn't leaving without an answer.

Chapter Five

"ARE YOU PAYING attention?"

Storm snapped his gaze from where Ithen was building the fire, to focus on Gregory. As the eldest of Gladys's grandchildren, Gregory took a central role in tonight's ceremony. He was closer to Storm's age at twenty-four, but this was important enough to forego the snark. "Sorry. I banged my head earlier," he said, rubbing the sore spot.

Gregory walked behind him and parted his hair. He tutted and poked around, ignoring the hiss of breath and Storm's instinctive bob to avoid contact. "If I can still see the bump, it must have been a hell of a hit. You seem okay, other than being distracted," he said, walking around to face Storm with appraising eyes. "Do magic for me to make sure you're ready for this. I can't send you to the abyss if you can't find your way back."

The compassion was unexpected. Gregory was the golden grandchild, the one the Glades thought could do no wrong. Married and settled into a secure job, living locally and learning to become the head of the coven whenever Gladys passed on, he was the quintessential white witch.

The overload of perfection made Storm's teeth itch.

"Hey!" Fingers snapped in front of his face, focusing his attention back on Gregory. "Do a simple spell. Lift the leaves off the ground and place them in my open hands. Say...six. Three to each hand."

Storm didn't bother arguing; this was something he could do in his sleep. Looking at the ground, he picked the best leaves for the task, mentally sent his magic into their cells and offered a jolt of magic to communicate his intentions.

Too many witches used the earth without thought, tearing leaves and adding them to potions or carelessly practising dangerous crafts in the woods. They didn't understand the pain and panic they caused, but Storm knew. The wind, the trees and the earth communicated with one another, whispering their fears, wondering if he would hurt them.

I'll lift you and place you on his hands. I promise I won't do anything else. He sent the words through the magical connection and waited patiently. The fear lessened and the cells responded, opening and welcoming his magic, accepting their role in this non-threatening task.

The leaves drifted lazily through the air to land on Gregory's palms. He nodded his approval, then turned his hands to let the leaves fall to the ground. Storm withdrew his magic, removing the brief consciousness he'd given the leaves before Gregory carelessly stepped on them.

"You seem ready." Offering a rare smile, Gregory glanced at the fire Ithen had built and the gathering coven. "Check in with Gladys and make sure there's nothing else you need to do to prepare," he suggested, walking away before Storm had the chance to respond.

Storm stepped away but hesitated to approach Gladys. He'd been avoiding her all day and didn't want to tell her about what happened until he had answers, which meant talking to Rowan.

He stopped by the fire, watching Ithen's muscles ripple invitingly under his white tank top as he added more wood. At twenty-eight, Ithen was his senior by ten years, the most academic of the Deontay coven. No one was better prepared for this ceremony than Ithen, who had offered to be Storm's mentor and guide, to help him navigate his new powers.

Ithen had studied everything he could find about the Tera coven, necromancy, and dark magic over the last ten years. He'd devoted his adult years to fulfilling the prophecy he claimed would save magic from destruction. Ithen should have trained to become a shaman, like his father, but his coven had died out long before his parents—the last surviving members—died in a tragic accident. Now he was a white witch, with a talent for commanding fire and water.

The only thing that worried Storm was the lack of first-hand, practical experience. He was the last Tera in this part of the world and Gladys insisted that his mum's family—those with the greatest power and knowledge to help him—wanted nothing to do with him.

That was their choice, but Storm was left with little guidance for his ceremony. He didn't have his parents to tell him what was expected, and the other covens would never dare practice dark magic just to prepare him to fulfil a prophecy only half of them believed in. Not when they didn't understand what would spark this final war Storm was supposed to fight and win.

The covens chose not to believe in the prophecy, because they could safely put their heads in the sand and pretend the war would never happen, but Storm believed in every word. He could feel his fate in his bones, hear it in the wind, feel the omens when the rain fell, in the current between the trees around his home, in the darkness that crept under his door and seeped into his dreams.

The danger was real and was coming whether anyone believed or not.

*

STANDING ON A platform in the centre of the circle of fire, in the middle of three standing stones, Storm looked over those gathered for his ascension.

Regardless of what he'd seen today, Denver and Foley still cared enough about him to support this massive step into adulthood. To the side, Gladys talked quietly with Gregory, who was minutes away from performing the spell to send Storm on his journey. Ithen stood tall and proud, directly in front of Storm, on the other side of the fire. He'd dressed for the occasion, the only one here tonight who looked like a witch.

While the males of the Glade coven had ordinary clothes, short well-groomed hair and looked like every other man on the street, Ithen stood tall, with a black waistcoat over his sleeveless white shirt and black trousers leading to black shoes. His six-foot height was accentuated by the outfit, his muscled arms bare, his thick, wavy black hair tamed into a ponytail. Everything about Ithen's choices were more subdued than would be expected of Storm's ancestors in New Orleans or his mother's side of the family, the brujería, Mexican witches who embraced the dark arts along with the light. According to Gladys, the combination of practices made Storm stronger than anyone she'd ever met, the two practices embracing and accepting the unity of dark and light, death and life, this life and the next.

Gladys walked to Ithen's side and dusted imaginary lint from his shoulder. "We may begin."

Shoring his courage, Storm was about to speak when a faint breeze tussled his hair. He closed his eyes and breathed deep as he listened.

Believe, said the wind.

Beware the demons, the trees whispered.

Mint drifted past his nose, something he couldn't place as

part of the ceremony, but reminding him of Rowan. He would often walk the Tera property and stop to watch from a distance as Rowan sat on the other side of the fence and spoke to the flowers, weaving magic with dextrous fingers. The scent stirred Storm's magic and sang softly beneath his skin, reacting to the support of the elements.

Storm created sparks of fire in his palm as he opened his eyes and watched the flames dance, swirling and weaving amongst one another. In gratitude, he offered the magic to the elements, a promise they would understand better than the confused coven.

Ready for this immense step toward his fate, Storm kept his eyes open and mind alert as he spoke the words of the ritual, first in Latin and then his mother tongue, so all aspects of who he was took part. "The Fates have named me the Chosen One, the Dark One, necromancer and mage. The gods have named me seer, light wielder and storm chaser. The demons call me master, life-giver, guardian of the lost and hopeless...for I am Storm Tera, last surviving Tera mage, commander of the dead," he called out into the night sky, gazing at the blood moon that marked his birthday, his birth rite: November second, the day of the dead.

*

DEJA VU ENCAPSULATED Storm as he stood within the standing stones and a storm rolled overhead. Ithen's face morphed from watchful and prepared to concerned, and Gladys grabbed his arm, visibly afraid and unsure. The ceremony was supposed to start with Storm stating his intentions, revealing his true nature and waiting for the dark gods to welcome him to the abyss. A light breeze would sweep out the fire; he would disappear into the smoke to pass through the abyss, where the full strength of his power would be released from the depths within; then he'd step from the circle unscathed.

This onslaught was unexpected, and if the prickle of his power was any judge, unnatural. Dark magic had summoned the storm, but not his.

Closing his eyes, Storm focused his mind. This ceremony hadn't been performed since his dad turned eighteen twenty years ago, and he hadn't been friends with Gladys back then. Cesa Copry was the only coven leader Storm knew of who had been there the night of his dad's ascension.

Magic swirled beneath Storm's skin, visible lines of smoky black coursing through his veins in response to the storm. The temperature dropped so low his breath misted, the wind cut through him, and thunder rumbled in the distance. Instinct made him gaze beyond the boundaries of the land backing into Copry fields. He was startled to find Rowan standing at the barrier.

Knowing Rowan was there was important.

The wind whispered warnings he couldn't hear above the sound of the thunder cracking the sky open to unleash a torrent of lightning. The sense of familiarity was strong, and he wondered if this had happened before. Lightning cracked to the ground two feet from the standing stone to Storm's right, forcing the coven members who had gathered to move away to avoid being hit. Another whiplash of light struck the centre cairn, leaving the ancient stone with a brutal black marred line twisting down the natural grooves of the stone.

Gladys cried out Latin words that sounded vaguely protective, while Ithen rushed around the circle, ushering people toward the most open area of the field. Once they were safe, he walked a circle around them, building a magical protection. Gladys stayed by the cairns, screaming into the wind to be heard by the Fates.

Storm felt helpless, trapped by the circle of fire and the necessities of the ceremony. While the others were safe from the repercussions of the storm, Rowan was standing by an electric fence, surrounded by trees. Extending an arm toward the fence, which Rowan had backed away from in panic, Storm sent tendrils of black magic swirling to his fingers. With his other hand, he encased Gladys in a protective bubble. Ithen could keep the others safe, but these two fools were more worried about him than themselves and would get killed.

As a bolt of lightning struck the electrical fence, sending a visible reaction of electric blue light sparking off every inch of the wire into the ground, Storm's vision turned hazy, darkened by gathering shadows. Fighting the loss of clear vision, worried he was passing out from the stress, a head wound and the overuse of magic during a ceremony that had clearly gone wrong, Storm could only pray that his protective spells kept Gladys and Rowan safe or he might wake up to find his world had changed irreparably.

*

"THAT WAS NEW."

Storm flinched and spun to find that he was in the stark darkness of the abyss, arms outstretched from his use of magic. Heaving a sigh of relief, he dropped his hands and turned in circles to find the source of the voice. He'd passed whatever test the storm had been, but there wasn't supposed to be anyone or anything with him in the abyss. Was this another test or something he didn't know to expect from his ceremony?

"What was new?" He never normally encouraged demons to keep talking, but he was curious about the words and their meaning. Only those of the darkness could pass through the abyss without being tempted or coerced by the voices or creatures hiding within. The one consolation of being a necromancer was that life and death were much the same and none of the dark creatures would hurt him.

A long talon slid over his bare forearm, the sleeve of his cable jumper pushed to his elbow for the ceremony. Storm shivered at the contact, familiar from years ago but unexpected in the darkness. Now he knew what he was dealing with: definitely a demon, the long nails marking them a lower demon. Higher demons possessed wings and shorter nails more suited to intricate tasks.

The demon responded lazily, "I said, this is new. So much has changed: the storm, your decision to protect Rowan, even his presence. He certainly didn't attend your ceremony the first time. I imagine your encounter this afternoon intrigued him." The voice was close enough now that Storm could make out their indistinct shape in the darkness.

Androgynous features denoted a lower demon drawn to the dark shadows: a whisperer, an influencer, who enjoyed toying with humans but had power and talent for death, both giving and taking. They were the perfect match for a necromancer, which left Storm wondering if the demon had sought him out or if his magic had searched for a suitable match amongst the demons he had encountered throughout his life.

"What a risk. Your magic positively *sizzled* for him," the demon hissed with the word, a smile lighting their face with glee and intrigue. This demon thought his magic had responded to Rowan's presence, but Storm wasn't sure whether to be thankful or to worry. Either way, he would evaluate that problem later, when he wasn't buzzing with magic and confused from his head injury.

"What did you mean by 'the first time'?" Storm asked, grateful for the laws of the abyss that dictated the rules for encounters like this. A demon could be trusted to always tell the truth, though they tended to speak in riddles and temptations. Rowan? He wasn't sure what side Rowan had chosen yet, or if Rowan even knew he'd *chosen* a side.

"When you first completed your ceremony," the demon replied, continuing the slow, curious walk around Storm, a talon occasionally testing boundaries and trailing over skin. "The storm never raged the first time, and Rowan wasn't there. I believe the two are connected...though I don't know why."

The demon passed Storm's right side to flash a smile and catch his eye. The red mist swirling in their eyes told Storm this demon wanted him not for any depraved reason but for magic. His powers were a mystery to them. If he ever bonded with a demon, they would be the only demon in the whole of the abyss to know the true extent of Storm's power. That wouldn't happen for a few years, because Storm had to be in full control of his power first, but demons lived for knowledge, and bonding a necromancer was their version of winning the lottery.

"As you know, we demons detest a mystery," the demon continued. "You have become one, for this is the third time you have passed through my domain but never found what you seek."

"I haven't been here before."

The demon sighed, deflating like a disappointed puppy. "But you have." Leaning close, they sniffed at the collar of his jumper, darted their tongue out to trail the tip over his cheek and hummed at whatever they discovered. "This time you have purpose: to gain your powers, to become a man worthy of your prophecy. You intrigue me, youngling. You are missing a piece of the puzzle that is in your mind, yet you walk willingly into the abyss, knowing the risk to you if you are not whole."

The meaning behind the words made Storm's skin prickle with awareness. He was in danger here; not from the demon but from his own ignorance and whatever his recent head wound had done to his memories. "I'm not...whole?"

The demon scraped a red-tipped talon—nail varnish, he

thought—across the tip of their tongue. With another hum, part frustration and part curiosity, they replied, "You are seeking something buried in your mind. I can fetch it for you...for a price."

Storm bit his tongue to keep from promising anything for answers. This was what demons did, and their twisty way with words often led young mages and witches into trouble they couldn't get out of. Demons offered what the mage wanted most, which would explain why the demon had licked him to read his sweat and decipher Storm's intentions and hopes. "Why would I make a deal with you?"

"Because what you seek was left in another life, not past or present but the future. You left your purpose in the future."

Chapter Six

A CHILL RAKED Storm's spine as remnants of memories flashed through his mind: an older version of himself, of Gladys being older, the fear she was about to die. The words came to his tongue instinctively: "If I'm *in* the past, any memories will be from my future."

"Yes!" The demon clasped their hands in delight, talons clicking in the otherwise silent abyss. "Pieces are floating around your head, but they don't make sense yet. I can help." They moved closer, the scant light revealing more of their features: a smart black suit, perfectly cut to slightly rounded hips and a slim waist, cropped short to show slender ankles leading to black stilettos. Empty white eyes, with a single point of ice blue, where the iris should be, stared, unblinking. This was a lower demon as he'd thought, but powerful, holding an old-fashioned cane. Only the strong were allowed self-expression, the others allocated black cloaks and near nakedness to symbolise their lowly, unwanted status.

The look suggested androgyny but the single lurid purple talon on their right hand denoted the demon as non-binary. Most demons were female, the more powerful of the species, and displayed their nature with black talons. Males displayed their gender through white talons, as their talons were a skin pigment present from birth. Storm had heard a rumour once that a demon's nails changed colour according to their gender preference, and that some switched genders at will so that one day they were male and another day non-binary. That demon had been bonded to a mage visiting the village, so Storm had never had the chance to ask the demon questions about how common such an ability might be.

The idea of bonding with a demon for answers intrigued Storm. His magic would increase threefold if he agreed, but he barely knew any real dark magic. "I imagine your price for this information would be bonding?"

"Hmm, not yet. I see what awaits you, and I don't want to hitch myself to a dying horse." The demon laughed while cocking their head to the right so that long white hair tumbled to their elbow. They paused and cocked their head in the other direction. "I would be willing to make a bargain. I will tell you something to help you fulfil the prophecy and, once complete, you will bond with me in payment."

Storm gave the offer serious thought. The bargain could benefit him, particularly in terms of fulfilling the prophecy. By rights, the prophecy acknowledged and accepted his darkness and bonding with a demon would make no difference, but he was young compared to the stories he'd heard. Most dark mages didn't bond with a demon until they were in their thirties, experienced and comfortable with their magic. "I guess you can't tell me the information first?"

"The youngling does not make deals with demons lightly, I see." They didn't seem insulted, turning away to stare into the darkness. At the last moment, before Storm spoke to break the silence, they glanced coyly over their right shoulder. "If my information fails to help you fulfil the prophecy, no harm done. I will have given you useless information, and I will not hold you to the bonding."

"Fair enough." Storm almost smiled at how surprisingly fortuitous this meeting was. No harm no foul, as Gladys would say. Though he wasn't sure she'd agree this was a situation that called for blasé decision-making. "My head *is* jumbled. I keep seeing things that...aren't there," he confessed, knowing the demon wouldn't judge him the way humans would.

With a quick turn they were in his face, leaning close, breathing clover-scented air against his cheek as wide white eyes gazed into his. "Oh, but they are. Or rather they were...in your future."

Storm shook his head, refusing to challenge the demon's information. "If the information proves to be the key to fulfilling the prophecy—something I could *not* figure out without you—I will bond with you, but only once the conditions of the prophecy are met."

The demon's lips twitched into a smile. "Clever mage." They chuckled, stepping back swiftly to offer a long arm, hand held out to shake. "Accepted. I am Yael."

Raising an eyebrow at the ease of the deal, he nodded his acceptance and grasped their cold, pale hand. "I am Storm Tera."

Yael fluttered their eyelashes extravagantly. "Wise witch," they gushed in approval, understanding the power they had exchanged by giving their true names. There was no power greater in the magical world than a witch or mages name and no greater currency to demons.

Yael pressed tight against Storm to whisper, "You have done this before, youngling. Fought to fulfil the prophecy, fought a war you did not win." They cocked their head as Storm internally winced at the idea of failing to win the war. "I know of one pivotal moment in the war, which you failed to see the significance of. To make sure the mistake is not repeated, you will need to become the Dark One they whisper about."

"That sounds like a riddle."

Yael squeezed his hand, playfully swinging the other arm behind them. "You will see danger and not act quickly enough, because it is not your fate to react. What you do next is vital, for you must resurrect the dead." Without waiting for a reaction, Yael dug a talon into his wrist, drawing blood in a warning not to question or interrupt. Knowing the wound would heal, Storm didn't question the violent censor.

"There is one whose fate decides the war, though none can fathom why. Only you will know, once the deed is done. Save this soul, and you will resurrect your chances of winning the war and fulfilling the prophecy. Without him, failure awaits. Do you understand?"

Storm reluctantly nodded. "Yes." He still had questions but most weren't important enough to press Yael. "You're telling me I need to learn necromancy. How do you know I didn't intend to?"

Yael huffed and shook their head. "Because you chose not to learn your family's craft the last time. When you fought the war, you had no such gift and no ability to use the magic calling to you. Thus came your downfall. Learn the craft, respect the dark arts, and you will succeed."

That sounded too easy, but the most complicated magic often required the simplest sacrifice. If learning necromancy—something he'd always shied away from—would fulfil the prophecy and save magic from destruction, he'd make the sacrifice.

"Who do I need to save? Ithen? Because he knows necromancy?"

"Ithen is not who you believe him to be. That much would have been revealed *after* the war; an opportunity to learn the truth that your past failure did not afford you," Yael warned, their eyes sad as they leaned closer. "The soul you must save is Rowan Copry."

Shock slammed into him, followed by the sense of im-pending doom when Rowan stood in the lightning storm. "You can't let Rowan die."

"You remembered my warning?" Yael looked delighted. "Yes. Rowan Copry's life holds the key to the prophecy. Save him and you will see victory."

Storm nodded, glad to have one question answered, even if most of what Yael had told him left more questions. Interestingly, Yael's warning meant they had been waiting here, aware of what the ceremony would entail and that they'd meet Storm to discuss this. As interesting as this conversation was, they wouldn't have long before Gladys panicked and plucked him from the abyss by force, likely with Ithen's help.

"How do you know this? What do you mean by saying that was *your* warning? I don't remember hearing those words... but...something isn't right in my head..."

Yael shrugged nonchalantly and grazed a talon over his wrist. "In time, youngling. Your mind is struggling to cope with two existences in one body. When you adapt, you will learn the truth." Their obvious compassion for his mental stability was almost a relief, because he did feel overwhelmed. To have that acknowledged told Storm how dangerous it would be to keep pushing. "I *know* because we demons are the only creatures besides your dark self who can exist in both planes—life and death, past and future. We see all. We *know* all. We have no hesitation over meddling with what has been if we do not like what will be."

"What about my ceremony?"

"You gained your powers as we spoke," Yael informed him as they released his hand with reluctance and clasped both hands behind their back. "You may go now. Return to your past and present. Return and fix what was broken. But first, complete a task for me."

"Don't you mean one *more*?"

Yael tipped their head coquettishly. "Be brave, youngling. Warn Gladys Glade to stay away from dark magic." Storm wanted to ask if Yael knew *for sure* Gladys had been meddling where she wasn't wanted. "She will understand." They retreated a single step, where they evaporated into the darkness. "We demons are not yet willing to see her light fade."

*

THE MOMENT YAEL'S voice faded, a symphony of noise assaulted Storm's ears, though he couldn't see anything but darkness. Smoke clogged his senses, gathering in his throat while clouding his vision. When shapes appeared, he didn't know if they were real or more ghosts trapped in the abyss. The smell of burning made him want to choke, and he instinctively turned his head to cough into his shoulder in a vain attempt to clear his airways. He was no longer standing on the podium, but kneeling, one hand on the wooden platform to stop him from face-planting.

Raising his head, he blinked to bring everything into focus. Gladys was frantically fighting the storm, Ithen was advising her to back away while keeping the rest of the coven within his protective bubble. Rowan stood in a secure bubble of magic, a black and silver shimmer to the air letting Storm know his magic was keeping Rowan safe.

He was on the wrong side of the fence. Storm remembered him being on Copry land the last he looked, but Rowan now stood firmly on their side of the fence, a foot from the cairn circle.

At his side, Foley spoke through the magical protections separating them, urging Rowan to leave and get to safety, while Denver argued that he was being heartless. Storm had no idea what that meant but he was getting a headache from the noise.

His magic swirled beneath his skin, teasing and testing his resistance, begging to be set free. Seeping from his eyes, black smoke wove through the air and floated on the breeze. Storm felt weak but this much was instinctive.

The wind stopped like a flame blown out, taking the raging fire of the circle; a rumble of thunder cut off mid-sound; a lightning flash disappeared halfway to the ground, and everything stopped. The world paused, no one daring to breathe as blessed silence descended.

Storm closed his eyes, feeling better for the pressure lifted from his mind. Prepared to face what had happened, he stood, craning his neck to one side then the other and stretching his arms. Every muscle ached, each one popped or cracked as he worked them loose, freeing them from the confines of a regular human body and infusing them with powerful magic that promised to reshape him, body and soul.

"By the Mother…" Rowan whispered as Storm dropped his arms to his sides and faced the onslaught of nervous gazes. "You're stunning."

Laughter bubbled up in stunned surprise, but Storm hid it behind a smile. That wasn't the reaction he'd expected, especially from Rowan, but he wouldn't deny that he felt incredible. The dark magic was mesmerising, slithering beneath his skin, rushing through his veins, whispering dark promises. His headache and confusion from earlier was gone, replaced by the questions Yael's words had implanted.

His thoughts took longer to settle. When Ithen approached the podium to extend a hand, Storm ignored the disingenuous offering. He could hear the Glade coven members muttering, Gladys saying a prayer as she crossed herself, and his friends hesitating to get close to the unknown entity he'd become.

The secrets Yael had shared lurked in the corners of his mind, screaming guidance and warnings. One rang clear above the others: he couldn't trust anyone. Demons couldn't lie to another dark creature so Storm could trust every word from Yael's mouth. Gladys must be toying with or planning to use dark magic, Ithen couldn't be trusted and was yet another person keeping secrets, while Rowan was just as important to the prophecy as Storm.

Feeling stronger and more comfortable in his body, Storm descended the podium by the two side steps—blocking the questions, the looks, the cowering—and walked straight to Rowan. He was an interloper to everyone else, but the only one Storm wanted to focus on. He looked at Storm like he had blossomed from a mage into a dark prince, and he'd never felt stronger, more powerful or more desirable than when that gaze locked on his and sent his blood churning with uncertainty.

Rowan's attention was intoxicating. Storm stopped a breath from Rowan, who stood a good few inches taller than him, then utilised a power he'd never had but that slid effortlessly into the forefront of his mind.

"I can't talk here, but I need to not see you until my magic settles. I'll explain everything as soon as I can," he promised, using an untapped pathway in his mind. He didn't have time to question his new powers, but they felt familiar, like a long-lost friend newly rediscovered.

"How are you doing this?" Rowan asked, his brow crinkling with confusion.

"I don't know."

Rowan raked a hand through his hair and averted his gaze. He tensed when he found Gladys staring, but met Storm's gaze unflinchingly. *"You saved my life tonight. I owe you this much."* Within the space of a blink, the confusion cleared and determination took over, along with a suspicious glance at Ithen. *"Be careful. What I saw this morning has been bothering me."* He didn't seem to be as shocked by the telepathy as Storm would expect. Either Rowan had always been capable or someone else was.

"I can explain everything, I promise." Storm intended to,

because Rowan was the only person he could trust. He just couldn't risk talking anywhere that Gladys or Ithen could overhear them. Right now, he wasn't sure if this telepathy would give him a headache or cause other side effects from utilising a little-explored power.

"Come to my summer house when you're ready. Use this... connection...to call me, okay?" Rowan suggested, sounding scared but cautious. Did he realise Storm may be safer on Copry land than with the people he thought he could trust?

Storm remembered one more task and let the fingers of his right hand weave the magic. *"I'm sorry."*

"For what?"

Rowan hissed and backed away. When he looked at his hand and found the burn mark on his palm, he glared at Storm. "What the hell?" he said aloud, asking in his mind, *"I guess this is for show?"*

"You're a Copry. Act like one just this once." Storm needed the security of natural animosity to continue for both their sakes.

"My father was right. You *are* dangerous," Rowan said aloud, taking a step back as he shook his head and glanced at his hand in confusion.

Having always been a neutral party—someone who tried not to participate in Cesa's ideas nor endorse them and who had always supported the covens—Gladys sucked in a shocked breath and rushed to Rowan. He would need to take the long way home with no way through the fence that didn't involve Storm's magic.

Gladys followed Rowan, muttering about the recklessness of boys, while Ithen crossed to Storm's side, his face showing no discernible emotion.

"I always knew he took after his father. The fact he's hidden behind supposed neutrality shows how much he takes after the old man," he remarked, surprisingly hostile toward someone who had never done him wrong.

Storm frowned at Ithen, wondering where the judgement was coming from. "What do you mean?" Was this why he couldn't trust Ithen or just a side of his personality he'd never seen?

"Cesa weaselled into your parents' lives when you were born, spying on you to find out how powerful you might be and if the prophecy was true," Ithen explained, completely contradicting everything Storm had been raised to believe about their families. They could hardly have been natural-born, lifelong enemies if Cesa had 'weaselled' his way into their lives. "He showed his true colours soon enough. They all do."

As do you, he thought, startled to realise he couldn't remember one decent thing about Ithen to explain his crush. *Just as Yael said.*

He couldn't help but question—if this was Ithen's true self, then what had Storm ever seen in him to inspire a crush? Now that those feelings no longer existed, he wondered if going through the abyss wiped them away or simply gave him clarity? The worst-case scenario was always possible, now Storm knew he couldn't trust Ithen—perhaps the crush had *never* been real but had been pressed upon him to give Ithen a reason to remain in his life...just the way he claimed Cesa had done with his dad.

Chapter Seven

One Week Later

November 9, 2026

FATIGUE WASHED OVER Storm but he held firm, grasping the arms of the wooden chair he'd been placed in at the start of the lesson.

When his ceremony ended and the chaos calmed after Rowan's dramatic exit, he'd thought his life would start to make sense. Instead, he'd been bombarded by questions and doubts, secrets, and dreams. He'd woken more than once from those memory-dreams to find Yael crouched on the end of his bed, staring curiously but nevertheless willing to explain what the dreams meant.

"You did something to your memories," they warned with

more curiosity than care. *"You performed a dark spell to bind your memories of your future, performed by an unaccomplished dark witch. Gladys, I think."*

Storm couldn't blame Yael for being intrigued. They couldn't lie and had revealed more than he'd expected. At least Yael was helping him, unlike everyone else who expected him to read his family grimoire and work it out.

Now that he knew the truth, he had to prevent that future from happening.

Once upon a time, he'd failed to fulfil the prophecy, the world had gone to hell, and he and Gladys had messed with the darkest magic to send him back to his past to fix his mistakes. Something had gone wrong with the spell, and he couldn't remember his past like he'd hoped. Without those memories, Storm didn't know what was true to his past actions and what he was doing differently, or how to change his fate to fulfil the prophecy.

Sadly, Yael didn't have answers, and they were beyond displeased about the way Ithen chose to teach him the dark arts.

By law, magic users—no matter what their talent, whether light or dark—weren't allowed to purposefully use magic against another person. Guarding them, shielding them, or creating a barrier to stop them were fine, but the magic had to be pushed onto an inhuman element. Directed at another human, their magic became corrupted, and the witch or mage would be stripped of their powers. Some slipped through the cracks—the ones who kept their darkness a secret from others and didn't let anyone who knew their secret live to tell the tale.

Storm wasn't sure what category Ithen fit into, but he was determined to find out. The man had pretended to be his best friend and mentor on the night of his ceremony, when Storm successfully bonded to his full power. The man standing in front of him was nothing but a monster.

He'd been excited the night of his ceremony, when Ithen and the others helped him celebrate with a small party. Hopped up on hormones and adrenaline, his good mood had been marred by the storm, his encounter with Yael and the secrets lurking in the people closest to him. When Ithen had handed him a drink, Storm had questioned whether to trust the man even with a simple beverage, for the first time in his life.

What magic do you want to learn? Ithen had asked, smiling as he lay a hand on Storm's arm. *I've studied your magic the best I can, without access to your family grimoire. I can teach you anything you need or want to know. The choice must be yours.*

Storm had been intrigued by the phrasing, about Ithen's insistence that the choice was his and wondered whether that was a protective barrier of dark magic, to ensure the prophesied one couldn't be forced to learn magic he wasn't comfortable with. He could only imagine how dangerous the world would become if the Chosen One could be magically manipulated.

While he'd once put stipulations on what he wanted to learn, he knew better. He'd answered the way Yael had guided him to, the way that would allow him to learn necromancy and fulfil the prophecy, the way that would equip him to protect and save Rowan's life. "*I want to know everything,*" he'd said, convinced he was doing the right thing.

He wanted to learn dark magic, control, stability, necromancy and how to commune with the spirits, how to bond with a demon...everything that was normal for a Tera and the Chosen One...but not this. He'd never agreed to this.

Storm gritted his teeth against the curse writhing over his body, seeking to latch onto his magic and morph into something unnatural. He didn't know what Ithen had done or why, but he needed to find a way to break the hold.

From everything Yael had shared—of the war, how it had ended and why—nothing suggested Ithen was a traitor to white magic. He'd been fighting on Storm's side and had died protecting him. Storm had thought that meant Ithen was one of the good guys. So why was he using dark magic powerful enough to combat Storm's? It felt wrong...sick...as that magic coursed through him.

Why do this when Storm was only a few days into learning how to harness his full magical abilities? Where did he come by these strange powers, and why was he using them against someone he'd once followed into a war?

Storm was still considered a rookie mage, a trainee, and Ithen shouldn't see him as a threat.

Needing answers, Storm fought against the attack as best he could. While he could move his body, he didn't want to for fear he would lose his concentration and break the mental barrier he'd built between himself and the invading curse.

Resisting Ithen's magic was draining him. Storm had endured half an hour of physical tasks, used his magic for another twenty minutes, and guessed that he'd been in this chair, assaulted by Ithen's magic, for twice as long. His body was weak, his mind strained and his magic furious.

For a week, he had suffered Ithen's lectures, the homework and reading assignments, wondering why he wasn't being shown how to *use* his new magic. He suspected this was the answer. Whatever Ithen was planning, he didn't want Storm to become powerful. The fact he wanted to learn *everything* about the dark arts, in this version of his life, had forced Ithen's hand. By refusing to learn necromancy and the finer black magic of his line in his previous life, Ithen hadn't felt threatened, because he knew Storm would fail to fulfil the prophecy. Eventually, he must have realised the foretold war would kill him if he *didn't* fight, and the Fates had forced his hand...ultimately taking his life in the process. That could have been their way of dealing with him, their idea of karma.

Now that Storm *wanted* to learn, maybe Ithen wanted him out of the way because he risked succeeding. And that was enough to make him fight harder.

Storm was beginning to understand so much that he'd been ignorant of before, evaluating the moment with the clarity of having a plan. Rising to his feet took more effort than he cared to admit, but Storm pushed against the magic holding him to the chair, while magic ravished his dark powers. Once standing, he had to pause, breathing heavily, chest heaving from the effort.

Ithen cocked an eyebrow and lifted his free hand from his trouser pocket. He brought his hands together in a clap that resonated in the remote area of the woods he'd chosen for this lesson. His magic tightened its hold on Storm, but he'd come this far and refused to surrender. If he'd gone to the trouble of travelling through time, he wouldn't let someone like Ithen stop him—a white witch, more magician than mage, with only the simplest academic knowledge of the dark arts.

Storm could never hold his head high again, as a Tera or a dark mage, if he let someone of Ithen's abilities best him.

Calling on everything he had, Storm strained his bruised lungs to take in a deep breath and pushed power into his magic. With one shove against the darkness, he reached to his right.

Ithen's eyes widened as Yael stepped from the abyss, wearing a white suit. They took one look at Ithen and clasped Storm's outstretched hand. With the surge of a demon's power to assist, Storm opened his mouth and blew out the breath he'd held for too long. He could see Ithen's magic retreating from the onslaught as the man stumbled, lost his footing and fell to the ground.

As a crow cawed in the distance, Storm sagged and realised how quiet it had been during his lesson. He hadn't felt the wind, heard the trees or registered any sign of life since they arrived.

"Ingenious," Yael said, swinging their joined hands like a gleeful child. They touched a fingertip against something invisible, which shimmered at the touch. "He created a barrier to prevent anyone sensing your magic." They prodded the shimmer a second time. On the third, the barrier exploded in a burst of colour, more like popping a bubble than a magical cage. The moment the barrier popped, Storm could breathe easily.

"How could he do that?"

Yael shrugged and rested their head on his shoulder. "He has strong voodoo magic in his veins. It's possible no one understood his powers. A true voodoo master hasn't been seen in this country in generations."

Storm squeezed their hand. "Thank you for coming." They didn't have to, because the bond hadn't been made yet. Yael could have ignored him.

Yael lifted their head and beamed. "You *asked*. Do you know the last time anyone asked for my permission? A strong, dark master such as yourself would never ask a lowly one such as I for their help. You may ask me any time."

"And you may refuse any time," Storm promised, hating how badly Yael had been treated in the past. Yael was...unlike anyone else. He'd known a few transgender and non-binary people through the LGBT club at his school, but he'd never met anyone as vulnerable or as open as Yael. They were dangerous, mischievous, yet gooey as chocolate mousse underneath the murder and mayhem. Storm couldn't have asked for a better ally.

Yael blinked innocently. "Are you going to kiss him?"

Ithen had fallen to the ground, knocked unconscious. Storm thought about what he wanted to know, the options for getting at the truth and the doubts festering over the last week about Gladys. Who else could he trust but Yael, who was incapable of lying?

"*You,*" said a voice in his head. "*You can trust yourself. Your magic.*"

A few mornings ago, Storm had woken with a start, shouting Rowan's name, and found Yael watching over him.

"*To discover who to trust, you would need to know the heart of the person, to know their mind, their heart and their intentions. Your new gift could be useful, but we demons know of another way.*"

Storm had presumed Yael's half smile of mischief would lead to making another bargain, but Yael had offered the information freely.

"*You have changed your future, youngling. I admit I cannot turn away,*" they had confessed, crawling across the bed to press their nose against his. "*I must see how you change the future and why this change has occurred. You are stronger of heart than the boy who first completed the ceremony and failed to win the war. Something inside you has changed, and I need to know what.*"

Knowing that Yael—and most demons—would do just about anything to solve a riddle, Storm had promised to share dreams or memories of the past and treat Yael like his therapist. In payment for the personal details Yael found fascinating, like jigsaw pieces to a puzzle, he shared demon secrets and quietly haunted his shack.

With the bargain struck, Storm had dared ask the question,

"How do I see the heart, mind and intentions of a person?"

The answer had been simple but sent shivers up his spine. Yael had leaned close to whisper the words against his cheek, talons tip-tapping along his forearm before stopping at his right wrist and carving a design into his flesh. With an evil grin, they had met his gaze and removed their hand to lick the tip of their talon, revealing a bloody heart on his wrist.

With a kiss.

With regret, he whispered his answer, "Yes."

This wasn't how he thought he'd kiss Ithen for the first time. His crush had formed almost immediately when they first met, when Storm was in awe of Ithen's vast knowledge about the dark arts.

His schoolboy crush was more like a dream as he straddled Ithen's chest, where he lay on the ground, still unconscious from the magical backlash. He could remember seeing Ithen for the first time: all long flowing hair, muscles galore, and a deep voice. Now, he felt nothing but revulsion for what he was about to do.

Shoring his courage, Storm pushed sentimentality aside, wiser now he had the truth in his grasp. Placing his hands on either side of Ithen's face, Storm spared a glance at Yael who crouched beside him, ready to grab onto him and drag him out of Ithen's heart if there was trouble.

Reassured by the reinforcements, Storm bit the bullet, reminding himself that a momentary kiss to spark a spell was far less of a violation of Ithen's will than the violent torture he'd put Storm through. He pressed his lips to Ithen's and closed his eyes, using his magic to set intention. *Show me the heart of all he is.*

There was no dark ether of nothing, like with the abyss, no flash of light like his ceremony, no swirling wind or grand storm to prove dark magic had taken place. As he sat back, breaking the brief kiss, he had the strange feeling of slipping out of his skin and into another: *wrong* and *tight* and *suffocating*.

When Storm opened his eyes, he was in another time and place. If the spell had gone right, he was in one of Ithen's memories *as* Ithen.

Chapter Eight

Twelve and a half years ago

September, 2013

The Tera Manor

FIFTEEN AND GANGLY, uncomfortable in his skin, with little natural magic, Ithen had been forced to study various dark and light magic to find something he was capable of, but he never thought Asher would ignore him.

The man was an enigma to Ithen: a doting father to Storm, the prophesied Chosen One; a loving husband to Veronica, a talented bruja of immense power; and an infuriatingly attractive man who proved immune to Ithen's charms. No matter what he said, did, or what kind of magic he used to garner Asher's attention, the man ignored him with an ease that bordered on the ridiculous. Even Storm's imaginary friend got more attention from Asher than Ithen could hope for.

Ithen hovered in the doorway to the playroom to watch Storm, wondering what made him so special. Since his family died, Ithen had been alone, left in the guardianship of the united covens. Though Asher was the most powerful and his son destined to lead all the covens into a secure future, he'd fobbed off his responsibility to Ithen by placing him into the Copry household. Duty should have brought Ithen here, into Asher's home, but he reasoned that his young son's unpredictable magic made it unsafe for strangers and the other covens had been cowardly enough to agree.

Cesa Copry wasn't so bad, focusing most of his attention on his young son, but Ithen was bored. He spent most of his days here, at Asher and Veronica's home, because that was where Cesa wanted to spend his time. The two families were close, their children friends until recently, but Ithen was struggling to root out their secrets.

He'd never expected to grow attached to Asher over the last few weeks, and the feelings could become a complication if he wasn't careful.

"You have your child! You have an heir now," Cesa's voice raged, behind the closed door of the nearby study.

Ithen had never known Cesa to raise his voice to Asher. Leaving the playroom behind, Ithen walked down the hallway to the study door and gave a flourish of his wrist to summon a spell that would create a portal in the wall. He would remain unseen from inside but could watch Cesa and Asher, hear every word, and perhaps finally discover the secrets of the Copry and Tera families.

Asher paced the window and raked both hands through his raven dark hair. When he faced Cesa, his deep green eyes were sad and pleading. "I love her, Cesa. I love Storm. You always knew that," he said, briefly touching Cesa's elbow, where they stood barely a foot apart. "You always knew we could never be together again after we separated." He leaned closer to rest his forehead against Cesa's, the man who had been his best friend for years.

Ithen's heart squeezed at the thought of Cesa and Asher being in love with each other or having once been in a relationship. He'd assumed Asher was disinterested in his attention, immune to his spells, because the man was straight, not that he didn't see Ithen as someone worthy of his love.

"I don't know if I can live without you," Cesa replied in a pained voice.

"You have Rowan to live for," Asher reminded him, though the words made Cesa grasp his arms and hold on tighter. "You know I still love you. Veronica knows and understands that what we had doesn't just disappear. But you know the danger. If we hadn't married other people, our magic would never let us be together."

There was nothing but sorrow and regret in his voice, but Cesa positively exploded with anger, pushing Asher away. "To hell with magic!" The anger and fight left him instantly, a shuddering breath preceding a few whispered words. "I would give up my powers for you."

"I know. And I for you, but we are the balance. You and I are the cornerstone of magic. I protect the amulet, and you protect the spell that makes it work. If we were together, we'd create chaos. If we abandon our magic and our positions, the humans would descend into war."

"I know."

Ithen frowned, having never heard of a magical amulet or spell. Now that he was within the inner circle of the two people meant to protect them, could he get his hands on the amulet? The magic of these covens held many secrets, as he'd discovered most covens did, and he had now stumbled upon an interesting one. A secret he would dig deeper to understand. If Cesa and Asher couldn't be together as a couple despite their love, the amulet was something Ithen wanted.

"This was *your* decision," Asher said, lacking the judgement and blame those words should have held, considering the implications.

Cesa turned away from Asher and walked to the drinks cabinet in the corner of the room to pour a whiskey. Asher followed to accept a glass from his ex-lover and friend. He ducked in to kiss Cesa's cheek, then walked to the two armchairs by the roaring fire, where he sat.

Crossing to the armchair opposite Asher's, Cesa gazed into

his glass. "I feel torn," he said, the casual tone implying that he was eager to change the subject. "Rowan's reached an age where he wants to go to school and be like the other kids. You know he can't do that."

Ithen wondered what was wrong with his son. This was the first he'd heard of Rowan being different to the other kids, though Storm was strange enough to make any other child look normal, no matter their problems. Still, he'd been around Rowan long enough that he should have seen if there was a reason for him to be different, but other than being friends with Storm and having an imaginary friend that they apparently shared, he'd never noticed anything untoward.

"No. His magic would kill someone or risk his sanity," Asher agreed. "Cesa, no matter what happens from now on, no matter how much I love my wife and child, you know I will always love you. We are soulmates...heart-bound...and nothing can change that."

Tears filled Cesa's eyes as he nodded his acceptance of the words.

When Asher finished his drink, he returned to the drinks cabinet and Cesa followed closely. Neither showed surprise at the proximity, nor by the tentative way Cesa rose on his tiptoes to graze his lips against Asher's.

Ithen thought Asher would push him away, to remind him he was married and happy with his family, but Asher cupped his cheek and returned the kiss. They kissed for long, slow moments that lasted an eternity, while Ithen clenched his fists, forced to watch in silence. He wondered if drawing Veronica's attention to the kiss would help, but he didn't like the woman and dealing with her could cause trouble. For a start, he'd need to explain how he knew what was happening inside the study.

Asher parted from Cesa with obvious reluctance, leaned their foreheads together and closed his eyes. "You are not a secret," he whispered, the tender reassurance no doubt causing the next tear that trailed down Cesa's cheek. "You are not unseen, not unloved. You are as much mine, as much my everything as Veronica and Storm have become. I will never leave you."

Cesa tilted his head to steal another kiss, offered Asher a smile and stepped back. "Goodnight, my love." He walked to the door with his head held high, but he clearly left his heart with Asher, just as Asher's obvious sadness implied he'd sent half of his with Cesa.

Ithen closed the portal and walked away from the study to ponder what he had seen.

*

Present Day

RETREATING FROM THE memory, Storm sank to the side, beside Ithen's unmoving body.

He barely knew what to make of what he'd learned, his head spinning with the implications of the intense memory. Ithen's crush on Asher—Storm's dad—was frighteningly similar to Storm's feelings for Ithen. The man wasn't the stranger he'd thought, only entering his life this year. Ithen had been in his house, practically part of his family, and in love with his dad when Storm was a child.

No wonder Ithen hadn't responded to Storm's flirtations; he thought them pathetic, or this was his revenge for Asher never noticing Ithen's attention. Storm had felt invisible to Ithen, and he now knew Ithen had felt the same to his dad.

The deeply buried anger and resentment had been clear to Storm, bubbling in the teenage Ithen long before he entered their lives. In contrast, Storm had been overwhelmed by the sheer intensity of genuine love in Asher's eyes when he looked at Cesa. The man was nothing like the Cesa Copry he knew, and the reason seemed simple: Cesa had turned to stone when Asher Tera died. Cesa had said he didn't think he could live without Asher, and Storm was watching the living proof of those words in the Cesa who drifted through life as nothing but a sad, bitter man full of anger.

Glancing at Yael, he couldn't find the words to explain what he'd seen.

Yael raised an eyebrow and cocked their head. "That was unexpected."

"You saw?" Storm asked, relieved he didn't need to find the words to explain the grief, love and pain he'd experienced.

Yael gave a careless shrug, so common to demons. "Yes. At the moment, you are projecting." A tentative smile played on their lips as they tipped their head, a lock of hair falling over their white eyes. "You want me to see what you see, because you know I can help you understand. Thank you. You are such a considerate mage."

As much as he cried for his dad's lost life and love, for the unfairness of what magic had done to two innocent people, Storm laughed for the way Yael could so easily put everything into perspective. He'd have to keep the silly demon safe before someone took advantage of the sweetness lurking beneath the surface.

"There is more to see," Yael reminded him, as if reading his thoughts.

Storm shook his head. "I'm not sure I want to go back in." His heart broke to see his dad, who he barely remembered with any real clarity, so full of life. As sad as the memory was, Asher still loved his family despite loving Cesa.

Seeing more may tempt fate.

"You must. You have not yet found your answers," Yael warned, with such compassion Storm smiled.

He nodded and gazed at Ithen. He hated the thought of kissing him, knowing what the man was like and what had motivated him to teach Storm magic, but he wanted answers. Repeating the spell and kiss, he stepped back into Ithen's memories, praying his dad's secret love would be the only surprise of the day.

A flurry of images shot through Storm's mind at once, like watching a movie on fast-forward with no way to slow down or come to a stop.

*

Ithen's Memories

SITTING IN GLADYS'S house, Ithen ran an appraising eye over the living room, from the kaftan on the sofa to the piles of books and magazines littered throughout the room. The place was a mess; herbs lay across a sideboard filled with voodoo dolls and candles, a list of spells had been scribbled on the bare walls on either side of the door, while sigils had been carved into the fireplace mantle.

Gladys was clearly paranoid.

Ithen knew little about the white witch, but she had known his father and had contacted him after his parents' deaths to offer him a place within the local coven circle. There were five covens in the county: the Copry, Tera, and Glade covens that he was familiar with, as well as the lighter witches of the Sorrell and Lasym covens. Gladys had known the Deontay family for nearly twenty years and wanted to include his magic into the coven circle, but the other covens could take years to trust him enough to allow him legitimate membership into the sacred council of coven leaders. He was willing to wait, amassing knowledge and power while they fussed over some prophecy that would probably never come true. If any of this was real, he doubted Storm would face the vengeance of the Fates until he was an adult, and Ithen planned to be long gone from this area by then.

Still, Gladys was the reason he was here, welcomed into the community and poised to get his hands on the mysterious amulet and the accompanying spell. He'd lived in this tiny house before moving in with Cesa, and it didn't compare to the manor. The house had deteriorated in such a short time, and the company left a lot to be desired. What caught his eye was the spell for creating a homunculus, scribbled onto a piece of paper on the table, partly hidden by a photograph of a young boy. No more than ten or eleven years old, the boy had albino features, startling ice-cold and dead behind the eyes. This was either a death photo or the child had died not long after.

Who was he to Gladys? What made her think a white witch could create the dark abomination of a living being? Did she hope to resurrect this child's spirit into another human, into a doll or animal as he had seen written in his family's grimoire?

"How do you take your tea?" Gladys asked as she stepped through from the kitchen.

"I don't." Ithen gestured for Gladys to sit, both rude and presumptuous, considering this wasn't his house and she had invited him, but he had questions and Gladys had enough secrets that Ithen could use to force her to answer. "I presume your attempts to resurrect the boy failed?"

Gladys visibly flinched, drawing her shawl around her fifty-year-old shoulders. "I don't believe that's any of your business," she said, her tone stern and motherly. "I invited you here because I know what you want. I read your cards." She gestured to the table by her armchair to the velvet pouch he presumed held her tarot deck.

"What did you see?"

"You plan to start a war," she answered without censure as she settled into her chair. "Murder is in your future. In your past too, I believe."

Ithen shrugged and rested his arms on the chair, tapping his finger thoughtfully against the worn fabric. "My parents weren't progressive witches. Rather short-sighted, in fact. They were displeased when I began studying the family grimoire without their permission and positively enraged when they found out I'd used a spell on a neighbourhood boy."

At barely nine years old, he hadn't been old enough to know what to do with the boy but had ended the brute's bullying words at school, enjoying the ability to make him hurt whenever he said something against Ithen's wishes.

He faced Gladys without flinching, not needing to fake shame for his actions. "When they threatened to bind my magic, I pretended to be weak, locked them in the barn and set a fire. I stayed until the fire burned out to make sure they were dead," he revealed, intrigued to see no sign of judgement in Gladys's eyes.

The woman nodded and gazed at the table and the photograph of the boy. "I have a photographic memory. All I need to do is focus to draw the words to me. Under the guise of helping the other covens read the ancient Latin spells, I memorised every grimoire. The Tera grimoire—" She stopped, lifted the photograph and gazed lovingly at the boy. "I sent myself to the abyss in the hopes of ascending to greater magic. I was lost for days, and my sweet Donald James paid the price. He followed me and encountered a higher demon, an unforgiving beast who didn't approve of my intrusion into their world.

"By the time I found my way home, Donald James was a shell. He had abilities he'd never been born to, saw what no one else could, and he'd lost his mind. In the end, he walked into the woods and surrendered to the demons." She drew her shawl around her shoulders, avoiding eye contact. She wasn't ashamed but Ithen suspected she feared his reaction, no doubt aware that he'd consider her responsible for her son's misfortune, despite her obvious denial.

Ithen was impressed. For a boy so young to brave the demon world to cure his madness was uncommon.

"I can return your son to you," Ithen said, sure he could manage the task, once he had the amulet and had increased his power. "Help me find the amulet and spell the Copry and Tera families guard, and I will return your son, more whole and complete than any homunculus."

*

IN THE STUDY at the Copry manor, Ithen stretched from his place on the sofa by the fire. Months since his agreement with Gladys, victory was in his sight.

Thanks to Gladys's experience with dark magic, Ithen had managed to break Cesa Copry's mental shields. A touch of manipulation, dark magic and a sprinkle of herbs to cloud the mind, and

Cesa was as much a puppet dancing to his whims as that boy at school had been.

Under his influence, he had created a solid barrier between the Copry and Tera families, with Cesa growing more bitter and angry toward his old lover in the last month. He had become stern with Rowan, sending him away more often than he spent time with the boy, leaving him in the hands of his tutors and the family grimoire rather than teaching him anything of worth.

Ithen was rewarded with that knowledge, expanding his magic with secrets from the Copry family line. Delighted by the growing distance he'd encouraged, Ithen kept Cesa from being in Asher's company as much as he could. Despite his new power, he knew that the strength of love they shared was probably the only thing in the world that could break through his curse and free Cesa from his sway. He couldn't allow Asher to ever find out that Cesa wasn't in control of his own mind.

A whisper, a lie, a glance in the wrong direction and Cesa was utterly convinced Asher didn't love him, had never loved him and had used dark magic to twist his mind. With the added bonus of Rowan studying hard and sulking over his lost friendship with Storm, Ithen was able to monopolise Cesa's time and convince him to be a magical mentor.

"Tell me about the amulet," he asked, keeping his voice quiet and curious as they sat on the sofa together, pouring over the Copry grimoire. "I want to know everything."

"I can't say how much is the truth, as the story is generations old, but...very well." Cesa nodded and cupped his hands around his knee, staring thoughtfully into the roaring fire. "There was a young Celt boy, whose village was attacked. Their women and children were slaughtered mercilessly, and because this boy had magic, he prayed to the Fates and the gods of magic, begging for a way to protect his village from more death and destruction.

"The boy wore a brooch, passed down through his family line. The Fates gave him a spell to make the brooch into a protective amulet that would increase his magic tenfold. As long as he protected rather than attacked, his magic would remain strong, but if he betrayed the Fates by misusing the amulet, he would pay the ultimate price and lose his magic forever."

"I see." Ithen nibbled his lower lip, wondering how he could use the amulet without corrupting the Fates' wishes. He didn't want to lose his magic but may succeed if he had someone else do his bidding; then they would lose their magic and he would still be able to use the amulet for his own intentions.

Cesa kept talking and Ithen didn't interrupt. The more he knew about the amulet's origin, the more he could plan his future endeavours. "The boy grew into a man, using his power for good. When he grew old, he passed the amulet to his son and so on for three generations...until one descendant used the amulet to conquer a town. They spilled so much blood that the man was stripped of his magic and lost the amulet in the snow.

"Thus came the end of the story, until two siblings found the amulet, a year later. The Fates spoke to them and promised that if they followed the same rules, they could take the amulet and spell, but they must part forever." Cesa sighed, his gaze far away and voice full of the weight of the responsibility that came from protecting such magic. "The girl was a natural dark witch and went on to marry a local mage, a Tera. The boy, a white witch, became the head of the Copry coven. Both dedicated their lives to hiding the existence of the amulet and spell from other covens, and the Fates swore that only the descendants of these two protectors could see or touch the amulet or know the spell. To pass both safely through the generations, the spell was written down, to avoid misinterpretation or failing memories."

Ithen nodded, glad to have some good news.

"Ever since, the Copry family have guarded the spell, and the Tera have protected the amulet. No Tera and Copry could marry, live together, nor perform magic together, for fear that the temptation to join the spell with the amulet would arise," he admitted, confirming Ithen's suspicions. This was the reason Asher and Cesa couldn't be together.

"That seems unfair."

Cesa graced him with a smile. "That is how it has been."

Ithen twisted to lean into Cesa, holding his gaze. "Will the prophecy change anything?" The prophecy didn't mention the amulet, but surely Storm must need the amulet to become the all-powerful mage prophesied to unite all the covens.

"The prophecy changes everything," Cesa agreed as his eyes lit with wonder. "If Storm is truly 'one who is the sum of all powers', in terms of magic he is a member of every coven. Meaning he would be—not by blood but certainly by magic—equal parts Tera and Copry."

"He could be the one to break the bonds of the agreement with the Fates? In terms of the amulet?" Ithen inwardly cursed, realising the little brat was the key to giving him everything he'd ever wanted. If he could get closer to Storm, he could make the boy give him both the amulet and spell, *if* Cesa proved unreasonable. Either way, Ithen would strip the covens of their power and rid the world of magic until he was the last to hold power.

He would make the world kneel at his feet, force Asher to love him and make Cesa obey him, even if he had to kill the little prophecy boy and any others who stood in his way.

Chapter Nine

Present Day
November 9, 2026

AS MUCH AS Storm hated what he was seeing, he didn't pull away from Ithen's true heart. He kept watching the roll of memories, needing to learn all he could about this man at the centre of everything important in his life.

For the first time, he pitied Cesa Copry. The man suffered bouts of clarity throughout the next few years, fighting the curse Ithen placed upon him. He was often kind and sweet to Rowan and thought of Asher with fondness. Yet, no matter how long his victory, he always reverted to how Ithen made him: bitter, angry and convinced the Tera family had stolen his power. Cesa became obsessed with finding the amulet.

Storm wanted to reach into the past, to give Cesa his sanity back, to remind him that Asher loved him. He hadn't known what love was before, but now he knew. He'd seen love in his parents, in Asher and Cesa's relationship, in the glimpses of Cesa and Rowan. They were all different kinds of love but each true and solid; no amount of magic in the world could stop them from loving each other.

No matter how cursed Cesa was, his love for Asher and Rowan broke through. The fact he kept fighting was the only reason Storm couldn't give up. He embraced the truth as he allowed Ithen's memories to wash over him.

*

Ithen's Memories: 2014

A BRUTAL STORM howled as Ithen arrived at the Tera manor for Storm's sixth birthday. The property was dark at only six o'clock on the November night and he was glad Cesa hadn't needed any convincing to stay home, despite Asher's continued attempts to reach out to his old lover. Ithen hoped tonight would be the night he could unearth the last piece of information about the amulet.

"Storm, will you please talk to the wind?" Veronica's voice floated through the entry hall behind the little boy running toward the stairs. She shook her head and crossed to Asher. "That is the strangest little boy I have ever met."

Asher caught her around the waist with one arm, gazing into

her eyes. "He is the best of both of us."

Storm walked to the open door, ignoring Ithen standing there, and cupped his hands around his mouth. "Wind, could you please calm down? Mum is shouting at me like it's my fault." He stood and waited as the wind calmed to a hard breeze. "Thank you!" A crackle of black mist floated from his hands, drifting out the open door as Storm turned and ran to the stairs. The magic sailed through the air, becoming a flutter of leaves, dancing in the calmer wind.

Clearly the boy had learned to befriend and play with the wind.

Ithen scowled when Storm turned at the bottom of the stairs, where Rowan stood waiting, chatting to someone invisible.

"Come on, Yael. We'll find you a new hat in the attic," Rowan said, leading the way up the grand staircase with Storm hot on his heels. A few steps later, Asher lifted Storm off his feet to raucous laughter.

"No demons in the attic. You know dark magic can hurt your friend. Take the box and your friend to your room," he advised, letting him go to continue his run upstairs. He didn't seem concerned that his son was playing with demons.

Ithen watched in confusion. Intrigued to discover if the demon was real or if Storm had an imaginary friend, he turned to Asher. "Storm sees demons so young?"

"Since he was a baby," Asher admitted with fondness. "He has a strong affinity for this one. What I find more curious is that

Rowan has the ability. An elemental witch wouldn't normally have contact with the darker arts at his age. The Fates must believe he'll need the gift in the future."

"To protect the amulet."

That remark bought him a dark look from Asher. He grabbed Ithen's arm and guided him into the privacy of the study, closing the doors behind him and flicking the lock. "How do you know of the amulet?"

"Cesa told me. He said I should know how to protect the spell, in case of an emergency," Ithen explained, though he still needed to know how to find the spell and where the amulet was.

"I see." Asher walked away and paused at the window. "Did he not tell you that you must be of Copry blood to protect the spell? Only a Copry can see the paper the spell is written on, just as a Tera is the only one who can see the amulet."

Ithen raised an eyebrow, pretending to be surprised, though the words confirmed what Cesa had told him. He was neither Tera nor Copry and Cesa wasn't likely to bend to his will, with the way he continually fell into old habits. Ithen had been forced to increase the hold over his mind, and he feared another push may break him entirely.

"I didn't know," Ithen lied, digging deep in his magic to find the darker spells, the ones to control and manipulate minds. With a flick of his wrist, he muttered the words to the spell until Asher froze mid-step and was fully under his control. "Bring the amulet to me."

Intriguingly, Asher resisted. No one had ever resisted him, not even in those fleeting moments Cesa regained his faculties. He always succumbed again because believing the lies Ithen had fed him came so easily.

Ithen pushed more magic into the spell, watching the alertness remain in those beautiful dark eyes. He needed to vanquish Asher's consciousness for the spell to take root, and if that required more magic then so be it.

After only two minutes, the sound of footsteps approached the door, followed by a polite knock. "Asher?" Veronica called, repeating her husband's name a few times.

Every time Veronica spoke, Asher fought harder and gained more control, able to curl his hands into fists. Ithen couldn't let him regain enough to utilise his magic. "I didn't want to do this," he admitted, dragging out the darkest magic from the Tera grimoire. The moment he called the shadows from the corners of the room, Asher's eyes widened with understanding.

Ithen bought a few inches of ground, shoving Asher's consciousness so far that his eyes flickered between awareness and emptiness. Just two more minutes and Asher would be his puppet.

"Asher! What's wrong? Cesa says you're in danger!" Veronica shouted, though her voice didn't inspire another resurgence of Asher's consciousness.

He was almost fully submerged in Ithen's will.

Another, harder knock battered the wooden door, and Cesa's voice shouted through in panic, "Asher, stay away from Ithen.

Fight him!"

The result was instant. If Ithen had ever doubted the fabled power of love, he saw its effect in full force. Asher loved his wife but seemed to love Cesa with a strength so powerful and deep that Asher broke through the spell with ease, almost before Ithen could register the switch.

With an enraged scream, Asher thrust out both hands, sending every ounce of his magic toward Ithen. Scrambling to save his life, Ithen focused on a defensive barrier. This had gone to hell, so he needed to find a way to escape, to find another path toward his goal.

Clearly, Asher was too strong to allow him to live.

*

Present Day

STORM STUMBLED FROM the memory into a place of darkness, similar to the abyss but nowhere near as dark or evil. He wasn't sure where he was, but pain raked along his spine like the mark of a talon, leaving him screaming and grabbing his head as words and images warred with one another.

In an instant, he was thrown from Ithen's memories into his own. Memories so distant and forgotten that Storm had never seen them.

*

Storm's Memories: 2014

SITTING ON THE floor with Rowan as Yael tried on their fancy-dress hats, Storm flinched as the wind battered the window, a tree branch beating the glass. Storm cocked his head to listen, but screams from downstairs distracted his focus. He looked at Rowan whose eyes widened.

"My father is here," he whispered, probably worried because he wasn't supposed to be here. Their fathers had fallen out, and Rowan was banned from visiting. Homeschooled as he was, he didn't have any other friends and Storm liked playing with him.

He was about to speak when his dad's voice broke into his mind, creating a crack that resonated through his head, opening a previously locked door. Storm cried out and held his head as the word *Run!* repeated over and over inside his head.

Yael squeaked and rushed to their feet, spreading their arms wide. Black smoke emanated from every inch of their body until Storm could barely see the rest of the room which became opaque and cloudy within minutes.

Rowan grabbed his arm and tugged until Storm huddled in the corner by the bed, remaining behind Yael's barrier of smoke.

The door banged open and Storm screamed. Rowan put a hand over Storm's mouth as Yael trembled but held strong.

Ithen marched into the room, blood trickling from his nose as he stomped around, searching every corner. Storm had never liked the man or how he spoke to people, so he remained in hiding.

When Gladys followed him into the room, Storm almost called out to her, trusting the witch like she was family. Then she spoke and his world shattered into uncertainty and confusion.

"This is a disaster," she snapped, helping Ithen search the room. "You knew only a Tera could find and use the amulet so you went and killed the only two we could control?"

Rowan glanced at Storm and held a finger to his lips. Storm nodded but didn't understand what was happening. Gladys was saying his parents were dead...killed by Ithen. Why?

"It wasn't on purpose," Ithen replied, sounding almost petulant, a word his mum had loved to use whenever Storm was moody and tired. "Asher fought me, and he was stronger. We're lucky I got out alive," he said, pausing at a scream from downstairs.

Rowan's eyes widened, and he mouthed, "My father."

Instead of being overcome with grief, clarity flowed through Storm. Their parents had been close before these last few months and that scream could only be from Cesa, who must have been so sad that his friends had died. Storm cried for them, but stayed quiet as Yael protected them from the people he had thought he could trust, who were now ravaging his parents' bedroom.

"I doubt we'd see the amulet even if it was right in front of us," Ithen grumbled, turning to where Gladys stood by the door. "You said the boy couldn't leave the house. Where is he?"

"I don't know. I put a spell over the exits so he couldn't leave, but he isn't anywhere to be found."

Rowan squeezed him tight, and Storm grasped his hand.

They were searching for him and an amulet; he couldn't let them find him, not if they had killed his family.

Ithen left the room, barking demands, but when Gladys followed, she glanced at where Yael stood and sniffed before leaving. A moment later, Yael sagged to the floor and faded into a shadow before disappearing.

"Yael!" Storm reached for them, but nothing remained. He didn't understand why, where they'd gone or why they'd left.

Rowan grabbed his hand and urged him to stand. They snuck downstairs and froze at the bottom of the steps as Gladys stepped out of the sitting room and pointed at them. She uttered strange words, and Storm felt his mind tremble.

"Storm, we've been searching for you." When she reached out, every instinct told him to run, but he let her hug him and hold him tight. "I'm sorry, sweetheart. A demon tried to force your father into a bond and killed him. Your mother died from the explosion of magic."

The words were spoken in comfort, but Storm's brain screamed, *Don't believe her,* and the wind howled, *Lies! Lies! Run!* He didn't know what to do. A prickle of something raised the hairs on his neck as Gladys drew an image on his back, and in an instant, his doubts were chased away and he felt silly for worrying.

Gladys was so kind, though she'd been sad ever since her son died, and DJ—the nickname the other boys gave him—would probably trade places with him in a heartbeat, to hug his mum again. Storm squeezed her tight and let her lead him toward the door.

"You'll live with me until you're old enough to live alone," Gladys said, wiping away his tears.

Storm wasn't sure why he was crying but a scream and a shout came from his dad's study. The door was open, and his dad lay on the floor, empty eyes staring unseeing at Storm, blood seeping from his eyes and mouth. The last tendrils of dark magic floated around him, not sure where to go without their host.

Cesa Copry lay across his prone body, crying out in grief and pain. Though Rowan ran to Cesa, the comfort of his son wasn't enough. Storm opened his mouth to ask Cesa to care for him so he could be with Rowan but hesitated when the magic surrounding his dad became a hazy figure rising from his body.

Asher Tera, his dad, stood from his body and gazed at Cesa with sad eyes. He bent to kiss his cheek, Cesa shivering in response to the contact he could feel but could never fully understand, then walked from the study toward Storm.

In the background of Storm's awareness, Ithen and Gladys were making plans, but he couldn't find the will to care. He stared at his dad as a misty hand lifted to cup his cheek.

"I love you, my little Storm. When you are ready, you will learn the truth, and I hope you are wise enough to not seek revenge. It cannot bring us back to you," he advised, glancing over to where Storm's mother stumbled from her body.

"Trust no one," Asher whispered, bending to look him in the eye. "The only people you can trust are Rowan and Yael. One day Yael will return to you, but they won't be safe here for some time.

You have to be brave while you're alone."

Storm nodded his promise and watched his dad glance at Cesa Copry, clearly distraught by the loss of his friends. Veronica walked away, fading into a stream of light that welcomed her.

Once she was gone, his dad kissed Storm's forehead and tapped his nose. "You won't understand this now but when you're older…if you can, save Cesa from the darkness clouding his mind and heart. For Rowan's sake and yours."

"For you, daddy," he said in his mind, knowing his dad couldn't rest easy in the abyss unless he did this.

Asher nodded but looked sad. "You're a smart boy. Love deeply, study hard and live well, my little Storm." Without another word, he faded into the light the way his mum had, after taking a last glance at Cesa before he caught Storm's eye and disappeared forever.

Following his gaze, Storm didn't know what else to do but sent some magic to soothe Cesa and Rowan, who sat by his father, crying quietly. When Cesa hugged his son, Storm saw the darkness fade from around him, glad he could do something good in this moment of madness.

*

Present Day

RETREATING FROM THE torment of memories, now he had the answers he needed, Storm sagged and slipped away from the traitor. An added kick to Ithen's side was instinctive, but he wasn't sure if he wanted Ithen further away or just to hurt him.

He wanted to scream, to run, to forget he'd ever witnessed these memories that revealed so much.

Everyone he'd ever counted on since his parents died, everyone he'd ever trusted since he was left alone in the world, had betrayed him by murdering his parents. The one man he had blamed for everything, the one man he hated more than anyone else, was a victim, just like Storm.

Tainted by Ithen's magic and manipulations twisting his mind, Cesa was trapped in a cage, locked away from the feelings of love and warmth he had for Storm's parents, while kept at a distance from his son.

Rowan needed to know the truth Gladys had kept from them, with her twisted dark magic. No wonder she'd aged well and hadn't handed over her coven to Gregory; she couldn't risk him finding out what she'd done or what she was capable of. Gregory could be counted on to treat her like a traitor. Thanks to Gladys's lack of motherly instinct, her detachment from anyone not herself, Gregory could do what needed to be done without sentiment getting in the way.

The tears slipping over his cheeks were a natural reaction to everything he'd seen and now knew, but Storm pushed them away. They wouldn't help. Lifting his head, he met Yael's gaze across Ithen's body, not surprised that they looked shocked.

"I remember nothing of my childhood. It is like a separate

life to demons. The way your life and death are separate." Yael would have mentioned if they remembered their past together, though they must have been terrified to realise there was so much of their life they couldn't remember.

Gladys must have sensed Yael that night and had either sent them away or known they would run, in case she used her magic against them. She stole them from each other, erasing them from Storm's mind so he couldn't remember Yael, while knowing that Yael wouldn't keep those memories.

What a bitch.

Storm crawled around Ithen's body to sit next to Yael, taking their hand in his. "I understand now." He watched the confusion clear as anger took over, an emotion he shared. "This explains why we're drawn to each other. We were childhood friends. And we're a team, right? We'll work together to make this right and bond as we were always meant to," he said, feeling more deeply than ever that this was their true path. They would be a team, not a master and servant. He could never put shackles on Yael and monitor their every move; that was Ithen's idea of magic but not Storm's.

Yael looked pleased, a slow smile forming, which morphed from delighted to coy. "Yes. I think I'd like that."

Storm didn't doubt they looked forward to dealing with Ithen and Gladys when the time came. "What will we do about him?"

Yael's gaze slid over Ithen's body, pure evil swirling behind their white eyes. "The higher demons might want him. They would find his magic interesting."

As fitting as punishment may be, Storm wanted Ithen some-where accessible and safe, in case they needed him later. "How about we stuff him in my shack?" he countered, smiling when Yael looked disappointed. "In case we want to delve into his head again or we need to use him. I can't go back to the shack. I need to stay somewhere they won't find me."

"Rowan." They spoke at the same time, so Storm didn't de-fend the decision. It was the only place he could think of, and his dad had been right the day he died: the only two people in the world he could trust were Yael and Rowan. Just as they had always been by his side, they would need to fight this war together.

He wished he didn't have to involve Rowan, but logic de-manded he open his eyes and cast his own feelings aside because Rowan was already involved. He had been ever since the start when his father was cursed and Ithen stole what relationship they had with a curse.

Now they had to undo the wrongs of the past: Cesa's curse, his parents' murders, his failure as the Chosen One, and their bro-ken friendship. Storm had a feeling that the real reason he'd lost the war the first time around was because he hadn't been at his strongest, and he hadn't been whole. Without Rowan and Yael, he wasn't surprised he'd failed to fulfil the prophesy, lost the war and descended into bitterness.

Without them, he wasn't truly Storm Tera, dark mage and necromancer, the Chosen One worthy of fulfilling the prophecy.

Chapter Ten

WHILE STORM PACKED his belongings—study books and personal items from his shack—Yael dragged Ithen inside and strengthened the existing protections and barriers around the building. Ithen wouldn't get out without assistance, even if he did wake before they got back.

Storm decided to wait until nightfall as Rowan had suggested, to avoid being caught by Cesa. He and Yael lazed in the sun for a few hours, lurking in the middle of the poppy field, assured of privacy as everyone expected him to be training with Ithen.

Staring at a blue sky contrary to his mood, Storm listened as Yael ran through all they had learned; who they could trust, who had been involved the night of his parents' murder, who remained innocent or undetermined, and what they knew about the amulet.

"Oh, I know this!" Yael sat up and stared at Storm with eager eyes. "The amulet was used in the war. The one in your—"

"Future, right. Who had the amulet back then?" he asked, not wanting to recap having lived this life. Neither he nor Yael could figure out what had changed, except that his magic had rebelled against the idea of repeating this life just to fulfil the prophecy. According to Yael, part of him wanted to change *everything*, so he immediately began acting contrary to his past life.

"Who do you know who is obsessed with power, position, and believes they are more worthy than any other?" Yael teased, with a knowing smile.

"Copry. Please tell me it's not Rowan." He refused to accept that someone else had betrayed him. Rowan was his last haven, and without him Storm was lost.

"It's not Rowan."

The sass made him smile. But if that was true, he might have to break the promise he'd made to Asher, during a night he couldn't remember. Cesa's involvement complicated everything.

"We demons hear many rumours. From what I remember, the last time you lived this life, the Copry family took possession of an ancient amulet, one the Tera family had become guardians of many generations ago, and used the amulet to begin a war between the covens," Yael explained, gazing into the distance, deep in thought. "I believe that when you chose not to learn the darkest of arts, Ithen had second thoughts about defeating you. He hoped by openly fighting on your side, he may obtain the amulet or your trust. If he had saved your life in the process, you may have felt indebted to him and trusted in his loyalty enough to ask for his guidance in how to safeguard the amulet."

Storm nodded, seeing how easily that plan might have worked. Despite his willingness to resort to murder, Ithen killed Asher by accident, because he fought back and possessed stronger magic. "Because I chose to learn everything this time, including necromancy, he saw a threat and tried to kill me." That would explain why Ithen only taught him theory, but something else niggled at Storm's brain. "Cesa is still under his spell."

"Is that a problem?"

"Just...sad, I guess." He shrugged, not knowing how else to explain how he felt. "He isn't evil. He's being manipulated by dark magic and controlled by a puppet master. Before I knew what happened, I used to look at Rowan and wonder how his father could be evil. How could he be, if he raised Rowan to become who he is?"

"Now you know that he raised Rowan the best he could under the circumstances," Yael said, understanding his train of thought. "Perhaps Rowan is who he is *despite* his father, as you are who you are despite the woman who helped raise you."

Storm didn't want to think about the people who had raised him; not his parents and certainly not Gladys. He didn't want to wonder what his life might be like if his parents had never died, if Ithen had never come into their lives, if they'd never been betrayed or if Cesa had taken him in after his parents died. He wasn't sure he wanted to know or would like the answers.

"Is Gladys dabbling in dark magic?" he asked, seeking clarity from Yael on the warning they'd given him.

Yael tilted their head to follow the path of a crow through the trees. "The higher beings want her to pay for dabbling in magic that does not belong to her. To wield magic not natural to oneself forces magic to become tainted, and those crimes must be paid for."

"Because magic is a balance and a partnership," Storm said, knowing how easily his magic had responded when he was a child and that Yael responded now because he dared to ask for permission. His dad always said Storm should look at magic like love; neither should be forced, and they were both a lifetime commitment, a partnership to be respected, and that required continual time and attention throughout his life.

Gladys had taught him the opposite—magic was the equivalent of a stubborn jar lid that sometimes required a good whack. That was probably how she treated dark magic. If so, she deserved whatever the demons had in mind.

He didn't want to think about Yael's claim that Gladys had sent him here. He couldn't understand why she'd send him back to fix his mistakes, but he *could* understand her motivation for delving into dark magic. Losing her son had broken her spirits.

"Oh gods," he gasped and faced Yael in horror. "I know her son. I met him…in the future. He's been in my dreams," he confessed, wondering if the sweet boy with frightened eyes and no compassion or understanding of his abilities was the same child Gladys had once lost. His name had been Donald in life: Donald

James Glade. He'd been the first not to bear the GG initials, because he wouldn't inherit the coven. Could he be the same DJ he'd met in the future?

"Yes. The boy I sent my message through," Yael agreed with an innocent blink that asked why Storm hadn't put the pieces together sooner.

"She made him a homunculus," he said, ignoring the haughty look he was sure Yael didn't mean.

"I believe so," Yael said, sounding cautious and uncertain, perhaps having the same doubts about how Gladys managed such a feat without true dark magic. "But that was in the past you have now prevented. By changing your actions when you returned, you have made the future obsolete. Just as we must make sure the rest never comes to pass."

If Gladys had the power to tamper with his memories—in the past and in the future—he could easily believe that she'd gained enough power to mess with time. By sending Storm back, she was amassing a level of magic no one wanted her to have; not humans, nor mages, and certainly not demons.

Demons used knowledge like currency to determine their rank in demon society. The more a demon knew—about magic, the past and the future—the more power they had and the more revered they were by other demons and even dark mages, who might choose to bond with them. Higher demons routinely chose seers for bonding partners because they could feed the demon knowledge and maintain their position as a higher demon.

Storm realised how hard this whole situation must be for Yael. They had discovered a childhood friendship, something they hadn't known about, and the future had been changed by the actions of one woman. She had turned the world upside down for demons. Everything they knew about the future, about what would happen and the outcomes, had been tainted by her spell to send him through time. Storm had changed everything when he returned.

"Not having answers must kill you."

"You have no idea." Yael sighed deeply. "Knowledge is power. That is the reason I am a lower demon and not a higher being. If I were higher, I would know more."

Curious, he leaned over his knees. "Can you...*become* a higher demon?"

Yael blinked and Storm wasn't sure why. Did demons never talk about rank or was this supposed to be common knowledge? Was it an insult to ask?

"If what you say is true, the one with knowledge has power. The more you learn, the more powerful a demon you become, right?" Storm rationalised the theory aloud, hoping to figure out if Yael knew the answer or if this was something they could use. "No one knows about this incident today. Like you said, no one could sense my magic. You only came because I asked, which means you know something a higher demon doesn't. And no one knows that we were friends growing up, because *you* didn't know."

If Yael hadn't known that, then the other demons had never

known, or else rumours would have reached Yael long before Storm came back from the future. He wondered if that information was enough leverage to convince a higher demon to help them, or promote Yael to a higher demon rank and, in the process, give them access to more knowledge.

Curiosity flared in white eyes, then teeth appeared as Yael flashed a frightening smile. "You are devious. I love it!" Yael leapt forward to kiss his cheek, grinning wildly. "We must find more answers until we know everything!"

Storm laughed and nodded. "If you happen to grow wings along the way...bonus?" he teased, pleased Yael positively preened at the thought. They laughed and he wondered how he'd been best friends with this creature as a child and never been scared. He wasn't scared now, but he was older and knew the power and heart of this demon.

Perhaps Yael's innocence endeared his childhood self as much as it did now. He wanted to protect that innocence so that Yael could remain exactly as they were, forever.

*

YAEL INSISTED ON slipping into the abyss, in the hope that any mages who passed through might have information about recent events or Ithen's past. Storm wasn't sure they would discover anything new, but Yael was excited about the idea of becoming a higher demon through the pursuit of knowledge. Storm didn't have the heart to disappoint them with the warning that obtaining a rise in rank could take more than a few hours.

After Yael left, Storm stopped by the shack to check on Ithen, who was still in a magically induced coma, chained to the wall where Storm had left him. He rechecked the spells, protections and charms on the shack and found everything in perfect order.

With one problem solved, he only had to worry about the other more complicated one.

Walking to the end of the Tera property line was simple; figuring out how to sneak through the electric fence without being killed, electrocuted or forced to walk three miles around was hard work. For ten minutes, he stared at the fence, exploring his new magic and working out how he'd brought Rowan safely from one side to the other during the storm on the night of his ascension.

Ithen had done a bang-up job of keeping him from learning the ins and outs of his magic. He'd kept Storm locked in reading, studying and going over the basics for so long he hadn't had a chance to *use* his magic. Other than a few scant lessons he'd learned from his dad, in a time he could barely remember because he'd been less than six years old, most of his magic was instinctual or learned from the family grimoire. Now he knew Gladys was a traitor to his family, he wasn't sure anything she'd taught him in the intervening years was worth much.

He had to start from scratch, relying on his best source: instinct. Closing his eyes, he reached for the magic that let him talk to the wind, the ability he'd mastered when he was barely old enough to understand what magic was.

I don't know what I'm doing. I barely know who I am, and Rowan is the only one I can trust. I need you to help me. Guide me. He let the magic swirl beneath his skin and seek out the wind to relay his message and hope something could provide the solution.

A breeze kissed his face, a caress both reassuring and hopeful. Storm held onto that feeling and waited, appreciating the help.

Storm, the wind whispered as the breeze lifted and stirred the autumn leaves around his feet. *Believe. Trust.*

The words soothed his near panic and reminded him he was never alone. No matter what happened in life, he could always count on the elements, the animals, and his demon. Yael had always been a part of his life, and Storm would do anything to keep it that way.

He breathed slow and steady, believed he could do what needed to be done, and put his trust in the wind. In increments, the wind rose, creating a cyclone of air around his feet, leaves caught in chaos. He opened his eyes to a billowing torrent of colour, his feet shrouded by a black mist of magic. His feet left the ground, his balance offsetting until he felt like he would topple over. Storm held his arms out to the sides to provide balance and stability as he rose higher. Carried over to the electric fence, he sailed harmlessly a foot above the jagged spikes.

When he landed on Copry land, on the other side of the fence, Storm felt dizzy but exhilarated. Who knew levitation was possible?

"Thank you," he said aloud, smiling when a leaf grazed his cheek in a caress of gratitude. As he had since he was a child, he lifted his hands to his mouth and blew the tendrils of untapped magic into the wind in thanks for its help. He'd never known why he made the offering or what the wind used the magic for, but his dad had told him to never stop showing his gratitude. His magic sailed off with the wind, set to do something incredible that he might never see.

A tension he hadn't been aware of carrying around eased as Storm turned in the direction for Rowan's summer house and began walking. He remembered the route from his last visit, but he was surprised by the state he found the building in. The door was unlocked and swinging in the breeze. He opened the glass-panelled door and went in, but nothing seemed amiss. A pile of books had been stashed in the corner next to the chaise, blankets and cushions occupied the armchair and a pile of papers lay on the coffee table.

How Rowan managed to fit so much into the room was astounding.

Storm dropped his bag on the chaise and made sure the door was securely shut. He headed for the pile of books, running a finger over the spines to find Rowan was a magical prodigy. Half the books in the first pile were ancient and advanced magic he could never hope to accomplish in the next five years. He found the stereo on a dresser and flicked on the record seated in the insert. A slow jazz tune made him smile.

Leaving the music playing, Storm drifted through the room, losing track of time as he explored the little summer house. Books about magic sat alongside gay romance novels, a collection of science fiction and fantasy comics were beside a wooden box that held Rowan's tarot deck.

Yael wouldn't return until tomorrow, so Storm got comfortable on the chaise, borrowed one of the comics and lay back to read as he waited for Rowan. He badly needed a distraction from Ithen's memories to forget his life was in chaos because everyone he'd ever thought he could trust had been a traitor.

The summer house filled with the sound of jazz music. When the rain began a pitter-patter on the windows, the soothing combination lulled Storm into sleep.

No ghosts haunted the summer house, and he slept peacefully. Long after the sense of being half awake crept in, the dreams changed from random images he could barely remember to what must have been his previous life, the one he'd been so determined to fix.

Storm watched in fascination and shame as he fell for Ithen's innocent act and thought he loved the man. He saw Denver die, all because he'd failed to learn anything useful, allowing his feelings and flirtations with Ithen to distract him from training. He'd been useless and hadn't dared learn necromancy, which meant that when Denver died, and then Foley and Ithen, he could do nothing but watch and let regret consume him.

His mind battled with his body, attempting to wake up, but

his senses were clouded by the smell of smoke clogging his nose and people screaming. He couldn't concentrate on waking through the noise and the chaos.

Watching from a distance, Cesa sent a curse at Storm, while Ithen died from the explosive clash of his magic with a spell from the Sorrel coven. Storm was shocked to see Ithen's spell had been a killing curse, just as Cesa was sending one to kill Storm. If his other self—the one who had lived through this battle—had seen the truth of Ithen's actions toward the other covens, he would have known Ithen wasn't worth grieving over. Instead, the other Storm had turned homicidal at the loss.

The dream-body, taking in the chaos of war, shook his head but didn't dislodge Storm from the dream. He just careened from one horror to another.

He stood on Copry soil, and Cesa looked enraged because Storm had dared to ask about the amulet and his place in protecting it. Perhaps his newfound knowledge of how deeply Cesa had loved his dad offered clarity, but the anger seemed to mask a deeper emotion. They argued, throwing accusations at each other until Storm made the grave mistake of accusing Cesa of murdering his parents. Cesa reacted brutally, throwing a curse at Storm that could have killed him, but Rowan darted from the house and placed himself in front of Storm with impossible speed.

Storm didn't understand how Rowan was capable of such an ability, but he rushed to protect Storm, a wave of silvery mist trailing behind his body like a ghostly shadow, equally beautiful and terrifying. The horror of Rowan being hit by the curse floored him, while Cesa dissolved into shock, stunned by what he'd inadvertently done.

His half-awake mind remained detached enough to ponder that strange glow of magic. Rowan was a child of the light, born on Midsummer—Litha, the longest day and shortest night of the year—a purer white witch than any other Storm had seen. Rowan's birth marked him for the light, just as being born on November second, the Day of the Dead, had made Storm the perfect dark mage.

As Rowan sank to the ground, hit by a brutal curse meant to torture its target, he didn't die instantly as he should have, as Storm would have. He lingered long enough to grasp Storm's hand as he held Rowan and sank to his knees to cradle Rowan's dying body.

"I never wanted any part of this," he whispered, eyes flashing with the coldest ice blue.

Waking from the shock of the revelation, Storm's sleeping and waking minds joined for a single moment, and he rose from his dreams screaming Rowan's name.

His waking mind needed time to register that he was no longer locked in the dreams and memories that ruined a peaceful sleep. The summer house was encased in night and the slow *tick tick tick* of the record waiting for the needle to be replaced offered a relief he didn't realise he needed.

"You called?"

Storm recognised the voice instantly. Though Rowan sounded nervous, Storm lifted his right hand and called forth magic to light the space. "Sorry. I was...dreaming," he said, hoping Rowan didn't think he was rude for falling asleep in his secret place. "It's been a hell of a day."

Rowan snorted but closed the door behind him and crossed to lift the multiple blankets and cushions from the armchair to sit down. "I'm sure I have you beat, but we'll see." A smile flirted with his lips as he sank into the seat and heaved a sigh. With the ease of familiarity, he pulled a satchel strap over his head, dumped the bag at the side of the chair and kicked off his sneakers. "I started my day with my father screaming as he woke from a nightmare," Rowan began, linking his hands on his stomach. "He rambled about regrets and not being strong enough to save 'him'. I came here, studied for my online course and found out someone had cheated on their last test, and so we were forced to redo the entire thing 'to be sure'." He rolled his eyes as he used air quotes to prove how shitty his day had been.

Storm stifled his smile as he pushed up to sit on the chaise, then crossed his ankles and listened with interest.

"By the time I remembered to eat, I was stuck in an online lecture for the next hour. When I finished, I had enough time to nip home, grab some food, feed my father and head out onto the farmland to collect the rent. You know, since my father isn't capable of taking care of the estate."

Storm understood why the estate was the bane of Rowan's

life and didn't interrupt. He could tell Rowan the truth about his father's mental state and why he flitted between insanity and clarity, but he felt that needed more tact than blurting it out. He could explain more once he'd broken the rest of the bad news.

"I bumped into poor old Mrs Sorrel—Scott's mother, not his sister—and found out she's newly diagnosed with Alzheimer's. In the midst of breaking the news, Scott made a *completely* inappropriate pass at me, offering to 'take care of me' if I just gave him a chance."

Storm lost his composure.

Rowan couldn't resist either. Chuckling at his misfortune, he shook his head. "I escaped unscathed and returned home to find my father sleeping in his armchair, so I put him to bed and got to relax on the sofa in front of the fire for a few hours before this annoying voice screamed my name and brought me running, thinking he was being murdered!"

"Sorry. That's one hell of an interesting day," Storm admitted, realising Rowan had every right to be frustrated and want a quiet night. Storm could be kind and say they could talk in the morning, but Rowan deserved to know the truth.

"No shit." Rowan snorted his amusement but kept eye contact.

"Want to hear about mine?" Storm asked, waiting for the affirmative nod. "I went to meet Ithen for my training lesson and was tortured by his dark magic. I fought him off, sent him into a magically induced coma and had to lock him in my shack with magical wards." He kept his explanation short because Rowan was exhausted and there was worse to come. Though Rowan was shocked, his eyes widening as he sat forward to protest, Storm kept talking. "A demon friend helped me spend the better part of the afternoon using a demon spell to see into Ithen's heart, which propelled my mind into his memories…where he cursed your father and murdered my parents."

Storm paused after dropping that emotional bomb, to give gave Rowan time to process, the shock visibly washing over his startled gaze, along with the obvious urge to ask questions and the need to find out more. Until they'd talked through every frame of every memory, they couldn't decide what to do next.

"I came here because you're the only person I can trust, and we have to figure this out together, for both our sakes. Except…I fell asleep while reading your comics."

Rowan shifted in his seat. He opened his mouth to speak, shut it again and muttered, "Well…shit."

"Yeah." That was exactly how he felt and why he'd fallen asleep. "Taking Scott's wholly inappropriate flirting into consideration, I'd say we're even," he said to keep things light, and he was relieved Rowan laughed, though he looked weary and confused. Swinging his legs off the side of the chaise, Storm planted his feet on the floor and nibbled at his bottom lip, wondering if he could wait for morning. He caught Rowan's eye and knew that wouldn't be fair. Standing, he crossed to the armchair, not sure what to do except be honest. He touched the fingertips of his right hand against the arm of the chair and braved the words he would never normally have the courage to say. "I need to know I can trust you."

"You can." Rowan nodded, narrowing his eyes as if to ask why Storm doubted him.

Storm knew what it had taken for Rowan to bring him here, to keep his trespass onto Copry land a secret from his father, and the guts required to witness his ascension in front of the Glade coven. Rowan had risked a lot, but Storm had just learned that he'd been trusting people blindly for years and couldn't risk making the same mistake twice. "I need you to prove it," he said, hating that this could ruin the tentative trust between them. They'd spent their entire lives believing lies, treating each other like the enemy, never remembering the years of strong friendship they'd formed before his parents died and their worlds collapsed.

"How?"

The fact he bothered to ask was a relief and let Storm know he was prepared to prove his loyalty. "A demon trick. I have to kiss you to see your heart. I guess it's their fancy way of showing me your intentions, your true self, and revealing your hidden secrets. I need you to be fully aware of what you're agreeing to." He hoped Rowan knew he would only ask because Storm already knew Rowan's heart was pure.

Rowan swallowed, licked his lips and nodded. He seemed as nervous as Storm felt, probably because they'd been enemies for so long, unaware they'd once been the best of friends. Now, they were planning to kiss for the first time, not by choice or even an accident but to fulfil a demon spell.

Storm felt awkward, cupping Rowan's face in his hand, being the younger of the two and having never kissed anyone before. Ithen didn't count because that had been part of a spell required to find the truth, and he'd been desperate for answers. This was different.

Dipping his head, he paused to check the look in Rowan's eyes, to make sure he was okay with this. When Storm found no hesitation, only nerves, he ducked in and pressed their lips in a tentative kiss.

The moment they made contact, his magic surged beneath the surface, responding to whatever magic made Rowan unique. The air pushed in tension, his ears popped and something foreign tickled the back of his mind. Opposing forces pushed at each other, elements twisted, distorting in his mind, becoming something equal parts dark and light.

The surge was irresistible...addictive...and threatened to sweep Storm away, but he focused his mind and did what he'd planned to do. *Show me his heart.*

Rowan was—*kind, considerate, passionate, a voracious reader, a lover of music; he loved the sound of rain, long naps, and had been hiding a kitten in this summer house for months; he dreamed of being free, of his family, of being safe around people, of not being alone*—a demon.

Storm broke the kiss, finally knowing the truth.

He didn't expect the tear tracking down Rowan's cheek.

"Half," he whispered, then cleared his throat. "I'm a half-demon. My father couldn't have children and asked the Tera patriarch, your father, to help. Using dark magic, they asked a demon for a favour, creating a child from my father's DNA. In return for the child crafted by the magic, he gave them precious information."

Storm's head was swimming with the repercussions of such a revelation. Rowan was a half-demon, with abilities that astounded him, but nothing changed who he was at heart, in his soul. Just as Yael had promised, the spell showed him exactly who Rowan Copry was at his very core. "Because information is power to demons."

"Right," Rowan replied, pausing to lick his lips. "He needed an heir because only a Copry can continue the coven, the family magic, and protect something we've been tasked to guard for generations."

The fact he thought he had to explain to Storm made him feel like the biggest ass in the world. He was sure that with demon blood Rowan had seen far too many of his truths during their kiss. The kiss would have shared both ways with Rowan being both conscious and part demon, making the magic something natural to him. Storm's secrets weren't pretty. He considered them far worse than Rowan being half-demon because he didn't have a choice to be what he was, but Storm had made every bad decision, taken every wrong turn.

If anyone was evil, it was him.

One more truth had been revealed during the surprisingly

short reading, one that sent his heart fluttering wildly. Taking a risk that he wasn't only seeing what he wanted to see, or misinterpreting the insight, Storm bent to kiss Rowan. He may not have lived through the pivotal moments of Rowan's life, but he was pure even for a demon. Nothing in Rowan's life could hurt him the way Ithen's memories had.

Rowan didn't respond, and he wondered if the flash he'd seen had been wrong or if circumstances had changed since he'd returned from the future.

Was he no longer the Storm that Rowan wanted?

As he was about to break away and apologise, two hands caught his biceps and urged him closer. Rowan parted his lips and flicked his tongue against Storm's, and he opened without question. It was the most electrifying moment of his life; nothing compared to the thunderstorm of magic that often crackled beneath his skin, a rainstorm drenching everything he was and dousing his erratic magic or the highest height. Of all the thrills Storm had sought in his life—the one he'd lived, the one he had memories of, the future he dreamt about—none matched this moment when Rowan...fit. Like the missing piece of his soul had been returned and his body, magic and spirit flared in relief.

A thought perforated the bubble and he stepped back with a gasp, hand lifting to his lips. "You wanted to kiss me," he said, latching onto the faintest whisper, the briefest glimpse of a thought, as Rowan stared with wide eyes. "When you died, I was your last thought. The last person you saw. You wished you could kiss me before you died. You never got to."

The shock of that revelation was startling enough, but when he saw Rowan's wide-eyed stare, Storm realised that Rowan wouldn't know what he meant. He hadn't explained about the strange memories, travelling through time, or that Rowan had died to fulfil the prophecy.

He was about to apologise when Rowan dipped his head and took a shuddering breath. When he looked up, Rowan's chin was trembling and a second tear tracked the mark left by the first. The ice blue belonging to demons fought through the natural human cornflower blue for a split second, the tear sparkling with that same silver magic he'd seen earlier but never questioned.

"The war isn't over until the prophecy is fulfilled," he whispered, maintaining eye contact as he said impossible words. "I can't die again. Please don't let me die."

Chapter Eleven

CRACKING OPEN BOTTLED water and a box of chocolate from the stash in the cooler, they sat on the floor together, beneath a blanket, as a storm raged outside the summer house. They'd been sitting quietly for so long, talking softly and taking a break from the reality of the danger ahead by focusing on their feelings that when the rain started, Rowan flinched.

"Midnight!" Rowan rushed into the steady patter of rain in a panic, while Storm sat confused, until Rowan returned with a tiny black kitten in his arms. He returned to his seat beside Storm, the bundle of fur snuggled tight against his chest while the half-demon and heir of the Copry coven stroked its ear. "This is Midnight. She was given to me by the demon who gave life to me as a way to share my power when it becomes overwhelming," he explained with a proud smile that melted Storm's heart.

"Is she also...part-demon?"

Rowan nodded, glancing up with a charming smile. "She takes the burden of my magic, whenever I feel like I might lose control. She always knows when she's needed. That's why I don't go to school. I stay at home, because my magic is unpredictable."

Storm hated that he was scared of his own heritage, but he understood better than Rowan thought. When magic was an integral part of someone, they learned how to understand and control it, but dark magic—which was, fundamentally, linked to demon magic—wasn't something that enjoyed being tamed and harnessed. Dark magic was a wild thing that longed to be free, no matter how many years Storm put into bonding with his magic. Cooperating with his magic had always been far more effective than trying to strong arm it, though he wondered if anyone had taught Rowan that useful distinction as a way of handling his own errant abilities.

"Sorry. You were telling me about what you discovered from Ithen," Rowan said, flashing a shy smile in apology for the interruption.

Storm didn't care, but he loved that Rowan's worry for the kitten had taken precedence over everything else. Since he'd asked, Storm talked through events, starting with waking up on Copry land, feeling disorientated and finding out he'd travelled through time because he'd failed to fulfil the prophecy the first time. He explained about Yael, that they'd made a tentative pact and how he'd been tortured by Ithen that morning.

The hardest part was telling Rowan about his encounter with Ithen, reading his heart, darker than the most accomplished dark mage, and all the crimes he'd committed. He confided the truth about the fake rivalry between their families and how deeply Asher and Cesa loved each other before the Fates tore them apart.

Rowan didn't seem surprised. "My demon blood lets me feel big changes in the magical world," he confessed, staring at Midnight, who pawed at a loose thread of his jumper. "When you fell from the abyss, I knew where to find you and what I'd find, but when *you* didn't know, I wasn't sure what to do.

"I tried not to let on that anything had changed, so I kept my distance until your ascension. When you spoke to me in your mind, I realised you were putting the pieces together." He raised his head to meet Storm's gaze with a glimmer of a smile. "You've had the ability since you were a kid."

"When we were best friends," he added, because Rowan needed to know he'd found the memories in Ithen's mind.

Rowan nodded, then winced, glaring at Midnight who he set on the ground before lifting his scratched hand to blow on the cut skin. The wound healed almost instantly, and he brushed off the incident. "I could never tell you because you didn't remember. I'm half-demon and can't be affected by witch magic for long. I fought the compulsion to forget, but by then everyone thought our families hated each other and I couldn't admit the truth without having to explain something I didn't understand."

"Admitting you remembered would have put you in danger,"

Storm said, letting him know he'd made the right choice. Even if he could help Storm remember their friendship, they were children and had no way of fighting back.

Storm noticed that Rowan had grown more physically distant since their kiss, so he offered his hand, palm up. They were in this together and always had been; it was time to remember what they'd forgotten and regain what had been taken from them.

Rowan nibbled his bottom lip and clasped Storm's hand, linking their fingers. "I'm sorry Ithen killed your parents."

"I'm sorry he cursed your father," Storm replied with genuine regret. "As much as I loved my parents, I barely remember them. Knowing they died means their suffering is over, but your father...I can't understand what's happened to his mind. I'm not sure I can fix him." He wished he could do that for Rowan and for Asher, who had trusted him to make this right.

Whatever plans Gladys had for sending him through time—regret, fear for magic users or a last-ditch effort to save her soul—she'd given him a precious gift: the chance to reclaim what she stole from his life. Rowan and Yael had been more than just friends, they'd been missing pieces that were an integral part of who he was, leaving him soul-bruised and incomplete in ways he'd never understood until now. The memories he would never have regained and a lifetime of friendships and chosen family he could trust were important, but nothing meant more to Storm than having Rowan and Yael back in his life. With them by his side, he could purge the people who would hurt him from his life and live the rest of his years—no matter how long—with people he truly cared about and who cared about him.

"I know you're meant to have this power, but I've tried to help him countless times and nothing has worked. If I'd known Ithen was the one responsible, I'd have—" Rowan's voice trailed off as he clenched his free hand into a fist, power crackling along his knuckles like a deadly arc of ice blue electricity.

"Your magic is beautiful."

With a rare blush to his cheeks, Rowan glanced up through dark eyelashes. "So is yours. I guess it's true what they say about opposites attracting. Being the purest white witch, despite my demon nature, means my magic is instinctively attracted to the darkest black magic in the world."

"What about you? Are you attracted to your opposite?" Storm asked, curious if Rowan was attracted to his opposite or if something else tugged them toward each other.

"I think I've loved you my entire life," he confessed without hesitation or embarrassment. His eyes were a delicate cornflower blue, no longer revealing his demon nature. Storm loved both sides and wished he could find the words to admit it. "I knew the truth about our friendship and our families, and I always knew your heart," Rowan continued, hovering a hand over Storm's heart.

Instinct had him covering Rowan's hand, encouraging him to touch, to not shy away from what he wanted. His heart was beating erratically, and that only intensified at the contact, desperate to escape the cage of his body and return to its rightful place, nestled beside Rowan's half-demon heart.

He gazed at the pale hand against his black T-shirt and glanced up to catch Rowan watching, waiting and prepared to hold eye contact. A current shot through his veins, stirred the magic beneath his skin and threatened to tear his soul in two with the overwhelming spark of power crackling between them. If he could survive, he may have stopped breathing to allow nothing else to exist but this connection holding them together, making their hearts beat in sync.

"This isn't new for me, you know. I've always crushed hard on you, but you were a Copry..." Storm whispered, not knowing how to finish. Rowan needed to know this wasn't an instant recip- rocation of his feelings. He hadn't hit his head and suffered an en- tire personality change. He'd been flighty, thinking his friendly af- fection for Denver and Foley—the love that made them feel like family, now he understood himself better—was actually love. He'd allowed Ithen's looks to turn his head and make him crush on someone who was pure evil, or—the worst case scenario—he could have been bewitched to feel that way for him.

Rowan was different. Everything he was had become beauti- ful to Storm. It started with how he looked because Storm had ac- cess to nothing else, a fleeting glance because their families were supposed enemies, a few brief conversations that revealed the in- credible mind and talent beneath the surface. In the days since he hit his head and Rowan helped him, he'd seen a new side to the boy who had always been around but whom Storm had never seen with any real clarity.

There was a look in Rowan's eyes that said he was scared to believe Storm, because it was new, unexpected, and he was worried the words were just a safeguard because Storm had nowhere else to go and no one else to trust.

"Nothing is what it used to be," Storm promised in a whisper. Leaning in, he touched his lips to Rowan's, feeling the dizzying thrill of being free to kiss him whenever he wanted. When Storm parted his lips for a second kiss, Rowan pressed forward. Curling his fingers into Rowan's hair, Storm forgot everything else, needing to pretend the rest of the world and its problems didn't exist.

In that moment, it was just the two of them, and he wished they could stay that way.

Sorely tempted to spend the rest of the night here, Storm was on his knees to move when a swipe of claws sent him reeling. Midnight raised her paw to take another aim at Storm before either he or Rowan could register the sudden switch of emotion.

He instinctively raised his hand and twisted his finger until the cat turned and her claws gouged the wooden chaise leg instead. "Nothing is what it used to be," he repeated breathlessly, glaring at the cat for interrupting his first ever make-out session. Storm caught Rowan fighting a smile and shook his head. "You're a half-demon, I have a demon best friend, my parents were murdered by someone I used to crush on, my two best friends are dating *each other*—" He paused when Rowan raised an eyebrow, as though he hadn't seen that coming either. "And you have a cat."

"What's wrong with Midnight?" Rowan teased, lifting the kitten and crossing the room to place her into a crate. He didn't shut the door, but the cat seemed to understand she was grounded.

"Honestly, I thought of you more as a dog person. Like a big Doberman," he admitted, eyeing the cat with curiosity. She certainly had enough vindictive demon nature to have been a gift from a higher demon, someone who knew Rowan was important and needed protection. That didn't mean Midnight needed to protect him from Storm; he'd *never* hurt Rowan.

"Snob," Rowan remarked with a raised eyebrow. He reclaimed his seat beside Storm and lay his head on Storm's shoulder, where they spent a few minutes in blissful quiet.

Eventually, Storm huffed, resting his head against Rowan's. "Do you think you can travel through time twice?"

"Would you risk it?"

He almost laughed at the thought, then nearly cried when he remembered what that meant. "No. But I'd love to drown Ithen at birth and return to this moment to find we'd always been together and the world was simple," he confessed, aware that neither he nor Rowan had the strength to mess with time without serious consequences.

Rowan laughed in a sad, tired way that acknowledged all they could do. "Come on, sunshine, we both need sleep. You can come to the house and sleep in my bed with me," he said, patting Storm's thigh as he pulled away and rose to his feet. He stretched, momentarily distracting Storm.

"Don't you have a spare room in that big mansion of yours?"

Pausing on his way to the door, Rowan glanced over his shoulder and smirked. "Do you *want* to sleep in a spare room?"

Clearing his throat, Storm fought the blush creeping up his neck and cheeks, resisting the urge to drag Rowan in for another kiss. "No." However embarrassed he was by the idea, nothing could make him refuse.

"Then shush." Rowan reached for his hand, leading the way into the stormy night.

Chapter Twelve

Three Days Later

November 12, 2026

FOR THREE DAYS, they lived side by side, sharing a bed, a room, their space and their secrets. Storm had confessed his feelings to Rowan and hadn't been laughed or screamed at because he was a Tera, a traitor and the enemy. None of those things were true anymore, and it astounded him every time he looked at Rowan. He'd known all along and still played the part of a distant enemy, so that he wouldn't shatter the magical illusion Storm had been imprisoned by.

Forcing someone out of a magical compulsion was extremely dangerous and was the reason Storm was avoiding Cesa until he could figure out a way to cure his curse. Having Yael back would help. He needed someone unconnected to Cesa's situation to bounce ideas off, and there was no one better to deal with a curse than a demon. But Yael had stopped by the morning after his confession to Rowan to warn Storm that they wouldn't return for nearly a week.

How strange that a single week in someone's company could make him miss them and forget what loneliness felt like. Even with Rowan busy studying for his online college course most of the day, Storm knew he wasn't alone. Yael and Rowan would always be there when he needed them.

Now he needed Denver and Foley and to know where they stood in this mess of a life.

Storm signed his name to the note he'd written and passed the rolled-up paper to the crow sitting on Rowan's windowsill. Gladys would have become concerned by Ithen's absence by now, and he didn't know what power either had or if his electronics had been used to track him. To be cautious, he'd left his phone and tablet at his shack, in a place hidden by magic and surrounded by protections to keep them inaccessible to Ithen and Gladys.

Watching the crow fly off with his message, he turned to where Midnight lay on Rowan's pillow. The cat had come to accept his presence as long as he didn't get between her and Rowan, and Storm wasn't particularly interested in pushing those boundaries. Most animals loved his dark magic as they were made from the abyss and recognised him as family, but this kitten was demon-made and a whole other problem.

Having plans for the day forced Storm to hurry; he showered, changed and stole one of Rowan's cable jumpers, since the wind had increased during the night. He'd need to go to the shack soon to collect his clothes, but he could make do with what he'd packed and a working washing machine, with the bonus of borrowing Rowan's clothes.

He left the house at eleven in the morning, walking over crunchy fallen leaves, bracing against the biting wind, to clear his head. Storm had been consumed with thoughts about Gladys and Ithen for the last three days, trying to fathom their plans and why they needed Cesa to be under their control. He was on a deadline, needing to figure out their plans, find the amulet and spell, and regain his memories of the future so he could avoid reliving the same fate, all before the date of the war. Storm only wished he knew when the final battle had taken place because then he would know if he had days or weeks to spend working through his problems.

The wind was unusually quiet as Storm walked the open field of Copry land. To be surrounded by blessed silence at a time when Storm expected the world to be in an uproar felt ominous. Was this the calm before the storm?

He walked to the shack without anything untoward happening and stopped to check on Ithen. He was still unconscious, which suggested he may have slipped into the abyss, in an attempt to escape Storm's magic and hadn't realised how endless the place could be. Without intention, he could remain lost for years.

As long as he stayed out of Storm's way, he wasn't bothered. With Ithen out of action, Storm had time to breathe and focus on one enemy at a time. Once he was sure Ithen was well protected, he walked to the poppy field and sat under his favourite tree: the willow at Adam's Grove. He'd borrowed one of Rowan's books about dark magic, a necessity for a half-demon with natural dark magic in his veins. The pages contained more advanced magic than anything Storm had salvaged from his parents' house or those Gladys had let him read and he was intrigued to see how the teachings differed. With dark magic and demon magic so similar but their methods so varied, he may find a better explanation than the old grimoires that used the old-fashioned phrasings.

Storm was holding onto a frayed thread of hope that the demons knew of the amulet and might know of a way to handle it safety.

*

AFTER AN HOUR, footsteps and voices heralded Denver's arrival at Adam's Grove. "Let's find out what he wants."

Storm's stomach sank, realising that neither Denver or Foley wanted to see him. He didn't know what had been said about his three-day absence, but Gladys could have been spreading rumours. Setting the book aside, Storm stood to greet them. "Thanks for coming."

"What's with the secrecy? You said not to tell anyone about meeting you, but everyone is saying you disappeared?" Foley asked, always the one to address issues head-on.

"I was at a lesson with Ithen the other day. I told you, right?" He wanted to make sure they knew the expected events before he threw them in at the deep end.

"Yeah."

There was no easy way to say it, so Storm didn't try to sugar-coat the news. "He tried to kill me." He watched as they processed the news; Denver blinked in shock while Foley positively burst with questions.

"What? Why? How could he—?"

Storm caught his hand to quieten him. "Because he killed my parents."

Silence fell and Denver ran a hand over his mouth, clearly lost for words. While they struggled to come to terms with the information, Storm countered Foley's questions and Denver's naïve disbelief that Ithen would ever hurt him by telling them everything.

Storm needed them to know the truth. He talked them through the entire sorry story: being sent back from the future—a future where he'd failed to save their lives and failed to fulfil the prophecy—and how events had changed. He spoke about Yael and how Rowan was linked to his past and future, about Cesa being cursed, his parents murder and Ithen being locked in his shack. He told them about Gladys, hoping to keep Foley safe. He was from a coven friendly with the Glades, and he didn't want Foley or his family running foul of her new dark magic.

"I have to tell you guys something else. I need you to be aware, in case the events of the future can't be avoided," Storm confessed because this was the real reason he had to speak to them. He had to make them understand the danger, to keep them safe for as long as he could.

"What could be worse?" Denver asked, glancing at Foley, who sat with a faint frown.

"First off, I know you two are dating," he admitted, smiling when Denver squirmed and looked to Foley for guidance. "I'm not mad. I just wish you told me the truth."

Denver blushed furiously, rubbing the back of his neck. His shyness only made Storm smile, but he genuinely had bigger problems than them keeping a relationship secret.

"I'm glad you found each other. I only ever wanted you both to be happy," he promised.

"Thanks." Denver glanced at Foley with a raised eyebrow.

He cleared his throat and bobbed his head at Storm. "We weren't sure how to tell you."

Storm wished they'd never had to wonder or worry. Maybe he'd been a different person before he returned from the future; less approachable, less open about his feelings. "In the future... during the war...something happened. During this prophecy moment where I'm supposed to save magic, a curse was cast and hit Rowan. He was killed."

Denver gasped and instinctively reached for Foley's hand.

"The curse went straight through him and into the person

standing behind him," he went on, not sure how best to continue. The images flashed through his mind to remind him that he'd lost both of these people, once upon a time.

With a knowing tilt of his head, Foley was quick to realise the meaning. "Which one?" He avoided Denver's gaze, probably because he didn't seem to understand what Storm was struggling to say.

"Denver." He refused to go into details about how and why, or how Denver had been kidnapped and magically tortured. As a human, Denver had been lucky to survive the magical overload, only to die a few hours later from a rebounded spell. The pain he must have felt didn't bear thinking about.

"You died a few weeks later. I then died on the final night of the war, and I killed every Copry in sight," he confessed because other than Rowan, he needed Foley's stern reasoning and Denver's foolhardiness to balance out his need to rewrite the past. "The Glade coven didn't fight in the war."

"Which, now you know Gladys is evil, makes total sense." Denver nodded, like the rational guy he was—one who liked to know what he was dealing with.

"Exactly."

"Denver died," Foley said, having come to terms with that news.

Storm nodded and reiterated how important it was *neither* of them die this time. "I needed you to know. In the other future, the one where everyone died, I don't think I ever knew you were

158 | Elaine White

together. So much has changed, but I still need you to know the risk."

Rowan had been right; distancing himself without explaining why would only bring Foley and Denver closer, no doubt to check on him or to argue about being left out. As Yael would say, with knowledge came power, and this time the power was having the ability to live a long life, as every teenager should. They shouldn't die for someone else's war.

"Rowan will help me study necromancy so I can resurrect anyone if I have to. I'd rather not need to. We're going to stop the war now that we have Ithen imprisoned, but Gladys is free, and Cesa is still under his curse."

"You also don't know where the amulet or the spell are," Foley said, sounding determined to help resolve that problem.

Storm nodded and leaned over his crossed legs, one elbow on each knee. "Yeah. My parents died before they could tell me, and I imagine Ithen and Gladys have been through all the family documents and searched in person and with spells." They would have tried everything to get to the amulet, probably even taking Storm's blood. A scratch or doctor's visit would have been easy because he didn't know he couldn't trust them. "Rowan has a few ideas. Until then, we're in danger and I need to stay missing."

"Definitely." Foley licked his lips and turned to Denver, his face portraying the gravity of the situation. "You shouldn't be around me."

"Are you serious?" Denver snapped, a purely instinctive

reaction but one that Storm understood. He didn't want to be away from Foley, but Storm also understood what Foley meant.

Foley stood so he could pace, his usual method of working off tension and nerves when he couldn't use magic. "You don't have any magic, Denver. You could get killed; not because *I'm* afraid or because you're human or because you *can't* defend yourself against magic, but because you *die* in the future! We don't know if Storm has done enough to avoid that yet." He gestured at Storm though neither looked to check if he had an answer. "You would be safer keeping your distance from both of us."

Before Denver could argue—and he would—Storm cut in. "He's right." He may not like it, but there was a lot he didn't like about this situation. There was nothing to do but keep moving because going back wasn't possible and standing still would get them killed. "I also know you won't listen, so I've asked Rowan to make a protective amulet for you. You *will* wear this with no compromises and no loopholes. Every second of every minute of every day, you will wear the amulet until this is over and the war is won. Understand?" he demanded, reaching into his bag.

When he handed the bracelet to Denver, he slipped it on without hesitation. "Deal." Wiping the triumphant glee off his face, he glared at Foley and gripped his hand tightly. "I'm *not* leaving you."

"Stubborn ass."

"I love you too," Denver responded and kissed his cheek.

Storm envied them that easiness but had to face the sad

reality of knowing he couldn't convince Rowan to take his own advice. As a half-demon, no protective amulet could help him, and he was as embroiled in this as Storm. Asking him to keep a safe distance from this chaos would be like saying he'd do the same.

Foley shook his head and wrapped an arm around Denver's waist. When he looked Storm in the eye, there was a mischievous glint in them that he should have seen coming. "So...Rowan, huh?"

The blush was automatic, but he shrugged and appreciated the friendly ribbing about falling for the enemy.

*

"DO YOU THINK she'll find the amulet? Do you even know where to start looking?" Rowan asked as he dragged Storm from the warm main house to trudge through the long grass to his hidden summer house.

Huddling into his jacket against the wind, more chilled and less wild over the hour since he'd left his friends, Storm looked at the sky. He could feel the weather brewing and wondered when the storm would hit.

"Nope." He didn't much *like* the answer, but that wasn't up for debate. "As for Gladys, I don't even know who she is. I never knew the real Gladys." That was a hard truth to swallow, but Storm wasn't naïve enough to deny the obvious. "A week ago, I would have said she'd never sniffed at dark magic but, now I know she's been using it and the demons have been watching, I'm worried. Yael says the demons want her to pay for her misuse of dark magic.

You'll know better than me that demons aren't allowed to kill or cause the death of a human."

Rowan nodded and tucked his hands into his jacket pockets. "Demons are the counterparts to humans; if one dies out the other can't exist. To make sure of that, they can't harm each other." He recounted the rules with a smirk and nudged Storm. "That's why I've been safe from Gladys and Ithen all these years. They can hurt me and curse me, but I'll shake the spell off eventually. They don't know that, and they've never bothered to check."

"It needs to stay that way, for your sake and your father's," Storm said, agreeing with Yael that the secrets they'd discovered were all the power they needed and could rely on. "They've been manipulating him for so long, I'm not sure what can break Ithen's hold. I don't know if the answer is to untangle the curse or if Ithen has to die, and I'm not ready to find out."

He hated to put a downer on the conversation, but he needed to confront the reality of not saving Cesa. He couldn't see any other way to cure Cesa without Ithen's help or removal; Rowan had admitted to trying everything in his formidable power. Storm wouldn't be averse to killing Ithen, to break the curse, if he knew enough necromancy to bring him back. He wasn't sure he was cut out for outright murder, the way he had been in the future.

Storm wished he could punch the man who had caused so much trouble for them, both in the past and the present. "Thanks to Ithen, I learned nothing during my training. I still don't know any *real* dark magic because I've been taught by two traitors who killed my parents. My dad only taught me small spells."

"Such as?"

Storm raked through what few memories he had, and the few he'd borrowed from Ithen. "Respect the elements, always ask permission of magic and never use magic against another mage unless I was prepared to die," he recounted, knowing the last was something he'd have to face sooner or later, just as his dad had when Ithen killed him. Asher fought back, hoping to protect those he loved, even if he had to give his life to secure their safety. "He laughed whenever I tried to conjure something from another room, which I never did manage."

Storm almost laughed at the fond memory, embarrassed to admit something like that to Rowan, who was so proficient and knowledgeable with magic.

Rowan removed a hand from his pocket, then raised it as though he was holding something he wanted Storm to see.

The wind whispered: *Conjurer. Half-demon child. Dead.* The last word was chanted like a child who had found a word they loved. *Dead. Dead. Dead. Dead.* The wind practically sang with joy.

The sound raised the hairs on the back of Storm's neck and sent a shiver up his spine, warning of an unnatural event heading his way. Before he could ask the wind for more information, a book appeared, floating in mid-air, then casually sailed through the wind to land on Rowan's hand.

"Don't worry, I can teach you what I know," Rowan offered,

his charming smile hinting that he hadn't heard the wind's ominous words. "Your demon will help you with the rest."

Storm shoved the wind's warnings aside and returned Rowan's smile as he tucked the book under his arm. "Yael technically isn't my demon. We haven't bonded yet. We've agreed not to until after the prophecy is fulfilled so they can't get hurt, if or when I die."

"Wise choice." Rowan linked his free arm through Storm's. "But they will help if you ask. As will I." His smile was warm enough to chase away the chill left by the wind's warning. He continued toward the summer house, just a few feet away, oblivious to the niggling warning Storm had been given.

When they reached the building, Storm opened the door for Rowan, pondering another problem. "We need to find the amulet and the spell, then make sure no one else can get their hands on them," he admitted, waiting for Rowan to head in from the cold before he followed. He had no choice but to ignore the flirtatious look Rowan sent over his shoulder and the glance he gave Storm's hand on the door. He hadn't thought about what he was doing but, if he could make Rowan look at him with such approval, he wasn't doing so bad.

He only wished they had time for flirting.

Rowan placed the book he'd summoned onto the arm of the chair as he sank into the cushion. "I'm still surprised my father hasn't succumbed to Ithen's curse and given him the spell. I'm hoping that's the part of him that calls for your father in his sleep."

Storm perched on the chaise to Rowan's right. "That's how you knew about them?" He'd wondered what had spilled the secret: Cesa rambling or moments of clarity amongst the hours, weeks and years of Ithen's curse taking hold. He hadn't expected Cesa to talk in his sleep or have nightmares about losing Asher.

With a negligent shrug and a yawn, Rowan sank into the seat, understandably tired after hours of working on his college course. "I put the pieces together and remembered a few things," he admitted, nibbling on his lower lip with uncertainty. "I don't know anything about the future you. Can you tell me what you remember? We might find hints that we can use to help?"

"Sure." Storm had no problem digging into those memories. Though he'd been an arrogant sod in the future, considering what he'd been through and everyone he'd lost, he figured he was entitled to a few years of bad behaviour. Thrusting the magical world into a living hell, however, was a dangerous move, but shit happened when a jaded dark mage became a sarcastic, alcoholic twat. He just hated the idea that he'd spent years pining for Ithen and thinking he'd loved the asshole.

Maybe he wouldn't tell Rowan that part. No, he should be honest. In a world where they only had each other to count on, lies and secrets could get them killed.

Again.

Chapter Thirteen

STORM FROWNED AS the book wobbled on the floor, refusing to lift. How could he manage to levitate *himself*, but he couldn't move a single bloody book? "What freaked me out was meeting Donald James Glade," he said, while Rowan sat in the armchair, absently flicking through a book for his course on Occult Sciences through Glasgow University. Though he wanted to ask what Occult Sciences was about, he had more important things on his plate. College wasn't even a glimmer of hope on the horizon.

"Do you think the DJ you met was a homunculus?" Rowan asked, his concern shining through. He would know better than anyone that sending the soul of a once-living being into a shell not created for the purpose was dangerous.

"Yael thought Ithen did it for her or she waited until after the prophecy. I mean, your father had the amulet in the war, and it had to go somewhere *after* the war. Yael can't say whether I destroyed the spell or if I even knew where the amulet was."

Right now, they couldn't rely on anything being set in stone. Though Storm had seen Ithen offer to make a homunculus for Gladys, there was nothing in the memories to say he'd held up his end of the bargain. Ithen may have been bluffing, to get Gladys on his side.

"What's sad is that DJ was this sweet, innocent kid. Gladys moved heaven and earth to resurrect him, but she didn't *love* him," he explained, not sure why anyone would go to the trouble of bringing their child back from the dead only to leave him floundering in uncertainty, unaware of what he was or what he could do. "He was as haunted by her house as I was when I lived there," Storm recalled, relieved DJ didn't exist in this timeline, though no one was sure if Gladys's plans for him were already in motion. "Why did she bring him back just to live a life of fear?"

Rowan slipped from the armchair and crossed to where Storm sat, just outside the door—using distance to force his magic to work harder. "We have to assume he had a purpose he'd already fulfilled, and Gladys couldn't bring herself to kill her son when that task was completed." His voice was full of understanding for the unfathomable bond Storm had with the boy. He knew that future didn't exist, but he and DJ were so similar he wondered if Gladys had been using Storm as a substitute for her dead son all these years.

"I need to find a way to save him." Storm couldn't bear to

lose the war again, knowing that some poor child—DJ's spirit or whatever homunculus Gladys created from magic—would end up suffering for his failure.

With that incentive in mind, Storm went back to the book and his pathetic attempt to summon objects. Give him the wind, the rain or leaves and he could summon them without even thinking, but ask him to move something solid and Storm's magic ground to a screeching halt.

After three hours of strenuous disagreements with his magic, Storm could lift the damned book far enough to reach. What Rowan called cheating—when the book dropped a foot away and he lunged to catch it—Storm called proactive disaster control. For a dark mage, cheating was in the eye of the beholder.

Rowan huffed when Storm made the mistake of admitting that out loud. "Honestly, you dark mages love to break the rules. You can't settle for bending them, you just walk right over them in your size-twelve boots, trampling on the foundations of magic until you—" He cut off with a gasp of surprise, saving Storm from an extended lecture as Yael stepped from the abyss.

"Hello, youngling. Demon-witch." Yael's greeting was hardly their best but far from their worst, and Rowan didn't look insulted. "I'm glad you had a powerful ally by your side while I was indisposed," they said, stepping from the portal to cross to Storm. They sank down beside him, crossed their legs and looked expectantly at Storm as though they hadn't been gone for days.

"I would say hello *lower demon*—" Rowan leaned over his

knees and rested his elbow on the arm of the chair. "—but I sense you're climbing the ranks. You've learned something interesting that no other demons know, haven't you?"

Intrigued by the development and that Yael was surprisingly quiet about his discovery, Storm turned to Yael. "What did you find out?" he asked, wondering why they hadn't said anything and why they wore a checked green hunting suit over tan trousers, with no shirt or shoes. Their style was both old-fashioned elegance and in major need of human sensibility.

Folding their hands on their lap, Yael sat tall and proud. "What I have learned has no direct bearing on current events. I will think upon the information to determine what must be told and what must remain secret." They glanced suspiciously at Rowan then faced Storm. "I am awaiting further information from other demons, who have been told to request my presence in the abyss or visit me if they know anything pertinent to your quest."

"Fine. Getting information from demons who will always want payment can be tricky."

Yael nodded and didn't seem in the least remorseful when they announced, "I have made many promises that you will pay these demons for their information, in either spellwork or knowledge."

Storm rolled his eyes and bit his tongue. There was no point arguing. Thank the gods demons didn't deal in money or he'd be broke. "Great. Thank you, Yael."

Putting that problem aside for another day, Storm spent a

few minutes filling Yael in on what had happened in their absence, from talking to Denver and Foley to living with Rowan and re-learning how to control his magic. He wanted them to all be on the same page about their goals and what was needed to achieve them.

Yael hummed, sounding ominously cautious. "I could feel you attempting magic, but I'm afraid you barely know where to start. You are not a demon, nor are you an ordinary witch, and certainly no ordinary mage. I have brought you this book to help you understand the darker arts more clearly." Reaching behind their back, they plucked a heavy tome from the air, no doubt uti-lising a demon trick.

"Where did you get this?"

Yael handed him the book. "The higher demon I visited was saying farewell to his current master. The man was dying and the demon gave this to me, on his behalf, to help you fulfil the proph-ecy," they explained, sounding like a huffy teenager.

Storm glanced at Rowan who struggled to hide his amuse-ment.

"We demons want to see the prophecy fulfilled as much as you do. If the future remains on the same path, magic will disap-pear. We demons will then be the only source of pure magic left." Yael glanced between them, the gravity of their words sobering the mood. "I'm sure I do not need to explain the consequences to our survival."

"No. I understand." Storm rubbed his brow as he offered Yael an apologetic smile and grasped their hand.

Yael stood and gestured to the book. "Begin reading and I will allow you to use magic against me to show you how to find control," they offered, seamlessly taking on the role of lecturer. "Where other witches and mages must command magic, your magic responds to your will and an instinctive request for partnership. You do not demand but *ask* magic if you can work together; that will be key to finding your control."

Storm nodded, glad to hear someone talking his language. Rowan's well-meaning guidance about calling on his magic and using his intent to communicate his needs had been helpful, but Storm didn't work that way. Even when dealing with the wind or rain his magic had always been easy, a matter of speaking to them, asking if they were willing and thinking of what he wanted only after merging their magic.

"It can't be any worse than this pathetic attempt." He pulled the tome onto his lap and began reading.

Yael walked into the summer house and lay on the chaise. "I think I will sleep. Wake me when he has completed the first chapter, Demon-witch. Then we will put his learning into practice."

They sounded like a lord of the manor, ordering the servants about, and Rowan wasn't the only one left speechless. Storm glanced at Rowan as he huffed and shook his head, silently agreeing that there was no point arguing. Yael had obviously never worked with a master before, or they wouldn't be so cocky about taking charge, but Storm loved that. The one thing he'd always hated about the idea of being a dark mage, destined to bond with a demon, was the thought of becoming some asshole master, knowing the demon was bound to obey even if they didn't want to.

Rowan had a small, almost amused smile playing on his lips when he picked up Midnight, who was sneaking out of the summer house. "No point getting sore," he whispered to the kitten. "Yael is more demon than you or I and they can't help the superiority complex. We have to be better than them and not retaliate, no matter how much we want to."

Storm stifled his laughter, realising Rowan struggled to tolerate Yael's attitude because he was also half-demon.

*

THE PREVIOUS OWNER of the book had obviously been making notes for an apprentice or younger member of his family. Numerous loose pages, scribbles in the margins and drawings to help visualise the spells, littered the ancient book. Whether Yael had to return the book or if Storm could keep it, he was grateful for the gift.

Pulling out a single sheaf labelled, *Necromancy Rules,* he studied the beautiful script and set about memorising every word.

Magic cannot be used for personal gain, therefore even the darker arts are constrained to the laws that maintain balance. In necromancy, the one cardinal rule is: you cannot resurrect someone you love. If they die, you must suffer their loss as any other mortal would. You cannot take without giving, because balance will find a way to maintain itself if you disobey this rule.

For example: in the eighteenth century a young male nec-romancer of my family had an illicit relationship with another man. Attacked for their proclivities, his lover died. My ancestor broke the laws of magic to return his love from the dead, and while the lover returned in body he was not the same man in mind or soul. The man was but a shadow of who he had once been and had no consciousness, no free will. He was no better than the modern Gothic invention: the zombie.

I wish to note that the mage was wise enough to regret his decision. He endured the pain of killing his lover and following him into the abyss, where they lived as spirits for many genera-tions before they passed into the light.

Storm raised an eyebrow at the story, unable to resist the urge to look at Rowan. His death lingered in the future, a distinct possibility if no longer a certainty, and Storm wasn't sure what he would do when the time came to act.

He'd been crushing on Rowan for years, and while this mage mentioned love, he didn't know if he was in love with Rowan. He wasn't sure what love was or how he'd know when he felt it.

What if he loved Rowan and couldn't resurrect him? What if he didn't love Rowan but thought he did and didn't even *try* to resurrect him? What if he trusted that he loved Rowan and they wouldn't face a zombie fate, then resurrected him and realised it *wasn't* love? What if Rowan being a half-demon meant his magic wouldn't work, even if he didn't love him, because resurrecting a demon disrupted the balance?

Suppressing the groan of frustration brewing beneath the surface, he returned to reading, hoping his jumbled thoughts would disappear as he learned more.

Necromancers are in a unique position that allows the trade of death for life or life for death. As well as resurrecting the dead—the ability most necromancers are known for—they are also able to send the living to the abyss.

I do not say kill, because the act resembles a wish fulfilled rather than a crime committed. If, as in the world of medicine, a person wishes to die—due to extreme pain, they are dying, or are certain of their decision—necromancers have their own form of magical euthanasia. Their method is less painful on the soul, the so-called victim, and the families than a suicide or medical euthanasia. A necromancer can touch the victim and ask the heart to stop beating; a transition rather than instantaneous death, allowing for goodbyes and preparations to be made. The spell can be performed at any time at the victim's request, planned weeks in advance if necessary.

This must only be done in extreme circumstances. If every necromancer offered a pain-free euthanasia to anyone who asked, there would be no necromancers left. As with all magic, a give and take must occur or the magic will not work. When bringing a soul from the abyss, the necromancer will sacrifice anything from one to five years of their life, but when sending a soul the number can double.

For this balance, necromancers must calculate the cost to their soul and their life before using this ability. If they lack the strength, energy and focus to be clear with what they are and are not willing to trade with the abyss, the results can be disastrous for the mage and victim alike.

A strong mage can prepare themselves for the sacrifice in advance, if they know they are soon to perform this feat. Fortifying the human body with twice the calories they would normally consume, avoiding alcohol and cigarettes beforehand, and performing a reading followed by a sage cleansing will prepare the mind and body for the journey through another's heart and death.

"What?"

Storm flinched at the sound of Rowan's voice, realising he'd been muttering out loud. "Sorry. It's talking about necromancy and the price we pay. They should just have a big flashing sign saying, 'Don't Do It'!"

Rowan chuckled and petted Midnight's ear as he turned the page of his paperback. "We may not have asked for these abilities, but you're doing the right thing by learning how to use and control them," he said, always supportive, as though they'd never been anything but allies and friends. "I had to tame the demon side of me, and you need to understand the side of your magic made to control death. I wouldn't trust anyone else with my life...or death."

A cloud passed over his eyes with the last word and Storm knew why. He wasn't the only one with Rowan's future death at the forefront of his mind. He nodded his agreement and returned to the book, hoping something would click.

He'd never needed anything as badly as he needed to understand and control his necromancy.

*

YAEL CRACKED THEIR knuckles as they waited for Storm to make his first attempt at using magic against a demon. According to Yael, he was the prophecy child and the only one capable of using 'friendly fire' against a demon and posing a serious threat. If Storm had been any other mage, he'd be better going home, but he wasn't, and Yael was convinced he could do this.

Gathering his hands in front of his stomach, Storm asked his magic to assist him as he created a ball of blue fire Yael insisted wouldn't hurt them. Before he could get any further, Yael huffed.

"Stop!" Yael looked like a teacher frustrated by a failing pupil. "The dark magic within you isn't dark because the craft is wrong or evil. You don't need to ask your magic *if* it is willing to help, as if what you're doing is wrong. You ask if it is *ready* to help," he said, giving Storm no time to consider their words. "Demon-witch! You have shared intimacy, please explain in a way he can understand."

"Hey!" Storm objected to the weird phrasing, but Yael didn't know how inappropriate those words were to humans. "You said 'please' this time."

Rowan set his book aside with a thoughtful frown. "I think I know what Yael means," he admitted, placing Midnight on the ground. He left the summer house and walked toward Storm. Already early evening, the warm look in Rowan's eyes made him want to return to the manor and snuggle in bed.

Rowan pressed against Storm, chest to chest, and dipped his head the brief distance between them to nudge their noses. When he kissed Storm, he was waiting, closing his eyes to the now familiar act that, barely a week ago, he would never have thought possible.

A Tera and a Copry.

Gods, history was repeating itself, but Storm refused to let Rowan go. He didn't want to live the same half existence, begging and pleading with Rowan the way Cesa had, knowing he'd never be whole without him.

When had a kiss become this?

Rowan broke the kiss with a smile, his eyes sparkling ice blue with emotion. "The first time you kissed me, you asked if I was willing. If I was okay with you kissing me because we'd never kissed before," he said, placing a hand over Storm's heart. "Now I can kiss you any time I like. I still *ask* if you want to—just in a different way. A way that doesn't need words."

The point eluded Storm after the thoughts overtaking his mind during their incredible kiss.

"Your magic is part of you; you know each other. Your powers gave blanket consent the moment you stepped out of the abyss with them. Your magic—the wild, intricate blend that only you possess—knows what you want and what you're planning to do. All you have to do is ask. Like you knew I would kiss you when I nudged your nose, your magic knows what you want the minute you call." Rowan's voice was soft and soothing as he tapped a finger over Storm's heart. He wanted to sink into Rowan's arms and not let go, mesmerised by the words that worked like a spell against his heart. "Just as you would have kissed me if I hadn't closed the distance because I'd let you know with my body language that I wanted to be kissed, your magic is waiting for you to lead the way and will put its foot down if you step out of line."

Gods, he'd never heard anything more beautiful or anything that made sense of his magic in a way he understood.

"Nicely done, Demon-witch."

Storm glared at Yael for interrupting the moment and was caught off guard when a wisp of dark smoke drifted from his fingertips to knock Yael on their ass. He caught the arched eyebrow from Rowan, asking if he'd meant that, and shrugged. "Serves them right. Getting in the way," he remarked, unable to resist stealing another kiss.

Yael huffed, sounding mildly irritated. "Let's try again."

As Rowan stepped out of the line of fire, Storm reached for his magic almost without thinking. He knew where his magic lived, swirling at the base of his spine and the pit of his gut;

mentally tapped on the door that opened to welcome him, pleased to be wanted, eager to put itself to use.

Storm cocked his head, evaluating Yael's body for a weak spot, and formed the fire in his mind. His magic sang beneath his skin, fingers tingling and flexing with the need to explore. Once the fire was fully formed, a single thought had it extending from his fingers like red smoke, sailing toward Yael.

The demon smirked and twisted their wrist to stretch their fingers, the movement effortlessly waving his fire aside. Before he could recover, Storm blew into the air, sending a gust of wind and hail.

Though Yael brushed the wind aside, they stepped aside to avoid the hail and flinched as a piece grazed their cheek. "Well done. Quick, unforgiving, unyielding; you reacted the moment you knew the fire would fail. You have learned to watch with your eyes and mind open, to adapt, and how to summon your magic. You must now learn how to harness your magic, how to strengthen your ability and when *not* to use your powers. That will be your most vital lesson.

"Read the book. Study the history of dark magic, the rules, the limitations and think about how you would have defended yourself from these attacks," Yael suggested, shaking their arms out to the side and drawing them to their stomach, their favourite cane appearing between one act and the next. "Once you have studied more, we can put what you have learned into use. I think your next lesson must be in necromancy. We will test your abilities once more, but we must focus on that gift to ensure that if the worst happens then you are prepared."

The fact Yael glanced at Rowan showed they were all holding Rowan's life at the forefront of their concerns.

"Homework." Storm realised he'd have a lot of reading in his future, but that was okay. Rowan had his course work, Yael was busy gathering information to make them more powerful, and that might help with the prophecy. Nothing they did from this point would be worth anything if he didn't know how to harness the art of necromancy.

It was time to get to work.

Chapter Fourteen

AT FIVE O'CLOCK they reluctantly ended the lessons and went their separate ways. Rowan spend time with his father, while Storm and Yael ate takeaway in the upstairs sitting room, then returned to work. Fully fuelled and with a whole night to focus, Storm was ten pages into the tome Yael had gifted him when the door opened and Rowan walked in.

"I put Dad in his sitting room. He'll go to bed soon," he said, sounding weary and worn out. Caring for Cesa and shouldering the full weight of his responsibilities—with the coven, the manor and the locals—was starting to take a toll. "If you're busy, I've got an essay to write."

"What's it about?" Storm asked, only to take his mind off his father.

"St Mary's Close in Edinburgh."

"I believe a natural entrance to hell exists there," Yael remarked, lying on the bed and prodding an unsure talon at Midnight, who had dared to crawl over their lap in curiosity.

Storm wasn't surprised by that news, as he'd always heard Edinburgh was a haunted town, never free to escape the memories of the old days. He listened absently as he lifted the tome onto Rowan's window seat since Rowan had his papers sprawled across his desk.

Yael hummed thoughtfully and poked at Midnight's bared belly. "I believe one of the death doctors was a demon. He lived amongst the humans for many years and knew of the supernatural abilities amongst those condemned as witches during the time. He treated plague victims and stumbled upon the gateway in the heart of the city, along one of the tunnels leading off the Close." They scratched their chin and frowned at Midnight when she tapped her paw against their leg.

Rowan turned in his chair. "If you can remember the name the doctor used, I could find documents about his behaviours and practices to include in my paper," he said, deep in study mode, looking attractive in his disarray: all mussed hair, wild eyed, and distracted.

"Why would you wish to?" Yael replied, gingerly lifting Midnight's paw from where a claw had tangled in their trousers.

"Just as knowledge is currency to demons, having unusual knowledge in a college paper can be good for my final grade," Rowan explained, using a comparison Yael could understand and appreciate.

An enlightened look crossed their face, their white eyes standing out more than usual. "Very well. I will endeavour to remember."

"Thanks." Rowan turned to his desk but barely waited a beat before glancing at Storm. "What? They're your demon. Don't blame me for taking advantage of the fact they're here and apparently not leaving."

Storm smiled because Rowan didn't really care about Yael hanging around, but he imagined the unwelcome bed mate who wouldn't give them any privacy was the real problem. Clearing his throat, Storm leaned against the recessed wall framing the window. "I've been meaning to ask, Yael. Where do you go when you're not with me? Where did you live?"

"Live? I don't particularly live anywhere," Yael responded, their tone implying this was common knowledge.

"Where did you sleep?"

A tentative, confused smile passed their lips as Yael shook their head. "We don't need to sleep unless we remain in the human world for many years. When I'm not here, I exist in the abyss until I return."

That answer gave Storm nothing to work with, in terms of getting Yael out of this bedroom. He tried another tactic. "You don't plan to go back?"

"Time is different in the abyss. A minute can be a day or a few weeks here. I couldn't help you if I kept flitting back and forth." Their innocent smile faltering, Yael glanced between Storm at the window and the desk where Rowan was staring intently. If he didn't say something soon, Yael would feel unwanted.

Rowan reacted first, always knowing what to say to an emotionally vulnerable and innocent demon. "Would you be okay sleeping in another room? The bed is only big enough for two, and we wouldn't want you to be uncomfortable. That way, you could have an entire room to yourself and a bathroom," he said, throwing every incentive he had at Yael, who blinked but didn't appear to know what to say.

"With a bath?"

"Sure." Rowan's tone suggested if there wasn't a bath in the room then he'd damned well find a way to give them one.

"I would like that," Yael said tentatively. "I do enjoy a bath. But if I am to leave you in this room, then this little demon must go with me." They stared at Storm with such wide eyes he was caught off guard. "Midnight is demon-spawn and you are the prophecy child who could spell our demise if you fail. She does not like you on principle. You are Tera blood and your Demon-witch is not. You are close, but every instinct tells her this is not possible."

"The cat hates me. Check." If Yael was willing to take the cat, Storm might get to sleep without being trodden on during the night. "You can take the cat with you if you want. Right, Rowan?" Midnight was his cat so the decision would always be his.

"Definitely. I still haven't gotten used to her walking over my chest in the morning," Rowan replied with a guilty frown. Midnight hissed at her owner and traipsed over to Yael's side to curl into a ball by their waist. Yael stroked her ear and Storm couldn't help but laugh. An emotionally childish demon, a vengeful cat that hated him and now felt unwanted, and a guy who wanted to share his bed but wasn't technically his boyfriend: Was this what being the Chosen One meant? To be surrounded by chaos, uncertainty, and to always have his world turned upside down?

Storm glanced around the room and smiled. It could have been worse.

*

FOLEY: *Gladys is telling everyone that Ithen took you on a trip to tap into your abilities to remove you from distractions.*

The text made Storm frown. Rowan had done something clever using Demon-magic that allowed messages sent to Storm's phone to forward to Rowan's. If Gladys was tracking Storm's phone or the messages, she would be wasting her time, as Rowan had implanted a secondary cloaking spell to the messages.

Storm only wished he had half of Rowan's magical capabilities. Maybe if Rowan had been the Chosen One, the magical world would never have fallen apart the first time they lived this life, and everyone could breathe easy.

He typed out a quick reply—

Storm: *Thanks for the update.*

Then he reminded him to stay safe, and to keep the lie they'd concocted about falling out after his ascension. If everyone thought they'd fought, the lie could protect Foley and Denver, and let everyone believe they didn't know where he was. If Gladys had gone to the length of creating a believable lie to explain his absence and Ithen's, she must be worried about Ithen's absence or lack of contact and plotting to find him.

Storm glanced to his right, where Rowan was sleeping beside him. The bedside lamp had a soft glow, enough to read by so Storm could stay up reading more of the magical tome in hopes of learning something to help his brain adapt to the new power surging beneath his skin, waiting to be set free.

Dark magic isn't evil. It takes a strength and belief in nature, yourself, and the Fates that most mages can't manage. The magic is dark because those too weak and ignorant to listen, to learn and to understand, shunned the craft. Dark magic is similar to light—a child you need to nourish—but where light magic is an eager learner, happy and bright, waiting to be taught, dark magic is wilful and stubborn. Light magic can be given at birth by the Fates, while dark magic can be learned by the simplest of humans if they have the will and respect to try their hand.

Dark magic can reject any soul deemed unworthy of its gifts and will take offence if you do not respect the craft. As such, magic may fail you in a time of great need, if you fail to understand and accept its terms.

Storm nodded at the explanation which sounded so simple when written in plain English and by someone who was clearly trained and prepared to teach a novice. He scribbled a note in his book, cutting through the lectures and examples.

Necromancy = easy enough humans can do it.

He turned the page and read the next entry.

Death is another plane of existence, just as life, dreams and wishes are real because our mind, our hearts and our spirits make them. Someone who is strong enough and wilful can exist—in one state or another—forever. If someone has the right resources and is willing to do anything, then immortality is possible...at a price.

The one fundamental law of magic remains: all magic bears a cost. All magic requires balance, an exchange of give and take. Some enlightened human cultures have come to realise this truth for themselves, acknowledging that life and death are two sides of the same coin: yin and yang. One cannot exist without the other. That is the balance of the world, of the earth, of the elements: dreams and reality, dark and light, good and evil. To learn necromancy, you must first master giving life, for in magic you must know how to give before you take.

The fundamental law of dark magic never changes: dark things are connected. Dark practices, beliefs, hearts, and dark minds are drawn to dark magic. Not all can master the darker arts because there is another little known law that none like to acknowledge: only the light can master the dark.

A prophecy speaks of a child who will control magic, who covens will turn to for guidance and laws, and who will bring us together in a way no other has managed. He will be a dark mage, a master of death, a necromancer with dark magic to rival the lightest magic. If such a child exists, I am sure he will prove to have the purest, lightest heart we have ever seen, for only such a child could become the dark master of necromancy.

Storm pushed aside the prophecy talk and focused on the information about dark magic. With a nod of understanding he made two notes:

- Necromancy is similar to cryogenics: the illusion of immortality.
- A true necromancy master must be pure of heart and full of light.

He wasn't sure he could manage the last part, to become the good omen of lightness, the miracle, this guy talked about, but he did know he could understand the first note. Cryogenics was easy to find on Google.

In the chapter on "Death and Other Existences," Storm found another short note slipped between the pages, a nice change from deciphering the black-inked writing on aged paper. Usually the notes were left at the end of a chapter, on the excess space beneath the printed material, but he liked the notes better.

We have one existence, one length of time in which our body and soul can exist. That time is split into two: life, the existence of our bodies; death, the existence of our souls. If you accept this one truth—that your body deteriorates upon death—you must accept the other: that your soul is freed and will go on to exist after the death of your body, the prison keeping your soul captive.

No matter what we accomplish in this life, our victories or failures, few leave a lasting impact on the world when we die. Those who do—who are tasked with great deeds, who accomplish great deeds or who have greatness thrust upon them—will reap no rewards in the next existence. They only have the honour of knowing they have left the living world richer and more wondrous for those left behind and who follow in the future. Their memory will live on long after their second existence has faded.

I would wish such a legacy; alas, I have but a higher demon who will miss me when I pass and two nephews whom I loved dearly but were never allowed to know me. I hope this book helps you better understand your uncle Reed Hadley.

Smiling at the personal note, Storm closed the book and made a mental note to show Rowan in the morning. He'd love the sentimentality and lament the fact that Reed Hadley had died without learning of the legacy his demon had made sure he would leave behind. Yael would like to know too.

Tucking the book into a satchel—to keep it out of sight from

Cesa, if he wandered in, and to protect it from Midnight—Storm tucked the bag under the bed and slipped down the mattress. He switched off the lamp, made sure Rowan's phone was off and snuggled under the duvet.

A faint sniff made him pause and smile when Rowan grasped his hand. "Go to sleep," he whispered, pulling Storm's hand to his chest, drawing his arm around Rowan's back and side. Storm had no choice but to curl against his back but every intention of never moving again.

*

A DREAM THAT wasn't a dream lurked in Storm's mind as he slept, drifting in the unspoken place between sleep and consciousness. Shadows surrounded him, indecipherable whispers lurked in the dark, and he wasn't startled when an almighty crash tore through the old mansion.

Rowan shot up in bed, the word 'Father' slipping from his lips in proof this was a regular occurrence. He threw the covers aside, while Storm was still untangling from a fog-like sleep, and rushed from the bedroom.

Storm rubbed at his eye and trudged after him, hoping this was an accident in the dead of the night and not something new to worry about. He glanced at the clock on his way out the door and groaned at the flashing 4:04.

Stepping outside the room, they froze to hear noises emanating from Yael's room, along with cat yowls that sounded furious and afraid. Yet a light was on in Cesa's bedroom, and Rowan was clearly torn on which way to go.

"I'll—" Storm said, pointing toward Yael's room. "You—"

Rowan didn't question his inarticulate state, following his final gesture toward Cesa's room. He took off without speaking, no doubt panicked his father's condition had worsened or he'd woken from another nightmare about losing Asher. That was something Storm wasn't awake enough to think about.

He walked to Yael's room and knocked to avoid startling them. "It's Storm. I'm coming in." When he didn't get an answer, he opened the wooden door, blinked at the state of the room and flinched when Midnight shot from under the bed with a screech. At the last minute, the kitten detoured out the room and along the corridor.

Storm watched Midnight disappear into Rowan's bedroom, no doubt to escape the cause of the crash or in search of safety. Once the kitten was safe, Storm glanced at Yael and blinked before stepping out of the room and shutting the door.

When Rowan emerged from his father's bedroom, Storm met him in the middle of the expansive hallway. "Dad is fine. He woke at the noise, but went to sleep when I told him I'd dropped something," Rowan explained, the relief written all over his face.

"There's a demon in the spare bedroom," Storm said, not sure how else to explain what he'd found in Yael's room. Shock didn't begin to explain how he felt, walking in to find Yael naked, bare ass in full view, and straddling a demon on the floor with a knife pressed to the intruder's throat.

This was not what he expected at four in the morning.

"I feel like I know that, but your face says I don't," Rowan replied, as frazzled as Storm was by the rude awakening.

"I mean...there's *another* demon in the spare bedroom," he corrected, not surprised Rowan groaned, rolled his head to gaze at the ceiling and counted under his breath. He barely reached six before he began marching toward Yael's room.

Yael had dressed in a kimono dressing gown and stood over a corner chair that housed the new demon. With the way Yael hovered over the poor, obviously terrified creature, Storm suspected the chair had become a prison; not that he'd ever say that out loud.

"Does someone want to explain what happened?" Storm asked as Rowan moved from his shocked pause in the doorway to close the door behind them. Storm crossed to perch on the edge of the double bed, staring at both demons as he waited.

Yael darted a glare toward the other demon. "This is Kyrie. I met him while I was scouting the abyss for information, but he swore he had nothing to tell me," they explained and raised an eyebrow at Kyrie in accusation.

Before this could become a demon-on-demon brawl, Storm cut in. "Kyrie," he said, waiting for the demon to turn, androgynous facial features and white talons letting him know this was a male demon of lower rank. The black clothing of tattered trousers and no shirt indicated that he was a bonded servant to a mage.

"You are...the Dark One."

"Yes. Can you tell us why you're here, how you got here, and if you need help?" he asked, convinced he'd stumbled through from the abyss, creating chaos when he walked into the furniture or stepped on the cat. If he'd arrived in any other way, he doubted Yael would have been taken off guard.

With a tentative nod, Kyrie sat straighter. "I am servant to a dark mage who resides in Paris. He summoned a higher demon to do his bidding last evening, who said that another sought information for the prophecy child. My master wanted to curry favour with the Dark One. He sent me into the abyss to find out what I could, to spy on those closest to you, in hopes of finding information," he confessed in a rush, desperate to get the words out.

Storm raised a hand to stop the flow of words. "Kyrie, do you want a drink? Are you hungry?" he asked, worried his fear might lead to a panic attack, if demons had such things.

Though Kyrie paused with a look of utter bewilderment, he soon winced and rubbed at his right wrist. Storm crossed to Kyrie with a horrible suspicion of what he'd find. Rowan stood and Yael leaned in to peek over Kyrie's shoulder.

"Are you hurt?" Rowan reached cautiously for Kyrie's wrist. "Let me see. I can treat a wound, if you've hurt yourself," he said, concerned and caring.

The way Kyrie lowered his gaze and covered his sore wrist with a hand gave the rest away: he hadn't hurt *himself*; someone else had hurt him.

With the confirmation Kyrie had been hurt, Rowan dis-ap-peared from the room to get the first aid kit. Yael let their long fingers flutter against the chair where Kyrie sat, eyes narrowed with disapproval.

"We'll handle this, but you need to keep a cool head. How about you bring Kyrie a drink and a cake?" Storm suggested, aware that sweet food helped calm demons. Something about human sugar boosted their healing abilities.

With an obliging tip of their head, Yael faded from sight.

Storm smiled at Kyrie, who stared in disbelief. "Your wrist," he said, needing to know what had happened.

"My master told me to come tell you what I knew, and leave immediately," Kyrie answered, glancing at the door when Rowan returned. "Master's touch burns me."

The barely whispered confession made Storm want to scream, cry and hurt someone. This poor demon had clearly been bound to his master and had no choice but to do his bidding, but he didn't seem to realise that his master's touch was an affront to their bond.

The moment Yael returned with a tea tray, handing Kyrie a cup of tea and a slice of chocolate cake, which made Storm's mouth water, he cleared his throat and got his mind on track.

"He's been bound to his master. Can we free him?" he asked Yael, who was the best judge of the situation.

Yael tipped their head and shrugged, but a smile played on

their lips. "You are the Dark One. You would be the one to know," they replied, lifting a second plate with another slice of cake to lay on the table by Kyrie's chair. "Eat. You must regain your strength to be of use to the Dark One."

Instead of making him worry, the words inspired obedience as Kyrie happily ate the cake and sipped at the tea.

Storm stepped aside to let Rowan kneel on the floor and bandage Kyrie's wrist, which showed bruises where the imprint of long fingers had wrapped around his wrist. The sight made him feel sick and stirred his anger. He couldn't help but close his eyes when his magic whispered, *We can fix him. Heal the demon and punish the master.*

No. We can't stoop to his level, by punishing people for not doing what we want. He could feel his magic floating in his mind, fluttering and thinking about what he'd said.

We could...discipline him in another way. A warning from the Dark One, to remind him of who you are, that you are the Dark One, the prophecy child, the one who must be obeyed.

Storm thought about the less violent reaction; a warning, not a threat nor a way of seeking payback or revenge, yet he wasn't sure he had the authority to meddle in the lives of demons. He could free Kyrie because he was being misused by dark magic, and that was definitely Storm's domain. Did he have the right to warn another mage and scold them for their misuse of magic?

His magic gave another tap against his brain. *It is who you are. Who you are meant to be: master of Death, master of dark mages, ruler of the dark magics, protector of demons.*

The titles were familiar, the same ones the covens had whispered around him for years, laying on one responsibility after another. But the last was new; and the implication of the title, 'Protector of Demons' was an expectation he would gladly live up to.

"Protector of Demons," he said aloud, testing the title to see what everyone else thought.

Surprise lit Rowan's eyes and they flashed ice blue with heightened emotion. To his left, Yael snuffed a laugh and choked on a bite of cake they'd stolen from the second plate.

Storm raised his eyebrow, but Yael tipped their head and cleared their throat.

"It is about time you realise your true place."

It was as if everyone was waiting for him to accept the role, the way a ruler would accept their place as king in a fairy tale.

Gods, how had he never known this? Why didn't anyone ever tell him? Ithen or Gladys would never let him hear a whisper because they wouldn't want him to realise how much power he had at his disposal—the support and gathering of demons who would flock to Storm if he only asked. His parents had died long before he was capable of understanding what the title meant, but Ithen's memories made sense now. Storm's dad had accepted his bond with Yael as a child and not blinked at his son being best friends with a full demon or Rowan, the half-demon he clearly knew about. Asher knew about his title and that he would become the 'Protector of Demons'. He accepted that Storm would spend more time with demons than any other mage—dark or light. Because this was his destiny.

"Well, shit."

Chapter Fifteen

STORM CROUCHED BESIDE Rowan, shaking his head at how truly dense he'd been for most of his life. "Moving on..." He cleared his throat and focused on Kyrie. "Once Rowan is finished, I can break your bond *if* you want. Though I hate to see you being treated like this, it has to be your choice." Storm refused to be another mage who forced his will on a demon.

Suddenly tearful, Kyrie nodded, set his cup of tea onto the tray and straightened his posture, clearly preparing for what was to come.

Storm didn't have a clue what he was doing, but he gave his magic a mental nudge and reached for Kyrie's hand slowly, giving him plenty of warning. Pausing an inch away, he looked into Kyrie's big white eyes. "I'm going to hold your hand to connect to your magic, so I can find and break the bond."

Kyrie nodded and licked his lips, glancing at Yael and then Storm. "What about my master? I wouldn't want him to get hurt. He didn't know any better. He was taught to treat demons this way," he rambled, desperate to justify how he'd been treated. Regardless of the mage's intentions or beliefs, he should have worked harder to find out the truth and used common sense.

In Storm's mind, demons shouldn't be treated any different to humans. If a person couldn't bear to see a human tortured and treated like a prisoner, why do the same to a demon?

"I won't hurt him." Storm never wanted to give his magic a taste of vengeance that could start something he couldn't control. "It's my job to take care of you...of demons...and make sure mages, dark or light, know how to treat you properly. I'll make sure he understands that what he did was wrong, and there will be a penalty if he repeats the behaviour. I'll use my words and a push of magic," he explained to keep him informed and let him know his master would be safe.

He wasn't prepared to use violence to resolve violence. He may have once—before he saw how that ended for his parents, for Ithen, and everyone else who thought dark magic was the easy answer to every problem. Now that Storm knew better, he would educate the rest of the magical world.

"Okay." Kyrie nodded, his voice quiet and meek.

Settling on his knees, he took hold of Kyrie's hand and tentatively sought to locate Kyrie's bond. Rowan sat beside him, patiently packing away the first aid supplies. Storm closed his eyes to block out Kyrie's worried gaze and let his magic loose. He let his mind piggyback the journey until his magic hovered above a thin red thread running through Kyrie's brain.

Opening his inner eye to view the thread as a human, he was shocked to find the bond between human and demon was like another strand of DNA, latching onto the blood of the demon. That implied the mage or witch commands became their will, flooding their brain with the appropriate chemicals to *want* to obey. Gods, that was sick, and no different to rewiring the brain—brainwashing them into becoming a puppet on a string. Yet demons were naturally inclined to make the bond with any mage or witch they chose to work with. Why? Did the thread go both ways?

Curious, Storm allowed a mental hand to reach out while his magic swirled around to block the thread from doing further harm. He could feel the intent to do harm, the intention of binding and imprisoning the demon, the will to dominate and be obeyed. His mental hand curled into a tight fist around the thread from anger. A frisson of something unknown flared on the other side, like shock and the pain of a sudden burn, like being struck by a match.

"Hello." He sent the thought through the thread in an attempt to find out if communication could work over such a distance.

"Who are you?" The response was angry and resentful but posed an interesting question, one Storm wasn't willing to answer. Not until he was sure he'd connected to the right person. *"Where*

is my demon?"

At least this mage was smart enough not to give Kyrie's name, even when caught by surprise. *"My name is Storm Tera."* He wanted to make sure this mage knew who he was talking to and what the consequences were. *"The Chosen One. The Dark One. Necromancer and mage. Commander of the dead. Protector of demons."*

Silence reigned on the other end of the tether. Storm could feel the mage lingering, not sure what to say, aware of who he was dealing with but not understanding why Storm was contacting him. He should.

Storm realised this was what Yael and Rowan had been telling him. He'd been too stubborn and resistant to the idea, but he was the last of the most powerful covens to have existed since magic began, the last with old, wild magic. All other covens, mages and witches bowed to him and his powers, whether he wanted them to or not.

"I'm going to cut to the chase." He was too tired to ease into what he wanted. *"I'm pissed. You bound Kyrie against his will and put a barrier between a demon and the abyss."* The truth of this poor demon's sad life was easy to read in the thread which dictated the boundaries of the bond. *"You broke the covenant between humans and demons. Whether you were raised to believe that behaviour was acceptable or not doesn't matter. You treated a demon like a piece of shit, and you will stop. If I ever hear you have taken another demon and treated them the way you've*

treated Kyrie, I will make sure you pay.

"*If you don't know how to treat another living being by now, you shouldn't be using magic. Your actions could have disrupted the balance of the world, and it ends now.*" Storm commanded, refusing to accept that this mage, who came through to his senses as a thirty- or forty-year-old man, didn't know better. "*I am breaking your bond to Kyrie. If he's wise, he'll stay far away from you. He is now free to choose his fate, including whether he takes another master. If he chooses to return to you then you will treat him like the precious gift he is. Am I clear?*"

The answer was barely a heartbeat from reaching him, the tone suitably contrite. "*Yes, Chosen One.*"

In addition, he sensed a bow of the head. Storm guessed this dark mage had decided not to cross him. "*Good. The next time you want to send me information, don't do it at four in the bloody morning.*"

Storm cut off contact because he wasn't interested in what the mage had to say. He retreated from the thread and glanced at his magic, waiting patiently to be given permission to do what needed to be done.

"*Have fun,*" he said, watching as his magic descended on the thread in desperation. This was the first time he'd truly felt disconnected from his magic, despite knowing his will created the intent for its actions.

Black mist spread across the thread, turning from red to grey to a deep, dark black of nothing. Storm sensed a momentary shift within his magic, moving Kyrie's bond from the mage to himself. Knowing his body and magic the way he did, he grabbed hold of the black thread connecting them and tugged. He tossed the broken connection into Kyrie's body where it withered, shrivelling into a useless coil of thread. Within minutes, the evidence of the bond had dissolved.

Storm retreated from Kyrie's magic between one breath and another to find Kyrie staring with wide eyes that darted between Storm's gaze and their joined hands. When he released Kyrie's hand, he had to flex his fingers, feeling like he'd been stuck in the position for hours. The patience on Rowan's face said he'd likely taken less than a few minutes.

"Done." He made the announcement, unsure if there had been any outward sign of what had happened. "You're free now. You can bond to another mage, if and when you want to, but you can do so of your free will next time," he promised, glad to see the look in Kyrie's eyes morphing from shock to a smile.

Silence reigned as tears formed. In a split second, Kyrie burst into a wreck of Latin whispers and sobs, cradling his injured wrist to his chest. When he began to rock, Storm backed away, worried he'd done something wrong.

The touch of Rowan's hand on his thigh redirected his attention to soft, curious eyes, and he followed the nod to where Yael was hovering behind Kyrie's chair.

"Tea, I think." They faded into the abyss before Storm could speak.

He was about to ask what was happening when Rowan kissed his cheek, then leaned his head on Storm's shoulder. Convinced he wouldn't be calm if something was wrong, Storm took the time to breathe, to think and to just *be*.

They only had a few minutes of peace, while Yael and Kyrie had tea and another two cakes each, before Storm managed to get Kyrie to talk. As much as he wanted to sleep, the quicker they found out why Kyrie had appeared in the manor, the quicker they could get him somewhere safe and all get back to sleep.

"When the higher demon told us the names of who you wished information about, my master...um, mage Auden...said he had heard of the lady Gladys," Kyrie explained, sounding much calmer since he'd had the chance to rest.

"The woman is far from a lady," Yael remarked, not quietly enough to go unnoticed.

When Kyrie paused with his teacup to his mouth, eyes wide, Storm offered a look of warning. "Go on," he said to Kyrie, with an encouraging smile.

Kyrie sipped his tea and spared a glance at Yael, who remained hovering behind his chair. "Auden had heard rumours amongst his coven of a la—" He cut off sharply and glanced at Yael. "—woman called Gladys Glade, who sought to learn the dark arts. This was ten years ago. He and the coven assumed she was hoping to teach you the dark arts, without trusting you in the hands of someone she didn't know.

"Auden gave permission for a lower member of his coven to

contact Gladys Glade to discuss her needs. When she asked about necromancy and how to create a homunculus, Auden demanded they cut off contact. No one in his coven knows how to use necromancy; few dark mages do. The Voodoo quarter in New Orleans would have information, and the Brujería of your mother's heritage, but both are private. They separate themselves from other dark mages to protect the ancient arts."

Storm nodded, understanding what he meant. "Something about containing the wild, ancient magic. It does something to the mind that other families can't handle. There's a specific strand of DNA in both families, which the Fates gifted them to hold wild magic, according to Gladys."

Kyrie nodded his agreement. "Auden said that only a Tera or an Amari could teach you the ancient magic and advised the last contact sent to Gladys Glade that you should be handed to your mother's family to be properly trained in the dark arts," he said, his eyes sad, probably because he hadn't been offered a chance to meet the other side of his family or learn his unique family craft.

Storm should feel disappointed, but he'd never met either side of his extended family. He had no feelings about meeting them, but he agreed with Kyrie that they were the best people to teach him the family magic. Maybe when the war was over he'd track them down.

A hand slid over his thigh, and Rowan's eyes were just as sad as Kyrie's. "I'm glad she didn't."

Storm squeezed his hand in reassurance because he would

never have gone.

"When this demon mentioned her to Auden," Kyrie continued with an averted gaze, as if to avoid intruding on their moment, "he became curious to find out what had become of her and if she had accomplished the strange magic. Auden told me to find out more about her." Kyrie flinched when Yael let out a low growl.

Storm raised an eyebrow at Yael, who turned away to ignore the silent question. Kyrie didn't seem to notice. "I was sent through the abyss to spy on her home. I found a child sitting on her living room sofa, vacant of life. I could detect nothing wholly human nor wholly dead inside him; the boy was somewhere in between."

"A homunculus?" Rowan guessed, glancing at Storm with curiosity.

"No." Kyrie glanced awkwardly at Storm. "A demon child."

Storm wondered how Gladys had managed to find one, capture them and not face the consequences. Rowan stiffened beside him and gripped his hand painfully hard. Yael grabbed and threw a wooden box from the window mantle, the carpet dimming the resulting noise to a dull thud.

Kyrie nodded. "A true demon child. He said his name was Donald and he was waiting for his mother. When I stepped in front of him, he asked me politely to move, because he was watching his favourite TV show...but the TV wasn't on," he continued, sadness sweeping over his face. "I became concerned and returned to Auden to tell him what I had found. He became angry with me and with Gladys Glade. He insisted that I return and make sure I wasn't caught because he must know everything about the boy."

Storm could imagine why. Auden probably hoped to take the demon child for his magic; whatever age they truly were, a demon child's magic wasn't yet shaped by adulthood and was far more pliable for a mage to manipulate.

"The boy was in a bedroom upstairs, lying on a bed but not sleeping. I used magic to reach out, but something foul lingered inside, some twisted magic and images. I saw a demon boy with his father, being taught magic; the same boy cowering behind his father as Gladys walked toward him, and his demon father lying on the ground unmoving as hands grabbed him. Then the boy was shut in a cage, begging to be let free. Finally, I saw the boy sitting on the sofa as I had found him, empty of life." Kyrie shook his head and looked at his hands.

He flinched when Yael passed a plate with a piece of cake. With a tentative smile, he accepted the gift and nodded a silent thanks. "I was shocked, but the pieces came together in his mind and allowed me to see the truth," he said, taking small bites. "He was a true born demon child—the first in decades—and his father said he was a good omen, the first of a new breed of demons, born because of the Chosen One."

Storm's breath caught. He didn't know what he had to do with any of this, but the look in Kyrie's eyes suggested this would be monumental and life changing.

"The Chosen One had been born and would save demons

from their lives of near slavery. This boy was the first sign of the future," Kyrie continued, smiling absently at the piece of cake in his hand. "He was happy to have his son be the first sign of your birth, your victory and your future as Protector of Demons." He shook his head and the smile disappeared. "Then Gladys summoned his horde. The child had wandered into the abyss unguided and lost himself in the In-Between. Gladys demanded they return her dead son."

As Kyrie spoke, Rowan's hand turned beneath Storm's to link their fingers. Storm strengthened his grip, aware this must be hard on him. Rowan was half-demon and must be imagining what Gladys would do if she knew, how he may have been in this demon child's position if she had ever discovered the truth.

"The father refused." Kyrie clasped his hands, rubbing his bandaged wrist with a frown. "He apologised but told her the truth; her son had been dead for days and his soul was gone from his body. She stole the demon's child and swore she would not return him until her Donald was whole and alive. When the father again told her that wasn't possible, she threw a curse at them. The boy thought his father was dead, but the curse was weak, and I suspect the horde must still be alive."

Storm bit down on a curse, realising the horde could still be searching for their 'good omen' child.

"Why didn't they return for their child?" Yael asked, the bite of their tone causing Kyrie to flinch.

Kyrie shrugged. "I believe the boy has been hidden, that he

only exists within Gladys Glade's home. If anyone outside seeks to find him, they cannot see past the protections of the home. If they seek *him,* he is lost within his mind and cannot be found." Apparently Kyrie had found his backbone since he was freed from his bond. "He fought to remember who he was, while Gladys Glade used dark magic to convince him that he was truly her son. He fought for years to remember his name, to remember he was a demon child but was unable to fight the magic.

"The magic took its toll and he lost hope. When he 'became' Donald—answering to the name, behaving as the human boy would have, as she had told him to—he was allowed out of his cage and without his shackles. He essentially became Donald and forgot who he truly is," Kyrie concluded, with a natural sag of his shoulders that spoke of unburdening himself.

Storm thought logically about their game plan. They needed sleep and his magic needed time to properly recover from the day's activities. When he turned to ask Rowan his thoughts, the tears on his cheeks sent logic out the window.

"Storm," he whispered, his bottom lip trembling as he struggled to hold his emotions in check.

"Yeah. I—" He paused to clear his throat and squeezed his hand. "I feel sick, but this would explain the DJ I met in the future. That kid was scared of everything. If she'd forced him to become someone he wasn't and he had demon gifts, no wonder she didn't want to explain his abilities." He thought of the innocent boy he'd spoken to, given advice to and comforted, when the demons and ghosts of the room frightened him. "I can't believe Gladys would...to a child. I mean..."

No words existed to explain what Gladys had done. He didn't care that she'd lost Donald or that she was grieving. She had stolen another person's child and hurt him, manipulated him, done such irreparable harm that he saw no way out but to submit to her will. This demon child was a baby, too young to know how to defend himself, and he'd been with his family at the time he was taken. Having to see his family—

It reminded Storm too much of Ithen's memories of the night his parents died. Having to see his dad's dead body, watching Cesa grieve while knowing he had no way to fight the curse washing over him... Gods, the cruelty was far too familiar.

"I am sorry." Kyrie reached out to brush aside a tear Storm hadn't felt falling over his cheek.

"It's not your fault. You brought me this valuable information, and I'm extremely grateful," he promised, reassuring Kyrie he'd done well.

"That may be why Auden was angry with me," Kyrie admitted, glancing at Yael with obvious concern. "I sent him a mind-message to say I had found what you wanted to know but I didn't explain. I...didn't want him to have that power...over Gladys or you or the boy."

"You were scared he'd want the demon child?" Rowan guessed, seeing the same danger Storm had.

When Kyrie nodded, Storm resolved to deal with Auden

permanently once this chaos was over. "He didn't always treat me badly," he said in a quiet voice. "He was a kind, lovely young man but his father was harsh because he couldn't master the darkest of arts. When his father died, Auden began to emulate his father to prove he could outdo him. A few years ago, he changed and...hurt me."

A strong hand landed on his shoulder, making him flinch. Yael didn't retract their touch but the hardness of their gaze softened. "You are free now. We will protect you."

Storm thought he had better cut in before Yael's stern tone made Kyrie worry they were angry. If he wasn't mistaken, Auden had inspired Yael's fury, and the strong reaction made Storm curious. "Even if you want to go back—though I admit, I don't see why you would want to—you can. That's your choice, and I'm sure I scared him witless so he won't hurt you again," he promised, letting Kyrie know they wouldn't keep him captive.

"I know." Kyrie smiled warmly, the tilt of his lips becoming coy as he glanced at Yael. "I think I'd like to stay. To help you save the boy."

"You need to rest," Yael decided, taking charge. "You will remain here and sleep as a human would. You will heal faster."

Rowan's eyes widened, no doubt wondering when the infestation of demons and troubles would end, and if they would ever be alone again. That was a question Storm would also love to ask, but he suspected he wouldn't like the answer. "Another house guest," Rowan said, feigning excitement. "Would you like your own room? We do have one more, if you want to be by yourself," he asked, giving Kyrie the chance to escape Yael if he wanted.

Before he could answer, Yael's hand tightened on his shoulder in what Storm thought was more of a possessive reaction than dominance, a silent *back off* they knew better than to say to Rowan.

"That won't be necessary." When Yael looked down at Kyrie, he blushed as best as a demon could, his eyes sparkling a dazzling ice blue. "I will guard Kyrie so he can sleep in peace, to ensure neither the cat nor his master return."

Rowan glared at Yael. "Did you just lump my innocent kitten in with a brutal dark mage?"

"Your demon kitten is the most evil creature I have ever seen in such a small package," Yael replied good-naturedly, as though that was a compliment.

Unable to resist, Storm gave his not-yet-boyfriend a nudge in the ribs. "See? I told you," he teased, then rounded on the group. "Before we separate...back to DJ?"

"It's disgusting." Rowan shook his head at the horrible topic.

Yael nodded and removed their hand from Kyrie's shoulder to grasp the chair instead. "This means the boy I sent my message through was the same demon child," they admitted, with something like distaste. "I did detect something strange within him, but he must have been her prisoner for so long that he lost all will to live. No demon scent surrounded the body. His soul must have receded into the curse willingly, leaving no elemental sign of who he once was." The way their eyes narrowed suggested they were struggling to accept how badly they'd misread the situation.

Storm didn't blame Yael. They were both powerful beings, with good awareness and senses but neither had realised what the little boy was or known he needed to be saved.

"It's—" Rowan stopped, the tension running through him almost making him visibly shake with a combination of fear and anger.

He was probably aware how easily it could have been him. A demon child didn't have the mastery of magic an adult did and couldn't save himself from the situation or cross to the abyss to escape.

Storm couldn't imagine being so young, so afraid, forced to bond with someone, losing all sense of self and being a prisoner. "We'll find the amulet, find the spell, get rid of Gladys and save this demon child," he said, adamant they make up for their past mistakes as much as they could. "If I'm the prophesied child, the Dark One all dark mages must obey, then they will start obeying me! No more forcing demons to become slaves, no more distorting magic."

He was decided. Storm couldn't let this shit keep happening. Demons were suffering, children were being hurt, Gladys had become someone he barely recognised, and he'd been ignorant and complacent in a life he'd lived but that had gone drastically wrong.

If he hadn't travelled through time—by Gladys's decision, whatever her motives—he wasn't sure what the future would hold.

He did know he couldn't live with himself once he found out the truth. Gladys had wrought nothing but chaos and destruction over the last twenty years, but he'd been a child until recently and an ignorant teenager who had been raised under her hand in her home. He'd been raised to not notice how strange her behaviour had become. Now that he was of an age to be independent, Storm was damned well going to do something. "I need to embrace my legacy."

He thought he'd been building toward this the whole time, but he saw now the half-hearted effort and belief; a what-if scenario surrounding a prophecy and a war he'd lived but couldn't remember; a distant thing with no substance or meaning; something not serious, that didn't impact him or the people he cared about.

It was real now and had always *been* real, but Storm had his eyes open. Asses needed to be kicked.

Before the thought could run away and his magic could get hopeful of revenge, Rowan kissed his cheek and squeezed his hand. Without a word, he nodded to Yael who tipped their head briefly in understanding.

Storm couldn't fathom what silent communication had gone on, but when Rowan got to his feet he followed, glancing back when they reached the door. Yael fussed over Kyrie, who agreed to sleep for the night. Since Yael had everything in hand, Storm left them to handle the situation; they clearly knew what they were doing, and he was sure he'd detected flirting between the two demons.

Eager to return to Rowan's soft, warm bed and the interrupted sleep, he let Rowan lead the way to his room and shut the door behind them. He shooed Midnight off the rumpled duvet, where Storm gladly slipped under the covers, facing the centre of the bed in contentment. A moan slipped out when Rowan slid onto the bed and kissed him, soft and gentle, a pleasant reminder that Storm *could* kiss him if he wanted to, *when* he wanted to.

"You were magnificent," Rowan whispered, moving closer to regain his space in the centre of the bed.

"Yeah?" Storm wasn't sure what he'd done, but he loved the look in Rowan's eyes, slightly hazy, a soft languid thing that was warm and inviting. He grazed their lips in another sleepy kiss, pleasantly surprised when Rowan nudged closer, a hand coming to his neck.

When he broke away, Rowan pressed their foreheads together. "I've been afraid to accept you're here...that you'll stay, after this is over. I've been scared you had nowhere else to go, but you *want* to be here. You really do care about me," he confessed, his voice faltering in relief. "You're not afraid of me."

"Why would I be?" Storm pulled away to look him in the eye, not sure what there was to be afraid of.

"I'm half-demon."

Shaking his head, Storm brushed his thumb over Rowan's bottom lip, wondering how such a smart, beautiful and strong guy could ever be so self-conscious. "You're Rowan and that's all I need you to be." He ducked in to steal—no, borrow—a tender kiss.

Whatever their kisses were, they weren't stolen; they were shared experiences, moments of understanding and he would most definitely return them whenever he borrowed one. "I just squint and pretend I can't see the Copry part."

Rowan laughed, a combination of disbelief and absolute certainty in his eyes. "I love—" He whispered with a light peck at his lips. "—that you're more afraid of the Copry in me than the demon."

Storm leaned away from the next kiss to stare at Rowan: ruffled inside and out, not caring how he looked, eyes ice blue with affection he wasn't sure he deserved and no barrier between them other than their clothes. "You know...it's in my nature, and my job description apparently."

"Hmm. Protector of Demons," Rowan said, with a happy sigh of approval. "Promise to protect me forever?" he asked, showing his vulnerable side for a rare moment.

Though forever was a bloody terrifying thought, Storm knew what his answer would be. Everything inside him—his magic, heart, head, and soul—told him this was what he'd always been meant for: to protect Rowan, to love him.

Brushing a strand of hair from Rowan's eyes, Storm enjoyed a last lingering kiss and shifted to rest his head on the pillow. Taking Rowan's hand in his, he whispered, "I promise."

Chapter Sixteen

Three Days Later
November 15, 2026

"THAT MAN IS incompetent," Yael said, glancing at Kyrie as Rowan helped him slip into a new coat. "I wouldn't trust him with a pet, never mind a coven of dark mages."

Storm tried not to smile at the judgement but nodded, trusting Yael. He needed to do something about Auden and his coven soon, but not yet. When the war was over, he would need to place another more experienced mage into the position of leader of the coven, someone who didn't treat demons like chattel.

Yael and Kyrie had just returned from visiting Auden's coven, where they'd been gathering information and observing the man's abilities from a distance. The report wasn't good but hardly a surprise.

"We'll deal with that as soon as this prophecy business is sorted," Storm promised, aware Yael had a personal stake. Neither demon had acted on the obvious mutual attraction, and Storm didn't know the etiquette on demon relationships well enough to ask. They would either figure it out, or Kyrie would make the first move; the young demon had grown in confidence during the three days he'd spent with Yael.

Right now, they had a more imminent task ahead. One Storm didn't relish.

"Might I suggest you remain close?" Yael said, drawing his attention from his thoughts.

"Any particular reason?"

Yael shrugged and watched Rowan fuss over Kyrie's clothing. "By all accounts, your father was an extraordinary dark mage with abilities of some renown. There's no telling what he may have dealt with during his practising years or what he may have intentionally or accidentally invited into his home. I think you should be prepared for anything."

Storm nodded, accepting the wisdom of the word the caution. "I trust you, Yael. If you think I need to be careful, I will."

"Thank you. I appreciate your trust in me," Yael replied, with a faint smile that was part amusement and part pleasure.

"Nonsense." Rowan appeared in good spirits and linked his arm through Storm's. "Next to Storm, you're the most powerful person in this room," he insisted, kissing Storm's cheek with big, innocent eyes. "Besides, this is a huge deal, and we grew up together—whether we can remember or not—so we should do this together."

Rowan's support of the fact they were going, despite Yael's hesitations, meant more than any words could. "You're adorable," Storm admitted, not surprised that Rowan blushed and shook his head at the compliment.

"Come on. If we leave now, we can avoid the rain," he said, glancing back to make sure Kyrie was following them to the front door of the mansion. They had the reassurance of Cesa being at another business meeting which Rowan had given his support for.

"You do remember that's not a problem, right?" Storm said, leaving the subject of the two demons trailing them from the house for another day. "If I ask, the rain could fall around us but never *on* us." He wondered if the chaos of the last few weeks or the revelations they'd unearthed had pushed the knowledge from Rowan's mind.

Raising a sceptical eyebrow, Rowan led the way along the path to the Tera property by the quickest route. "I've seen you get soaked by the rain a million times."

Resisting the temptation to kiss the adorable pout off his lips, Storm cleared his throat. "Yeah, but...I like the rain. It's how we communicate," he confessed, despite the doubtful look Rowan shot him. "If I don't want to get wet, I won't."

"Okay, let's do that," Rowan decided, glancing pointedly at Kyrie, bundled into a heavy overcoat. "I do *not* want to get sick when we have so much to do."

"Do you *get* sick?"

With a nonchalant shrug, Rowan replied with a light tone, "No idea, but I don't want *now* to be the time I find out."

"Smart man." Storm appreciated the attempt to make this easier. Even if there wasn't a way to forget what they were doing, the fact Rowan cared enough to understand what he was thinking and feeling and wanted to help lighten the load, reminded Storm how special Rowan was.

Who knew an elemental half-witch/half-demon could crack the guards around his heart and show him what true love looked like.

*

STEPPING ONTO TERA property, Storm could feel the earth humming beneath his feet, sending vibrations throughout his body, welcoming him home. The ground embraced his magic, fawning over him while the trees rustled and whispered, "*The lost one. Forest child. Stolen son.*" The words were like a knife to his heart. The trees didn't mean to hurt him, but they reminded Storm of everything he'd been running from.

Deep down, he was still a child trying to escape the murder of his family, unaware he was walking straight into the arms of their murderer's accomplice. He was still hiding from the prophecy that shrouded his every move with expectation and whispers of the great deeds he was made for.

Storm had overcome those fears and found comfort in the truth. He understood what was expected and why, now that he'd lived a life where the prophecy remained unfulfilled. Even then, the atmosphere and pressure that knowledge left him wading through was suffocating as he re-entered the house he'd been born into, the legacy home that should have been his until the day he died. To Storm, it was nothing but a place of nightmares, ghosts and dark whispers from the shadows.

"Are you okay?" Rowan stepped closer and squeezed his clasped hand.

Storm looked at their intertwined fingers and couldn't remember when they'd slipped naturally from Rowan holding his arm to holding hands. "Yeah. It's—" He didn't know how to explain, but the ghosts of the house had crowded in on him the minute he stepped through the door.

The memories from Ithen's mind played out in stark clarity, showing him where he'd stood when he last spoke to his dad... where his dad's dead body had lain while Cesa had sobbed and grieved over his lost lover...where his mum had faded into the light and the abyss.

A shiver raked his spine, forcing him to face reality. Rowan stood by his side, where he'd been since Storm fell from the abyss and into his life. Yael was on his other side, offering strength and power, a promise of safety. Kyrie, the young demon, waited patiently beside Yael, ready to walk into this chaos because Storm had broken his bond to Auden. Kyrie was loyal, despite Storm not wanting or expecting repayment. He would never have known of Kyrie's situation if not for Yael, someone the young demon idolised. Eventually, he might sense demons—higher and lower—and become the true Protector of Demons, but he suspected that would come with time and experience, when he proved he was worthy of the position, perhaps when he saved the demon child that had become Donald.

For now, he had another task in mind.

"We need to find this amulet, which is supposed to react to a Tera descendant, so how do we do this?" Storm asked, glancing at the group in hope of a logical solution.

Yael gestured to the study door, still standing open from the day his dad had died. Even from here, Storm could see blood stains still on the carpet. Gladys's promise to have the place cleaned after the murder and maintained until he was ready to return had clearly been a lie. "I believe someone is waiting for you in the study."

Frowning at the fact they'd gone enigmatic, Storm squared his shoulders and released Rowan's hand.

A few deep breaths steadied his racing heart, a wipe against his jeans helped rid his sweaty-palm problem, and then he walked into the room. He only stopped after stepping over the blood stains that marked the place his dad had died, not wanting to look at them or acknowledge the memories of his dad lying there.

A breeze swept through the room, whispering words that niggled at Storm's brain.

Run!

...a Tera is the only one who can see the amulet.

An elemental witch wouldn't normally have contact with the darker arts at his age. The Fates must believe he'll need the gift in the future.

Storm remembered the words from Ithen's memory of the night his parents were killed, the night his life changed. What did they mean and why was the wind repeating them? What purpose did they have? The last one wasn't even about him but about Rowan.

Storm looked out the room and found Rowan standing in the doorway, one hand clutching the wooden frame, the other pressed to his heart.

Rowan licked his lips. "Turn around, Storm. There's...by your dad's desk."

Storm didn't want to turn around, but he didn't have the luxury to refuse. He was the Dark One: the one destined to control and guide all magic, the one the demons counted on to protect them, to return their stolen child and restore balance to the magical world. If he couldn't turn around, he was no good to any of them.

Closing his eyes, he took a steadying breath and faced the mahogany desk by the right side of the room. He opened his eyes, tears welling at the thought of what might be there, what *couldn't* be there but what he knew with everything in him *was* there.

"Hello, son."

Chapter Seventeen

STORM WASN'T AWARE he was shaking until a hand slipped into his. He didn't look because he didn't need to; the hint of mint, the sense of being stronger and more complete, the invisible thread linking them as surely as any demon-mage bond made the slightest touch electric and palpable. Rowan was by his side, as he always was when Storm needed him.

"Did you know?" he asked, unable to tear his gaze away but needing an answer.

His dad frowned and Rowan stiffened, his grip tightening as if realising that Storm wasn't asking him.

"No," Yael replied, not even sounding hurt or aware of the unintentional accusation in Storm's words. "I sensed a presence when we entered the house. Your father was...kind enough to introduce himself before we went any further."

The room remained silent with everyone waiting for Storm to speak. They could keep waiting, because he hadn't the first clue what to say. This man sitting behind the desk looked solid, but Storm knew he wasn't real; he was a ghost, spirit, or something completely unnatural, something *not* his dad.

He took time to look at this man he barely remembered, reconciling the sight with the man he'd glimpsed in Ithen's memories. Asher had been twenty-seven when he died, still young to be married with a six-year-old child. Maybe he'd been waiting for his ascension magic to settle, or he'd spent what years he could with Cesa, keeping their relationship a secret before leaving the man he loved to marry someone else.

Storm knew the love between his parents was real, but he'd never known someone could love two different people so fiercely. He understood that Asher hadn't had a choice. It didn't matter if his dad had been in love with a man and emotionally unfaithful to Storm's mother, because he hadn't been cruel or selfish. They'd been separated by forces beyond their control, and he imagined that trying to stop loving someone was impossible.

Storm had to admit, this wasn't the man he'd expected to be his dad. The few memories he had were of a man who dressed smartly, stool tall and proud, and had a commanding voice but was always soft and slightly amused when he spoke to Storm. The man in Ithen's memories hadn't been much different: the same strong bone structure, the same dark features. The only difference was that Ithen remembered the numerous tattoos that didn't exist in Storm's vague memories, the complete sleeves on both arms, the designs creeping up the front of his neck. Storm thought he saw some of the tattoos moving.

"I know this must be hard," his dad said, walking around the desk.

Storm took an instinctive step back, not sure what he was dealing with. "Hard?" He wondered what exactly Asher thought was hard: the appearance of a man he hadn't seen in twelve years; the fact the man was his dad and possibly a spirit; or that he'd been right to abandon this house, its ghosts and its secrets?

Pausing at the corner of the desk, the man who had once been Asher Tera looked at the wooden top and knocked his knuckles against the surface. "I'm sorry. I've been waiting for you to return and...I forgot you wouldn't have anyone to teach you about this," he apologised, still talking like his dad would.

"You've been waiting?" Storm asked, focusing on the words rather than the burning rage swirling under his skin. His dad—if this wasn't a trick—didn't deserve his anger.

Asher nodded and gestured to Yael. "Your friend can tell you, if you're not ready to believe me, but when a mage dies as I did...violently...using dark magic—"

"Murdered." Storm felt the need to interrupt now Asher was pretending this was normal and expected. The man who looked like his dad paused and met his gaze with a curious tilt of his head. "You were murdered," he elaborated, in case Asher didn't understand. If he hadn't left this house since he died, he likely thought

Storm believed the lies Gladys had poured into him. "I read Ithen's heart. I know what happened." A wave of sadness and loss enveloped his dad. The way his body sagged was indicative of a father in pain, and Storm didn't know what to do.

"Are you okay, Mr Tera?" Rowan asked, and started to step forward, then paused to look at Storm. He didn't know if the look was to ask for permission, or if he was hoping Storm would be the one to go to his dad.

No one moved.

Asher cleared his throat and looked at Yael, who hovered at the side of the room, an arm guiding Kyrie behind them while Kyrie watched with a vague, lost curiosity. "You let him read Ithen's heart? Knowing what he would see?" he demanded, harsh and angry, as black mist circled around him, proof that his magic, a part of his brutal death, had lingered.

Storm's stomach twisted in a knot, and he couldn't separate the man from his dad any longer. Whatever else he may be, he was his dad, trapped here in this damned house that Storm had avoided like the plague, because he was afraid to face the reality of what happened. If he'd been braver and stronger, he might have known the truth sooner and had time with his dad.

"I knew nothing," Yael replied, unaffected by the accusation. "Your son has a strange concept of how to work with a demon. He inadvertently took my mind along, when he read Ithen. That was when we both became aware of our history together."

"Because you were a child," Asher said in realisation, shaking his head and pressing both hands into the desk. He seemed to shrink, at once a great dark mage threatening a demon and a grieving father who never had the chance to raise his son. "I hoped the Fates had made you different, given you the ability to remember...so you would be with him."

That was where Storm had to interrupt. They were arguing with each other about purpose, responsibility and what happened in the past but had forgotten he was here. "I've been with Gladys. She cast a curse on me the night you died, forcing me to forget what I knew and believe the story she told me. I went to live with her."

His gut roiled to realise his dad must have thought Gladys an innocent visitor that night, someone called by Cesa or summoned by the disruption of balance in magic, not someone who had lied to Storm to save him from the truth. All these years, Asher thought Storm had been protected by her, unaware of how evil she was.

"I didn't leave her house until I was fourteen," he continued to help Asher understand why he'd never come home. "I didn't want to come here. She told me you were murdered by a demon. I didn't want to face the prophecy. I lived in the shack on our land."

"You stayed connected to the magic here but didn't embrace who you truly are," Asher said, understanding and not judging him. "Why return now?"

"Have you been waiting for me?" He needed one person on his side, one thing to hold onto, to remind him he was a true Tera and could believe in his magic. He needed to know what a mistake he'd made by being a coward.

"Yes, my little Storm," his dad answered, the nickname raising the hairs on his neck. "I couldn't leave this house. It was my dying wish."

Storm didn't quite understand why he sounded apologetic, as if he regretted that choice, until Yael moved, a slight shift of discomfort. "A dark mage such as yourself should have known better." They clearly didn't approve of what Asher had done. Whatever dying wish translated to in magical terms, Yael understood and thought him foolish.

"I know. I needed to be here for him when he had questions, when he was lost," Asher replied, unintentionally layering more shame onto what Storm already felt. His dad had stayed a spirit instead of passing into his next life to be here in case Storm needed him, and he'd been too much of a coward to even step one foot into the house.

"Were you alone?" he asked, needing to assuage his guilt with the knowledge that his dad had company while stuck here, waiting for the son who never came to visit.

"Your mother moved on a long time ago," his dad replied, with a faint smile that said he didn't blame her. "She knew why I stayed, but her spirit was free. She didn't know the truth of what happened the night we died, and I didn't have the heart to tell her. She was convinced Gladys would care for and protect you, and I knew she was selfish enough that you'd be safe as long as you remained useful to her."

Storm nodded, realising he'd been right. As long as Storm was the last surviving Tera, he was the only way Gladys could get her hands on the amulet. At least he had a straightforward answer to one question: his mum hadn't stayed because she thought he was being protected by Gladys. A few weeks ago, he might have said Gladys had done her best.

"And Cesa?"

"I'm sorry?"

Asher's surprise told Storm all he needed to know: he still thought no one knew about their relationship. "I know you loved him. Did you stay for him too?" Storm would never say he was wrong or judge his dad for staying just to be close to Cesa, to see him from a distance, or even to be in the place where they shared private moments.

"I'm sorry you had to find out the way you did." Asher perched on the edge of his desk and dug his hands into his pockets. "Cesa has visited this house often over the years. They're not pleasant visits, and I suggest you don't let on that you know about them or stop him if you ever see him coming here."

Whatever Cesa said or did here probably involved a lot of screaming, grieving, and sobbing, if Storm's theory was right. Cesa had never been able to escape the night Asher died.

"He's been cursed by Ithen," Storm confessed, needing his dad to know why Cesa wasn't in his right mind half the time. He fought so hard against the curse, but even Rowan knew there was no easy cure.

"I know." Asher shook his head, and the way he clenched his fist suggested he wished he could do something, could have known sooner, or beaten Ithen instead of dying the night they faced each other in this room.

Rowan stole the words from his mouth, his voice shaking with anger. "We don't know how to cure him. The hold on my father is so strong that none of my magic helps."

Asher straightened and frowned in obvious confusion. "He's *still* cursed? Why?" Either he didn't know they knew about the amulet and the spell, or he genuinely didn't understand Ithen's plans.

"He hasn't given Ithen the spell."

"For the amulet? You know about that?"

"From Ithen's memories," Storm said, curious about the slight anger in his dad's voice, as if he was never supposed to know. Was it Asher's plan to protect Storm from the threat of Gladys and Ithen by *never* telling him about the amulet? That was dangerous, but he supposed even if they'd used magic to interrogate him, he couldn't tell them something he didn't know. "We came to find the amulet."

Asher's face softened with surprise and affection. "Oh, my little Storm." He raked his eyes over Storm. "You've embraced who you are. You're ready to accept your legacy, your titles, your place in this world. I couldn't be more proud," he confessed, his gaze lingering on Storm's hand clasped tightly in Rowan's. "And you have a Copry by your side."

The remark was sad and thoughtful, reminding Storm of

how badly his dad had wanted to live his life with a Copry by his side. Storm reacted without thinking, not wanting to hear anything about prophesies or expectations. "I won't give him up. Not for anyone or anything," he swore, tightening his hold on Rowan's hand, pleased that Rowan squeezed his fingers with a supportive smile.

Shaking his head, his dad sounded sad. "I envy you because you can have it. No one will separate you," he promised, turning away as though the sight and the knowledge of his relationship with Rowan was painful.

Storm realised that was probably true. Asher was dealing with the visual proof that his son could have the relationship he wanted with the man he wanted without anyone getting in the way. That had to hurt, after all Asher had sacrificed to honour his position as a protector of the amulet, especially because Rowan was Cesa's son. His relationship with Cesa had been doomed from the start, all so that Storm could have this time with Rowan.

If his dad and Cesa had been allowed to be together, neither he nor Rowan would exist.

Rowan cleared his throat, glancing around nervously when all eyes darted his way. "Because he's the prophecy child, right? Because he's part of magic itself and I'm half Copry?" He put the pieces together, but his tone said he wasn't ready to trust his theory.

"Yes. You've both broken the rules of magic," Asher replied, relaxing against the desk now they'd moved on from talking about his life. He smiled at Storm, full of warmth and admiration. "When you were born, the Fates told us of the life that lay ahead. We let you be a child as long as you wanted, encouraged you to be wild, free, and silly because we knew the burden you would have to shoulder when you were older. As much as we let you get away with, you never purposefully broke the rules. You always knew where to draw the line even when it came to your magic and to your demon."

"They're not my demon," Storm answered instinctively, surprised Yael's lips twitched in what looked like amusement and pride.

Asher raised an eyebrow in what he assumed was a challenge.

Yael explained with obvious pride, "We're friends."

Storm smiled, loving that Yael sounded so happy. He was proud too. Yael may be a demon, but they were the best friend he could remember having, and he never wanted that to change.

Delight danced in Asher's eyes as he glanced between Storm and Yael, neither of whom had moved, presenting a united front by the study door. He wasn't sure if they'd decided not to move in case Asher escaped or if the shock of his ghost being here had kept them rooted to the spot. Asher didn't seem to mind.

"You used to get mad at anyone who called them your demon when you were little. You would tell everyone who would listen that Yael didn't belong to anyone and never would," Asher explained, easing the tension Storm had been harbouring and realising his dad respected their friendship, then and now. "Cesa separated you from Rowan, fearing you would go through the same impossible choice of losing each other that we had..." He paused, glancing away as if the thought of what he was about to say brought painful memories.

Storm wanted to go to him, an instinctive and automatic re-action, but he forced the feeling aside and remained where he was—in a position to protect the people he was with. He couldn't make the mistake of trusting the wrong person again, not even his dad, not with Yael, Kyrie and Rowan counting on him.

Asher shook off the melancholy and met Storm's gaze. "One night I came into your room to say goodnight and you were tucked in bed reading a book. I was shocked," he confessed with a chuckle and warm eyes that pulled on Storm's heart. "A storm blew out-side, and you would normally sit at your window to watch the lightning. I decided to wait and used magic to see what happened after I left the room."

Asher gestured to Rowan, who'd been leaning against Storm's arm but straightened as though he'd been caught doing something he shouldn't. "Storm went to open the window and asked the wind to bring you to his room," he revealed, staring at the youngest Copry with the same warmth he'd given Storm. "You came sailing in like a levitating angel and rushed to his bed. The pair of you snuggled in together, and I could see you'd likely been sneaking in for some time. You'd been reading the book together, taking turns reading aloud."

"I don't remember," Storm muttered, more to Rowan than to his dad. Those cornflower eyes were trained on him and showed no recognition of the memory, which was a shame; he would have liked to have one of them remember such an innocent moment from their childhood.

"You were only around four or five." Asher seemed unaware of how much Storm hated not knowing so much about his life. "Still innocent but determined to be together."

The fondness and sadness for his loss brought Storm's mind back to why they were here. He had to stop letting sentiment and the past get in the way. They had a purpose for being here, and he was the one diverting them. No one would stop him from talking to his dad for the first time in twelve years, so Storm had to be the one that put them back on track.

"Dad, where is the amulet?"

"It's been in your hands all along." Asher pushed from the desk to step closer. When Storm didn't retreat, he dug his hands into his trouser pockets as if to resist the urge to reach out. "I had to keep the amulet somewhere safe and hidden. After we learned of the prophecy, I knew *you* would be the one who needed it most, so I made sure you would always have it with you," he explained, glancing pointedly at Yael. "All you had to do was ask nicely."

"I have nothing resembling an amulet," Yael replied instantly, the indignation making Asher chuckle.

"Show him your treasure, Yael," he said, encouraging and fond in a way Storm had come to think of as a dad voice.

A rosy blush flourished over Yael's cheeks as they reached behind them and returned with their favourite cane clasped tightly beneath their fingers. They offered the cane to Asher, who shook his head and gestured to Storm.

"Reveal its heart."

With care, Storm took the cane from Yael's grip to press to his lips for an awkward, brief contact. *Show me your heart,* he said in his mind, calling forth his magic to seek whatever his dad thought he'd find here.

A flash of images fluttered throughout his mind, so many, moving so fast that Storm had no chance to grasp onto a single one and explore. They weren't unclear but thousands of images hinted at how long Yael's life was; the past, present and future zipping through his mind. Storm forced his eyes open, still standing where he'd been but feeling older and confused as though time had passed.

Asher's gaze was trained to the rounded handle of the cane, open in a petal formation to reveal a tiny black amulet sitting inside its protective cage. Storm wasn't sure how or why, but when he looked at his dad, Asher smiled in amusement.

Yael stared without comprehension at the amulet sitting on a perch inside the handle of his cane—the one he'd been carrying around for as long as Storm had known him.

"You've been protecting Storm all these years."

Speechless, Storm tipped the amulet into his hand.

"I was a child. I remember nothing," Yael responded to

justify the fact they hadn't known. They'd never thought to even *look* inside their cane, because why would they?

When they looked to Asher for an explanation, he appeared sad. "A few days before I died, I heard crying from Storm's bedroom. Yael was huddled in the armchair by the window, watching Storm sleep," he recounted, pain clouding his voice as he focused on Yael. "I thought Storm was crying. Then you showed yourself to me. You asked me to protect him, to never lay the Tera legacy into his hands until he was an adult, to keep him safe." He gazed at the threadbare carpet of his study thoughtfully, perhaps only realising in his last moments that Yael had known he would die and never told him. Demons weren't allowed to mess with time or any sequence of events involving mages, even those of the dark arts. Even if Yael had understood what he'd seen, he wouldn't have had the power or ability to hint at what might come.

Storm wanted to cry. A child—demon or not—had known something awful was about to happen to Asher but didn't understand or wasn't able to tell him. The burden of that knowledge must have been so heavy on their shoulders as a child alone in the world. Storm had never heard Yael mention a parent or guardian, and considering how much time they'd spent together as children they likely had nowhere else to go. Maybe that was why Asher had never asked Yael to leave Storm's side or to stop being his friend.

"When I asked what danger he faced—" Asher stared at Yael with sad, fatherly eyes that wished he could take the pain away from the child they'd once been. "—you cried and told me that

Storm must never hold the amulet before his eighteenth birthday. Then you disappeared and I never got to ask you to explain. I think you knew what was about to happen but didn't have the words to explain to a human."

Storm touched Yael's arm, not sure how they felt about hearing this, knowing they couldn't remember being that astute.

"Why the cane?" Yael asked, ignoring everything else in that stoic, brave way of theirs. "I didn't have a cane until I was older. I liked the style, and it fitted my clothing preference."

"You always did," Asher replied fondly. "Whenever you played dress-up with Storm, he would tell me how you looked, that you loved a sharp suit and a long cane. You had found one in the attic that you liked, and Storm wanted to give it to you. I knew where to hide the amulet because I knew you would keep both the cane and amulet safe until you were reunited." He turned his gaze on Storm as his eyes clouded with a deeper emotion.

Something spoke to the kid inside Storm who missed his dad and wished for more time with his family, the little boy who had hated them for leaving. Resentment throbbed painfully in his chest to the beat of the amulet's magical hum.

"You kept your promise," Asher said after clearing his throat. "For *my* son, for *your* best friend, for someone you loved and who loved you. You kept the amulet safe; then you kept him safe, even if you didn't understand why."

The weight of his words had an immediate effect on Yael's tender emotions, the side they tried not to show. When they turned away to find Kyrie gazing at them with adoration, Yael stared at the carpet as though hoping no one would notice they were crying.

Storm pulled Yael into his arms for a hug and held on tight. He understood, felt the regret of not having those memories, the bond between them as strong now as always. The pain of knowing they'd been connected their entire lives but someone had stolen the bond from them, stolen them from *each other,* was insurmountable.

He didn't know how or when, but he would make sure Gladys paid for what she'd taken. For Yael, for Rowan, and even for Kyrie, who had been treated with the same disregard she'd shown everyone else in her life. He'd do it for Donald, wherever his spirit may be, and for the demon-child who took his place in Gladys's life, a prisoner in his own mind.

Gladys had a hell of a lot to answer for.

Rowan rubbed Yael's arm consolingly, murmuring words of support. He said the words Storm should have spoken, but he was scared to open his mouth, afraid he'd be a bigger wreck than Yael if he did and all his conflicted emotions spilled out. Instead, he held on tight and thanked the Fates for allowing this version of his life to be different, for letting him reclaim what had been stolen. He wanted to ask how they could have let him suffer, but the Fates were in charge for a reason so there must be a point to this.

When Yael pulled away, composed and wearing an expressionless mask, they spared a momentary flash of a smile for Kyrie and straightened their suit jacket. Taking the cane from Storm, which he held forgotten in his hand, Yael closed the handle.

"Dad, I think you fulfilled your dying wish. You can go now. I'm okay," he promised, hoping he didn't think he was unwanted. Storm couldn't bear to know he'd inadvertently kept him prisoner in this house. When his dad opened his mouth to speak, Storm cut him off. "Go be with Cesa while you can, go after mum to the abyss, or just leave this house. You don't need to be stuck here." There was so much his dad hadn't seen or done, people he hadn't visited because he'd been lingering here, waiting for the son who never came. Now that Storm had seen him, had been given his dying message, his dad was free from that burden and duty. Asher had to be curious about the world, about how Cesa was coping with his daily life when he wasn't locked in grief.

"Will you return? I have so much I want to say."

"Yes." Storm was relieved his dad wanted him to come back. He'd been waiting twelve years, but he found it surreal that he could come here and Asher would be waiting. "Maybe in a few days. I'll come by every day, and if you're not here, that's okay. You don't have to be a prisoner in this house. Go explore, see how the world has changed. I'll be here when you get back."

Death was never meant to be a punishment, not even for a dark mage.

Asher nodded, then took a step. When Storm didn't retreat, his dad came closer and hovered a hand an inch from his cheek. "I will always come back for you, little Storm. Death can't stop me from loving you."

He hadn't realised how much he needed to hear the words until now. He'd never forget them now they were in his heart and head, in his memories. Storm reacted on instinct, lifting his hand in hopes of taking his dad's, to touch his wrist and prove he was real. The moment he moved, Yael grasped his wrist to stop him.

"That would not be wise, youngling," they advised, resorting to their habit of dishing out advice like an old woman. "While your father can touch the items in this house, his essence recognises this room as his. I'm afraid any contact between you would be draining for both of you." The softening in their white eyes let Storm know they regretted having to stop him. "I don't know the harm that touching death may do a necromancer."

"Sorry." He wasn't sure if he was apologising for attempting to try, for not knowing, or if he was apologising to his dad for not making contact. Storm was so consumed with a mix of feelings he couldn't separate them.

"I'd say touching you again would be worth any pain," Asher said with a teasing smile for Yael, "but I want to see you and talk to you for more than just tonight." He backed away a step to remove the temptation to reach out. "Take care of yourself, and let these three take care of you. Just because you're a dark mage doesn't mean you can't ask for help. Many of us fall into that trap, and it never ends well. Be better and smarter than we were," he counselled, the *we* carving a hole into Storm's heart.

Asher hadn't asked for help in dealing with Ithen and had

lost his life, the life of his wife, the future with his family, and his secret lover's sanity. He'd lost so much and though Storm knew Ithen was at fault, because of his greed and jealousy, his dad honestly believed that asking for help may have changed his fate. They would never know if he was right, but Storm wouldn't make the same mistake.

Storm nodded. "I will."

Chapter Eighteen

The Next Day
November 16, 2026

THE WALK TO his shack was quiet but laden with tension, like the calm before chaos, and Storm couldn't help but wonder what ominous event was on the way. He'd spent a pleasant morning with Denver and Foley, while Rowan studied and accompanied his father on estate business. He'd only left them ten minutes ago and already felt like he'd waded deep into more trouble than he wanted to face today.

Worried, he quickened his pace over the fallen leaves and dry, crisp grass to find the shack was still standing. Storm breathed a sigh of relief that the warning wasn't about Ithen's escape, even if that did mean something else was on the horizon.

Circling the building, he inspected every wall, crevice and spell before standing at the door and peering through the window in the front door. He didn't risk standing by the full living room window in case Ithen saw him, instead choosing the discreet option that kept him out of sight and mind.

Standing on his tiptoes, he peeked inside to see that Ithen was sitting against the wall, pale and drained, like he hadn't slept or eaten. This was the first time Storm had checked on him to find Ithen awake, but he'd left packaged food and bottles of water within reach because he wasn't the same violent, vindictive monster Ithen was. Inside the shack, Ithen lifted his free hand to the shackle holding his left wrist to the wall and tugged, muttering a few curse words, and attempted to strong arm the metal. When that failed, he used dark magic to weave shadows and mist until the magic was sucked into the protective spell.

Storm almost laughed to see the shock on Ithen's face.

While reading his heart through the demon spell, Yael had gotten a feel for his magic that allowed Storm to set a special spell on the lock that counteracted Ithen's magical abilities. Since neither had known the extent of what Ithen could do, what magic he'd had access to over the years, they'd been cautious not to get cocky and presume they had the upper hand. This spell was particularly clever, feeding on whatever magic Ithen exuded, effectively making Ithen his own jailer. Yael had preened like a peacock when Storm made the mistake of admitting how ingenious the plan was.

"He is awake?" Yael spoke softly by his ear.

Having grown accustomed to Yael's propensity to pop out of nowhere, Storm glanced over his shoulder to find Yael wearing a black suit with blood-red accents on the collars and cuffs. Their long white hair was styled into a long plait and a fringe curved around the right side of their face. Yael loved to play with their appearance but preferred this form, changing their hair from dark brown, blond and red. Storm had seen this version the most and liked the familiarity.

"He tried to spell the lock on the shackles."

Yael's eyes sparkled with amusement as they nudged Storm aside to press against the shack and breathe against the window. The glass steamed up, poised for the long talon that rose to draw delicate, intricate sigils in the breath mist. "*Famulus.*"

Storm knew enough Latin to decipher the command for *servant.* Watching over Yael's shoulder, he saw Ithen freeze and stare ahead, long hair tumbling over his shoulder when he turned his head sharply as if to catch something flitting out the corner of his eye.

"*Maero,*" they continued, their voice soft and lulling.

"To grieve?"

Yael retreated from the window. "Sorrow," they corrected, taking a gentle hold of Storm's arm to guide him toward the poppy field. "If he's to be a prisoner and awake, I want him too busy thinking of his sorrows to bother escaping." The argument was so reasonable Storm raised an eyebrow, surprised they'd insinuated Ithen *could* escape. "I doubt he could, but everything will be easier if he doesn't *want to*."

"Won't forcing him to relive his sorrows make him *want* to leave?"

"No, youngling. We are demons and the Dark One," they said, giving him an amused side-eyed glance as they walked to Adam's Grove. "We are made of the same dark magic. We *are* sorrow, suffering, death, and desire. We are secrets and lies."

Storm's magic practically sang its agreement beneath his skin, tempting him to use magic, teasing him with how easily he could be brutal, dark and capable of evil. Yet neither he nor Yael had crossed the line with their magic. As all witches and mages were capable of bad deeds, the dark mages were capable of restraint.

"It is who we are, as the dark ones; the chosen of the dark arts; the ones who can bend will and hearts as easily as we breathe."

"Disturbing," Storm remarked, not sure if he meant how right this felt or how it sounded coming from a demon capable of anything.

Yael didn't pander to his mood. "Good. The magical world *should* be scared of us," they agreed, without stopping to think of how borderline evil that sounded. "Especially when we work together as we will this afternoon."

Storm nodded and let out a self-depreciating laugh at his ignorant thought that this was nothing more than a visit to check on Ithen, and see how Storm was doing after Yael had insisted they had an errand to run. "It's nice to see you too, but could you *not* pop up just to lecture, train me, or drop an emotional bomb?"

With a mock gasp, Yael walked backwards, a hand over where their heart would be if they were human. "Did my friend miss me?" they asked dramatically, irritatingly human in their expressions.

Storm half wanted to strangle them and half laugh. The moment Yael reached out, he raised his hand in warning. "If you pinch my cheek, I will curse you!" He'd had enough of that from Gladys when he first moved in with her and every elderly witch in the area came to check on him.

"Save your strength."

Worried about the ominous words, Storm followed Yael to the poppy field that was his sanctuary during these chaotic days, stopping short of Adam's Grove when he found a body lying amongst the autumn leaves that had fallen late this year. "Please tell me I'm hallucinating and that isn't a dead body."

The silence that followed his question was less than inspiring. Swallowing his fear of what this 'lesson' may be, he turned to Yael, who stood at his side with their arms behind their back, swaying with a playful smile. "You must learn how to master your necromancy. Preferably sooner than later," Yael replied, letting their arms hang lax as they walked toward the body and crouched. "This man is...or *was*...an inventor. The higher demons are happy for you to resurrect him so they can make use of his knowledge. However, if you fail, they appreciate the sacrifice of helping you come into your full powers."

Yael turned the man onto his back without warning.

Storm winced at the thud of the body being rolled over, unseeing eyes gazing at the sky. Pressing his stomach, he fought his natural reaction. This was his purpose, who he'd been born to be. He couldn't get queasy every time he came across a dead body if he was ever going to *use* his necromancy. The future was uncertain, and no one knew if he'd done enough to prevent the deaths of everyone he loved: Rowan, Denver, and Foley. If they were destined to die no matter what he did, Storm *had* to resurrect them as any decent necromancer should.

Cracking his knuckles, he stretched his neck and shoulders, shook his arms and rolled his back, preparing for however long this might take. He ignored Yael's pleased smile and knelt by the man, trying not to look into his empty eyes. "How do I start?"

Yael's grin widened, delighting in Storm's surrender. "As I taught you, tap into your magic. It will know what you wish to do, and I am sure it is more than ready to welcome the task." They began unbuttoning the man's bloodstained white shirt to expose his chest. "Skin to skin contact will help the first few times and allow you to connect to the deceased through the faint electrical charge left over after death."

No doubt Gladys was scrying for Ithen, searching for him in any way she could. She wouldn't be held off much longer. He needed to do this right; he *needed* to master the art of necromancy.

"Everyone who dies in such a way—" Yael continued quietly, respectful of the dead body between them. "—murder or sickness, in this case a lung disease, will want to live again. They don't automatically consider or acknowledge the desire, but the will to live lingers in their body for a matter of eight to ten hours after death." With a thoughtful tip of their head, they met Storm's gaze. "This should be easier for you, as the body is an hour old."

"He has to want to live again?" Storm asked, surprised something like necromancy—which most witches thought evil and against nature—required the consent of the deceased person. "I mean, say someone I didn't know died in the street and I rushed in to save them. If they didn't want to live, could I still resurrect them?" He wanted to know where the boundaries lay before delving into practising on a real person.

"You could," Yael replied, sounding hesitant. "Your magic is strong. I believe your will could outweigh theirs, but you best not try. Forcing the will of the deceased could be as dangerous for you as resurrecting one you love."

"Right. That was in Reed Hadley's book. Necromancy will take years from me and potentially steal my magic when done wrong." Storm wasn't surprised something as dangerous as necromancy required a greater cost than other magic.

"Exactly. Best we not risk such harm to you," Yael advised, patting his hand before sitting on their heels and gesturing to the body.

"Agreed." There was too much to do to risk losing a few more years of life. Storm didn't know the consequences of travelling through time, and he didn't want to tempt the Fates any more. "Let's give this a shot."

Storm called on his magic, already dancing in his mind, full of glee for being called upon. Thinking of his magic as a living, thinking entity was strange. Sure they were of one mind, he opened his eyes and focused on the man lying dead and waiting for someone to bring him back to life.

He pressed his hands to the man's exposed chest and dug deep with his magic. At first, only the emptiness of death greeted him, then the ghostly image of the man appeared a foot beyond Yael's shoulder. His spirit was still following his body in the same vain hope of life that Yael had talked about; this man wasn't ready to let go.

Since Storm didn't know what to do—as the teachings in Reed Hadley's book were vague—he thought about how he'd want to be treated if he were in this man's shoes. "Hello," he said, hating how uncertain he sounded. Clearing his throat, he tried again. "Hello. I'm Storm Tera. Can you tell me your name?"

Out the corner of his eye, he could see Yael studying him intensely but showing no sign of approval or disapproval.

The man turned his gaze toward Storm, his ghostly eyes as white as the demon's. "Jordan Miller." He looked around the field with a frown. "I was in my office."

"I'm sorry," he said, holding eye contact despite the coldness of an empty gaze. "You died. But if you want, I can bring you back.

All you have to do is reach into your body and touch my magic. I can do the rest." He wasn't sure what 'the rest' may be, but he was willing to give his best.

Jordan looked at his body as he approached and crouched by his physical shoulder. He tentatively reached for Storm's hands where they connected to bare skin. "Resurrection?" he murmured with enough curiosity that Storm suspected he wasn't expected to answer the question.

He gave Jordan time to accept the situation, watching as his ghostly body turned and sat on top of his real body. With a last uncertain glance at Storm, he sank into his body.

A second later, Storm felt a tug at his magic and closed his eyes to focus. He could feel the curiosity, the interest in necromancy and resurrection. Beneath that lay a will to live, a searching mind, the essence of someone who never stopped asking questions.

Mend the soul and body; join them in harmony. Bond the mind, heart, body and soul until Jordan Miller is whole again. He sent his will through his magic, trying to be specific so there were no misunderstandings or misinterpreting of his wishes. *Return this brilliant mind, open heart, and gentle soul to the world of the living, so he may continue his good work and create a brighter world.*

Not knowing what else was needed, Storm sent a pulse of magic through the human body and opened his eyes to see the ghostly figure of Jordan Miller fade.

Gods, he hoped that was supposed to happen.

Glancing at Yael, he found them studying Jordan's face, leaning closer to determine the presence of life.

Storm removed his hands as fatigue washed through him. He felt like he'd been sitting in the same position for days, carrying a great weight. Sagging where he sat, he slid to the side and lay on the grass, lacking the strength to move. He lay facing Jordan's body, his breath catching as a faint twitch of the jaw gave him hope. The most haunting intake of breath followed the twitch, and Storm almost stopped breathing.

Yael cocked their head at the inventor, their eyes hopeful until the breath repeated, this time clearly the distinctive sound of relief.

Storm knew without having to ask.

He'd failed and Jordan Miller was dead. Again.

Chapter Nineteen

"I'M NOT STRONG enough," Storm said, his throat feeling dry as a desert.

"No." Yael's tone was a clear agreement as they closed Jordan's eyes and folded his arms over his chest. "Your body and magic are strong enough, but your mind has yet to accept who you are. You are the Dark One, the prophecy child, the one all others must bow to, the one that other dark mages must obey."

Storm sighed, realising this failure was his doing because he didn't believe everyone in the magical world should bow to him. But if he'd never master necromancy until he accepted that, they were up shit creek, because Storm would never feel comfortable being some almighty leader to be bowed to and obeyed without question; in his mind, that was a dictator not a leader.

Yael bent over Jordan's body to look Storm in the eye. "Until you believe—until you understand what it means to be Storm Tera—you will never overcome this shortfall." They flashed a consoling smile, equal parts scolding and amusement. "I will find more bodies for you to experiment on when you are ready," they promised, grabbing Jordan Miller's body by the ankle and dragging him away.

Before he could raise his arm in protest, Yael had taken the body through to the abyss, leaving him with his guilt and grief.

*

AFTER THE IMMENSE failure of not resurrecting Jordan Miller, Storm needed time alone. Though Yael didn't linger in the abyss, he agreed to give Storm space, leaving him in the field while they returned to the house to help Kyrie recover, no doubt by smothering him with cakes and tea, something Storm was sure the lower demon would love.

Storm made his way to his parents' house. If he wanted to learn more about necromancy, he'd be best starting with the library and his dad's study, hoping he found something useful to figure out what had gone wrong. If only he could find something to convince him he deserved this position of power and the legacy the Fates had given him.

Being the Chosen One wasn't all it was cracked up to be. What had Storm ever done to make the Fates think he was capable of being what they wanted? He'd done nothing except be born, and even that wasn't by choice. Being the Chosen One had literally nothing to do with his accomplishments or abilities. The Fates just picked a kid at random, one born to a dark mage family, and decided he would lead the magical world into a new era of equality and fairness, all because he was a damned Tera.

What had being a Tera ever done for him?

Storm kicked a few fallen leaves from the front door of the house and stepped inside, out of the wind. Shaking off the few that had fallen into his hair, he slipped off his jacket to place on the console table by the front door. Turning left into the study, he slid open the wooden door and paused.

Asher was still here, sitting at his desk with his feet on the corner, fingers flicking through a book.

"Dad?" Storm called, not sure if he wanted to be disturbed. He could always cross the hallway to the library if his dad wanted to be alone.

Asher closed his book as he dropped his feet to the floor and stood. "You came back," he said, sounding stunned and relieved. He cleared his throat and gestured to the sofa by the window. "Do you have time to sit and talk?"

Gods, did he ever, and he wanted to. He hadn't even realised this was why he'd come, hoping his dad would still be here to tell him how to fix what had gone wrong, why he was the Dark One and not someone else, someone more worthy.

"You look troubled," his dad noticed as Storm crossed to sit on the sofa. Asher was more careful about his movements, having to focus hard on the items in the room to interact while in his ghostly body. "Has something happened?"

Storm sat beside his dad and poured out every word of doubt and guilt from his failed attempt to resurrect Jordan Miller, a name he'd remember for the rest of his life.

Other than a few comments, his dad was relatively quiet while Storm talked. He hadn't had the chance to purge like this since his first night with Rowan, when they told each other their secrets. Storm hadn't realised how badly he'd needed to talk, especially with someone who hadn't been there to experience his failure first-hand.

There was something cathartic and reassuring about letting the words fall from his mouth unchecked and watching his dad listen with a thoughtful frown, the occasional comment and not an ounce of judgement.

"I first attempted resurrection on an old man from one of our covens," Asher said once Storm had finished rambling. "He'd asked to be my first test because he had a strong will to live and the desire to help every dark mage learn their craft. Only by *doing* can a dark mage train in and master necromancy. It makes for a dangerous craft to learn with a huge margin for error." The hand resting on his knee tapped to an unheard rhythm.

Storm knew how he felt, the nervous twitch a reminder that they couldn't touch. He wished his dad could hug him, take his hand, or pat his knee the way Yael tended to do. Sometimes contact was more comforting than words.

"He told me necromancy was the hardest magic for a reason,

because any witch could create a homunculus. Replicating the functions of a human body is easy, because you can insert a mechanical heart into any dead body. What humans call zombies are ten to the dozen if the craft isn't strong enough." He looked at Storm with deep penetrating eyes that begged him to listen and understand. "To truly resurrect a person, they need their mind whole, their heart beating, and their soul intact. Only *we* can do that for them."

Storm didn't want to complain but he needed his dad to accept that he'd fallen at the first hurdle. "I didn't though." Was that what went wrong? Did he not properly stitch the pieces together? "I mean, he took a breath and his jaw twitched, then he died." The image and sound of his last breath would linger in his mind for the rest of his life.

"Perhaps his will to live wasn't as strong as the demons thought?"

"Or I suck at resurrection?"

Instead of laughing, Asher tipped his head and eyed Storm seriously. "Do you know how many dark mages have mastered necromancy?"

"There's a logbook somewhere?"

Asher shook his head and eyed Storm with a mix of amusement and scolding, the same way Yael did. "Since the beginning of magic, a dozen have mastered the darkest of arts. They were twice your age before they accomplished their first successful resurrection," he explained, leaving Storm wondering if someone of his age and ability even he had any right to learn. "How many do you think managed to return life on their first attempt?"

They really did keep track of the art of necromancy if his dad felt confident he could give a definitive answer. "Half?"

Asher raised an eyebrow. "None. Not a single one. Some get as far as bonding the spirit and the body, some are drained before they get that far. The magic is *so* strong and the will inside you must be *so* strong because we must surrender everything to resurrect another human into the same whole being they once were," he admitted, the respect he had for the ability showing through every word.

Storm stared in surprise, beginning to realise he *had* accomplished something miraculous.

"From what you said, you managed more," his dad continued, a smile appearing because he could tell Storm was starting to see what he'd done. "The few who managed life on the third attempt—the earliest anyone has ever managed—had a recently deceased body. Their demons didn't wait for a person to die before handing over a body to their dark mage."

Shock flooded his system, and his magic shrank from the idea of what his dad was suggesting. "You mean...they killed just to give the dark mage a body to work with?" The concept alone was abhorrent and didn't abide by the laws of magic required for necromancy.

Asher nodded, not realising the direction his thoughts had taken, and lifted his hand as though to brush at Storm's hair, stopping with an awkward smile. "Be grateful Yael isn't like them."

"Gods. The sight was bad enough an hour after death. I couldn't have handled a live...body." The thought gave him shivers. If he'd had to see that, he would have thrown up.

Asher watched him with fondness. "Tell me about Rowan," he asked, a twinkle in his dead eyes that said he'd been waiting ages to ask.

Storm blushed but internally admitted he needed to talk. He couldn't tell Rowan the conflicting thoughts and doubts, the fears that he would lose Rowan sooner than he wanted to, that he wasn't worthy of the white witch half-demon.

Ignoring his embarrassment, he told his dad what had happened from the point of being sent from the future where he'd failed to fulfil the prophecy to how he'd been found on Copry land by Rowan. Though he had to give some events context, he kept to the relationship aspect in hopes of keeping the conversation light and happy. When he explained the awkward, amazing feeling of waking up beside Rowan every morning, Storm realised this was a normal father-son chat, something he couldn't remember ever having.

"What about you and Cesa?"

Instantly losing the happy, proud smile he'd been sporting while Storm talked about his new relationship, Asher cleared his throat. "I'm sorry?" He blinked, as if the question was unfathomable and had come from nowhere.

"How did you two get together? How did you meet?" he

asked, eager to find out more about his dad, the way Asher wanted to hear about his life. "Gladys told me our families had been enemies for generations. But I've seen pictures in the coven archives showing past generations with their arms around each other or shaking hands, laughing together." He'd gone to the museum in town many times over the years to look at the secret room in the back that explored coven history. The covens contributed items devoid of magical energy so that future generations could come together to see where the circle of covens started.

"We were never enemies," Asher replied, almost laughing, though his tone suggested he didn't understand Gladys's motives for telling him otherwise. Storm thought he did, but it wasn't the right time to talk. "We were brothers in arms, one family protecting the amulet, the other protecting the spell. That was only possible if we worked together and lived close to each other. In truth, we're the oldest and closest of the covens."

Whatever he'd thought, he stood and crossed to the bookcase behind his desk, the ones Storm had realised from Ithen's memories held the most private family tomes. Asher chose a leather-bound book and returned to sit beside Storm. "What Yael told you about seeing the heart of something is true, but we dark mages have our version. A not-so-awkward one," he confessed, with a cheeky smile that made Storm blush.

If he hadn't taken the risk of seeing into Rowan's heart with the demon way, he may never have gathered the courage to kiss Rowan, but he'd love to know an alternative for other situations.

"There's a loose sheet of paper on the inside of this book that will explain the spell," his dad said, holding out the book but making sure not to have his ghostly fingers anywhere near Storm's skin. The sensible precaution caused Storm's stomach to tighten, hating that he had to avoid touching his dad. "Once you confirm the spell works as expected, you can try this book."

Storm nodded at the advice and lay the book on his lap, wondering if he should leave. Asher lay his hand on the book, the closest they would come to touching each other, drawing Storm's gaze to his dad's sad, dark eyes.

"Cesa gave me this book the first day we kissed," he confessed, smiling as he pushed the tome toward Storm. "Maybe you'll see a side of him you never had the chance to. The book is linked to both of us and likely connected to more than one memory."

Storm smiled, realising this was Asher's way of sharing the story of his love for Cesa. He supposed that was for the best, because Storm didn't want to hurt his dad, but he couldn't just push aside his curiosity. Not when his relationship with Rowan wouldn't have been possible if his dad had been allowed to love Cesa openly, without the Fates purposefully keeping them apart.

Storm would never forget that he was the reason his dad had never been truly happy.

Chapter Twenty

Two Days Later
November 18, 2026

"FATHER IS HANDLING estate business and I have to go with him," Rowan said, packing two notebooks into a satchel that he buckled and tossed over his head, settling the strap over his chest. "We'll be gone a couple of hours, checking on the land. Rent is direct debit, but I want to see how everyone is coping with the weather and check if they need extra help. Father has to be there or the farmers will start to talk and they'll threaten to put him in a hospital."

Storm caught his shoulders and stared into Rowan's blue eyes, breathing steadily until Rowan matched him. Once the panic had subsided, he offered a calming, distracting kiss.

Rowan clutched at Storm's jumper and pulled him closer, sinking into the moment as though they'd never get another chance. Technically, they weren't alone; Kyrie and Yael stood barely a foot away, but as always, whenever he kissed Rowan the rest of the world disappeared. His magic crackled beneath his skin, whispering and pushing, telling him to go to Rowan, to surrender and join their magic.

Storm broke the kiss and stared at Rowan, whose lips quirked into a teasing smile.

"I think I would be more willing to listen to your magic if we didn't have an audience and I wasn't about to walk out the door," Rowan whispered, not helping the rush of hormones that made Storm want to shut the door on the rest of the world. When Rowan nipped at Storm's bottom lip and kissed him, he accepted but didn't reciprocate. They couldn't afford to be distracted today, not even by each other.

Eyes glittering with ice blue affection, Rowan broke the kiss and touched Storm's chest to gently push him away. "I'll see you in a few hours." Stepping away, Rowan called over his shoulder to Yael as he headed for the bedroom door. "Bring him back in one piece." One step out the door, he paused and waved at the demons, winking at Storm before he closed the door.

Storm understood the warning, however sweetly delivered, because Yael insisted on trying his necromancy skills again but with Kyrie in tow in case assistance was required. The care and concern from Rowan wasn't new, but after a lifetime of Gladys's emotional distance and lack of motherly instincts, Storm still blushed whenever Rowan was openly affectionate.

He cleared his throat and turned to the two demons, where Kyrie grinned in amusement and Yael raised an eyebrow as if to ask if the romantic displays were necessary. "Let's go practice the dark arts," he said, avoiding both demons as he turned for the door and resolutely refused to look back.

He was the Dark One, for crying out loud; he didn't need to ask permission to have a boyfriend...or an almost...sort-of...boy-friend.

*

"WHEN YOU SAID we were practising my necromancy skills, I didn't think we'd end up here," Storm said, glaring at Yael. They knew he didn't want to be here; he swore he wouldn't return to this house until Gladys was dead.

Yael pushed open the front door. "I borrowed your talking contraption and sent a message to Foley, asking him to have Gladys visit his house for tea," they explained with an accusing tone that said Storm should know better than to question them.

"She'll poison him!"

"I warned him about her particular talent for mind-manipu-lation," they insisted, now sounding *and* looking like Storm was lacking more than a few brain cells. "I suggested his parents should be in attendance. She isn't likely to curse him with two strong white witches in the same room." Yael shook their head and gestured for

Storm to walk into the house, holding the door open for him.

Reluctantly, he went inside, relieved Gladys wasn't here. He wanted to be at full strength with his dark magic at his beck and call and with no doubt he could do what needed to be done when the inevitable confrontation happened.

"He's also invited Denver on the pretence of being concerned about your absence," Yael added as Kyrie stepped into the house, then shut the door and surveyed the room. "They're going to lay the groundwork of your fight, that you've been distant since your ascension, and you haven't seen them since you came into your powers. That should keep them safe."

"Fine. You thought of everything," he grumbled, resisting an eye roll to focus on the room. "What are we doing here?"

"Rescuing a captive."

The straightforward answer took him by surprise. He was used to Yael being cryptic and confusing, lecturing him and dropping hints, so this was somewhat of a relief. Storm had wanted to do something about the Donald situation ever since Kyrie first told them.

"Donald is a demon," they said, realising from his face that he'd caught on. "He will have the power you require to complete the task. He is not dead, according to Kyrie's reading, which I trust to be extremely accurate. The boy is simply hibernating inside the skin of a curse which you have the power to break." The way Yael looked at him, this would be considered part of his necromancy lessons and Storm would be expected to correct his previous failure. "If you succeed at this, you can then feel confident enough to complete your necromancy training."

"You keep saying 'training'. What do you mean? The other times you talk about me learning magic you call them lessons. Why is this different?"

Yael stepped forward to awkwardly place a hand on Storm's shoulder, as if copying a gesture they didn't entirely understand. "Because you are training for the greatest and most important moment of your life," they said, dropping their consoling touch to his arm. "You must bring back the love of your life from the dead. In this, there can be no mistakes."

Storm swallowed the emotion that rose at the thought of losing Rowan. Yael said the words like Rowan's death was set in stone. Ever since he'd returned from the future, he'd never stopped to wonder if losing the person who mattered most was the one event impervious to change.

He braced for whatever was about to happen, fighting the emotion surrounding his thoughts about Rowan, and followed when Yael headed for the staircase at the left of Gladys's living room.

He'd expected Yael to lead the way *up*stairs, but they climbed the first four steps to the landing and pushed open the door to the basement. Yael walked through first with Storm following Kyrie to keep the innocent demon between them. If anything happened to Kyrie after the trust he'd put in Storm, he'd never forgive himself.

Storm wasn't sure what he expected to find when he followed

Yael and Kyrie into the basement, descending a dozen steps into the darkness. He'd been so sure Kyrie's explanation of how he found Donald had been a demon's exaggeration or natural dramatics, but this was horrifyingly real.

The usual junk filled the first half of the basement; the washer and dryer on the left of the stairs that led into the middle of the room, the boiler and storage cases on the right. Yael knew where they were going, bypassing the normal items to head for the back wall, where an eight-by-eight foot cage occupied the rest of the basement.

"How did I not know this was here?"

Kyrie rested a hand on his arm. "The cage is shrouded in dark magic. Maybe you couldn't penetrate the spell until you ascended to your full powers?"

Shame flooded him, knowing why he'd never seen this cage. He'd moved out at age fourteen, fed up with Gladys's hovering, lectures, and the way she cared but never loved. She made him feel empty when he saw other teenagers with their parents. He'd hated knowing she wasn't his mum even when she sometimes acted like a parent without ever showing him love. Storm had no one else to call family or home, and life had been simpler by himself where he didn't need to accept how alone he was in the world.

Right now, he realised he'd done the same to DJ as he'd done to his dad; he'd avoided the family home for fear of his personal demons and never returned to Gladys's house for more than a visit or the rare meal. He didn't want to get sucked into the life he'd left behind or to confront the reasons he'd left.

Seeing the huddled figure inside the cage filled him with remorse. He'd run from Gladys and never thought about what he was leaving behind. Storm looked around the basement at the ghosts who had gathered, trapped in this house either because this had been where they lived and died or because they were bound here.

"Yael," he whispered, eyes welling with tears as he realised how haunted this house truly was. He could feel the anger and pain and hear the screams of these people dying in this house. Without waiting for Yael's response or to think about what he was doing, Storm rolled up the sleeves of his jumper and brought his magic to the surface, an automatic reaction to the emotion clogging his throat and crushing his heart.

The apparitions turned as if summoned by his movement and pressed closer, reaching out and whispering his name. Others shied away from the dark magic that no doubt had a hand in their deaths. "I can help you," he said aloud, needing them to not be afraid. "Take what you need from me." He held out his hands to the ghost nearest him, willing to help them move on from this nightmare of an existence. They deserved more, no matter how they had lived or why they had died, and Storm was the only one who could give them freedom.

Yael's sharp word—his name—resonated the moment their ghostly fingers touched his, and the world descended into white light and shadows.

*

"STORM?"

Scrunching his eyes against the bright light, Storm winced as his entire body throbbed with pain, and he absently wondered why his dad's voice was ringing in his ears. He didn't remember his dad being here or why he was lying on a cold stone floor.

"Youngling?"

Storm let Yael's voice wash over him. Yael and his dad sounded pissed, so maybe he shouldn't wake up yet.

"Dark One?" Kyrie's tentative voice joined the chorus of screams and last breaths ringing inside his head.

As his consciousness gradually sharpened and returned to full strength, the sounds transformed into something else.

"Thank you, Dark One." An old man bowed and walked away.

A girl, no more than four years old, grasped his hand and beamed brightly. "Thank you, necromancer." She knelt beside Storm and hugged him tightly before taking the hand of a woman who waited nearby, her eyes cautious and curious.

"Thank you, young Tera," she said with a brief nod, then led the girl away.

Storm felt dizzy as a horde of once screaming, tear-streaked faces became smiles and relief. The spirits left the darkness of the basement for a patch of light streaming in through the bars of the cage on the far side of the room. Opening his outer eyes, he squinted at the darkness. The basement lacked windows and had no overhead light because Gladys insisted it hurt her old eyes. He knew the truth now and had a feeling he'd done something unexpectedly reckless.

"Are you with us, son?" his dad's voice asked, a hand reaching for his shoulder.

"Asher!" Yael shouted so loud that Storm winced. "The boy has just allowed a coven of spirits to pass through him, do you think he should risk touching another? In the state he is in?"

Storm resisted the urge to take his dad's hand and focused on getting to his feet, grateful when Kyrie offered his hand for extra support. His legs felt like jelly and halfway up, he fell flat on his ass. For the sake of his dignity, he stayed on the floor.

"You may have become his best friend, his demon, protector, and teacher... You can do what I cannot—" Asher shot a glare at Yael that could have melted ice, but Yael ignored him to offer Storm another hand to lean on. "—but I am still his father, and you will not take that from me!"

The warning was clear, though Storm's brain was so fried he couldn't fathom who the warning was for or why. To his surprise, Yael had the decency to blush.

Storm took Yael's hand, their free hand going to his elbow while Kyrie took his right side and helped hoist Storm to his feet, where he wobbled before stumbling toward the cage. Clinging to the bars for stability hardly helped preserve his dignity.

Clearing their throat, Yael bobbed their head to Asher. "I apologise, Dark Mage," they said, keeping their eyes on the ground, their posture diminutive and subservient. The very sight of Yael holding such a pose sent flutters of concern through Storm's stomach. "You are right. I am not, nor do I wish to be, a father or father figure to Storm. He is my friend and will one day be my mage. I am here only to serve him and his family."

Gods, that sounded awful.

"No." The word came out of Storm so sharply he winced and raised a hand to his forehead. "No serving anyone," he objected, glaring at the relative area where Yael stood. He was beginning to see double and figured he'd banged his head on his way to the floor. "You're my friend, and that's where we begin and end. If we decide to do magic together, that's something friends do. Foley and I do magic together all the time."

"I see." Yael raised an eyebrow, clearly surprised by that information. "Very well."

Storm realised something else needed to be said. Turning to his dad, his ghostly presence standing near the cage, Storm narrowed his eyes at the three swaying figures to find a central point close to his dad's face. "Don't be mad at Yael. I don't know what I did, but I *was* going to take your hand. For now, can we please just focus on Donald?"

Everyone remained quiet in what he presumed was agreement until Kyrie awkwardly raised his hand. "That may be a problem." He helped Storm turn and pointed to the lump of a body on the concrete floor. "The boy is unconscious."

"Damn."

Chapter Twenty-One

EVERYONE AGREED STORM needed to rest and regain his strength before they could help Donald—the demon trapped inside DJ's body. He only caved because they had to wait until Donald was conscious before they could attempt to help him.

By mutual consent, Storm leaned on Kyrie all the way to Rowan's house while Yael carried Donald, and his dad returned to the manor. They would meet again tomorrow to figure out Donald's situation, talk through their options, and fill Asher in on what was happening.

Storm was banished to Rowan's bedroom with reading material and told to study hard but rest and eat. The last part wasn't difficult, but the rest would take effort. "Yael," he called as they headed for the door, intending to spend time with Kyrie in the abyss in search of information that may be useful. "I was thinking about Donald. If he's not dead, then his soul must be wandering. We can't fix him until we can stitch his soul and body together."

Yael cocked their head in curiosity and nodded. "A reasonable assumption, yes. Do you wish Kyrie and I to search for him? We've become accustomed to his scent and essence."

"Sure."

Word spread through the demon ranks in the abyss. If they had any hope of locating Donald's relatives, letting the demons know they'd found a demon child who had been kidnapped by Gladys Glade in the last twenty years was the best way to an answer. If nothing else, they would be eager to help the Chosen One, but Storm suspected they would all be aware of which demon child they'd located and be eager to reunite the child of such importance to his horde. "Mention that we have information to offer for the location of his horde or contact with his family."

Either the promise of information—more valuable to demons than currency—or the hope of elevating their tied mage into the same circles as the Chosen One would inspire all sorts of demons to start looking for the horde, even if they didn't have the first clue where to start. All Storm cared about was helping Donald, the child demon, no matter the personal cost, and his family were the most likely to bring him out of whatever coma he'd slipped into within DJ's mind.

"Very wise. I will ask if any higher demons are willing to help cleanse his soul once found; then you can match the right soul to the right body, with no risk that any magic other than yours has tainted the process."

Storm nodded, seeing the sense in that decision. He would nap the afternoon away until Rowan returned, to make sure he was physically and magically capable of doing what was needed. He thought about what had to be done—dealing with Ithen and Gladys, fulfilling the prophecy, saving Rowan and Donald, protecting his friends—and what those tasks required. When Yael reached the door, ready to leave, Storm realised something was missing from that list.

"Hey," he called weakly, feeling sleep pushing his consciousness aside. "If you find out something juicy, *you* could be the higher demon to cleanse Donald?" Storm couldn't trust just anyone with such a monumental task of helping to put Donald back together into the demon child he should have been.

Storm knew little about demon children except that they remained children for about twenty years. They looked like babies for a year, became a toddler for two and lived as an eight- to ten-year-old for the rest of their childhood. The demon learned everything about their kind, magic and mages during those long years. When they were deemed sufficiently smart enough to become adults, they ascended to claws, talons, and crossing through the abyss. Whatever happened to Yael's parents and horde, they'd been left alone since they first became a child, living with Storm until his parents died and Gladys threatened his safety. It mustn't have been easy to lack guidance from another demon, to not have anyone to tell them of their childhood, to learn from or share their experiences with. Worse, after Storm's parents died, Yael had been alone again.

Maybe they could give Donald the guidance he needed until they found his horde?

Lips touched his cheek, stirring Storm to the present, only to find Yael standing by the bed with tears in their white eyes. "I would be honoured to help this poor creature. Thank you for asking me." With a sad smile, they pulled the duvet from the end of the bed over Storm's legs and chest. They took the books he'd been holding and put them on the other side of the bed, lacking only the pat on the head that came with tucking someone in. "Sleep well, dark one. You can read later," they said, leaving the room and clicking the door shut behind them.

What a strange, adorable demon.

*

STORM WOKE WITH a clear memory of what happened in the basement, as though his mind had needed time to process what he'd done. Seeing those lost spirits had stirred the anger in his magic, horrified by what they found in Gladys's basement. Despite the urge to rip the old woman to shreds, to hunt and curse her, Storm and his magic had agreed on one thing: to free her prisoners.

They were stuck with Donald because he wasn't dead, but the rest of her captives were gone. They'd left their life behind and moved on to their undead existence, trapped in that basement because of what had been done to them. Their violent and often untimely deaths left them with no freedom to escape to the abyss and become the soul to fill a new baby being born somewhere in the world.

They'd been unfairly locked onto Gladys's existence because she was the one who had handed them to death. Freeing them from their invisible cage had been a matter of anger plus magic equals necromancy. Without any conscious decision, his feelings and magic had combined, exploding in a white light that sent all the ghosts who were ready to move on into the abyss so they could be free.

Luckily, his dad hadn't been ready to move on or he might have been caught in the unintentionally naïve spell. Either that or he'd only arrived after Storm had knocked himself unconscious. Thinking about his dad presented another problem; just what was keeping him tied to his life, this world, and preventing him from moving on? As much as he would love to believe it, Storm wasn't the one holding his dad here.

Checking the time on the clock by the bed, he saw that he'd slept for two hours. As he was about to decide what to start studying and whether he could be bothered to get a drink, his gaze landed on the book his dad had given him; the book Cesa had given his dad when they first kissed.

If he hoped to understand Asher Tera and his reasons for lingering as a ghost, surely the answers would be in this book.

Did he dare?

Before reaching for the book, Storm looked around the

room, relieved to find a bottle of water and a glass on a tray on the table by the armchair in the corner of the room. Using Rowan's trick of levitating was too adventurous, so Storm reluctantly tossed aside the cosy duvet, put his feet on the floor and tested the strength in his knees before making a move. He downed the two paracetamol by the glass and felt marginally better. He carried the book to the window seat and stalled long enough to change into loose, comfortable joggers and an overlarge T-shirt.

Set for a long, lazy afternoon by the window, until Rowan returned from his tour of the estate with his father, Storm settled. By the time he finished the bottle of water he'd been needing the loo and could grab something from the kitchen. He was too curious to wait any longer.

Laying the book on his lap, he opened the front cover and found the piece of paper his dad had mentioned.

A spell to reveal the heart of any item or person.
Adapted from the demon spell requiring a kiss.

The note was pretty self-explanatory, likely written after his dad died, judging by the fresh ink and the fact Storm would need answers to a whole host of questions about his childhood.

"Thanks, Dad." Storm read the instructions clearly and cursed. Standing from his comfortable spot, he limped to the dresser where Rowan kept magical supplies in the bottom drawer. His left leg was half asleep, either from sleeping or he'd given himself a good whack when he fell in Gladys's basement.

Gathering a few of the herbs from the plastic tubs Rowan kept them in, he combined them on the dresser top. Keeping the piece of paper firmly grasped in one hand, he read over the list and grabbed a touch of sage to add to the concoction of lavender, mint and sandalwood. He scooped everything into an empty pouch, planning to thank Rowan for his well-stocked drawer and the handy bags waiting to be used.

He went to the bedside table, took out the red candle that he presumed Rowan used for scrying and reading tarot. He lit the candle and collected fresh wax, added the shavings to the bag of herbs and then held the bag open. Storm sniffed the collection, a scent reminiscent of coven meetings and family, of magic and Rowan. How could even his herbs smell like him?

Storm settled his will in his mind and blew magic into the bag. "*Show me the heart of anything you touch. Show me the heart of anything you feel,*" he whispered, breath misting from his mouth, swirling throughout the ingredients of the bag. "*Show me the heart of anything you can illuminate,*" he said to the candle wax, breaking apart at the contact of his magic until everything formed a clump in the bottom of the bag.

Storm watched, curious and intrigued, as the herbs disintegrated, the wax melted into liquid and his breathy magic swarmed throughout, eliminating whatever was left until a tiny piece of charcoal remained. Glancing at the piece of paper, he realised the spell had worked as expected. Tipping the bag, he caught the piece of charcoal in one hand and returned to his seat at the window.

He sipped from the water bottle to replenish the healing he'd undone by performing another spell—something he would resolutely *not* tell Yael about later—and gripped the charcoal in his dominant right hand. "Okay. Here goes," he said, putting charcoal to the old pages to write what he wanted to see.

Asher and Cesa.

Asher and Cesa.

Storm continued writing the three words until the page was filled from left to right, top to bottom. Asher had said to try something where he would know the spell had worked, but he was short on time, oddly and completely alone, and weak. He didn't want to risk doing this twice. He could try again another time, but his magic was excited and swirling from freeing a dozen or more spirits from Gladys's dark magic.

If this was ever going to work, it had to be now.

A black mist of dark magic spread across the page of the book, the words blurred and blended. Storm wasn't sure the spell had worked until the words disappeared, soaked up by his magic to reveal a blank page, shimmering and sparkling.

As he focused on the strange magic, the rest of the world around him faded. By the time he looked up, he was in another place and his dad was standing on a platform in the centre of a fire. He gasped, instantly understanding the scene: this was the night of Asher Tera's ascension.

November first. *Día de los Inocentes.* The Day of the Innocents.

Perhaps because Storm was seeing his dad's life through the book's contact and not directly from his mind, he didn't play the part of his dad as he had with Ithen's memories, instead feeling like a distant observer.

Asher looked proud and tall, standing on a podium with his arms raised, as he called on the Fates to grant his full powers, rhyming off his place in the world the same way Storm had. "Asher Tera, the last of my line: necromancer, dark mage. I am the Guardian of Demons, Guard to the Amulet, secret keeper of the spell and leader of the Tera coven," he called, proud of his titles, of his magic and all the Fates had asked of him.

Storm had never known these titles belonged to his dad. Guardian of Demons made sense when he thought of how his dad had trusted Storm's friendship with Yael, when he was too young to be surrounded by demons. The title made sense of why Gladys lied to the covens, insisting his dad had summoned a demon who had killed him in a rage. If his dad was the Guardian of Demons, he wasn't likely to strike out at a demon even in self-defence. He would certainly be known to speak with them, to summon them, to work with multiple demons without the strength of a bond.

Storm wished he could approach his dad and warn him of what was to come, to encourage him to change his destiny the way Storm had, but that wasn't possible. Asher was dead and any chance of changing his fate had disappeared the moment he died. There was no living Asher Tera to endure the spell and relive his life, to change his fate, to prevent his death.

Storm swallowed a swell of emotion as a storm grew over-head. From the looks of the gathered coven members, this storm was unexpected and impressive. A fog rolled in with the thunder, swallowing Asher, disguising and protecting his sacred path to the abyss, where the Fates would grant his powers and challenge his wits.

He was relieved he'd never known the story of his dad's as-cension. If he had, he might not have gone through with the cere-mony and that would have ruined everything. That night gave him Yael back and showed him a side of Rowan he'd never known ex-isted.

Asher set his jaw as he disappeared into the fog.

Glancing at the gathering, Storm found Cesa standing near the front, with the rest of the Copry coven. He didn't look like he hated anyone, just looked worried, a sentiment Storm could better understand since discovering his secret relationship with Asher and learning the truth of his dad's gifts.

He was still watching Cesa when a faint crack resonated and Cesa's face morphed from worry into relief. Storm watched his dad step from the abyss with confidence as the stone podium he stood on cracked, causing a flutter of muttering from the gathered cov-ens. Everyone looked pleased that he was in one piece and radi-ated magic.

As the covens crowded his dad, blocking him from view to offer congratulations and well wishes, advice and warnings about the dark arts, Storm turned his gaze to Cesa. He stood apart from the others, watching Asher closely. He must have been seventeen, a year younger than Asher, just as Storm was a year younger than Rowan. Their age difference perfectly opposed the difference between their fathers, as their feelings for each other were destined to be the reverse.

The Fates could be so cruel.

Cesa faked a smile when his parents forced him to join in the celebrations. Coven gatherings had never been his favourite either, but Cesa's hesitation was different, rooted deep inside in the feelings he had for Asher, feelings that no one else knew or could know existed.

The scene continued for a few minutes, with his dad accepting the praise and well wishes with grace while shooting curious glances at Cesa. After everyone walked to the Tera house for a proper party of food and mingling between the covens, the mood changed. Asher's jaw tensed, Cesa slipped into the woods, and they both managed to act normal even as Asher sidestepped his way out of the crowd and into the trees.

Storm followed his dad step by step, weaving through trees, deviating from the route Cesa had taken to emerge a foot ahead, blocking his path.

"Where do you think you're going?" Asher asked, crossing his arms over his chest.

"I wanted a minute alone," Cesa confessed, avoiding Asher's gaze.

In a single step, he moved closer to Cesa, who tensed in

response. One more step brought his dad chest-to-chest with the Copry teenager, who was forced to look up the half foot difference of height between them. "We've been friends our entire life, Cesa Copry. We've been boyfriends for six months. There is nothing we don't share," Asher said, his voice trembling in obvious concern. He glanced around as if expecting someone to hear, but Storm was the only witness. "Do you remember when we first kissed?"

Looking away from the intense awkward scene, Storm listened but didn't pry into this personal moment in his dad's life.

"I told you I loved you," Cesa said, meeting his gaze unflinchingly, not in the least ashamed. "I gave you the book my father found at the auction because it was about the dark arts, and I had no use for it." He smiled as he lifted his right hand to press against Asher's, their fingers intertwining naturally.

"I told you no one had ever given me anything as precious. That I'd always cherish this book because it came from my best friend," he said, his smile twitching in what Storm had learned was fond recollection.

"And I told you I didn't want to be your best friend," Cesa replied, recounting the moment, this conversation, like they'd done it a thousand times. For all they had only been dating for six months, they knew each other, had been friends their entire lives, were part of each other, and neither could be whole without the other.

The realisation of what they shared made Storm's throat close, thinking about what lay ahead. In less than a decade, they would go from this to one man grieving, locked in a cursed insanity, and the other dead; neither whole, loved or capable of existing without the other.

"I knew, didn't I?" Asher sounded tender and cautious, like he was afraid to frighten Cesa with the wrong words. "I knew you loved me; not that you didn't want to be my friend. I knew you wanted more. I kissed you and you kissed me back." He said the words with awe for Cesa's bravery, for kissing him back, as though he'd only risked crossing the line between friendship and boyfriends because he was scared Cesa never would.

Storm opened his mouth to speak as a tear slid over his eyelash, but words eluded him. He wanted to shout a warning, to do *something* to stop this from playing out.

Cesa nodded, looking innocently enraptured by Asher. Even if they could see or hear him, they would never believe Storm or accept their fate. They were doomed to a life of grief and pain. For two people innocently in love, they would think the future ahead was impossible.

Neither flinched from the eye contact that made Storm feel like an intruder. This was a precious moment where they looked into each other's souls, charged with heat, love and wonder. When his dad dipped his head to kiss Cesa, the entire woods shivered with magic.

Just as Storm's magic rippled and responded to Rowan's, to his very essence, Storm *felt* the intensity of what was between Asher and Cesa. The whole world acknowledged their love; strong, powerful and magnetic, causing a hush over the woods, silencing the birds. The trees held their breath, the wind froze, standing still and allowing this moment to become lost in a single kiss.

When they parted, Storm's ears popped from the obvious and deafening return of life to the woods, rattling his thoughts and disorientating his senses. Looking at where they stood, now holding hands and staring at each other, Storm's throat tightened to see that Cesa was crying.

"I have to get married."

In the space of a heartbeat, Storm could hear the world spinning, knocking Asher off his axis and shattering everything he thought was real. The feeling was so palpable Asher almost physically stumbled as he stepped away, dropping Cesa's hands.

"What?"

"My parents have decided. They've chosen someone," Cesa explained, his eyes dripping tears. He stared at Asher as though the sight could ease the pain. "Rosa Bellamy. She's the only white witch in her coven. We're to marry on the night of my ascension," he revealed, speaking fast, fear mixing with the pain.

The look in his dad's eyes made Storm want to throw up; the utter loss, betrayal and the doubts, probably wondering if any of Cesa's feelings for him had been true.

"You don't like girls."

"I don't have a choice." Cesa pulled the sleeves of his jumper over his hands, a finger nervously looping over the fabric. "You know we can never be together. The Fates won't allow it," he said, averting his gaze, struggling to say the words and mean them when faced with Asher's anger.

"We can fight them," Asher insisted, reaching for Cesa's hand.

Cesa stepped back, shaking his head, crying and tugging on his sleeves. "No one fights the Fates," he argued, sparing one more look for Asher before he turned and walked out of the woods.

Silence descended, leaving a hush over the woods that felt ominous and threatening. Slow-growing black mist leaked from Asher's fingertips as he clenched them into fists, his jaw tense, clearly struggling to hold in his anger, his magic and everything he was feeling.

Where Storm would have crumbled into a sobbing wreck on the forest floor, his dad proved how strong and powerful he'd become. With an almighty scream, he curled inward to hold his stomach and a torrent of black magic snaked from his eyes, mouth and fingertips. A magical tornado stirred the leaves, forcing birds from the trees, crackling against the wind, like two forces fighting: deadly, terrifying and heartbreaking.

All Storm could do was sink to the ground and wait, watching his dad fall apart, with dark magic and anger, while protecting Cesa from his actions. Storm couldn't even tell him that Asher would be doing that for the rest of his short life, and none of his power and his love would make a difference.

Asher Tera would never save Cesa Copry.

And history might be about to repeat itself through their sons.

Chapter Twenty-Two

STORM WAS SHAKING by the time the scene faded from his dad breaking apart in front of him to what must have been a year later, standing at the side of a heavily decorated floral arbour. Cesa stood beside him, watching his future bride walk down the aisle.

Cesa's gaze was firmly fixed on what must have been Rosa Bellamy and his dad stared straight ahead, like the dedicated, serious best man he was. They were so desperately trying *not* to stare at each other that Storm doubted they could see anything going on around them. Cesa flinched when Rosa reached him and held her hand out. He faked a smile and turned with her to face the priest, but Storm didn't miss the dart of his gaze toward Asher or the evident tension between them as the ceremony continued.

He watched the events happen like a movie, something detached from real life. All Storm could think was why? How could they stand side by side and not fight to be with each other? How could Cesa say his vows to someone else? How could his dad not do *something* to stop this?

Storm knew how he would feel if Rowan was marrying someone else. He wasn't sure what he felt for Rowan yet, but he didn't want to be with anyone else. He wanted to give their relationship time to evolve, and he couldn't bear the thought of letting Rowan go without knowing what they might have together.

Storm knew what was here, what existed between Asher and Cesa, so why were they accepting this? Why didn't they kick and scream for every second they were forced apart since it hurt so damned much they couldn't breathe? Their pain resonated, obvious to anyone who looked at them, an unavoidable truth everyone conveniently ignored.

This night under the stars was when their lives fell apart, when their world shattered, and they both had to pretend they weren't being ripped apart by grief.

Scenes flitted by, showing him brief moments of the day and night: Asher and Cesa talking but determinedly not touching each other at the wedding reception; Cesa having his first dance with his new wife while Asher stood on the opposite side of the dance floor; heated glances passing between them, despite their attempts to resist.

Asher took the hand of a girl and lead her onto the dance floor, where they talked quietly. Though Storm didn't hear a word of their conversation, his dad had the best poker face he'd ever seen, laughing, mingling and acting like everything was fine. Neither Cesa nor Asher showed any sign of their inner pain; when their gazes collided across the room or when they snuck a glance at each other, the truth flaring in their eyes.

Storm's breath hitched as a vision in pale blue stepped closer to his dad.

"If you'd like to walk me through the garden, you can take a minute to compose yourself," she said, her voice soft and beautiful.

The sound made him ache, having never seen his mum this young. Veronica was as beautiful in this moment as she'd been when he last saw her, crossing into the abyss. Tonight, she was an unknown pretty face to Asher, wearing a summer dress, her long, dark hair hanging over one shoulder, and clutching a purse in both hands.

When Asher looked at her there was no spark, no instant connection, just a man startled by her attention and a flash of fear that he'd been caught. He was smart enough to nod, offer his arm and escort Veronica Amari out the open French doors of the Copry manor into the garden.

"You think I need to compose myself?" he asked as they walked away from the house through the path lined with roses.

Veronica tipped her head to gaze at Asher with a fond smile. "I know love when I see it. You could say it's my gift," she claimed, brushing her fingertips across the petals of nearby dying sunflowers. The moment she made contact, they flourished into full bloom, shining in the night light.

Asher smiled knowingly. "I know who you are and what you can do. I'm just surprised," he confessed, politely ignoring her magical introduction. "I won't deny that I love him or that he loves me. But he believes we're destined to never find peace together, and I can't change his mind. Why torture myself with loneliness when I can keep his friendship?"

Storm wanted to shake him, and apparently his mum agreed.

Veronica shook her head and huffed in disapproval. "Men. You talk like you can't change fate, that the Fates can't be beaten. I come from a long line of necromancers like you do. You should know better," she said, watching him with frighteningly intelligent eyes.

Storm smiled at her frank opinion, stunned when she glanced up. If he hadn't known he didn't exist to them, he'd have thought she'd seen him.

Asher hesitated, but emotion shook his voice, exposing the sadness he'd been hiding. "*I* know better. *He* can't be convinced, and I refuse to fight for a man who won't fight for me. If he can give up on us, then our love can't be real and perhaps never was."

Storm followed as they walked through the garden, debating love, the Fates, and magic for what felt like hours. No one came searching for them, and though they walked slowly, they didn't have to repeat their circle of the rose garden. The moment they reached the doors to the wedding reception, they didn't hesitate to go inside where they danced together, both seeming lighter and happier for their brief interlude in the garden.

Storm had thought watching his dad avoid Cesa while he married someone else had been painful. Watching his parents slow dance to a romantic song, and knowing they didn't have much time left, was worse. They would start dating in eight months, marry six months later, and have only seven short years together: one year with each other, taking over the Tera estate and building a married life, then welcoming him into the world.

It wasn't long enough, and their lives would end in blood and betrayal.

*

THE MOMENTS BETWEEN Asher and Cesa flitted by fast after the wedding. Precious hours of being friends and nothing more, days spent discussing coven business now they ruled their respective covens. They spent evenings at home with their separate families, casting longing gazes out of windows, and endured silences when they thought of each other but said nothing.

Storm could have cried for them but felt too empty for tears. He had to watch his mum come into her own, taking charge of the estate as she and Asher fell in love, married, and welcomed him into the world. They truly did love each other by the time they married. Ever the smart witch, Veronica Amari knew and accepted that she could never be first in Asher's heart, and she didn't ask to be.

Over time, Storm heard snippets of conversations, saw

flashes of his parents lives together, but the book was bound to Asher and Cesa's love. The memories couldn't stop to show him what he most wanted to see, only pausing when their love flared to life and was given the chance to fly free or when their emotions reached a crescendo.

"Why did you marry her if you love someone else?" a male voice asked, one Storm didn't recognise.

The sound came before the location, gradually forming his dad's study in the mansion, placing Storm at the door across from his dad, who paced the window. The unfamiliar man was an older version of his dad, minus the tattoos, and Storm could only assume this was his grandfather, sitting in the armchair in front of the desk.

"You're simplifying the situation." Asher gazed at the darkness of night beyond the window. "Ronnie and I wouldn't have married if we didn't care about each other. She isn't a second-rate prize," he objected with enough heat to make his point.

His grandfather stiffened and gritted his teeth. "She says you're in love with Cesa Copry," he said, his tone practically screaming his disapproval and disgust.

As his dad hung his head and bit his lower lip, clearly hoping to contain his anger or sadness at the accusation of the words, the door creaked open. Storm's gaze followed the sound to see Veronica standing in the open doorway, dressed in dark trousers and a white shirt hanging loose over a tank top. She was covered in paint splashes that reminded Storm of her talent for the creative arts;

she'd made beautiful pieces of art, infusing her magic into the paint that made the manor a home.

"I'm sorry, Asher. I didn't realise your father didn't know," she apologised, sounding genuinely sorry for the oversight.

"Don't worry, love. Are you all right?" Asher asked with no sign of anger but a warm affection that made Veronica blush.

"You have a visitor in the library," she replied, glancing at Asher's father awkwardly in a sign that he wouldn't want her to say who the visitor was. "You should finish here first."

The look that crossed Asher's dark eyes was enough to tell Storm what was happening. Cesa was waiting to see him, and Veronica was strong enough to invite him into her home, fully aware of his past with her husband. Yet she didn't seem inclined to do anything to discourage their friendship.

"Thank you." Asher straightened and bobbed his head, watching as Veronica left the room and shut the door. A last glare in the direction of Asher's father let Storm know exactly what she thought about his judgements. "Father, I will say this once." He turned, his posture full of authority that Storm could never imagine using against his dad. "Cesa and I began a relationship months before my ascension, and we were happy. On the night I ascended, he told me his parents had arranged his marriage to Rosa. He didn't see any way out since we're destined to be separated by the Fates," he explained, managing to remain strong and determined without showing a trace of the pain that night had caused.

"I suppose that's true," his grandfather muttered without

compassion.

"I wish he'd given me a choice. Cesa isn't interested in women. He doesn't feel about women the way you or I can."

"You?"

Storm rolled his eyes at how obtuse his grandfather was. Thank the gods both of his grandparents had been out of the country when his parents died, or Storm would have been raised by them. Gods help him, but he might have been kicked out for being gay. The thought made him shiver, though he refused to thank Gladys for saving him when she was the reason he wasn't raised in a loving, accepting household by his parents in the first place.

"I'm bisexual, Father," his dad said, confirming Storm's suspicion. "Which is why I wish he'd let me marry for duty. If one of us had to, I could find a way, but Cesa... He's always obeyed his parents. Even in this he couldn't stand to ask for my help, to fight for what he wanted."

Silence reigned until the room was closing in around them, oppressive, like a sharp sting in the air. Storm wanted to march across to his grandfather, to shake him until he recognised the obvious pain his son was in and attempt to do something to console or comfort him...to care!

"Is that why he's been distant during coven gatherings? Why he's separated his family from ours?"

Asher sagged against the window frame. "No. I think he can't bear being close to me," he confessed, swiping the heel of his hand across his eye. Though he was crying, he still managed to speak without breaking down or leaking magic as he had in the forest. "It hurts too much."

Storm wanted to hold him and lie, to tell him everything would be okay, just to heal that pain. Asher would never believe him even if Storm could tell him his fate; that he couldn't be with the man he loved, that his wife tolerated their love in a way Storm didn't understand but which made her more wonderful than he'd ever imagined.

"For you too?"

"Yes. I love Ronnie, but I'll always love Cesa more. She accepts that truth, because she knows the sting of betrayal."

"What do you mean?" His grandfather's panic was written all over his face: the fear that Veronica Tera might be a lesbian and acting as Asher's beard. His reputation and legacy seemed to be all that mattered; how he looked to the other covens and how Asher's behaviour reflected on the family name. Storm hated him.

"Ronnie was in love with a boy from her coven," Asher revealed with an ease that said this was something he'd known and accepted for a long time. "But he was promised to a girl from another coven. *Betrothed*. Just as Rosa and Cesa were matched according to their gifts, this boy was matched at birth to a girl his parents wanted an alliance with. Neither had any say," he continued, gaze drifting toward the study door, no doubt thinking about the man who waited on the other side. "He didn't fight the union when he found out, and Veronica gave up on her dreams of their happily ever after. He's the reason she knew what I was going through when Cesa got married. She was separated from someone she loved, willing to fight for them but he wasn't, just as I would have fought for Cesa, but he wasn't prepared to fight for me."

Asher drew his emotions in tight and faced his father. "If you'll excuse me, I have a visitor." He left the room without waiting for another comment about his life.

Storm could only imagine the difficulty of maintaining the illusion of strength and composure until the door shut between them. He stayed in the study, conflicted. He wanted to go after his dad, waiting for the spell to move him like a chess piece on the board, but nothing happened. Rain battered the windows and a storm picked up, no doubt sensitive to his dad's emotions.

The reality of what he'd found tonight was a conflict in his mind. His parents weren't star-crossed lovers or teenagers who had been madly in love; that wasn't why they'd married so young. Veronica had lost her true love to another woman because he was too much of a coward to fight for her. Asher had stood next to Cesa as he married a woman he didn't know, just to appease parents who would never be happy with his choices.

No, his parents weren't madly in love with each other, but they didn't have to be. They'd comforted each other through a shared pain, becoming friends, a support system, and secret keepers. Love came later, gradually, because they'd allowed themselves to grow from friends to something more without resistance.

Storm retreated from the memories attached to the book, returning his mind to the body sitting on the window seat of Rowan's bedroom. He fought the overwhelming rush of tears threatening to overtake him because he knew the truth. Veronica and Asher were strangers who became friends, and they died with hearts broken by empty promises from lost lovers.

Chapter Twenty-Three

YAEL PAUSED WITH one foot in the room, staring with wide eyes at Storm, who was huddled on the bed, hugging his knees. "What in the Mother happened to you?" they asked, rushing across the room to perch on the bed and place a hand against his forehead.

Storm shook his head, but the words wouldn't come. He'd been sitting here for an hour and still couldn't move. "I—" He shook his head, unable to find the right words. So much ran through his mind: fears and doubts, pain he didn't know what to do with. He had to let the pain out but thought about his dad standing in the woods, screaming out his rage and letting his magic run free because he couldn't suffer in silence.

As he opened his mouth to make another attempt, a cry emanated from across the hall and he flinched.

Yael patted his hand. "Rowan returned with his father some

time ago. We left you to rest and put his father to bed with something to help him sleep. I assume the tonic failed." Cradling Storm's chin in strong fingers, they cocked their head. "Rowan left to shop for dinner. Will you be all right if I tend to his father?"

The thought of Yael willingly checking on Cesa was enough to snap him out of the shock. Instinct made him shake his head and slip his feet off the bed. "No. I'll go," he said, not sure where the words came from other than a feeling that he had to try this even if he failed. "I'm okay. In shock, I guess. I..." He waved in the general direction of the book still sitting on the windowsill but didn't have the words to explain.

Either Yael understood or didn't care to press the issue. They allowed Storm to get to the bedroom door and followed him to Cesa's bedroom. Storm walked in, sure Cesa would be too traumatised by his nightmare to care that Storm was in his house.

The man was still locked in his nightmare when Storm entered the room. The sheets twisted around his body, and Cesa was sweating profusely. Cries and sounds of pain emanated from Cesa's tightly pressed lips, sounds that were unnatural for a strong, powerful white witch such as Cesa should have been. What Ithen had done was so dark and twisted that Storm didn't know if he could be saved, but he'd promised his dad he would try.

Storm stepped into the room and crossed to the bed, where Cesa was beginning to murmur in his sleep. Keeping his voice low, he used the one tool he had to his advantage—his voice. The one lesson he'd learned from stepping into his dad's past was that he sounded like Asher had when he was younger. Asher's voice had deepened after his ascension, but now Storm sounded like a young Asher Tera, the one Cesa Copry was innocently in love with when they were nothing but two teenagers who could never be together but could never stop loving each other.

Yael hovered between the bed and the door, likely prepared to rush in if Cesa lashed out, but Storm didn't think he could.

"Do you remember when we first kissed?" he asked in a whisper, hating the way his voice cracked.

Almost instantly, Cesa stilled and rolled to his side, to rub his cheek against the pillow. "I told you I loved you," he answered, likely wrapped in the comforting dream of a memory that had only hurt him. The way he smiled as he continued to relive the past gave Storm the confidence to keep going. Cesa and Asher had replayed this conversation too many times to fail. "I gave you the book my father found at the auction because it was about the dark arts, and I had no use for it."

Fighting tears, Storm brushed aside the sweat-soaked hair from Cesa's face. "I told you no one had ever given me anything as precious. That I'd always cherish this book because it came from my best friend."

"And I told you I didn't want to be your best friend."

He was following the script so well, Storm wondered what he was dreaming of. Was he in the woods, reliving the good bits before his world fell to pieces, or was he living out the first time they'd ever said this, in some memory, time and place Storm had never seen?

"I knew, didn't I?" he whispered, studying Cesa Copry for the first time in his life. He looked so like Rowan. His son was the younger, carefree version of Cesa that Storm had seen in the book's memories, but this older man retained a naturally handsome quality which must have drawn his dad in. If he hadn't been locked in insanity for years, hadn't stopped caring about his appearance, he could have easily stepped from a Caravaggio painting.

He was nearing forty but was still beautiful in a different way than Storm had ever thought to consider. Cesa's heart was pure and he resisted Ithen's curse every day, as best he could. He was still caring and loving toward his son, despite Ithen's influence, and clearly held onto his love for Asher. No matter what he did, Ithen could never steal the pure love they'd shared.

A tear escaped out the corner of his eye as Cesa whispered, "He knew I loved him."

The clarity broke Storm's heart. He had no choice but to grasp the hand clutching tight to the bed sheet and curl his fingers around the weak grip Cesa offered. He waited patiently as Cesa's breathing slowly eased into a deep sleep. Storm gave his hand one gentle squeeze and let go. He would sleep now, completely unaware he'd broken a piece of Storm's heart that would never recover.

Rising from the bed, he left the room to find Yael standing by the door, their arms crossed over their chest with a knowing look in their white eyes. "I believe I know why you were in such a state," they remarked, opening the bedroom door for Storm and following as he returned to Rowan's room. "Your father allowed you access to his heart?"

"The book," Storm admitted, seeing no reason to keep the secret. He walked to the window seat and lifted the book.

Yael raised their right hand to hover over the closed cover, tentatively tracing a fingertip over the engraved title. "Be careful of this spell, youngling. You may see what you are not meant to see," they warned, without the anger he'd expected or a sign they would stop him from using the spell. A serious, silent warning in their eyes made Storm want to step back. "At other times, you could see what you *should* not."

A day ago, he'd have argued that no harm could come from the past. Tonight, he nodded and took the book to the bed, intending to get comfortable, then take one last trip.

"Will you stay with me? I want to see more. Just until Rowan comes back. I'm hoping there's something that will tell me where to find the amulet's spell," he said, feeling like the book wanted to show him something else. Or perhaps his dad wanted to show him something. Either way, he'd been sure he would be taken somewhere new by the memories when he chose to leave, and he needed to follow the instinct, no matter what he might see.

"If you wish. The decision must always be yours," Yael replied, a soft smile warming their face as they crossed to the window seat and curled up on the far side where they could keep an eye on him.

Storm nodded his thanks, lay against the pillows and placed his hand on the book cover to allow his magic to return him to where he'd been, reassured the spell would work on the same object until he performed the counter spell. Whenever he touched this book and focused his magic on his goal, he would return to his dad's memories. But, he figured Yael was right; this should be his last visit to the past, before he saw something he couldn't unsee.

Storm was surprised to return to exactly where he'd been before his sadness pulled him from the memories. As he'd suspected, there was something else he was meant to see on this night, something he was meant to understand.

His grandfather still sat in the armchair where Asher had left him, a faint shake of his head suggesting he was considering what he'd heard about Asher's feelings for Cesa and Veronica's lost love.

Leaving the study, Storm didn't walk into the hallway as he was supposed to but straight into the library, where his dad had just entered the room. Cesa was pacing in front of the fireplace.

The moment Cesa saw him, he visibly deflated and paused his pacing. "Asher!" he exclaimed, relief colouring his voice.

Asher's step faltered as though the sound hit him with a physical force. "What are you doing here?" he asked, rushing toward Cesa in panic. The moment Asher touched his shoulders to offer comfort, he recoiled and shook his head. "Gods, you're soaked!"

Storm saw the indecision of whether Asher should stay or rush to get a towel. The question disappeared before his eyes as

Cesa began to cry.

"They want an heir!"

Asher's hands fell, dropping to his side as a heart-pounding silence descended upon the room. "What?" Disbelief, fear and something close to panic laced his voice with enough emotion to let Storm know this had never been expected.

Cesa grasped desperately at Asher's arms. "They're telling Rosa if she doesn't supply an heir soon, they'll force her to go through IVF," he explained, the wide-eyed fear touching something inside Storm.

He hadn't realised how privileged he'd been to have parents who would never demand these violations. The realisation that Cesa's family were old-fashioned to a criminal degree was both disgusting and terrifying. Thank the gods that Cesa retained enough sanity that Rowan hadn't been forced to live with them since Ithen's curse took hold. Storm couldn't imagine how he would have survived.

"But...that's barbaric," Asher objected, opening his mouth to say more, but no words escaped; no doubts, no arguments, not a single promise that they'd be okay because they wouldn't. Words wouldn't help; nothing would.

"They're relentless. What will I do?" Cesa pleaded, falling against Asher's chest and clutching onto him so hard his knuckles grew white, and Storm was sure nothing would make him let go. "We've never...what I mean is, Rosa accepts our marriage. She knows that I could never... We were honest from the start, but this is unbearable." He confessed in stops and starts, gasps and heavy breathing. Every breath spoke of how near the edge to a full-blown panic attack he truly was.

With a hand on Cesa's head, Asher's eyes turned dark in proof he was tempted to use his magic. "Breathe for me, my love."

Cesa raised his head and gazed so openly with such vulnerability that Storm wasn't surprised when Asher kissed him. If Rowan had been in such pain, he would have done the same. A kiss didn't help or make the problem easier to bear, but the gentle act could remind Cesa that he didn't have to be alone with this burden.

When Cesa broke the kiss to hide his face in Asher's shoulder, Storm could almost see the cogs turning as his dad put together a plan. "We'll figure this out, I promise. Ronnie and I won't let you be put through this. Neither of you deserve this. This is unacceptable, and I'll make sure the other covens step in," he promised, saying the right words, even though they didn't solve the problem.

Watching them cling to each other, knowing what they faced, Storm couldn't see a solution. They had eventually come upon the idea of, and succeeded in, using demon magic to create Rowan, but Storm would likely never know what that choice cost them.

Asher pried Cesa away, helped him into an armchair by the fire and poured him a glass of whiskey. He crossed to the bookcase on the far side of the room, where he plucked a black tome from the bottom shelf. "I'm a dark mage. I can fix this. We *will* fix this."

The waver in his voice told Storm that even Asher wasn't sure of the promises he'd made or his ability to keep his word. A moment after he began flicking through the pages, Cesa rose from the armchair and crossed to his side. With a first tentative touch, he eased against Asher's back, leaning against him, holding him and taking comfort from Asher's strength.

"I can't do this without you."

Asher stopped flicking through the pages, tipped his head back to rest against Cesa's and closed his eyes. He seemed to cherish and hate the words, probably relieved to know he could be a saviour when Cesa needed one but guilty that his love for Cesa was a betrayal of his marriage vows. The conflict within him revealed itself in a single tear at the corner of his eye, proof of the two paths his heart pulled him in and the brutal fact that kept him frozen: he could never follow both roads.

*

STORM HAD NEVER believed a crisis could pull people together, but he watched his parents rally to help Cesa and Rosa.

The images and memories flashed by, threatening to leave Storm disorientated as the four friends formed a plan. Love bound them together when Rowan was delivered, a human baby with DNA from a demon and Cesa, creating an official heir to the Copry legacy. Rosa and Cesa grew closer as they raise him, and a new friendship formed a year later when Storm was born, and Rowan showed an instant fascination. Storm was embarrassed to see himself as a baby and a toddler, how a sneeze could cause a gale through the room or that the rain pelted down when he cried during the night. Cesa would laugh when Rowan would take Storm's hand or cuddle him to calm the panic and sadness but showed no sign of wanting to separate them as children.

All four parents shone with happiness as their children played and grew up together, forming a family that should have been at odds with itself but never was. Asher and Cesa didn't display their love often, and if they ever surrendered, during moments of pain or when the world grew too hard to cope with, Storm never witnessed those memories. Storm's parents grew visibly more in love as the years passed, their friendship as strong as their love. Then Rosa got sick when Rowan was three years old, wasting away before their eyes for a full year. Her death broke something in Cesa that not even Asher could fix.

Storm watched in horror as the man descended from grief to despair. Arriving at the Tera home in the dead of night, Cesa was clearly drunk as he begged Asher to help him. The look in Veronica's eyes when she let Cesa into the house and left him with Asher was heartbreaking. She must have known they would share something close to intimacy but never stepped in to set boundaries or tell Asher to choose between them. Storm had never realised just how strong his mum was. She'd harboured her lost love in her heart, knowing she would never see him again, yet she wouldn't deny Asher and Cesa their love.

He could tell, even at this distance and having not known

either of his parents well, that Veronica wouldn't have denied them anything. Asher and Cesa could have had an affair, become lovers, and she would never have stopped them, but neither made her suffer the betrayal and deception. What rare kisses they shared were given in comfort, to soothe, to remember the past and that their feelings for each other would never fade. Storm never saw them succumb to lust; what they shared was deeper than the physical, more tender and sacred.

The memories grew sadder, though Storm wasn't sure if that was because of his feelings or because no more happy days remained for Asher and Cesa. They were happy with their families for a time, Cesa lighting up whenever he was with Rowan, but loneliness enveloped them, and a distance grew that meant their stolen kisses and the times they held each other grew less.

Until Cesa stopped visiting.

The memories slowed as Cesa stood in Asher's study for the first time in months, both men standing so far apart Storm knew this wouldn't be like the other visits. There was too much between them now, too much space and time, ghosts and secrets.

"As much as I love Rowan, I was wrong," Cesa said, turning away from the window that showed Rowan and Storm playing in the front garden.

Asher's eyes welled but he remained at his desk, not moving from where he sat, staring at the bookcase across the room and showing no sign of having heard the words, bar those unshed tears.

"I wish I'd fought harder for us."

Closing his eyes so tight the tear escaped, to trail his cheek in proof of his pain, Asher nodded. "I know." He didn't open his eyes until Cesa left the room, shut the door behind him, and told Rowan they were going home.

Storm knew just as surely as his dad did that Cesa was never coming back.

The disappointment of knowing everything had changed for both men and they'd never found their way back to each other was enough to convince Storm he'd seen enough. The memories didn't feel like they were pulling him in a specific direction, so he let go of the magic and returned to where he lay on the bed in Rowan's bedroom.

Blinking to clear his misty vision, Storm pushed the book to the other side of the mattress. He doubted his dad had wanted him to see those memories, but the book didn't seem to remember being given to Asher, being found by Cesa or anything about their first six months together. The book only held the strongest emotions: the life-changing events of their relationship.

Storm wished he could speak to his dad about what he'd seen or find out what his mum had thought. He was sure she'd never loved his dad as much as she'd loved her first love, the same way she didn't expect Asher to love her the way he loved Cesa. They'd found happiness together anyway, and that was amazing.

Now he knew what haunted Cesa's nightmares; the doubts, the fears and the mistakes he'd made in the past. He was probably reliving or second-guessing his choices, wishing life had been different.

How often did he wake from a dream of the past or a nightmare of what they'd gone through, wondering if Asher would still be alive if he'd fought for them or if they'd run away together? How many times did he question whether he should have ever loved Asher, if he'd never lost his heart to a Tera or if he'd never obeyed his parents and married Rosa? What might the future have held for them, if they'd held onto each other and defied the Fates?

Storm sat there and composed his thoughts, unable to prevent the tears from welling. So much would have been different if his dad had been given the same chance he had—to be with the man he loved.

Pushing strands of hair from his forehead, he leaned an elbow on his raised knee and gazed out the window to find something to distract his mind. He found Rowan sitting on the window seat, headphones on and phone in his hand.

Despite the tears, he smiled. Rowan was practically glowing in the sunlight streaming in the window, his hair mussed. He looked ready for a lazy afternoon, dressed in joggers and a too-large T-shirt that still managed to look good on him.

Storm grabbed the pillow from behind him and tossed it at Rowan to capture his attention. With a smile that lit up the room, Rowan removed his headphones, put his phone on the window seat and stood to cross to the bed. Sitting by Storm's knee, Rowan lay a hand on his ankle, offering a consoling touch he hadn't realised he needed, one that released the horde of tears he'd been keeping at bay.

With the bare warning of a wobble of his chin, Storm descended into tears and sank forward to hide his face in Rowan's neck. He hadn't intended to fall apart, but that touch found the button to unleash his emotions.

Strong arms encased him, fingers drifting into his hair as Rowan shushed him. With stuttering breath and stumbling words, Storm explained what had happened, that he'd tried the spell his dad had told him about, and he'd seen so much of his relationship with Cesa. Everything he'd discovered about their families hurt.

Hugging Rowan tight—because he *was* his boyfriend— Storm took a steadying breath. With a growing sense of guilt, he lifted his head, wiped his eyes and stared into Rowan's open, accepting blue eyes. "I hate myself for being glad they didn't get to be with each other."

"What?" Rowan frowned in a soft way that said he didn't understand but wasn't jumping to conclusions. He fixed Storm's hair as though it could help, and damn him for being right, because those fingers in his hair did something to make the world right again.

"If they had each other, I wouldn't have you." He was ashamed to admit that he didn't know if he loved Rowan or not, but he thought he might. He suspected the feelings might have been there all this time, buried under Gladys's spell that made him forget an entire childhood they'd spent together, becoming closer to each other than he'd ever been with anyone else. Closer than his older self, from the future, had ever allowed him to be with anyone.

No wonder he'd been bitter and hated magic, by the time the war was lost. That Storm had never been loved or cherished the way that only his parents and Rowan had cared for him.

The realisation sent a lead weight to Storm's stomach as the reality of what faced them hit home. As long as he loved Rowan—and the magic wasn't clear enough to differentiate between romantic and familial love—it was already too late. No matter what he did, Storm would never resurrect Rowan, even if all that existed between them was a childhood love. If the worst happened, he'd have to do what Cesa had done—stand by and watch the man he loved die and spend the rest of his life grieving for a love that was never given the chance to bloom.

Rowan cupped his cheek, focusing his thoughts. "I know," he said, with acceptance for the horrible words he'd said.

The words made him cry harder, because they were the last words Asher had said to Cesa as they ended their relationship. He couldn't bear to hear them from Rowan with his emotions on the surface, raw and lost inside his head. He didn't want to hear those two words again because they would forever mean goodbye.

Chapter Twenty-Four

"PSST."

Storm nudged further into the pillow and duvet, warm and cosy. He'd fallen asleep in the early hours of the morning in Rowan's arms, with his fingers trailing patterns over Storm's neck. He wasn't ready to wake up and remember all the chaos and bad shit that awaited them in real life.

"Storm."

Storm turned onto his side and reached for Rowan, to draw him closer and suggest they stay in bed. A kiss to his lips distracted him, prompting him to pop his eyes open and raise an eyebrow at Rowan.

"Morning." Rowan looked happy, flashing a beaming smile, his eyes twinkling with mischief. Storm was tempted to say something about how he'd feign sleeping more often if Rowan insisted on waking him like that, but that thought could only lead to trouble.

"Is there a reason you're waking me at the ass crack of dawn?" he asked, wishing he'd had warning of the early morning. They'd talked late into the night, discussing what he'd seen in his dad's memories, then moved onto Donald's situation when Yael returned from wherever they'd disappeared to. Yael had finally left them to sleep at close to two in the morning. According to the clock that was only six hours sleep, which was not nearly enough.

"Don't be dramatic," Rowan replied, rolling his eyes as he tossed the covers aside to let the morning chill in. "Come on. There's something I want to show you." He bounded from the bed, crossed to the dresser and pulled a winter jumper from the middle drawer.

Storm couldn't help but notice that he was fully dressed in jeans and a T-shirt. Realising how important this must be for Rowan to insist, he left the warm bed, slipped into the bathroom to get the basics out of the way and allowed Rowan to drag him from the room still dressed in the joggers and T-shirt he'd fallen asleep in.

To his surprise, Rowan led the way downstairs to the main house. "I thought we were going to see Donald?" He'd been sure something had happened that Rowan wanted to share with him, something related to what they had intended to do today.

"We will. There's something you have to see first," he said, glancing briefly over his shoulder before continuing down the extensive staircase. At the bottom, he turned left and headed for the back end of the house that Storm had never been in and passed through the kitchen into what looked to be a conservatory.

Cesa Copry was sitting at a small breakfast table with a cup of tea and an open box.

Storm was tempted to put the brakes on since they'd been keeping his presence in the house a secret, but Rowan was determined, and he didn't see a way to stop him without bursting this bubble of excitement.

Cesa turned to Rowan with a warm smile, lifting a photograph from the box. "This was when your first tooth fell out," he said, shaking his head with undisguised fondness as he handed the photograph to Rowan. He was still a shadow of the man who had loved Asher, but as far from the walking zombie Ithen had turned him into as Storm had ever seen him.

Rowan practically glowed at the sight of his father, sparing a glance at the photograph only to laugh. The man muttered something about a photograph of Rowan using magic for the first time as he rummaged through the box of memories, and Storm found himself the focus of Rowan's warm, steady gaze.

"You did this," he whispered, squeezing Storm's hand as a smile wavered on his lips, equal parts sadness, joy and relief. "Whatever you said last night... I have my dad back. I don't care how long this lasts. There will never be the words to thank you, but I needed you to see that you were able to do this." Heaving a happy sigh, Rowan leaned against Storm's shoulder and watched his father during this rare moment of lucidity.

He'd never expected this. What he'd said to Cesa last night had come instinctively from a need to help the man heal from a pain that would never leave him. As much as Storm wanted to tell Rowan that this was his father's doing—the magic of the love between Cesa and Asher that refused to fade—this lucid moment may not last. Why burst his bubble when reality would come crashing down soon enough?

He watched Cesa mutter about the picture he was searching for, sorting through an entire shoebox of stacked photographs. The man was happy for the first time in years; aware, sane and completely in control of his thoughts and movements. He was the dad Rowan deserved and should have had all these years.

"Why don't you stay here today?" Storm suggested, not needing to think through the consequences of being without Rowan. What they had to do for Donald was important, and though Rowan stared as though Storm had told him he wasn't needed, that wasn't what he meant. "Spend time with your dad while he's like this. Like you say, we don't know how long this will last, but you need to be here. This might be your only chance to see him like this until we break the curse." Rowan smiled faintly and turned his focus to Cesa, who was smiling over a photograph. "I can handle Donald, and I'll have Yael and Kyrie with me if anything goes wrong. We'll be fine. You need this time with your dad."

Cocking his head, Rowan's eyes softened and threatened to spill everything he was feeling over Storm's shoulder, where he propped his chin. He didn't say anything, and Storm realised with a clench of his stomach that it didn't matter. Rowan could cry on him if he wanted to, he could lean on him and count on Storm to be there in these moments when he needed him the most.

Rowan released Storm's hand. "Thank you."

"You know where to find me if you need me."

*

STORM FOUND KYRIE standing outside Donald's room. "Morning, Kyrie. You look much better."

"Thank you, Dark One," Kyrie replied, evidently not ready to call him by his name, no matter how often Storm reminded him to. "I have information to share once you are ready." Turning, he opened the door to Donald's room and waited for Storm to enter before trailing behind.

He was surprised to find Donald lying on the bed, neither moving nor conscious. The fact Donald had been unconscious since Storm released the ghosts from Gladys's basement had been spinning through his mind. Between the panic over his feelings for Rowan, the fear of history repeating itself, and the weirdness of stepping into his dad's memories, there was so much to worry about that he was getting a headache.

"When this is over, I need to do nothing for a month." Storm rubbed his temples where a tension headache was steadily building.

"Here." Yael stepped through the door Storm was sure Kyrie

had shut behind him. They handed over a cup of herbal tea with a self-satisfied smile.

Storm cursed his failure to grab food from the kitchen before coming back upstairs to get ready. He sipped the tea and crossed to a dining chair by the bed, left for Yael and Kyrie who had been holding vigil over Donald. "I've been thinking about what happened in the basement," he said, deciding to share his thoughts with the two people most likely to know if he was talking total shit. He paused when Yael casually walked to his side and held out a plate with a bacon roll. Storm nodded his thanks, accepted the plate and took a bite of the roll. He finished chewing and swallowed. "As I was saying...when we were in the basement, I freed all the spirits, right? Wouldn't I have inadvertently freed DJ's spirit? As long as the spirit was ready to pass on. Wasn't that why my dad didn't disappear along with the others?"

With a thoughtful arch of their eyebrow, Yael sat and crossed their legs, flaunting the smart and sophisticated jumpsuit they'd chosen today, the deep burgundy accenting their choice of long white hair. They tapped a blood-red painted nail against their bottom lip. "I thought we believed Gladys glamoured the boy to appear and act like DJ?"

Storm took another bite of his roll while he searched for the best way to explain. "Why would the demon child lose himself just because he was trapped? Isn't that the deal with demons? They're usually older when they find themselves trapped in a bond, but the concept wouldn't have been unfamiliar, and he would know he'd grow strong enough to break the curse, right?"

If a demon child took a decade or more to grow into an adult, they were born with the patience of a saint. Donald wouldn't have surrendered his entire being, his soul and body; he would have held on for the decade, knowing he'd eventually become an adult, strong enough to fight back.

"I suppose," Yael agreed, not sounding convinced.

"Suppose the *real* reason he couldn't fight was because DJ— the real Donald James Glade—was attracted to his body?" he suggested, watching Kyrie sink into the armchair in the corner with wide, sad eyes. "His soul could have returned because his mother refused to let him go. That's another way spirits are created, right? They're held by the family who can't bear to lose them. Maybe DJ was haunting her house, unable to cross over because Gladys wouldn't let him. When she brought a perfect vessel, maybe his will was as strong as Gladys's and he took this demon child's body which strengthened Gladys's curse." He hoped he was on the right track because he had an idea of what to do next.

"That may explain why he lost hope," Kyrie said, glancing at Yael for approval. "His family horde couldn't find or detect him because his essence had been suppressed by the presence of DJ's spirit."

"Which isn't there."

"It's not?" Kyrie asked, eyes large with surprise.

Storm shook his head, took the last bite of his roll, and dusted his hands on his jeans. "No. Because I freed all *trapped* spirits from the basement, where Donald was being held in a cage."

Yael nodded. "You believe DJ was trapped by his mother's will and couldn't move on through his *own* will. He took over the demon child's body from necessity and a desire to be with his mother. When you offered a way to cross over, DJ accepted."

"I think so."

"If that is true, then we have a problem."

"Yeah. The demon child's body is without a soul," Storm agreed, only staying positive because he had a plan. "I know you guys have been coming up short, but I think I could...call...him home? You know, now that the body is empty." Souls were naturally drawn to their bodies, their essence, so in theory, now that the demon child's body was free of DJ's soul, they should be free to return with a nudge from Storm to guide them.

"It is certainly worth a try," Yael agreed, more sceptical than he'd hoped.

Kyrie positively beamed as he cleared his throat to capture their attention. "I found the demon child's horde. If they were here, surely the boy's spirit could be called to them?"

Thinking about his suggestion, Storm came upon a realisation. "Maybe his soul has been following them, unable to find his body."

Yael's eyes lit with understanding. "We must do this immediately before any more time passes."

"Just what I was about to say."

Yael stood and gestured to Kyrie, the two demons darting into the abyss before Storm had even finished speaking. "Nothing new there," he mumbled, and patted the demon child's hand. "Don't worry, kiddo. I'm much better at magic than thinking."

*

YAEL AND KYRIE returned from the abyss after an hour, walking back into the room with a hulk of a demon in tow. He bowed his head respectfully when Kyrie introduced him as the leader of the horde and addressed Storm as the Dark One. He swore that one day he would meet a demon besides Yael who could address him as something else. Anything would do.

Storm nodded and offered the demon a polite greeting, aware that being the leader must mean that this demon was Donald's father. Once the pleasantries were done, he turned to Yael. "Are the whole horde coming or can we start?" he asked, genuinely interested to know if he'd have to warn Rowan about a half dozen demons loitering in the spare room.

Yael turned to the higher demon who had accompanied them and raised an eyebrow.

"I believe Yael is rudely asking you to supply an answer," Storm informed the demon with a pleasant, if fake, smile.

The higher demon glanced at them in turn before facing Storm, obviously not sure of the etiquette of talking to a dark mage without being bound to them or asked first. "I can summon the rest of the horde, but to assume they were welcome in the home of a white witch would be rude."

"I thank you for the consideration on Rowan's behalf. He is half-demon and would more than welcome your horde," Storm confessed, having discussed the possibility with Rowan to make sure he was comfortable being exposed to them as a half-breed. "We can do this with you, since you were there the day your son was taken. If we don't succeed, then we can try with the entire horde."

Mother demons were notoriously strict with the fathers being the soft touch. If the boy would run to anyone in his horde for help after being kidnapped and cursed, Storm imagined he would want his father.

The higher demon bobbed his head in acceptance and moved when Yael suggested he stand at the side of the bed on the opposite side to where Storm sat.

"Most of my magic is silent," he informed the demon to keep him aware of the process. "Yael will let you know if there's anything to be concerned about. Until I speak to you, or they reveal concern, please trust that I'm focused and working hard to help your son." He didn't want to come across rude but didn't want anyone interfering either, just because he'd been silent too long or was making noises. He wasn't quite sure what he was like when his mind was deep in his magic, and he didn't want a concerned parent panicking because of innocent sounds or words that may slip through his consciousness.

After the demon leader nodded, Kyrie took up a position at

the door to the bedroom.

"His name is Haven," the higher demon said as Storm touched the demon boy's face.

He smiled at the trust he'd been given. "Thank you." Knowing the boy's name meant he, as a dark mage, had an unprecedented power over Haven. As a necromancer, he could use his magic to call on the boy's spirit by name, which vastly increased his chances of success.

The risk the father had taken by giving him the name was immense, both an honour and an incredible duty that Storm vowed to adhere to. He focused on Haven and touched the still chest, placing his other hand to the crown of his head. Storm made light contact with his fingertips against bare skin to strengthen their connection. He was counting on the connection they'd made in the future to do the rest.

Closing his eyes, he escaped into his magic. *Let's bring Haven home.*

His magic knew what needed to be done, searching through Haven's body for any sign of life, any lingering essence of the boy's true demon soul, while Storm called on the other side of his dark magic and spoke in his mind.

Storm Tera—protector of demons, master of demons, guardian of the lost and hopeless—calls forth the soul of Haven, demon child, from the abyss. I call for you to return to your rightful body, your true host.

Your body is free to be reclaimed. The soul which pushed

you into the depths of darkness has crossed over. Once you re-turn, I promise we will cleanse your spirit and body, returning you to the symbol of hope you are for your people.

Come home, Haven.

For too long, Storm felt nothing, heard nothing; darkness clouded his mind. His magic couldn't detect a flicker of anything belonging to Haven. The curse lingered over the vessel, showing only the visage of Donald James Glade, as though Haven had never existed.

Chapter Twenty-Five

AFTER INTERMINABLE MOMENTS, a faint shimmer appeared, like a presence caught out the corner of his eye. Storm squeezed his eyes shut, realising what had made an impact on his magic and the spell.

Come home, Haven. This is Storm calling on you. We know each other, you and I. You know me and can trust me. I will never let Gladys hurt you again.

There was another flicker of light just outside his field of vision.

Does the house haunt your dreams too? a voice whispered inside his head, escaping the darkness to reveal the tiny sound.

Storm's heart thudded as he remembered those words from his future. *Yes! Haven, it's me. Come home.*

I'm scared.

334 | Elaine White

You're not in Gladys's house. You're in Rowan's home. The house of a half-demon, white witch. You're with me. I have two demon friends here with me: Kyrie and Yael. Your father is here, he explained, hoping to draw him to his body.

Those last few words sparked hope so tangible Storm could feel it tingling in his veins, a glimmer of a shadow moving in the darkness amongst his magic. *It's safe?*

Yes. You can come home.

He waited, afraid of leaving Haven even for a second or to replenish his strength. It took what felt like hours but couldn't have been long as he didn't feel that familiar tingle of fatigue in his limbs. Eventually, a small hand reached from the darkness, the skin like black marble. Storm grabbed hold of the tiny fingers, linked them with his and held on tight.

He could feel how weak Haven was, that his soul had taken a battering from Gladys's curse, and Haven didn't know how to do what needed to be done. Storm would need to take over. Holding the tiny hand, he slipped into Haven's body and pulled Haven's spirit with him.

An audible crack in his mind startled him, but Storm focused on leading Haven's spirit through the trail his magic had left behind. As he'd suspected, the path led straight to the place where his soul belonged. Once he reached the cage meant to protect the soul from magic, he found the barrier torn to shreds, the bars warped and broken.

Storm guided Haven's spirit inside, watching the boy shiver

as he eyed the cage with terror. He touched the bars with a mental hand and used a pulse of magic to transform them. He plucked an idea from Haven's mind and allowed his magic to morph the metal bars into tree branches, the base of the metal cage into the trunk of a tree, and covered every inch in blue petals; Haven's favourite colour.

With a tired laugh, Haven gazed at the leaves and reached out with a spirit hand to touch one. *They're pretty,* he said, turning his gaze to meet Storm's. *I'll be safe here now. Because of you. Thank you.*

Pressing his hands to Storm's spirit-chest, Haven gave a gentle push that sent Storm careening from the demon body and into his own mind. The journey was almost instant, a head rush that left him disorientated but more secure in his skin. Maybe when Haven woke from his coma, Storm would thank him for the nudge in the right direction because he hadn't thought ahead to how he would get out of Haven's body after recklessly and willingly entering a demon's host body.

It took time to feel solid in his mind, to feel connected to his body, brain and magic. Once he sensed the firm ground-beneath-his-feet surety of the connection, he pulled away from his magic and Haven. Storm sat back in the seat, relieved to find Yael standing across the bed with a satisfied smile.

"Welcome back, youngling." Turning their attention to the bed, Yael watched Haven take a slow, deep breath and sleepily rub his eye. "You did well, Protector of Demons."

Haven didn't wake immediately. The rub of his eyes was followed by a sigh and the boy turned his head to snuggle into the pillow beneath his head.

Storm was glad he was safe and content to sleep, because he wasn't finished.

Yael took charge, reading Storm's mind or his fatigued magic. "The Dark One will replenish his strength for a few minutes, then work on the curse forcing Haven's body to display contrary to his natural appearance." Though the higher demon hadn't looked away from Haven's body since the boy had taken his first breath, once they received a nod, Yael turned to Kyrie. "Could I impose on you to bring the Dark One a hot chocolate and the cakes you found? He will need the energy to do what comes next," they asked, their tone polite and considerate, a tone they generally reserved for Kyrie.

Storm would have shaken his head at the preferential treatment, but he was afraid his head might fall off. Kyrie jumped to obey Yael, giving Storm time and an excuse to sink into his seat and catch a few moments of rest.

"I remembered something when you spoke to the boy."

Storm cracked an eye open and waited for Yael to continue. He hoped he hadn't been talking aloud when he was using his magic, but perhaps he'd let Yael piggyback on his experience.

Yael folded their arms over their chest, eyeing the higher demon with a look suggesting they'd rather not say this with an audience but had no choice. "The war began on November twenty-second. That was the day Denver was kidnapped by the Copry coven. As we now know Ithen is the true influence behind the coven, we can safely assume that we have avoided that deadline."

"I certainly hope so."

Yael tapped a talon against their chin. "We must acknowledge the dates and see the days pass in vastly different ways than before...or later." They didn't wait for Storm to apologise or agree again because they knew he wouldn't bother. "The next event took place on November twenty-third: the date Denver and Rowan die, in the future timeline."

Storm would find a way of making sure that never happened. Just as he thought he'd found the appropriate words, Haven's father cleared his throat and glanced between them.

"The timeline has not yet been changed."

Storm's heart sank. "Really?"

"No. The date and those events are bound. We higher demons have been attempting to decipher why, ever since you returned from the future," he revealed, facing Yael with a look of warning that Yael tipped their head at, clearly curious. "As far as we can tell, a magical battle will still take place in the evening. That has been decided."

That was Storm's greatest fear—that the Fates were determined that Rowan or Denver would die. Whatever the Fates had decided, they weren't ready to abandon whichever event killed both of the people he loved. Storm had to work harder to master necromancy so he could resurrect them.

"Brilliant," Storm muttered, wondering when he'd have time to focus on necromancy amongst the other shit he had to do.

"Sarcasm," Yael said, his focus on Haven's father, then he glared at Storm. "Such behaviour is unhelpful, youngling. This is good information to keep in mind. As long as we know what's meant to happen, we can prepare ourselves and make sure we are properly armed. There is no better armour than knowledge."

Storm wanted to curse them just for being so positive when he felt like the world was being tugged from beneath his feet.

Without noticing his contempt, Yael stared into the distance. "The final battle takes place on December twenty-third. If we can survive until Christmas with no magical incidents, we may count ourselves lucky and believe you have fulfilled the prophecy. Or will shortly."

The door opened before they could continue to reveal Kyrie walking in with a beaming smile and a tray piled with a plate of cakes and cups of tea. The smell of chocolate suggested he'd taken Yael's request of a hot chocolate to heart.

Ignoring the food, Storm focused on Yael's words. "Christmas is still a month away." Sixteen days had passed since he returned from the future and a whole hell of a lot of shit had happened.

"Five weeks and three days. Plenty of time for you to master necromancy," Yael replied with infuriating calm. Yael accepted a cup of tea from Kyrie and a cake, then offered Haven's father something from the tray. Kyrie walked around the bed and placed a cup and a plate on the bedside table beside Storm's chair.

He ate the three cupcakes, surprised by how hungry he was. Though the Christmas decoration on the icing was hideous, the cakes were delicious. By the time he'd gotten halfway through his mug of hot chocolate, he was ready to get back to work.

Storm cracked his knuckles and reached for Haven's hand, warm and flushed pink with renewed life, but still the pale body of Donald James Glade. With a push of magic to test the waters, Storm found his magic welcomed. Haven's will had grown strong during the short break since returning to his body.

Storm located the dirty brown thread of the curse Gladys had laid on his body. The glamour was sick, breaking down since DJ's spirit had left and Haven's had returned, like the curse had never been intended to be used over such a long time.

Tracking back to the centre connective point in Haven's brain, Storm gave a tentative tug with his magic and found the curse flaked away without effort, falling to the imaginary floor of Haven's mind. Determined to remove every last trace, he pulled, tugged and picked at every scabbed, rusted piece of dark magic left. It was a laborious job, but not otherwise taxing for his magic, which relished pulling the spell to pieces, as if the curse and its failure to endure was an affront to dark magic.

The sickness came away easily. When Storm was done, a pile of rotting black magic lay at the base of Haven's brain, weak and too tired to fade away. Fashioning his magic, the way he used to when he spoke to the wind, he blew on the flakes of the curse waiting to be disposed of. They transformed into slivers of pure magic and became absorbed by his spiritual presence, where his magic obliterated the pieces rather than assimilating them into his powers. He didn't want any part of the curse to survive.

Retreating from Haven's mind, Storm blinked to find the light in the room had changed. A glance over his shoulder at the window which showed a storm brewing and rain pitter-patting against the window. "Thank the gods," he muttered, dragging a hand over his face. "I thought it was night already."

"It is shortly after noon," Yael said, letting him know he'd spent a hell of a long time inside Haven's head. "You took twice as long to break the curse as to call on Haven's spirit. It is not ideal but proves you are more skilled with your necromancy than during your last lesson."

Storm rolled his eyes at the thought that this was being used as an unplanned teaching moment. He shouldn't have been surprised. "I guess that's good." Turning his attention to Haven, he saw the albino boy who had lain there when he drifted into his magic had faded away. The boy was clearly a demon; rich, honey skin and wheat-coloured hair in the lanky stage of being between a child and an adult; his little hands were long-fingered, with matte-white fingernails. The only deviation from what Storm was used to was the sapphire-blue paint at the tip of each talon.

"Blue?" he asked Yael, while Haven's father rushed to his now recognisable son and muttered words of comfort to the sleeping demon.

Yael made a face, something between a frown and a thoughtful pout. "A curious deviation," they agreed, glancing at the father demon and eyeing him appraisingly. When they saw no sign of an explanation, Kyrie nodded and pressed a finger to his lips with a pointed look at the demon father.

Storm nodded his agreement, while Yael began a one-sided staring contest with Kyrie.

They waited for Haven's father to express his relief and exclaim his joy before suggesting he take Haven to the safety of his horde. Though the boy hadn't woken, Storm had seen how much the curse had taken from his soul and advised his father that Haven might not wake for hours. He would need to rest and heal for a long time before he could be the boy demon they'd last seen.

Despite the promises made in gratitude by Haven's father— to owe Storm his allegiance and the assistance of his horde whenever he called, no matter the reason—Storm waved him away with promises never to call in the debt. He would have helped anyone in Haven's position, and he didn't need a demon horde at his beck and call.

When Haven and his father had been politely herded through to the abyss and out of Rowan's spare bedroom, Storm sank onto the bed and lay staring at the ceiling. "I think I'll sleep for a week."

"Kyrie," Yael said, the word enough of a reminder that Storm sat up and gave the nervous demon the signal to speak.

Kyrie nibbled his bottom lip and eyed Yael with caution.

"There is talk of a demon child who is special, in the same way as the Dark One: a prophecy child of demons," he explained, glancing between them as if afraid of their reaction. "He will be the guide who brings the Dark One to his true power and will become a leader of demons in the way the Dark One will become the leader of witches and mages."

"I've heard nothing of this," Yael snapped with a mixture of arrogance and hurt pride. Perhaps because they didn't have this important knowledge to make them more powerful. Storm suspected Kyrie having not yet shared the information with them after they'd grown so close may be the problem.

"Technically, no one believes the prophecy," Kyrie admitted, with a faint shrug. "My...Auden...discovered the information when he was a young boy. I'm not sure any demons would know of the rumour, only dark mages." He dropped his gaze to the floor, looking and sounding guilty for not sharing this information sooner.

Storm would have to have a word with Yael about those unspoken accusations in their tone and how they were naturally intimidating to demons like Kyrie, who didn't know Yael was a pussycat beneath the outer veneer. "Knowledge is power, right? The mages don't want demons having the power of this knowledge?" he guessed, helping Kyrie explain now that he understood better.

"I would suspect so."

Yael tapped their talons against the dresser they stood beside. "That would suggest you were meant to meet Haven, both in the future and this present. You are equals, the opposites to each other. He is destined to be the Leader of Demons and you are the Leader of Magic," they said, eyeing Storm with interest. "Perhaps this suggests the title you've been desperately resisting is fated."

"Which is?"

"Master of Demons," Yael replied, their teeth on display in a grin so menacing Storm would once have rolled his eyes. "You believe such a title will force you to treat us as chattel, but this new development suggests more. In this case, master does not mean you will dominate us or use us as servants, but the other meaning of the word."

"What's that?" The word master in this context meant two things—teacher or leader. He wasn't prepared to accept the role of either.

Yael pushed from the dresser and folded their arms, their self-satisfied smirk never wavering. They replied with a word that had never flitted past Storm's understanding of the word master but that gave him so much relief he was rendered speechless: "Champion."

Chapter Twenty-Six

One Week Later
November 23, 2026

"ARE YOU SURE you're not just thinking the worst because this is the day you expect everything to go wrong?" Foley asked, glancing over his shoulder as they walked.

Storm wanted to smack him because they'd agreed they wouldn't mention what this day was meant to be since they'd only tempt the Fates. "I'm telling you," he replied, glancing at Rowan who walked by his side, hand in his. "I woke up feeling sick, and Yael suspects my magic is warning me. We're going to check in the hope that I'm wrong." He genuinely wanted to be wrong, because if he wasn't, this would be a day he'd never forget.

Rowan was tense beside him, and Storm wasn't sure what

was worse: Cesa reverting to the curse or that this was the day Rowan died, according to the future they were fighting against. Storm couldn't bear to stand by and do nothing. He was willing to try everything possible to prevent his death, which meant going to the shack and checking on Ithen.

"He's right. We should know what we're dealing with," Denver said, nudging Foley and linking an arm through his.

"*You* shouldn't be here!" Foley replied without hesitation, still pissed that Denver wouldn't keep his distance.

"Neither should you."

Storm couldn't blame Foley for being annoyed, because if this was the day Rowan was meant to die, then Denver was equally at risk of repeating the future. But Denver wasn't wrong either. The best way to keep Denver safe would be for Foley to keep his distance and distract him, but the fact he'd shown up at the house meant there was no way he could stop Denver from following.

Storm looked over his shoulder. "Both of you need to stop. Neither of you should be here, but I know you'd follow whether we wanted you to or not." He sighed, hoping he wouldn't need to listen to their bickering until they reached Adam's Grove.

"I don't see why the demon couldn't have done this," Foley muttered.

Denver groaned and removed his arm from Foley's to walk by Rowan's side. "Geez, if you can't say something nice, shut up."

Storm decided just to explain to stop the bickering. "Yael can't go wandering off to the abyss whenever they want. If they go through, they could be there for hours or days. Time works differently in the abyss," he explained, not for the first time over the last few weeks. "You should know that." Even if Denver didn't understand, Foley should have understood the abyss and its limitations.

They managed three steps before Denver piped up, "I still don't understand the logistics."

Rowan huffed in exasperation and shot Storm a glance. "*Do you think we can ditch them somewhere between here and the shack?*" he asked, utilising the mind-speak they'd shared during his ascension.

Storm figured they hadn't needed the ability since then because they'd never spent a day apart. "*I'd love to, but you know they're like puppies... They'd follow us anyway.*"

"The abyss acts like a holding station between our world and the others. Heaven and hell, if they exist, would need you to stop off in the abyss first," Storm added to help Denver relate the method to something he understood. "Demons linger there, meet up and pass through the abyss like it's the front lobby of their office. Folks like me drop in from time to time to collect magic and leave, like a video game entry level."

Denver made the *aah* sound and stared at Storm with worried eyes. "Why do you go through when you ascend?"

"We don't," Rowan admitted with a chuff of laughter. "Those of us with dark magic in our families go into the abyss as a way of proving our worth and that we can handle being surrounded by dark magic. The whole of the abyss is made of dark magic, so it's the perfect place to 'collect' our magic when we ascend," he explained, offering Storm a consoling smile, probably because he knew what Storm had been through. Storm loved how Rowan could make him feel like he wasn't alone.

Denver looked past them to Foley. "You didn't go through on your ascension?"

He proudly shook his head and dug his hands in his pocket, the centre of Denver's attention. "Nope. White witches get sucked into a vortex of white and magic, spat out again a second later. We're decidedly *not* dramatic," he confessed, giving Storm a light shove. "Not like this one."

They all laughed because Storm's ascension was the exception to the rule.

"Just remember that's the 'dark one' you're shoving around," Rowan remarked, not bothering to look at Foley as they came within a few feet of the shack. "He had a horde of demons offering to be his pets a week ago. He may decide to accept and send them after your dreams."

Foley shivered at the teasing. "No thanks. I have *never* and don't intend to *ever* have anything to do with demons."

The temptation to warn him that worse creatures lurked in the abyss rose in Storm, but he knew better. Being ignorant about demons wasn't Foley's fault. His parents were old-fashioned and thought anything that wasn't pure white magic should be forbidden.

"It is too late."

Foley's face instantly paled on hearing Yael's voice, and he flinched so hard he nearly jumped out of his skin.

Storm dissolved into laughter along with Rowan, while Denver did a damned good job of hiding his behind the press of his lips. "Yael, if you give him a heart attack, I'm the one who has to resurrect him," he warned in case Yael intended to have fun with Foley now they knew his opinions about demons.

Yael stepped out from behind Foley, directly in their path, to bring the group to a halt. "Kyrie made a short trip this morning and returned with a message from Haven," they revealed, the serious look in their eyes and the presence of their cane in one hand causing the hairs on Storm's neck to stand on end. "We have a problem."

Storm nodded and waited to hear what had gone wrong this time.

"The message began with a code Haven claimed that only you would understand. *I feel them in my bones. The house is in pain. If I don't help, the spirits will hurt me.*"

Hearing the words recalled the image of Haven in DJ's body from the future, the fear in his eyes and the shake of his voice. "Yeah." He nodded to let Yael know that he agreed the message was from Haven.

"The message itself is more of a warning," Yael confessed awkwardly. "The boy says, 'To master necromancy, you must feel inside yourself, push aside other emotion and focus on one distinct memory of the person you are resurrecting.' If you call to them the way you called his spirit, then you will succeed."

Storm realised Haven's words had arrived on the day he'd most need them. He may be a demon child, but Haven must have realised Rowan would die today, and Storm hadn't had the time or training to master his necromancy despite trying everything Yael had taught him. "You don't sound convinced."

"This is not how I have experienced necromancy. Kyrie also agrees this is not how the procedure is usually performed," Yael admitted with a reluctant uncertainty. "However, you are exceptional in power and have accomplished feats I have never seen. You have accepted your place in the world and have a natural affinity for the undead. This boy may know your heart in the way you know his."

Storm cleared his throat when Rowan raised an eyebrow. "We didn't...do that."

"No, but you touched his soul, and he touched yours, which is the same, only much more dangerous," Yael said, without the usual censure over the risk he'd taken. "I believe we can trust his word on this matter if he truly is your equal and the Demon Lord to your Dark Mage."

"All right." Storm was pleased they'd decided to trust Haven, and this wouldn't be yet another argument about boundaries. "I'll keep that in mind." Even if he didn't understand what the hell Haven's warning meant, Storm wouldn't cast the words aside. Without Haven, he wasn't sure the spell to send him back in time would have even worked.

As Yael said, knowledge was a weapon, and Haven had given him a way to resurrect Rowan if the worst happened.

Haven's words stayed with Storm the short distance to the shack. When he saw the door hanging off the hinges and the shattered glass on the ground, he knew Ithen had escaped or been let loose. They didn't need to go any further to know Ithen wouldn't be inside, but Yael stormed through the mess of broken wood with Kyrie hot on their heels.

Storm didn't dare go inside. He knew what they would find and didn't need to see. He could feel Rowan practically shaking beside him, their hands still connected, and he wasn't letting go. "I won't let him hurt you."

Rowan swallowed and shook his head. "I'm not sure you have any say."

The frank honesty of the words made his heart stutter. He gripped Rowan's hand and stepped chest to chest, nose to nose with him. "I will *not* let him hurt you. He won't even touch you." Storm had taken too long to realise that while he was looking at Rowan, believing they were mortal enemies and could never be together, Rowan had been staring back and thinking the same. He wouldn't waste any more time.

The sound of footsteps joined the touch of a hand on his back and Yael's voice. "Ithen is gone. Kyrie can scent Gladys's twisted magic around the shack. She must have scried for him." The unspoken confusion that said Yael had no clue how that had happened didn't need to be said aloud. Storm knew the efforts they'd exerted to make sure Ithen was safe and undetectable to Gladys and would never be a threat to them. They'd done everything but bind his magic. Yael had wanted to kill Ithen as demon logic for how to remove an obstacle. Storm just didn't have the capacity for murder—not in this lifetime anyway.

"Hey." Rowan tipped his head until their noses brushed. "We'll figure this out. Now she's freed Ithen, we should be able to find him easily. We know what's going to happen, so we have an advantage."

"We should go to your house." Storm pulled away to glance at the worried faces. "Ithen will need to recover. We have a few hours before he'll go after Cesa and the spell. He might head to my house for the amulet." They couldn't waste any more time learning or searching or being the better person. They couldn't be distracted, no matter what they learned or how strong Yael became. They had to go on the defensive before Ithen brought the inevitable fight to their door.

Beside them, Denver clutched at Foley's hand. Storm crossed the first task off his now urgent to-do list. "You two need to leave. Neither of you are safe as long as Ithen is walking about. Go to Foley's house, barricade yourselves in with magic, make sure your parents stay to protect you, and do *not* leave!" he ordered, watching them for signs of defiance. He wasn't against threatening to curse them if they didn't do as they were told when their lives were on the line.

Foley bobbed his head and pulled Denver's hand. As long as

they kept walking in the opposite direction, he wouldn't think to stop them. He only wished he could send Rowan with them.

"What do you wish to do first?" Yael asked, with a determined set of their jaw and a look in their white eyes that suggested they would follow him into hell itself.

Storm thought about his answer seriously. His first instinct was emotional: he wanted to find Gladys and shake her until the lies turned into truths and he knew why Ithen wanted the amulet. In reality, he knew why: power, the need to be greater than anyone else, to become the best, because stealing the power was the only way he could make that happen.

"We need to return to the manor to make Cesa talk sense, find out where the spell is, and get Rowan connected," Storm said, planning the process. "If he can become the protector of the spell and I have the amulet, we can use them or our combined place as guardians to fight Ithen."

No one had combined the amulet and the spell since they'd first been separated. No one knew if the best way to protect them was to use them or whether they had to break the amulet and destroy the spell so they could never be united. Destroying them would give Storm a huge sense of relief and satisfaction, knowing that no one else could use them, but he might end up losing his only weapon and bargaining chip.

"Kyrie," Storm called and found him lurking in the doorway of the shack. "Can you find Ithen? Locate him without letting him know?" He'd proven capable of finding others in the past, finding

Haven and helping to free DJ's soul.

Cocking his head, Kyrie turned his head to the sky and closed his eyes. When he met Storm's gaze, his eyes shone whiter than ever with a sliver of black smoke emanating from the edges. "Command me and I can do anything you ask," Kyrie replied, reminding Storm of one of the notes in Reed Hadley's book.

"Kyrie, Demon of Scent," he said, using the demon's full name, though his skin itched with wrongness. "I, Storm Tera, command you to find Ithen Deontay, betrayer to the master of demons."

With a bob of his head and a cruel smile to rival Yael's best, Kyrie backed away a single step and disappeared into the abyss.

Yael watched his departure and turned to Storm with a matching grin. "I never thought I would see the day," they teased, taking a half step and dipping low into an old-fashioned bow. When they straightened, they removed the suit jacket with a slight tail design and tossed it to the ground. "Command me, oh, master of demons."

Storm glanced at Rowan and nodded. "You're coming with us."

*

STORM FELT LIKE a badass hero from a movie as they marched to Rowan's home, intent on finding the lost spell, hunting Ithen, and resolving this prophecy business. Three steps from the mansion's front door, he tripped over his own feet, stumbled and only saved his dignity at the last moment because the wind buffeted him to stop him from landing on his ass. Embarrassed by his clumsiness, he was about to head for the house when Yael caught his arm and looked around.

The ringing of Rowan's phone made him flinch, until Rowan pulled his phone from his pocket with a frown. "I swear I put this on silent." In a rush of movement, he pressed a button and put the phone to his ear. "Dad, where are you? You were supposed to be at home."

Storm could feel the weight of the ominous phone call in his gut. Whatever Cesa said was irrelevant because there was only one inescapable outcome: Rowan's death.

"Dad, slow down. You're not making sense," Rowan complained, pacing as he listened, pressing a hand to his other ear to block out the wind. "You're with Ithen?"

Storm swore, realising how awful the news was. Proximity strengthened Ithen's hold over Cesa, and they still had no way to safely break the curse. Though Storm had helped Haven, the glamour had been old, made against a demon child, and Gladys was never meant to work dark magic. Ithen had been born to use dark magic, and there was no telling what else he was capable of.

Leaving Rowan to talk sense into his father, Storm racked his brain for any way to counteract the curse long enough to get a sensible answer from Cesa. Nothing he thought of would be safe because Cesa's mind was already showing signs of strain. If Storm pushed him, even by *easing* his curse too fast, the pressure could destroy Cesa's mind forever. He couldn't do that to Rowan.

"Come home. We can talk about everything when you get here, okay?" Rowan's voice drifted back into focus as he raised helpless, lost blue eyes to find Storm's.

Storm had to be strong enough for them all. While Rowan encouraged his father to return home, he headed into the manor. There had to be a way to find the spell without Cesa. He could call his dad and ask him, but he had a feeling if Asher had known where the spell was kept, he would have told them when he revealed the amulet's location. Cesa may have moved its hidden location during a rare moment of lucidity since Ithen first cursed him.

Being familiar with the house from the past few weeks, Storm felt confident he'd find the spell hidden somewhere in Cesa's study, the one place the man spent his time when not with Rowan or in his bedroom. Rowan had already started digging around in the attic, the safe in his father's bedroom, and the appropriate places they could access without his father growing suspicious. They hadn't had a chance to touch the study because Cesa was always in there, and they didn't want to tip off Ithen.

Yael had been the one to warn them against asking Cesa outright. Ithen could have taken precautions against Cesa revealing the location of the spell. Ithen had already proven intolerably cruel, and Storm wouldn't be surprised if he could escalate Cesa's insanity, or provoke him to murder his own son, just by planting a few words in his brain to be triggered by the discovery of the spell. They hadn't been ready to risk that, but now that Cesa was with Ithen, his sanity wasn't the only thing in danger. If the time came to decide between saving Cesa's sanity or Rowan's life, Storm already knew what he'd choose. Rowan had paid the price for his failure in one life, he wouldn't let it happen again.

"You believe you can find the spell, even though you are not a Copry?" Yael asked, following him into the room.

Storm stood in the doorway, taking in the mahogany wood panelling, the window on the opposite side of the room, and the desk on the left. His dad's study was bigger, but this was nice and cosy with an entire wall of bookcases. The likelihood of finding the spell amongst the papers in here was slim at best, and they'd need weeks to check every book for a sheet of paper.

"I figure I can at least try. I am supposed to be part of *every* coven, and that includes the Copry coven." He didn't care about the Fates or their plans. If Haven's father was right, Rowan was destined to die tonight, and the spell may be the only way to prevent it. Storm wasn't leaving this house until he found and reunited the spell with the amulet.

"You do remember you're not meant to unite them? You're meant to *prevent* them from being united."

"I don't give a damn what I'm meant to do," he snapped, heading for the desk to start opening drawers in the hopes of finding something out of place. "This is all I have that Ithen doesn't. He knows the magic I'm capable of and has more tricks than I can hope to learn in a lifetime. If I have any hope of preventing

Rowan's death, I need to find the damn spell. Will you please stop talking and start looking?" he asked, stopping when he realised he was breathless. He looked up to apologise to Yael and found Rowan standing next to them, his eyes sad and soft.

"*You* need to remember what Haven told you," Rowan said with authority, "while *I* search this place top to bottom."

*

THEY SPENT THE next four hours searching for the spell.

When Storm realised he wasn't being helpful because the spell wouldn't reveal itself to a Tera, he sat in the centre of the room and sent his magic searching for an anomaly. Yael sat in an armchair by the window, waiting patiently while running through the likeliest places to hide a spell.

Rowan searched every inch of the study, adamant his father would never trust an important item to another room.

Storm tried scrying and using his magic to find the spell, but that only irritated Yael when their cane vibrated to tell them the location of the amulet. Apparently magic couldn't tell the two apart.

The fact Rowan hadn't heard from his father since the search began, and the man hadn't returned home as planned, had them all on edge. No one understood what Ithen's game was, what he was doing with Cesa, or where they might be and why.

Yael grew more agitated the longer Kyrie was gone, concerned he'd run into trouble and couldn't call for help. He wouldn't defend his decision not to bond with Kyrie because Yael knew better, but the constant grumbles over the last few hours had run Storm's patience ragged.

"It's getting dark out," Rowan said, drawing Storm's gaze from the floor, where he'd sent his magic beneath the floorboards in a last-ditch search for the spell. Rowan stared out the window and sank into his father's desk chair. "We've been here for hours. I don't know where my dad is, and this is proving pointless!" In an understandable fit of pique, he shoved a pile of papers off the desk and yelped in pain.

Storm got to his feet, wincing at the ache and stiffness of being still for so long, and grabbed a tissue from the desk. "Hurting yourself won't help," he complained, walking around the desk. When Rowan held out his hand, the blood had pooled on the cut along the side of his palm. A drop fell onto the leather desktop which made Rowan groan and rush to clean up before the blood stained.

As Storm was about to suggest getting a plaster and abandoning their search in favour of finding Ithen and Cesa, Yael's hand shot across the desk to catch Rowan's wrist. "Stop."

Rowan scrambled up, pushing the seat from the desk and rising to his feet as a faint shimmer of magic struck the desktop. He looked to Storm but he wasn't sure what was happening and watched as Rowan held his bleeding hand over the desk. A second drop of blood fell onto the leather padding of the writing desk; the shimmer spread and a ripple of magic made the top of the desk fade to reveal a plain wooden top and a single brass handle.

"Wow." Storm could barely calculate the amount of magic involved in creating what was essentially a hidden door.

Rowan pulled the brass handle, stumbling when his hard tug proved too much effort for the slick drawer. Six inches deep, the top of the drawer clicked and slid to the side on a spring, revealing a fingerprint pad. Rowan placed his hand the pad, but nothing happened. "Do I need to say something, like a password?"

Yael huffed and pressed the bloody cut to the scanner. "There is no safer way for a witch to protect their valuables—particularly a dangerous spell they have been tasked with guarding—than with blood," they explained, holding Rowan's hand in place to continue dripping blood. At the last moment, when Storm's patience had worn thin, the door clicked.

Yael released Rowan's hand and nodded.

They both watched intently as Rowan took the tissue from Storm's hand and covered his bloody cut, using his clean hand to open the door. He gasped and pulled out a scroll of antique paper.

"This is the spell?" Rowan said in disbelief, weighing the scroll in both hands.

A gust of wind rushed through the room, despite the windows and doors being shut tight in an attempt to keep Ithen from spying on them.

"I guess." Storm watched the wind swirl around Rowan and die away into nothing. "The wind is thrilled." He tipped his head to the side and put a fingertip in his ear to dispel the sense of his ear having popped.

Yael handed their cane to Rowan. "Place the paper inside. I cannot touch the spell, but perhaps I can protect what you entrust to me."

Rowan nodded, aware that no one would get past Yael. The cane was infused with their magic, and Storm doubted anyone else could even touch it. Rowan placed the scroll against the top of his cane and the secret compartment opened to reveal the amulet. The scroll floated from Rowan's hand and shrunk to fit into the hidden compartment of the cane, nestled beside the amulet.

"The two are connected. They belong to Storm now."

"Because he has all forms of magic, the Fates and the spell will recognise him as being part of all covens," Rowan said, apparently finding a logical conclusion.

Storm disagreed but the voices in the room had grown louder since the amulet and spell were reunited, and he wasn't sure he could shut them out much longer. He slapped his hand against his right ear to dislodge whatever sensation made him feel like he was underwater. "I can hear whispers, but it's not the wind."

The whispers stopped, the underwater feeling faded, but one voice remained, coming from the fireplace. Storm would have apologised for zoning out, if not for the last whisper and the chanting chorus of voices that picked up. There must be about twenty different voices. "They're all whispering the same words, apart from one. That one," he explained, pointing toward the flame now burning in what had been an empty grate. "*The two are now* connected. *Life and Death. Blood and Water. Guardian and De-mon.*

"That one's saying something different." Finally free of the horrible sensation in his ears, Storm faced Rowan and tried not to cry. This was a final warning that despite what they'd done, this would be the worst night of his life.

"*The half-demon will arise a light wielder, commander of the dead, the one who is made of light.*"

Rowan frowned, clearly not understanding yet. "Those are your titles." Beside him, Yael's eyes widened slightly, understanding dawning.

"You missed the important part." Storm couldn't say anything about Yael's hard gaze because the words spun around in his mind, and he couldn't get past the lump in his throat.

Arise. The half-demon will arise. *After* death.

As if that wasn't bad enough, the voice spoke again and tore his heart in two. The words fell from Storm's mouth, a mirror from before.

"*The Chosen One will kill the half-demon and will fail to be-come the Life-Giver.*"

Chapter Twenty-Seven

WHILE THE WARNING from the voices rang in Storm's mind, cautioning him that he could never resurrect Rowan because his death was inevitable, silence shrouded the room. He ignored Yael's heavy stare and the lack of judgement in Rowan's eyes with difficulty. Something monumentally life-changing was about to happen, and he couldn't do a damn thing to prevent it, despite being the Chosen One and harnessing the ability to control all magic.

A phone rang, disturbing the peace while Storm fought back the nausea rising at the thought of being responsible for Rowan's death, yet knowing with certainty that he would never bring him back. He'd been pinning all his hopes on resurrecting Rowan if anything happened, but to learn that he would never become 'the life-giver' meant that was a pipe dream. Rowan was meant to die tonight.

Why? Because Storm loved him, and a necromancer couldn't bring back someone they loved? Because he'd failed at everything necromancy related since coming into his powers? If so, what the hell was the point in being the Chosen One, the Dark One?

"Storm." Rowan's voice, full of confusion, captured his attention. "Your house is calling," he said, holding his phone out with a shaking hand.

When Storm took the device, his home phone number was displayed on the screen with the words, 'Tera House'. Putting the phone to his ear, he could hear a voice talking fast. "Hello?"

"Thank the gods," his dad replied, sounding panicked. "Don't talk, just listen. Cesa is here with Gladys, tearing the study apart in search of the amulet. Ithen just left."

The time for searching, learning, and thinking had dissolved in his hands. Storm had been distracted, his attention diverted from the real problem until the inevitable happened: he ran out of time. Just as in the future, the two biggest events of his life took place tonight—Rowan and Denver's deaths.

"I'm supposed to kill Rowan," slipped from Storm's mouth. Maybe he confessed because he was talking to his dad who would understand and could comfort him, or maybe because Storm was beginning to realise he was alone in this.

"What?"

"Nothing. Thanks for the warning but..." He was about to warn his dad that the information wouldn't help them defeat Ithen when a rush of air beat against the study window, followed by the flicker of a flame. "Ithen's here, at the Copry house. I have to go." He was about to hang up when he remembered to say what he hadn't the chance to all those years before. "I love you, Dad."

"Storm, I—"

Storm hung up, afraid his dad would only talk him out of doing what had to be done. This was what everything had been leading to. He'd done everything he could to live this life different to the future where he failed to fulfil the prophecy, but Haven's father was right—some fates were set in stone.

Knowing Rowan would go whether he wanted him to or not, Storm crossed to his boyfriend of a few weeks and held out his hand. "Let's do this together."

With sad eyes but a determined nod, Rowan took his hand and looked at Yael, who had walked to the window.

"Ithen has half of the Copry coven outside," they said, glancing back so that their eyes shone ominously in the flickering light. "There are people we have never seen. They may be from his coven, if one exists." Yael didn't seem concerned about being outnumbered or knowing Rowan would die tonight.

Rowan tugged his hand. "We can use the spell to activate the amulet. You're the only one who can use them for their original purpose."

Storm shook his head. "The whole reason they were separated was because they could be misused. It wouldn't be a war or a fair fight but a slaughter with no guarantee who would get hurt," he admitted, thinking of the ancestor of the original guardian who had misused the amulet. Women and children had been slaughtered because he didn't care about the consequences, because he craved power. "I don't know if I could resist or if the amulet would *use* me to cause more damage. What if the plan is to unite the amulet and spell and *that's* why you die? To rebalance the scales."

Storm had to face facts: if Rowan's death was inevitable, he couldn't risk adding his magic to the amulet's power. They didn't have enough information about the amulet and its powers, if his powers could be manipulated, or if he would become power hungry at the first touch. The amulet was far too dangerous to fall into anyone's hands. He'd much rather destroy the amulet, but it was his only bargaining chip right now.

Rowan looked deflated but didn't argue.

Storm had one more person to disappoint. Yael stared out the window at the mob waiting for them. "Yael, Demon of Wisdom."

Yael spun, their eyes wide with alarm and confusion, but Storm couldn't let them speak and interrupt him. He knew what Yael would do and what they would want, but he couldn't take the chance.

"I, Storm Tera, command you to leave me to guard the amulet and spell in the abyss until I call for you."

"Storm," Rowan protested, shaking his head in obvious disbelief. "You can't send Yael away."

"I have to." Storm didn't take his eyes off Yael as they stepped forward, only to pause and grit their teeth, their jaw tightening in anger as they realised they couldn't disobey his orders. They didn't have to speak because Storm saw the faint shimmer of light blocking Yael from coming closer.

With a half step back toward the window, Yael's white eyes glimmered with the onset of tears. "If you die, I will be trapped in the abyss forever." A single tear tracked their cheek. The silent words they couldn't bring themselves to utter—the *I need you, Don't die,* and *Take care of yourself*—were human emotions and not the single-minded selfishness natural to demons.

"If I die, you'll be free of my commands, released from my magic, and you can come back here to avenge me!" he countered, letting Yael know he didn't want to do this but had to. If he couldn't stop Rowan from dying, he could keep Yael safe, protect the amulet and the spell, and become the Protector of Demons in the only way that mattered. "Come back and kill Ithen. Protect Rowan and Kyrie, and make sure Haven does a better job of fulfilling his fate than I have."

Yael's gaze softened as they took one final step into the abyss, a second tear falling as they disappeared, dropping to the wooden floor where Yael no longer stood.

"I'd send you with them if I could, just to keep you safe," Storm confessed, gazing down at Rowan with worry. If he'd thought there was any way to keep him trapped in the abyss until this was all over, Storm would have, but Rowan was half-demon and wasn't bound to obey him the way Yael was.

Rowan squeezed his hand and brushed at Storm's cheek,

removing tears he hadn't realised were there. "We'll see them again. When it's safe for all of us."

He wasn't sure if they would. Storm nodded, about to suggest they face Ithen, when a shimmer of light drew his attention to the window. In a split second, his brain registered the ripple of magic that was the abyss opening up, but he had no time to put together a defensive spell before a talon ripped a hole through the air.

Tensing at the intrusion and the potential for attack, Storm moved Rowan behind him, watching the talon turn into a hand, an arm and a body. Kyrie fell to the floor, his foot escaping the darkness just before the abyss disappeared in a cloud of inky magic.

Clearly rattled, Kyrie glanced at the space in shock before lifting his head. "Thank the gods you're here," he said, pushing his hands to the floor as he struggled to rise to his feet.

Storm rushed to help, dragging him up.

"Ithen is determined you're not escaping," Kyrie said, taking deep breaths, as though he'd expended a lot of energy. "He's put a spell around the house to stop you from escaping to the abyss or anyone from coming to help you. I barely made it." He gestured to the doorway he'd forced his way through, as a warning of how close they'd come from being separated.

"Where have you been?"

"Ithen has been busy over the years. I managed to find him in Gladys's house, but those clowns stepped from the abyss and into her living room, so I stayed to find out who they were," he explained, gesturing at the window, where Yael had said unknown accomplices had joined Ithen. They had since become a mob, shouting insults and calling for them to leave the house.

War was coming faster than even the demons had anticipated.

Ignoring them, Kyrie kept talking, giving Storm the information he needed about the man they were about to face. "He's been living in the city since your parents died, building a coven. He's picked up stray witches and mages who stepped out of the boundaries created by their covens. He's made promises that they could do whatever they wanted as long as they deferred to his will," he admitted, though he didn't sound impressed. "A couple are cursed the way Cesa is. I think he needed their abilities and forced their compliance, but these guys are determined to kill you, gain the amulet for Ithen, and become the only people left in the world with magic."

"What about demons?" Rowan asked, drawing Kyrie's attention.

"They plan to drain us of our magic or enslave us," he said, digging into his right jogger pocket to remove a wrapped sweet. "The higher demons are in an uproar, because they wanted to come through with me to help you, but they're the ones who discovered this place is completely shut off from magic." He popped the chocolate treat from its wrapper into his mouth and chewed.

Storm didn't rush him, aware he would need to replenish his energies.

Swallowing the sweet, Kyrie picked up where he'd left off. "No one with magic can enter or exit the Copry or Tera property lines. I'm a lower demon and you commanded me to return, but no one else is coming and they are pissed," he explained, pulling another sweet from his pocket to pop into his mouth.

"You've changed," Storm noticed, sensing something about his stance and mannerisms that wasn't as shy and coy as when he left.

Kyrie frowned. "You know how mages gain their power from the abyss? We gain maturity and independence. That's why Auden didn't let me go in unless he was desperate. Technically, I've grown a few years in the time I've been gone."

"Cool." Storm mentally reminded himself to kick Auden's ass for keeping Kyrie from his natural growth. Shoving that aside, he focused on what awaited them outside. "I guess that means we're on our own, which I expected but...still sucks." He suspected the Sorrell and Lasym covens wouldn't help, but as long as Denver stayed with Foley, both would be out of harm's way and couldn't come rushing in to get killed.

"No offence, but you are the one always saying you're in this alone," Rowan reminded him.

"Yeah, but I didn't intend it to be some self-fulfilling prophecy shit," Storm protested, smiling at the sight of Rowan's bright eyes and sudden calm. "You know...whining. For my eighteenth birthday, I got a demon best friend, a mortal enemy, I was betrayed by the few people I trusted, found out my dead dad is a ghost..."

Rowan kissed his cheek. "You got me."

"And me," Kyrie chimed in, popping a third sweet into his mouth with a charming smile.

"Awesome. *Two* demon best friends." He was too tired to be happy, but the warm look in Rowan's eyes, even as they turned ice blue with a rush of emotion, was enough to rebalance him. "The boyfriend is sweet. The best damn birthday gift I've ever had."

Rowan shook his head, but his eyes agreed that they'd found each other when they most needed, and they wouldn't let go without a fight. "Come on. We can kick Ithen's ass, and that will make everything better. Like an early Christmas present," he teased, taking his hand to link their fingers.

They walked out of the study toward the front door, ready to face the mob of angry mages and witches waiting for them. Stepping outside, Storm's step faltered at the sheer number of people that easily surpassed Yael's previous count. Four men stood around the hood of a car to the left of the house, blaring high beams at the front door. On the right, to hem them in, sat Gladys's beat-up truck, though the woman herself was nowhere to be seen.

A faint breeze whispered a warning to Storm: *Six witches in the woods are strengthening the barrier.*

Storm couldn't send magic in thanks for the information, because he'd need everything he had to get through tonight in one piece, but he added to the mental logbook of their debts. With his index finger, he tapped Rowan's palm six times to let him know more bodies lurked in the woods and hoped he understood the signal.

Adding six made the total count close to twenty; four women and two more men stood straight ahead, loitering a few feet behind Ithen. He was dressed elaborately in a mimic of New Orleans voodoo: a black waistcoat over his bare chest, black trousers leading to bare feet, and a long black cane held in both hands, the white-tipped point on the ground, white round handle in his grasp. The top hat adorned with a single feather was an unfathomable addition along with the gaudy make-up of white face paint, a skull mimicked by black around the eyes, nose and mouth. The fake stitches along his jaw and up to his ears was a pathetic, Halloween-esque caricature of voodoo. Everything about the cheap costume was an affront to Storm's heritage and every true voodoo practitioner, and only proved that Ithen knew nothing of *real* magic.

To Ithen's right, Cesa was being held by the arm by a young woman who looked like the Grace Glade from his future, but older and more confident. Her tight grip said she wasn't just supporting Cesa in his confused state, but literally holding him captive. Storm counted him as both a victim and a potential threat. If Cesa needed to be restrained to stay by Ithen's side, that implied the curse was wavering, and with that could go his sanity and his grip on reality as there was no telling where Cesa's mind was.

Taking them into account, Storm was left with two threats he could sense but not see, one of which was likely Gladys, attempting to stay out of sight. She probably wasn't aware that Storm knew about her involvement, since Ithen had been unconscious when Storm read his heart, but there was no telling what he might know or surmise from his captivity.

In the beginning, Storm had hoped Ithen would suspect Yael of being responsible for his capture and would believe Storm was nothing but a shocked, confused novice who'd done something well beyond his abilities by accident. If they believed that, he had an advantage, but that was pointless now. Gladys would be prepared to do what she'd always done—plan and execute her betrayal from a distance, then appear in time to clean up the mess and play the innocent when it didn't go to plan. He couldn't let her lie and manipulate them, only to walk away and have no one know what she'd done.

Right now, he couldn't think of any way to expose her that didn't involve being honest. So he opened his mouth and challenged Gladys to show courage and admit her complicity for the first time in her pathetic life. "Come out, Gladys. I know about your plot with Ithen," Storm called, refusing to play their game of lies. He stopped six feet from where Ithen stood, glad Rowan remained in step with him. Kyrie took two paces forward with a slightly crooked smile that said anyone would need to get past him to reach them.

What sent a thrill through Storm was the flicker of Ithen's gaze toward Kyrie, no doubt aware this wasn't the same demon who had held him captive and come to Storm's aid. The shock and anger that lit Ithen's eyes was all the better for realising that he thought Storm had bonded two demons and was only now realising how powerful that made him.

Chapter Twenty-Eight

THE SOUND OF a car door opening made heads turn. Gladys stepped from her truck and straightened her gypsy skirt before slamming the door behind her. With confidence, she crossed to Ithen but placed herself in front of him, another sign she was the true power between them.

"How did you find out?"

Storm nodded at Ithen, feigning confidence. "I read his heart and saw everything you've been plotting: kidnapping a demon child, cursing DJ, murdering my parents," he recounted, letting her know the specifics in case she thought he was bluffing.

The three men at the car exchanged indecipherable words and curious looks. In less than a minute, the three young witches realised they were in over their heads. Clearly, they wanted the rule-breaking that came with being in Ithen's coven but hadn't signed up for murder.

"Demon tricks!" Gladys spat as if disgusted by the idea.

"You would know. You've had more dealings with demons than I have," he reminded her in case her followers had a healthy fear of demons and refused to get involved. "I admit, I've learned a lot from mine. You scared them away a long time ago, but they will always return to me, just as I'll always find them." He gave her a moment to let that information sink in, to worry and wonder where Yael was, since they obviously weren't standing by Storm's side. Then, after almost two interminable minutes of silence, he added the final blow. "We freed the demon child and set DJ free," he said, needing to see if she cared.

With a glare, Gladys held her hand out to Ithen and turned her wrist sharply. Cesa immediately cried out in pain and sank to his knees, forcing the woman holding him to dip or release him. She was too smart to disobey her orders, so she sank to one knee and held on tight, while sparing a confused glance at Gladys.

Beside him, Rowan was tense and ready to move but holding just as still as Storm because they'd agreed that curing Cesa would only come *after* the war was won and Ithen was dealt with. Until then, they couldn't safely break the curse holding him captive.

"You can use all the demon tricks you like—" Gladys warned, flicking her gaze at Kyrie before meeting Storm's gaze. "—but we both know I'm the one with the power." The arrogance was sickening but proved Gladys hadn't changed one bit from the woman who had raised him. She was still predictable.

Feigning a frown, Storm tugged on Rowan's hand, like he was being held back, glad Rowan played along and pretended to tighten his grip. "You dare to look me in the eye when you *murdered* my parents?" he questioned, almost relieved to see the smirk on her face that was as good as any confession. "You raised me! You made me think I could trust you."

As expected, she shrugged and crossed her arms, eyeing him with disdain. "I had no hand in killing your parents. I simply cleaned up Ithen's mess when his temper got the best of him," she admitted, tipping her head at Ithen while he stood staring at her in surprise. The fact he was taken aback by her candour and that she would willingly blame anyone but herself only proved Ithen didn't know Gladys like he'd thought.

"You're going to throw the blame on Ithen, like you do every other time?" Storm wanted to be clear, in case Ithen had any illusions about her loyalty. He shook his head and added another dig at the age-old wound lurking beneath the surface. "Say what you want, but we both know he's the one pulling the strings. You're just the old hag with the demon slaves and a photographic memory."

"Maybe best *not* to piss her off," Rowan whispered in warning.

"Trust me." He knew Gladys better than anyone and that was her own doing. By taking him in and raising him like a son—just as unloved as DJ and Haven had been, left to grow as a wild weed rather than given any tender care—Gladys had exposed her greatest weaknesses. She hated nothing more than thinking some-one else had bested her or proven her useless; she couldn't abide being the last to know something or to not notice what was happening right under her nose.

Storm had a lot to say that would push her towards her breaking point, but he was smart enough to head straight for the jugular the first time. "All you're capable of is summoning demons. You couldn't even keep DJ safe. You had to kidnap a demon and put DJ's soul into a demon body." He made sure the disgust showed in his voice.

Gladys let loose in anger.

Prepared, Storm curled around Rowan, pulling him two steps to the side, out of harm's way from the fire spell. Though he heard Rowan's distinct tut, probably aware Storm had provoked her on purpose, he didn't judge. Storm released him with an apologetic smile, relieved Gladys was on the offensive, losing her temper and growing reckless. He hadn't even started with the heavy blows.

"Gladys!" Ithen shouted, spurred into participating in this farce of a showdown and grabbed her arm. "Behave yourself."

The demand went unhindered as Gladys shrugged him off with a scowl. She tossed her long fringe over her head and met Ithen's gaze in a silent warning that she wouldn't be ordered around.

While they squared off, Storm gave Rowan a nudge and tipped his head toward the car, where the three youngest mages were walking away. He didn't need the whispers of *Betrayers* from the wind to tell him they wanted no part in this.

Rowan heaved a relieved sigh and nodded, squeezing Storm's hand to show he was still supportive of his plan to pit Gladys and Ithen against each other. Just as his dad had suggested when he advised how to tackle a multi-threat, Storm planned to divide and conquer.

Storm's first plan had been to target Ithen next, but Gladys was still riled up and Ithen had always been the cooler head. By reacting, Gladys revealed who had the upper hand and who was the easier target. Ithen gestured to a woman nearby, who handed him a pouch, so Storm left them, not sure whether to act first or find out what they were doing. He could smell the salt and sage, even detect the intent to use the mixture.

He decided to take one more shot at Gladys, to buy time and gather more information. He knew who would strike first from the young witches and mages who had followed Ithen here, who were likely to run rather than fight, and who were cursed to follow Ithen's will. 'Know thy enemy' had been his mother's only, and best, lesson in magical warfare.

"I never thought I'd see the day when you let someone else boss you around, Gladys. Times have changed," Storm goaded, making sure to stare at Gladys so she couldn't avoid the contempt he felt.

Ithen shook his head, probably aware Storm was taunting her on purpose. Gladys glared at Storm as though he was a mere irritant. She turned and tucked her hands tight to her chest, pulling at the air with clawing fingers. When she made the first crack in the thin layer between this world and the abyss, Storm's hopes skyrocketed.

Once a visible tear appeared in the abyss, Gladys raised her hands into the air. "Demon horde, come forth and serve me as I command," she called, clearly having lost her mind or else she was playing up the role of the mighty, powerful witch for the youngsters, because Storm had never seen a true dark mage work so ostentatiously.

Ithen spared a huff for the old woman, apparently just as unimpressed by her performance, and focused on the pouch he was muttering over. Neither saw Kyrie glance at Storm and, on his nod of approval, edge around the side of the group.

"Predictable, as always. All I have to do is mention DJ and you lose your shit," Storm goaded, while Rowan kept his attention firmly focused on his father, who was still kneeling by the young woman, and refusing to rise to his feet. As agreed, Rowan was waiting for his moment to rush in and get his father to safety, leaving the dangerous work to Storm, who as the Chosen One had more resources at his disposal. Selfishly, he hoped their plan would keep Rowan at a safe distance.

The one thing that worried him was how Cesa was sitting; was he faking his weakness while he waited for a moment to dart away to freedom, or was he truly hurt by that malicious little bitch who kept tugging on him? Or, was this the worst case, that he'd lost his mind and simply didn't care that he was sitting in the dirt and muck?

Storm bought more time while Kyrie got into position, deliberately hitting Gladys's weak spot with something he'd learned when he was inside Haven's body, putting his soul back. "You know what, Gladys? Your DJ was an evil shit. He used to kick animals and beat the kids at school. He was a violent little bastard, and I'm glad he's dead."

"How dare you!" Gladys screamed, her eyes turning an unnatural black, as though nothing remained of her but the twisted, dark magic she'd stolen from others. Raising her arms, she chanted in a high-pitched scream, "Demon horde! Come to me!"

Ithen turned with an exasperated mutter of her name and froze as a chilled wind roared through the open and expansive driveway.

The split separating this world from the abyss grew larger, and ghostly hands that Storm was sure only he could see began pulling at the tear from the inside. Whatever Gladys had wanted to come through, she'd gotten more than she bargained for. The spirits he'd freed from her home reached their hands through the void, desperate to reach the woman who had cursed their souls.

"Come to me!" Gladys screeched, unprepared for the taloned hand that broke through the tear, leading to a pale arm. The talon slid over Gladys's shoulder, long fingers curled around the bone as an arm snaked out and wrapped around her waist. In a split second, the demon dragged Gladys Glade off her feet and through the void of the abyss. The ghostly hands disappeared in pursuit of their victim.

Panic erupted within seconds, those nearest the tear so terrified of the thought of demons emerging from the abyss that they screamed and ran before Ithen could even gather his wits. He wasn't reckless, however, grabbing Cesa's arm and dragged him to his feet, where he instantly placed a protective barrier around them.

Storm was about to tap into his magic to undo the barrier and, hopefully, give Rowan a chance to rescue his father, when a knee-high stiletto boot stepped through the tear in the abyss. The boots led to tight, black shorts, a black striped waistcoat that ruffled around an elegant neck, and an angry grimace over blazing white eyes.

"Bugger." Storm cocked an eyebrow at Yael, while Rowan stifled laughter behind his hand, both silently staring at the demon to ask what the hell they were doing back here, without outwardly admitting this had never been part of the plan.

Yael tossed their long white hair, currently tied into a fishtail, over their shoulder. They lifted what looked to be a scythe the length of a sword to point at Storm, the unspoken accusation that he was in deep shit quite clear. "I obey *no* mage!" They planted the tip of the scythe in the ground and cocked a hand on their hip. "I *do* protect my friends."

Storm heard Rowan's breathless, relieved laugh against his neck and added his own. However pissed he was, Yael was a godsend—and a gift from the Fates. He wouldn't want to do this without them.

Before he could thank Yael for returning, especially at such an opportune moment, their face slipped from amused to concerned and they spun to gaze into the forest. With an expertly crafted eye roll, Yael lifted their scythe to point at the trees. "Your brainless friends are rushing headlong into battle with no weapons," they said, taking charge before Storm could process the words. Yael whistled, a sound that instantly stopped Kyrie's progress toward Ithen. Like an obedient puppy, he stood still, his spine straightened, and he spun to face Yael with a grin. "Human and white witch."

Kyrie offered a cheeky salute that made Yael smile and took off to follow their orders.

Storm stood frozen, speechless as he tracked Kyrie's movements to find Denver hiding at the edge of the treeline. Foley was already throwing a spell at one of Ithen's followers, who had probably heard Yael's warning or been about to attack Foley when they were caught by the demon.

Storm focused on Yael, since Kyrie had everything in hand. "As my friend, I ask you to make sure they don't get themselves killed. As the Chosen One, please tell me that *you-know-what* is far from here?" he asked, because protecting the amulet and spell had been the whole purpose of sending them away.

"In time and space," Yael replied, stepping closer, where they decided to take Storm's hand and link their fingers. "I entrusted

384 | Elaine White

our fate to someone I would trust with my life, who will return my cane in a week when we play dress-up." The whispered words almost brought tears to his eyes as they shared a secret Storm had never even thought to consider.

He'd given the amulet back to Storm, all the way in the past, when they were children playing together, right under Asher Tera's nose. "Thank the gods."

Yael's eyes crinkled with amusement as they released his hand and cupped his cheek. "Not the gods. The Fates," they corrected, shaking their head and taking a step back. "They are on your side. When I stepped into the abyss, the door to our past was open. All I had to do was cross the threshold."

"Chances are, they didn't do this only to let me get killed." He almost laughed in relief. There was still too much at risk and no guarantee that the Fates would protect everyone else he loved. Turning, he found Rowan watching him with sad but hope-filled eyes. Storm knew the risks, but he ignored the chaos around him to bask in the moment and kissed Rowan. This may be their last chance.

Rowan grasped his jumper and held him close, as if to prove a theory Storm had come to in the last few days: the soft, slow kisses were so much sweeter.

A scream broke the moment, and Storm forced a smile as he prepared to do something he didn't want to. "Protect your father, and I'll get to Ithen," he said, knowing in his heart that something awful was about to happen. He didn't want to separate from

Rowan, to let him out of his sight, but in case he was the reason Rowan died tonight, they should stay far away from each other.

Even as Rowan nodded and stole a last kiss before rushing off toward his father, Storm watched him with a heavy heart. He hadn't done much right since returning from the future. He'd tried to change everything and still ended up in the same place, but this was one thing he could do.

He could *not* kill Rowan and make damned sure no one else killed him either.

Chapter Twenty-Nine

A DAGGER FROZE two centimetres from Storm's face. His hands shook from the effort of using quick-thinking magic to stop himself from being impaled. Until now, all magic use had been practised, familiar and well-intentioned. War made all those lessons obsolete; there was no time to think on the battlefield, only react. Catching the dagger was a close call, but Ithen was a nasty piece of work. He had six daggers, all spelled to follow his muttered commands while he hid safely behind Gladys's truck, with Cesa shoved into the front seat and locked inside.

Rowan had been an arm's reach from rescuing his father from Ithen's clutches when the mage magically lifted Rowan off his feet and threw him against a tree. Despite the crack of a bone breaking, Rowan managed to stand and counter-attack to cover his retreat to a place of safety.

Whatever the curse had done to Cesa, nothing could erase his fatherly instincts; the moment Rowan was attacked, no curse could stop him from getting to his son or attacking Ithen in an attempt to protect Rowan.

For those precious few moments, Ithen had been forced to fight three mages—Cesa, Rowan, and Foley—with Storm rushing along the six-foot space between them to add his magic to the attack. Then the daggers wove through the air, and he was cut off.

In two minutes, Ithen had bought time and space. He'd run to safety, trapped Cesa, who was too weak to fight back, and sent his daggers after Rowan and Storm, effectively separating them.

Taking a moment to breathe and recover his energies, Storm looked around the unlikely war zone. Haven's father had wrapped a strong hand around the neck of one of Ithen's minions, off to the left, squeezing the consciousness from the cursed mage. He tossed the limp body aside and moved on to find another target.

At the treeline, Foley and Kyrie fought back-to-back against three witches who had cornered them. Yael held onto Denver with one arm and used their scythe with the other, wisely choosing to protect the one who didn't have magic, even if that meant leaving Foley vulnerable.

Knowing he couldn't do anything for his friends, Storm reached into the magic surrounding the dagger facing him and unravelled the spell. Once adapted to his will, he wrapped a hand around the handle to hold by his side. The dagger made a vicious weapon with a sharp, long point but he wanted the spell.

Storm ducked behind the car on the furthest edge of the front lawn to the house. He felt drained and exhausted but didn't have the luxury of resting. Focusing on the spell he'd unravelled, Storm gave a short sharp whistle. The wind grazed his cheek with a curious caress, wondering why he'd called on them in a way he never normally would. "I need your help," he whispered, struggling to slow his breathing and heart rate. "I'm going to do something you won't like, but I need you to work with me, okay? I need you to bring the fog and buy me a clear path to the truck." He nodded toward Gladys's truck, where Cesa was frantically pulling at the inner door handles and kicking the windows in an attempt to escape. He wouldn't, because Ithen had trapped him with magic, but the man had little-to-no sanity left.

With a ruffle of his hair, the wind raised the leaves that littered the lawn. It was hard to keep his eyes open with the strength of the wind, leaves blowing in his face.

Kyrie dragged Foley into the cover of the trees, smart enough to anticipate that Storm was controlling the weather and could be trusted to handle the situation. Rowan ducked behind the trees at the side of the house, too far away to help. Mages lurked in the trees, and Yael had amassed the few demons who had come through the abyss to surround Denver, pushing him against a wall that separated the parking spaces from the garden to keep him safe.

Once Storm was sure they were all safe, he gave the wind the signal to do its worst. The fog rolled in around his feet, and he needed to push with every ounce of energy he had to fight the wind. Using the cover, Storm made his way across the expansive lawn to the truck. Not even the most talented elemental witch could have managed, but the wind had a soft spot for Storm.

When he reached the truck, he tucked the point of the dagger into the lock and slammed his right palm against the butt of the handle. Despite the pain, he couldn't stop, because only the combination of Ithen's magic from the dagger and Storm's will would get the damned door open. He used the force of every hit to reinforce his will. Black misty magic seeped through the lock into the truck, swirling around Cesa who was too busy kicking at the window to notice. When the magic returned and the dagger cracked the door lock in half, Storm was disappointed to find that Cesa was in worse shape than he'd thought. Ithen's curse was weakened but only because he was losing his mind from being under the curse's influence for too many years.

Storm held onto the fact he could still save Cesa, even if he couldn't save his sanity. He could remove him from Ithen's clutches, remove the curse, and reunite him with Rowan. It was better to be free and unstable than trapped and lucid.

Shoving aside the melancholy he didn't have time for, Storm opened the door. "Cesa!" he called as loudly as he dared, with the wind hopefully disguising the sound. When the man didn't acknowledge him, Storm reached into the truck and grabbed his ankle.

Cesa screamed and automatically kicked out, but when he

turned and saw Storm, he slipped into the front seat and followed him out the open door and into the open air.

Yanking the dagger from the door, Storm handed it hilt-first to Cesa. "Take this and follow the wind to Rowan."

Though Cesa stared at the knife, he took the weapon without protest. He could easily have turned on Storm, but he nodded and spoke with a voice made hoarse from shouting, "What are you doing?"

Not sure if that was a general question about his plans or genuine concern over Storm handing a dagger to a man with little sanity left, he shrugged. "The best I bloody can." He nudged Cesa into the wind, then drew upon his magic and replicated his recent trick of levitation. With the wind and the fog giving him a rare moment of serenity, Storm lifted Cesa off his feet and left him in the trusted clutches of the wind.

Their plan had worked for the short term. Time to figure out Plan B.

*

"THE DEMONS HAVE gone." Denver glanced over his shoulder, interrupting Storm's concentration as he created a new spell.

Of course the demons were gone; they'd helped thin the herd but wouldn't risk tipping the balance between Light and Dark magic by choosing a side. No one knew if the Fates were watching and what they'd do if the demons showed a preference, even for the one they were supposed to obey.

Haven's horde had arrived, probably to repay the debt they imagined existed between them. They would know the risk of facing Ithen but would also want a hand in retribution for the harm done to Haven. Thankfully, Storm also knew they would be smart enough to only do what was necessary, aware there would be no point of getting Haven back if his whole horde died in a war that wasn't any of their business.

"Do you see Rowan?" Storm asked to distract Denver, hoping to keep his attention on the main action. He worked with a few ingredients he'd managed to call from the main house, finally using Rowan's summoning charm properly, and hoped that Denver could see what was happening out there.

Denver ducked his head around the tree for a quick but clear view. "Nope." He sniffed and rubbed his arm against the cold of the late night. "I haven't seen him since you sent his dad." His voice didn't shake, but Storm could hear the worry and barely tamed panic. He was worried about Foley and probably hated not knowing what was going on as much as Storm. Reminding him that Kyrie was protecting Foley would have been pointless, because Denver didn't understand how important that was or how powerful Foley was as a white witch.

Storm glanced up to see Yael leaning against a tree, unmindful of the curses that Ithen kept throwing in their direction. Ithen knew where they were but was too afraid of exposing his position to get any closer, and the few mages working with him must have been keeping Rowan and Foley busy or they would have been back.

"The boy is right. The demons left because the followers are dealt with," Yael informed him, sounding thoughtful. "I count three dead and five who ran away. The others have been incapacitated. The numbers are in our favour, but Ithen is unnaturally powerful for a man of his lineage. I imagine he siphoned power from his followers or made a deal to gain more. He is certainly strong enough to wield the amulet."

Storm nodded at the warning but focused on adding the last ingredient to the spell. "I would say 'over my dead body', but I know you'll kill Ithen before he even gets a finger on the amulet to avenge me," he said, partly teasing because he'd already decided to break the damned amulet and destroy the spell if the only alternative was to let them fall into Ithen's hands.

With his spell complete, Storm lifted the ring he'd borrowed from Denver to show Yael, who nodded their approval.

"What's that?" Denver asked, frowning at what had been a replica ring from his favourite anime that he'd kept on a chain around his neck for years. The necklace had become a lucky charm because his favourite rugby team always won their games when he wore it.

Storm hoped for a different lucky charm tonight. "Something I learned from Reed Hadley," he confessed, unclasping the chain to slip around Denver's neck. He'd fashioned the ring to look like the amulet, hoping the disguise would last long enough to distract Ithen. Although Ithen had never seen the amulet, Storm didn't know if Cesa could have described it, and he'd rather be extra cautious. If Ithen attempted to use magic against Denver or the amulet, he would find his curse rebounded.

After setting the necklace over his top to remain clearly in view, Storm inspected Denver. He'd remembered to wear the protective bracelet Rowan had made him, meaning Storm's plan should go off without a hitch.

"We'll have to find that demon and thank him," he admitted, glancing at Yael with a smile, because he couldn't have managed this without Reed Hadley.

"Do you want his ungrateful nephews to know you have the family grimoire?" Yael shot back, pushing away from the tree and narrowly but effortlessly avoiding one of Ithen's better-aimed spells.

"I'll give them the book back...eventually."

Dusting off Storm's shoulders, Yael grinned. "You would have made a wonderful demon, youngling. So greedy for knowledge."

"Thanks."

"You two are weird," Denver shot over his shoulder, barely sparing them a glance.

Storm playfully patted him on the head. "Come on. Show off the necklace for me, and I'll buy you a new one if it gets damaged."

"You mean *when*," Denver complained, still muttering when he took the first tentative step out from the shelter of the trees.

Ithen stopped throwing spells and waited. Maybe he was afraid Denver was tricking him or that someone had disguised themselves as Denver. Storm wished he knew how to make himself look like Denver, then he wouldn't feel so guilty sending him out there as bait, even if the plan was to keep him far safer than the rest of them were about to be.

The pause gave them time, and Foley had the reckless courage to reveal his location, shouting at Denver, "Get back!"

Denver grumbled something Storm couldn't make out, but he didn't miss the slight twitch of his fingers, like he wanted to wave at Foley. He figured that meant the other witch was visible from his position. "Ithen," Denver shouted, sounding scared and nervous. "I have the amulet, so Storm said I-I'd be safe, but I'm willing to trade if you let Foley and me walk away without harm."

"What the hell, Denver?" Rowan shouted his protest, sparking an argument between him and Foley.

Storm wouldn't let their bickering bother him because he'd written this role and had his own part to play. He stepped out from the trees, as though this was all a surprise. "You're going to betray me?" he played along, grateful Denver had taken those acting classes two years ago for the school play. He was damned good at being the villain when he needed to be.

"This isn't my fight. I don't have any magic," he argued, gesturing around in proof of the danger. "I'm not dying for you."

Storm couldn't be more proud of him for having the guts to say those words to his face and mean them. He didn't want Denver to die for him either. He watched Denver face the open driveway and front garden of the Cesa property that had so recently become a war zone, showing no outward fear though he must have been terrified. Everything was now encased in the dark of night and empty of life but for their group and Ithen; the innocuous landscape becoming mysterious and full of the unknown with the lack of sunlight.

"Do you want the amulet or not?" Denver grabbed the ring around his neck as Storm had suggested.

"I'll take what belongs to me, yes." Ithen stood from behind the truck and turned his attention to Denver. A shimmer surrounded him, indicating a protective spell. "I think I'd prefer you and the amulet much closer to me." Extending his arm, he used magic to drag Denver toward him, his feet digging into the dirt as he was forcefully pulled across the ground, thankfully still standing.

Storm almost swore at the disappointment of Ithen not daring to use magic to summon the amulet, but he supposed that made sense. Ithen probably rightly theorised that if the amulet couldn't be summoned from its hiding place, then no magic could be used to manipulate or move it except the original spell. However, as a living thing and separate to the amulet, Denver could be utilised.

As soon as Denver was within reach, Ithen grabbed the amulet in one hand and tugged to break the chain from around Denver's neck. Though the plan hadn't gone as he'd intended, Storm was still hopeful that Ithen would be too busy studying the amulet to care about Denver, who was now surplus to requirements and in a much safer position to escape if an opportunity presented itself.

Denver glanced back at Storm, clearly confused by the changed plan. He gave Denver a discreet nod to the side, to remind him where he should go now Ithen was no longer interested, i.e., he should run like hell for the trees. He glanced back at Storm with a frown, then gave a determined nod. Without hesitating, Denver turned and ran for the trees, grabbed Foley's hand, and left.

A weird swell of pride filled Storm's chest as he saw Foley paused with Denver just long enough to glance at Rowan—looking stricken, confused and betrayed—before making brief eye contact with Storm. Foley knew what needed to be done, even if he felt guilty for leaving, and he didn't hesitate to turn and drag Denver deep into the woods, where they would find their way to safety, hopefully sooner rather than later.

Storm was glad Foley wasn't taking any chances that Denver's death might be as set in stone as Rowan's.

"I think I want insurance before I use this," Ithen said, so thoughtful and cautious that Storm didn't know what to expect. The eye contact across the distance between them didn't bother him half so much as the look Ithen gave him: not a smile or a grimace but stuck somewhere in between. He was ready when Ithen lifted his hand and blew smoke from his palm.

The expanse of ground between them, a good twelve feet, gave Storm mere moments to process the magic making its way toward him, long enough to realise the swirling cloud contained a death curse. This wasn't like anything he'd seen in his family grimoire but resembled a warning spell Reed Hadley had written about—a cruel and twisted curse intended to make the victim bleed internally, causing a slow but clean death that could take ten interminable minutes of agony.

Storm didn't dare move after the precautions he and Yael had taken. They wanted Ithen to hurt him, because any spell he sent would rebound off the second spell he'd spent so much time crafting, to match the one on Denver's ring. Storm had placed the secondary spell on his jumper, already a barrier between his skin and Ithen's spell—as Ithen was the type to aim for the heart—the curse would bounce off, rebound and hit Ithen.

Until now, he hadn't wanted to kill Ithen, but he couldn't let him walk away from this without paying for his crimes. People he cared about were at risk. If Ithen died because of his own curse, that was his problem.

Time slowed as the spell came rushing toward him, likely taking mere seconds for his thoughts to consider the options. Before he could fake an attempt to dodge or defend himself, movement from his left made him spin, panic flooding his veins. Rowan ran toward him, a hand outstretched with white magic crinkling the air, prepared to protect him from the curse. At the rate he was going, using demon speed, he would careen straight into the path of the curse.

Storm looked at Yael in hope they could help without foiling the plan, but they stared at Rowan with a look of dread that said not even Kyrie could reach Rowan in time.

This was the inevitable moment they had all been dreading.

Storm planted his feet to hold his ground, making sure the curse would hit him and only him, then rebound on Ithen as planned, and he raised a hand toward Rowan. With every ounce of will, hope and prayer he had left in his body, he screamed a single word, hoping the wind, the trees or the damned air itself would come to his aid: "STOP!"

The world froze, the wind stopped, and Rowan stilled mid-step.

In the blink of an eye, the entire world around Storm came to a standstill. Ithen's spell paused in mid-air; Cesa stood by the trees, with an arm outstretched and his mouth open in an attempt to stop his son; and Rowan remained frozen in time.

Storm blinked, but nothing changed. Dropping his hand, he looked at his fingers but saw nothing different. He raised his head and found Kyrie sporting a curious smile as he stepped from the cover of the trees. Kyrie looked like a child discovering snow for the first time, unsure at first, and then too intrigued to keep his distance. He poked his finger into Rowan's arm and laughed when Rowan didn't register the contact.

"Um...what happened?" Storm asked, relieved both demons could move, think and experience this, to prove he hadn't momentarily flipped out.

"No idea, but it's neat!" Kyrie shook his head and grinned at Yael.

"It's dangerous," they countered, crossing to stand in front of Storm with a raised eyebrow, as if he'd meant to do this shit.

"I did *not* know this would happen, but let's do something useful. Don't just stand there," he insisted, realising this was a perfect opportunity.

No one showed any signs of realising that time had stopped. They could stop the death curse from hitting Rowan and killing him. This was their chance to make a difference, to do something to win this fight without casualties.

Kyrie looked to Yael and shrugged a casual agreement. He walked over to Cesa, who had a full view of the current situation, and wisely lifted the man by the waist to move him into the cover of the trees. From there, he could still see Rowan so they didn't damage his mind any more, but he would be out of harm's way if anything went awry.

Storm approached the hovering curse and cupped his hands at a safe distance, deciding to do something far more useful than just moving the players on the board. Calling upon his magic, he set his intention to contain the curse. Once a spell or curse was crafted, the desire to fulfil its purpose until the mission was accomplished was all-consuming. Storm needed the curse to be harmless, without the risk that time would restart before he'd finished what he intended to do. There was no telling what he'd inadvertently done.

He gathered his will to render the curse safe—replacing the intent to kill with the idea of falling rain. As much as he wanted to dissolve the curse, the magic was too strong to be destroyed. He had to maintain balance and prevent the risk of the curse fighting back.

When he blew his will and magic onto the curse, Storm prayed this worked, because he wouldn't find out until time regained its usual process.

Yael walked behind Ithen and lifted themselves to sit on the hood of the car he'd been hiding behind until Denver coaxed him out. "I could kill him now," they admitted, meeting Storm's gaze with unfazed, unblinking eyes.

"We're not killing him," Storm said, glancing around to make sure Kyrie heard him. They'd had the same conversation multiple times over the last few weeks, and he wasn't repeating himself. "We don't kill people." Ignoring them, he pushed more magic into the newly transformed spell. "He'll face the witches council and the covens," he explained, lowering his hands and taking a careful step back from the reinvented curse. "I'll strip him of his magic in a minute, I just need to...I need..."

A sharp spike of pain in his head made Storm pause and blink, wondering where the sudden, piercing headache had come from. Lightning danced through his brain, and he cried out as he grabbed his head in both hands. His vision blurred and no matter how many times he blinked or widened his eyes, he couldn't seem to get the cloudiness to fade. His first step toward Yael faltered, and his right foot turned beneath him, folding like a pack of flimsy cards.

"Kyrie!"

Hands were on his shoulders and Storm blinked, surprised to find Kyrie standing behind Ithen, while Yael grabbed Storm's face in strong fingers and forced his head up. Storm didn't have the strength to fight the fingers that pinched his nose, and while he wanted to hit out, his entire body felt disconnected and weak. Yael was speaking but the words were garbled and distant, making no sense to Storm's muddled thoughts. Eventually, necessity forced his mouth open to gather breath, and Yael wasted no time darting in to place their mouth over his. Instead of kissing or suck-ing out his soul, Yael breathed *into* Storm.

He could feel their familiar magic flooding him, widening his eyes, smacking his brain into shape, and pulling on his limbs until they moved properly. The jolt felt like someone had hard wired him to an electric pole, where everything was suddenly bright, loud and right in his face...just like Yael.

Never taking his eyes from Storm, Yael drew back and broke the awkward breath-kiss thing. Without having to ask, they lightly smacked his cheeks to wake his senses. "You depleted your energy. The spell was reckless, but I understand you did not call such power on purpose. Now you know you can bend time and space, you will *not* do so again without proper training."

That last part was an order. Storm managed a weak nod of agreement and glanced out the corner of his eye to see Kyrie star-ing at them, still worried. Storm tried to lift his arm, to wave in reassurance that he was fine, but he barely got past his hip before flopping uselessly, and Yael huffed.

"Take more," they insisted, giving him no chance to resist.

When Yael backed away, Storm tried not to make a show of

wiping his mouth. "You make a rotten demon." He was glad Yael smiled in approval of the compliment for the weirdo he'd grown too attached to. "Any other demon would have encouraged me to bond with them when I was too weak to resist. They would have used me to get control of the amulet and the spell."

Yael leaned in close to whisper, "Demons have no interest in the toys of mages. Even one as dark as you."

"Oh? I'm darker than other dark mages?"

Yael shook their head and patted his cheek fondly. "You are the darkest I have ever seen."

They traded places with Kyrie, but Storm didn't mind; he'd heard the pride in their voice. When Yael said 'You are the darkest I have ever seen,' that was the equivalent of one of Rowan's warm, flirtatious gazes when he called Storm adorable or ridiculous—something worth cherishing.

Storm pointedly ignored the exchange between Kyrie and Yael, one asking after his health while the other gave a biting remark akin to Storm meddling where he wasn't supposed to. Neither the words nor the sentiments were new, so he focused on standing and finding stability. He only realised the danger when a hand grabbed his arm and he looked into Rowan's worried eyes.

"What happened?" Rowan barely had time to glance around before Ithen's curse hit his arm and he flinched, like he'd forgotten all about the curse in the two seconds before contact. His eyes instantly widened with fear, no doubt expecting danger or pain, but the curse exploded into a shower of sweet rain and Storm smiled, relieved he'd managed to do one thing right, even if everything else had gone to hell.

"Wha—" Ithen watched the curse dissolve into a mist of water with the same shock Rowan displayed. He swept his gaze over the surrounding area and paused first on Cesa, who was staring at the trees in confusion. Then Ithen spun in a circle and flinched to find Yael sitting behind him.

Storm figured this was the right time to lay his last cards on the table. He allowed Rowan to take his hand, while Ithen panicked and called upon another curse.

"I'm serious. What happened?" Rowan bit out, glaring as he helped Storm steady his balance.

"He tapped into new magic," Yael called out, answering for Storm though no one had invited them to. "Powerful magic not meant for humans."

Storm almost chastised them for saying that, until he realised the point: not just an answer for Rowan but a threat to Ithen, who had one more thing to worry about, and one more piece of knowledge he hadn't anticipated. Storm mentally promised to explain everything to Rowan later. "Give up, Ithen. I have the amulet and the spell. I can also now bend time so...you've got nothing left." He hoped to make an impact on the stubborn fool who kept resisting the inevitable. "We both know I won't stop. No matter how many times I have to travel through time, relive this life or pause and rewind this moment, I *will* win, and you *will* lose. Let's save me the hassle, okay?"

He was pretty sure those were one-time deals, but Storm was beyond caring. He was tired, ached in various places, and he'd just stopped time. Now was the only chance he'd ever get to play that card.

Ithen visibly considered his options, eyeing Kyrie with curiosity as he moved closer to Cesa and talked calmly, in an attempt to keep him out of harm's way. Yael sat behind Ithen, an obvious threat, their scythe tossed over their shoulder. Then Ithen faced Storm and the faintest flicker of a smile made him worry. Ithen held his arms out and offered his wrists. "Take me in, Dark One. Have me put in front of the covens."

Storm hesitated, because Ithen wasn't a man who surrendered, not even to the inevitable. He couldn't admit defeat, and from the worried looks and suspicion on both Kyrie and Yael's faces, neither trusted Ithen's sudden compliance. Determined to be reasonable, Storm stepped forward, unprepared when his head spun. It took every ounce of effort to not show the weakness, to not give Ithen any ammunition to use against him.

"Storm," Rowan's voice wavered as a finger touched his top lip. With worried ice blue eyes, Rowan turned his finger to reveal blood.

Storm stopped moving and lifted a free hand to touch his nose, his fingers coated in more blood than was healthy.

Yael said his name, concerned and distracted, while Rowan focused on Storm. In the background of his thoughts, he could hear Kyrie asking what was wrong, followed by the sound of Cesa screaming so loud his ears hurt.

In the silence that followed, Rowan jolted as though he'd been hit. He was standing right in front of Storm, almost touching him, yet he suddenly felt a thousand miles away. Those blue eyes pulled away from his, drawing Storm's gaze to a faint shimmer surrounding the obsidian blade of a dagger sticking through Rowan's chest.

Chapter Thirty

SHOCK HAD STORM convinced this couldn't be real; this must be a hallucination, because he'd used too much magic by stopping time. But the longer he held Rowan's gaze, the less he could believe the lie, watching Rowan's eyes well with tears as if he'd accepted this was happening.

Storm wiped away Rowan's tears, wanting to tell him it was okay, that this wasn't what they thought. Then Rowan gasped and lurched forward, as the blade was pulled out, no doubt causing more damage.

This wasn't real. Maybe Storm wasn't as smart as he'd thought and he hadn't unravelled Ithen's spell properly. Was this part of the death curse? Or was he still unconscious after stopping time, and this was nothing but a nightmare of hallucinations caused by using too much magic?

Rowan's knees gave way and he tilted forward, leaving Storm no time for thinking or reasoning. He caught Rowan, refusing to let him fall, but the weight of his body, no longer able to support itself, pulled Storm to his knees.

Storm arranged Rowan across his lap, shaking his head as blood bubbled between Rowan's lips. "No," he said, his hearing rushing back in a wave. "No." Storm focused on the wound in Rowan's chest that seemed to be growing bigger with each breath. In the background of his thoughts, Yael screamed, Cesa sobbed, and Kyrie was shouting questions. He didn't know what had happened to Ithen and he didn't care.

He had to save Rowan. Storm had promised he wouldn't let him die again. He suddenly realised it wasn't the wound growing—the gaping black hole in Rowan's chest was blood, pooling thick and fast, flooding from his body and draining his ice blue eyes into cornflower blue sadness.

Touching Rowan's cheek, Storm gasped at the rush of information his magic instinctively picked up: the blade had been spelled with a death curse, forcing his organs to bleed out internally, leaving no mess or sign of the true injury. Any human would see a natural death, slow and painless, but Storm felt the mortal wound in his heart.

There was no stopping this curse, no way to change or twist a spell that had fulfilled its purpose.

The demons were right: Rowan's death had been set in stone from the beginning. Though Storm had dismantled this curse, he'd failed to reason that things were meant to happen in a certain way for the prophesy to be fulfilled. Now they were here, where they were supposedly always meant to be, Storm had to think fast and do something to change their fates.

"Okay." He nodded, racking his brain for what he needed to do. He caressed a hand over Rowan's hair as Rowan coughed, blood trickling out with the weak sound. Storm looked for Yael but they had disappeared after his earlier shout, leaving Kyrie staring at a spot where Storm would have expected to find Yael.

Fine. Yael must have a plan, or they'd gone to find help. Gods, if only Reed Hadley were still alive or even a spirit that Storm could ask to help him. But no, yet again he had to do this on his own, with no idea what to do and no guidance.

Turning his attention to Kyrie, Storm was relieved the young demon had more sense than to fall apart the way Storm had. Kyrie had encased Cesa in magic, holding him in the treeline where he stood like a statue, visibly calm, though tears fell from his eyes that never strayed from where Rowan lay.

If Rowan was about to die, his father had the right to say goodbye in whatever way he could. Kyrie had done the right thing by resisting the temptation to spare him this pain.

Guilt weighed heavily on Storm's shoulders. He'd promised Asher that he'd cure Cesa and had failed; he'd sworn to Rowan that he wouldn't let him die again, and now he'd failed. Nothing he'd planned, intended or hoped for had come true since returning from the future to correct the mistakes of the past. He'd been so afraid of making the same mistakes that he never stopped to consider he'd end up making *new* mistakes that led him down the same path to disaster.

"I killed you." He should never have separated from Rowan. He could have explained his plan about rebounding the spell so that Rowan didn't rush to the rescue, just as he'd done in the future. Storm shouldn't have wasted his energy on stopping time; that had been reckless and, though unintentional, if he'd only been faster and stronger, this would never have happened.

Gods, if only what he'd said was true. If he could reverse time a few minutes, he could fix this, but he was too weak to lift his arms, from cradling Rowan's body as he lay bleeding out.

As always, Rowan was strong enough for both of them. He lifted his hand as far as Storm's wrist before losing strength, but it was enough to draw Storm's attention to those sad blue eyes. "I never wanted any of this to come true," he whispered, his voice hoarse and deep with the strain of speaking, "but I think this was meant to be. For you. Because I believe in the prophecy. I believe in *you*, even if you don't."

His first instinct was to shout at Rowan for wasting his breath, for dying...for leaving him. Then the words sank in, and he realised what Rowan wanted him to do. What he would have done if he'd been thinking even halfway like normal. Lifting his head, he searched for Yael, for Kyrie, for someone who could help him find the right place to start.

Stepping out of the abyss like an avenging demon, Yael

walked towards Storm with purpose, their favourite cane in their right hand. They didn't stop until they reached Rowan's side, sinking down beside him to kneel and present the cane like a sword to be bestowed in battle.

Storm took the cane and stared in surprise; it was such an innocent thing, a toy when they were children, and now the key to everything, the temptation he'd never wanted to give into. He was a necromancer; he should have been capable of bringing Rowan back from the dead, but he was so depleted by the spell to stop time he wasn't sure he could summon a leaf. This was his chance.

Storm wiped his cheeks free of tears and pushed Rowan's hair from his eyes. "You're dying. The wound is made of light magic, twisted by hate. No one can undo this, do you understand? You *will* die," he said, needing Rowan to understand that he wasn't callously watching him die because he didn't know what to do or was afraid.

Rowan nodded and squeezed his wrist, the strength of his grip barely changing. Storm forced a smile and pretended he'd felt the contact. "Do your job, necromancer. This is the moment we find out whether you love me. When you give me what I want most, before I die."

He didn't bother arguing because he knew what Rowan meant. He'd always known he'd have to do this, and he was half-way prepared. Storm brushed the blood from Rowan's mouth, wiped away his tears and bent to give him the last kiss he wanted. Whether he succeeded or not, Rowan had asked for this, and

Storm would give him that final wish. This time he wouldn't die with regrets.

Dark eyelashes flickered shut against Rowan's pale blue eyes. He was running out of time.

Storm licked his lips and shoved aside every concern he'd ever had that this wasn't allowed and was dangerous. He didn't care. Firmly holding the cane, he sent his magic toward the secret compartment in the handle, which opened like a petal, no longer a surprise or something to marvel over but a painfully slow process that made his heart stutter in desperation. With one palm open, ready to catch the amulet, Storm tipped the cane...and nothing happened.

Even Yael frowned in confusion and leaned closer.

Storm stared into the hidden compartment and his heart sank to the depth of his soul, his hopes dying at the realisation that all was lost. "It's not there," he confessed, the answer coming quickly and glaringly obvious. "The Fates showed you the door. They did this on purpose. They knew I'd use the amulet if I had to."

"No," Yael disagreed with a look of utter guilt. "They knew I would let you."

Storm had never hated the Fates more. They'd been cruel to allow him to crush on someone who turned out to be his enemy, brutally allowed him to be a necromancer, the Dark One, the prophecy child, then stop him from using the gift. The worst they ever did was to let him fall in love with Rowan only to steal him away. He couldn't use necromancy because he loved Rowan. This was stronger than anything he'd ever felt in his life, yet he could never use necromancy to resurrect someone he loved.

Storm sat with Rowan in his arms, watching as blood pooled on his chest. A trickle escaped his lips whenever he breathed too deep for his lungs to handle, and all Storm could do was wipe the blood away.

Ithen had won; he'd taken the one thing from Storm's life that he couldn't bear to lose. With a final, sharp breath, Rowan died, and Storm's heart broke.

Lowering his forehead to Rowan's, he let the tears fall unhindered, finally knowing grief. He'd never experienced death, always too young or too detached from the reality of the loss. With his final breath, Rowan stole every last ounce of his strength.

Storm didn't dare look up, afraid to see Rowan's spirit leaving his body, not wanting to see whether he was angry with Storm for failing or if he was still full of compassion. "This isn't fair," he said, staring at Rowan's peaceful face, devoid of life, as his tears mingled with Rowan's blood.

Tucking a strand of hair behind his ear, pulled back from those unseeing blue eyes, Storm memorised every last inch of his face; to hold onto the warm smile that would only ever exist in his memories, the laughter that was always so damned infectious and cute, the sweet kisses and the way Rowan's eyes would turn ice blue whenever he was overcome with emotion. He'd never thought this half-demon would be the one who could push past the bullshit and see the real Storm, to not be afraid to embrace his dark powers and the danger lurking in his veins.

Someone cleared their throat, and Storm remembered Ithen was still out there, on the loose, on the run. He'd killed Rowan and knew Storm would be coming.

Looking up, Storm frowned to see Kyrie standing beside Haven's father.

"Haven sent him," Kyrie said softly, crouching to touch his arm. "He helped me contain Ithen. You can take all the time you need. He's not getting away."

Storm nodded, glad someone was thinking clearly because he had a whole hell of hurt waiting for Ithen when he was ready. For now, he looked at Haven's father, wondering why he would intrude on his grief. He would understand better than anyone that Storm would want to be alone with Rowan, to hold onto what he could.

Haven's father awkwardly thrust out a hand, holding a piece of paper, as his eyes darted toward Rowan's body. "Haven sent a message for you. He said this was important...to both of you," he explained with a faint tip of his head toward Rowan.

Storm may have shouted that it was too late, but he had a feeling Haven knew more than most. He was supposed to be Storm's equal, so maybe he had a solution to this, some way Rowan didn't have to stay dead. He took and opened the note and frowned at the words.

Build a wall inside your head.

The words were simple, sparking a memory from the future they'd shared where Storm had helped DJ—as he'd been then—build a wall of defence from the nightmares and the ghosts. Was he telling Storm to protect himself from Rowan's ghost? If he was, Haven knew this would happen.

Storm looked for Yael to help him figure this out, but though he glanced around the immediate area, he couldn't see them. He checked on Cesa and found Yael standing by his side, brushing a hand over the man's head, rendering him unconscious. With the greatest care, Yael helped Cesa to the ground and lay him by the trees. His care for Cesa wasn't the thing that clenched Storm's heart, but the way they crouched by his unconscious body and shook. Was Yael crying? For Rowan?

"Yael." Storm shouted, his voice rough with tears. As soon as he had Yael's attention, he gestured for them to come closer and handed them the note from Haven.

"Might this relate to his last message?" Yael theorised, their tone gentle and tainted with grief as they brushed a hand over Rowan's head.

Storm couldn't fight the fresh rush of tears, realising Rowan's death hurt Yael just as much. He had to blink hard and focus on the note or miss whatever opportunity Haven had sent him. "Something about necromancy," he recalled, his head too foggy to remember exactly.

"To master necromancy, you must feel inside yourself, push aside other emotion and focus on one distinct memory of the

person you are resurrecting." Yael recounted the message word for word, their white eyes widening as they understood.

"He knew Rowan would die. That's why he said to pick a memory of the person because I had memories *with* them." Storm could have screamed in relief, but he held onto every last bit of energy he had, as Yael helped lay Rowan on the bare ground.

Kyrie thanked Haven's father when the demon insisted he should leave them to their personal task. Storm would find a way to thank him and Haven later; right now all his focus belonged on Rowan.

"I believe in you, Storm Tera."

Storm glanced up at Yael in surprise, refusing to cry as he realised that this was the first time Yael had ever called him by his name, which was an immense sign of respect from a demon. Storm pushed emotion aside and thought back on the pivotal moments of his time with Rowan. It felt like they'd been close all their lives and he still couldn't fit the strength of his feelings into the twenty-one days they'd had together.

He thought about their first kiss and how he'd seen the heart of Rowan...their second kiss, when Rowan was afraid Storm would hate him for being half-demon. Storm had taken the risk of kissing him because Rowan was beautiful inside and out. That was a good memory, but he thought there was a better memory, one more tender, more important to what they'd become to each other.

Closing his eyes, Storm focused on the memory as he shifted to kneel beside Rowan's body and placed one hand on his cheek, the other beneath his T-shirt, to press skin against skin to his stomach. He needed all the help he could get.

Help me, he whispered to his magic, desperate and on edge. He thought about Rowan, his smile and laughter, his kisses, the warmth of his body curled into Storm's arms at night, and the strange flutter in his chest when he woke every morning to find Rowan beside him.

Storm wasn't sure what he'd done, but he loved the look in Rowan's eyes, slightly hazy, a soft languid thing that was warm and inviting. He grazed their lips in another sleepy kiss, pleasantly surprised when Rowan nudged closer, a hand coming to his neck.

When he broke away, Rowan pressed their foreheads together. "I've been afraid to accept you're here...that you'll stay, after this is over. I've been scared you had nowhere else to go, but you want to be here. You really do care about me," he confessed, his voice faltering in relief. "You're not afraid of me."

"Why would I be?" Storm pulled away to look him in the eye, not sure what there was to be afraid of.

"I'm half-demon."

Shaking his head, Storm brushed his thumb over Rowan's bottom lip, wondering how such a smart, beautiful and strong guy could ever be so self-conscious. "You're Rowan and that's all I need you to be."

Storm held onto every second of that warm, tender memory and sent his magic searching through Rowan's body for any trace of what made Rowan Copry the man he was.

Yael held his gaze, their eyes strong and determined, the whites reflecting Storm's dark image. The set of his jaw, the tears still on his cheeks, and the second his magic surged to the forefront of his consciousness were all mirrored in Yael's gaze, as dark as Storm's magic. He saw his own face, pale, no doubt from the fact he was weak and barely had control. Yael hardened their gaze, as if to remind him to stay strong.

Storm pushed every thought and feeling aside, let go of his doubts and fears, and thought only of Rowan.

Give him back to me, he said, in the only place magic cared about—in his heart and his head. He balled every drop of free will he had to shove into the space where his magic slept. He wanted every trace of magic in his body to react to his will. Lifting his head to the sky, he thought about the Fates and linked them in his mind to Rowan. He refused to allow them to hide. They'd done this and would undo it, even if Storm had to unravel time itself.

You know this is your doing. You think you can force me to be your dark one, to make me the prophecy child you foretold. Storm knew they were watching and needed the Fates to remember who they were dealing with. *I don't want any part of this. Not without him. Without Rowan, there is no point. Give him to me. You return him exactly as he was, and I'll be your puppet; I'll do anything you want.*

The promise could get him into a whole hell of a lot of trouble, but he didn't care. Even if he had to walk away from Rowan, never see him again, and live with a broken heart for the rest of his life, Rowan would be alive.

You can see inside my head, you can read my will, and see my magic. You know the lengths I'll go to bring Rowan back. Storm was fully prepared to do what was running through his head if they didn't pay attention. *You return him as the same Rowan Copry who died for me, or I'll give him everything I have—all my power, every heartbeat and ounce of blood, every bit of strength and breath I have to give.*

The Fates would know he wasn't bluffing because Reed Hadley's book was a goldmine of interesting, but seemingly irrelevant, information. The only reason Storm hadn't given Rowan everything—blood, body, and breath—that he had to spare yet was because Rowan wouldn't want him to. Storm's death would devastate Yael, hurt Denver and Foley, disappoint Kyrie and Haven. So many people loved him, when less than a month ago he'd been alone.

He would die for Rowan but he wanted the Fates to *want* him to live.

"Choose!"

Chapter Thirty-One

STORM STARED AT where Rowan lay, wondering if he'd been abandoned by the Fates, ignored and cast aside in retaliation for his threats. Then, after just a moment, he heard a single long hiss of breath.

Refusing to release his magic or the contact, in case he accidentally undid whatever had happened, Storm watched and waited, his heart thudding painfully, his breath ragged and close to hyperventilation. A slow breath in, a rise of the chest, and Rowan's eyes moved, his gaze shifting in search of Storm. When their eyes met, both realising he was alive, they laughed.

Tears fell as Rowan took a deliberate breath, blowing out and frowning at the black mist. Their gazes clashed as realisation sank in that the Fates had done nothing; that black mist was proof that Storm's magic was responsible for this miraculous resurrection.

Storm had resurrected Rowan, which led to one inescapable truth: Storm didn't love him. Necromancers couldn't resurrect someone they loved. Seeing that understanding in Rowan's eyes, the truth hurt more than the thought of losing Rowan forever.

"Congratulations, youngling. You mastered your necromancy," Yael said, congratulating him without knowing the full truth.

Storm wished he had, then he wouldn't have this empty hole in his heart, mixing up everything he thought he knew, turning truth into lies, the known into the unknown. Instinct said to run, to escape, to not stay around and see the recrimination in Rowan's eyes, the knowledge that he wasn't loved. Before he could move, a hand raised and cupped his cheek. Almost without effort, Rowan sat up and held his face in both hands, keeping Storm still as he forced eye contact that had always come naturally to them.

"I know what you're thinking," Rowan whispered, leaning close enough to kiss but stopping just out of reach. "You think because you resurrected me that means you don't love me. Maybe you don't, but it doesn't mean you *can't*." He smiled as he brushed his thumb across Storm's jaw. Rowan crossed the last, short distance between them and pressed their foreheads together. "Nothing says you can't love me *now,* in a few days, in *weeks*. We need to be thankful you don't love me, or I wouldn't be telling you this." He continued the soothing caress of a thumb across Storm's cheek and jawline, lost to the moment. "From now on, you choose your future. *You* choose your fate. If that means you don't love me yet but can love me *later,* that's good enough for me."

Storm breathed freely, the pain fading as he accepted the embrace and rejoiced over having Rowan back. "I can't believe they were going to let you die," he confessed, tears welling and clogging his throat at the thought of what might have happened if he hadn't been strong enough.

"I'm more surprised they were willing to let *you* die," Rowan disagreed, dropping his hands to Storm's chest. "You were willing to give up everything for me. You almost did. I could feel your soul pushing into my body...almost losing yours, because you're still weak."

Storm shrugged because he had no words, no awareness of what he'd been doing, except that he'd been willing to do anything, to *give* anything, to have Rowan back.

Rowan's gaze sharpened, and he hit Storm's chest with a weak blow. "Don't be reckless with your life! I know you panicked but, Storm, you have a purpose. You have the prophecy to fulfil, and Yael and Kyrie to take care of."

Storm smiled, loving this side of him. Gods, he hadn't realised how much he needed Rowan to champion him, to believe in him, to bitch.

"Hey!" Yael objected with less grace than usual.

"We both know they need a leash half the time," Rowan said, ignoring Yael's huff. He shifted to sit on his knees, pulling his T-shirt away from his chest with a crinkled nose of disgust. "Don't think you have no worth just because the Fates didn't help. Maybe they *knew* you needed a push. Maybe they're heartless bitches and don't care about anyone. Either way, *I* care about you. Whether you love me or not, you *were* willing to die for me. Think more of yourself, okay?"

Storm swallowed at the look in those big, bright, alive eyes. He hadn't realised he was willing to die for Rowan, just that the thought of being without him hurt too much. "I'll try."

"Good."

Yael's tone dripped with criticism as they cut through the cute moment. "After all this time, you still believe the Fates care nothing for you?" They eyed Storm with disappointment. "You have travelled through time, rewritten your future, and broken every rule I have known to govern magic. You befriended a demon, and you *ask* to combine our magic, yet you believe the only reason you resurrected Rowan was because you do *not* love him? Why must this be the one rule you obey?"

Storm blinked at Rowan, rolling those words through his brain, but they refused to make sense. "Are you saying that I brought him back despite already loving him?"

"What does your heart say?"

Rowan's lips twitched into a smile. "I know what mine tells me. That you're a miracle, as you've always been."

But that would mean...he loved Rowan. Was the strength of his love the reason he'd been able to break the rules? Did the rules even apply to him anymore?

"Gods have mercy!" Yael rolled their eyes and turned away

in disgust as a black blur came rushing toward them. As Midnight became discernible from the black fur, jumping against Rowan's thigh, they sighed, sounding horrified. "How did *you* survive?"

The kitten meowed at Rowan, who instantly lifted the monster he unfathomably loved to pieces. "Don't be mean," he warned, butting his head against Midnight's. "I'm fine, but you'll have to be nicer to Storm. He's the reason I'm okay." He grinned up at Storm with such a look of adoration he shivered. Storm figured that look made up for the fact Midnight could rub all over Rowan in relief that he was alive, but Storm couldn't.

He reached for the black ball of fur, grateful she hadn't died or run away during the chaos, but stopped when Midnight started hacking. "I guess that sums up how she feels about me." Unstable mage, horde of demons—Storm could handle them. But Midnight was an evil little bitch, and he wasn't taking the risk of getting further onto her bad side.

Rowan had the cheek to laugh, though the humour was short-lived, turning into shocked silence when Midnight hacked up something large and black. "What have you been eating, you bad kitty?"

There was no way he would suggest taking Midnight while Rowan looked to see what she'd brought up, so Storm reluctantly pushed a finger into the ball of spit, to roll the black object across the ground. He was rendered speechless by the black amulet laying on the ground between them. Glancing up, he was about to ask if he was hallucinating the amulet, but the shock on their faces was answer enough.

Yael didn't have to be asked. They summoned their cane to hand to Storm and watched, their white eyes screaming a protest that this shouldn't have been possible.

Storm accepted the cane and used his magic to open the hidden compartment. He was disappointed to see the scroll inside, where the compartment had been empty just minutes ago. "I won't ask why the Fates stole the spell and amulet, then returned them... or why I had to touch something your cat coughed up." Storm shoved the amulet inside with less care than he should have, his patience for this day having grown thin long ago. Once the spell and amulet were secured, he handed the cane to Yael. "This day has been weird enough, and I don't think I want to know."

Rowan chuckled fondly as he petted Midnight and praised her for saving the amulet.

Storm didn't doubt the little bitch had been following orders. *And we both know who gave them, don't we?* he said, glancing at the sky to make sure the Fates were listening.

*

ONCE THEY KNEW Rowan could move, speak, and think clearly, without any pain or discomfort, they decided not to waste time.

Handing Midnight to Yael was never going to happen, so Rowan entrusted the kitten to Kyrie, to keep the cat safe while they dealt with Ithen.

Storm wasn't sure what to do about the corrupt mage, but

his magic sang beneath his skin and he could feel the growing presence of magic around the property. An inner instinct knew what was about to happen, what *needed* to happen.

Kyrie stood guard by Ithen, making sure the demon barrier around him didn't wilt or weaken, which reminded Storm that he had Haven and his father's horde to thank for capturing him. He owed them a debt greater than any amount of money or power could buy; they'd saved his life tonight—and Rowan's.

Storm stepped in front of the barrier holding Ithen at bay and met his angry gaze. Raising his hands out to his sides, he turned his palms and allowed magic to crackle like lightning, re-charged by Rowan's resurrection and ready to do damage. His will stopped the magic from crushing Ithen like a bug, harnessing the power to push out until the barrier surrounding the property crumbled to ash.

"The Fates have named me the Chosen One, Dark One, nec-romancer, and dark mage. The gods have named me seer, light wielder and storm chaser. The demons call me master, life-giver, guardian of the lost and hopeless...for I am Storm Tera, last sur-viving Tera mage, commander of the dead and protector of de-mons." Storm felt the power and heady weight of those titles for the first time and didn't feel like crumbling under the expectation. Instead, he stood tall and proud as magic swept through his veins, rejoicing in the claim, his magic singing its relief.

The bubble of magic surrounding Ithen vanished with an au-dible pop, and the man's eyes narrowed with victory. He had no idea who he was dealing with. Storm's magic surged, pulsating and growing in strength, lifting Ithen off his feet into the air, where his body was spread like a sacrifice, arms wide, legs encased by invisible ropes of magic.

"Ithen Deontay, you will face judgement for your crimes against magic," he called, pausing when he caught movement out the corner of his eye.

Gregory Glade emerged from the trees, standing by his coven members like a true leader and gestured for them to wait at the forest boundary. He walked forward with confidence and only a touch of fear as he approached Rowan, standing two feet to Storm's right. Gregory met Storm's gaze without pause and gave a brief nod. "Dark One," he said with a faint twitch of his lips in allegiance, friendship, and the same casual nodding acquaintance they'd always shared.

"Gregory Glade, your coven are welcome to sit on judgement." Storm hated sounding so formal and didn't know where the words came from, but they felt and sounded right. Most importantly, Gregory nodded and signalled to the rest of his coven.

Because he could sense them, Storm called out a welcome to the others, starting with Rowan, who gave a mock bow. "Rowan Copry, Scott Sorrell, and Florence Lasym, you are welcome to bring your covens to give judgement on Ithen Deontay's crimes." He sounded arrogant, all-knowing and all-powerful, but there was no way to stop the magic guiding him. Before he turned away, he sensed one more magical signature in the woods, hesitant but intrigued. If Storm wasn't wrong, the interloper had brought a show of allegiance. "Auden Bellamy," he called, glancing at Kyrie to see that he tensed on hearing the name, "you are welcome to join the covens."

Outsiders weren't usually asked to join the local coven gatherings, and Storm's welcome to Auden, without consulting the others, brought whispers from the Sorrell and Lasym covens who were eager to show their displeasure. Gregory either knew Auden or had warned his coven to keep quiet, no doubt for their own sakes.

Silence reigned as Auden made his way out from the cover of the trees, carrying himself with dignity, clutching at a satchel slung over his shoulder.

As they waited for him to reach the gathering, Gregory took a half step closer. "I'm sorry about my grandmother."

Storm blinked, surprised he didn't seem upset by the fact Gladys had been kidnapped by a horde of demons to pay for her crimes against magic.

"I didn't know what she was doing. We haven't spoken in years, outside of coven business," he confessed with a shrug and a glance at his coven. When he looked at Storm again, he smiled. "I look forward to having your guidance as I step into the role of coven leader. We need a good role model who knows how to respect magic."

The words were unexpected but appreciated more than Gregory realised. Storm was about to thank him for the confidence when Auden appeared at his left side, stopping far closer than the other covens had.

"As leader of the Bellamy coven, I hope you will forgive past mistakes, accept our loyalty to dark magic and show us how to properly connect with the magic binding us together," Auden said, taking one more step closer as he removed the satchel from over his head.

Yael immediately lowered their scythe between Auden and Storm. They didn't blink at the protective role they'd chosen or flinch when Auden glared, momentarily startled. He was quick to recognise defeat, tipped his head at Yael in apology and handed them the bag.

Yael passed the bag to Kyrie, who placed Midnight on his shoulder to free his hands. He took the bag with obvious curiosity, only to glance at Auden in surprise. "He has given you the family grimoire," Kyrie explained, turning to Storm with wide eyes. "The passages are written in the old tongue, which only a demon can read. No Bellamy has deciphered them, no demon has understood its words, and the family believe the grimoire was cursed to hide its secrets from all who had magic." The raised eyebrow suggested this was a valuable and rare gift, one that asked for leniency for past indiscretions and was meant to show fealty.

Storm wasn't sure how he felt about any of that. On one hand, Auden had the gall to approach them tonight with a gift that implied he'd been made welcome and forgiven, but his presence at the most opportune moment meant he'd been lingering. Had

Auden been waiting to see how the war panned out and head home if Storm lost, or had he been biding his time, convinced the Chosen One could deal with the problem?

Either way, he'd left them without much-needed aid, and if Storm hadn't successfully brought Rowan back from the dead, Storm would have sent Auden to join Rowan in the abyss before he could utter a single word of apology.

"My demon," Auden began, pausing when Yael growled a warning.

They would never stop protecting Kyrie, but Storm figured he may have to teach Yael that their fierce, possessive streak would get them in trouble one day, if the utter joy in Kyrie's ice blue eyes was any indication. Kyrie was in awe and hearts-and-flowers about Yael, but if Yael didn't notice that soon and act, there would be hell to pay.

"My apologies." Auden tipped his head to Yael but didn't sound apologetic. "The grimoire was considered too dangerous for any human to possess, and those with magic who attempt to read it are weakened and can't use magic for days," he said, smart enough not to reveal Kyrie's name in front of other witches and mages. "I thought the strongest and darkest of dark mages may wish to keep the grimoire safe. Use it, if you can."

Though the words sounded like a challenge, Storm also thought he detected hope, as though he would read the grimoire and share what he knew with Auden. That was unlikely, but by the feel of the man, Storm knew Auden wouldn't be the head of his coven for much longer. "Thank you," Storm said with a smile to remind Auden who was in charge. "We will keep these secrets from being misused."

The 'we' took him off guard, but Auden glanced at Rowan first, presuming he was the sole reason. He eyed Kyrie critically and finished with a brief glance at Yael, the fear and curiosity evident. "Of course." He stepped into the ranks of the other covens, leaving Storm in the uncomfortable and unfamiliar position of being the centre of attention.

"Hey!"

Storm wasn't the only one who flinched at the shout, spinning to look towards the trees at the far end of the front of the property. He could barely believe his eyes when Denver hobbled out, grinning like a loon and waving while Foley held him steady. He gave a cheeky thumbs up that made even Yael smile.

"I didn't die this time!"

Chapter Thirty-Two

FOLEY AND HIS cousin helped light candles and place them around the area, so they could hold a true coven council without leaving the front lawn of the Copry household. Rowan had checked on his father and found him still unconscious from Yael's spell, and they both agreed to leave him. There was no telling what may happen if he saw Ithen, or if he would attack Storm after what had happened to Rowan.

For now, Cesa was safe and content, but Storm was determined to resolve his curse by the end of the night, once Ithen had been taken care of.

With the coven members rallied, Storm began the meeting with what mattered most: explaining everything. Foley's mother Florence volunteered her seer gift to prove that the answers they were given were honest and first-hand accounts. Rowan offered to read the cards of the meeting, drawing the upright Judgement to represent reflection, reckoning and awakening; Justice followed, to represent cause and effect, clarity and truth; and the Hermit finalised the reading to show that Storm offered contemplation, a search for the truth and inner guidance.

Once the leaders were satisfied that they could believe Storm's every word, he walked them through the entire story, from being sent back in time to his changed friendship with Rowan, discovering Ithen's crimes and how Ithen and Gladys had been working together. As Yael was a demon still not bound to any mage, the coven leaders accepted their word as impartial. Whenever they wanted a question answered, they asked Yael or Kyrie, trusting that neither could lie when asked a direct question.

Storm left nothing out, speaking about the rogue witches and mages who had worked with Ithen, that demons had become his allies, and that he was sure Gladys and Ithen had manipulated him during his first run at this life to prevent him from fulfilling the prophesy. His prevailing theory was that Gladys had only sent him back when magic began to fail, and the elementals suffered. Then and now, Gladys and Ithen saw Storm as nothing more than a pawn, finding no reason to remove him from the equation or fear his magic until his decision to study necromancy interfered with their plans.

Most of the covens listened without interruption. Gregory, Denver, Auden, or Scott would occasionally ask for clarification or to pause and focus on a certain event. Storm was happy to oblige, as all but Denver were coven leaders and had every right to question his story. He enjoyed the looks on their faces when Denver asked intelligent questions to clarify Ithen's part in events and made observations none of the rest had considered.

Storm kept to the point, but some events were interwoven, and he had to recap others to provide context. He felt like he'd relived the entire last month in half an hour, but the covens soon had a full account of everything Storm knew about Ithen, his motives, actions and the crimes he had committed against magic and against the local covens who had welcomed him into their circle.

With the truth laid bare, Storm called for the covens to make their judgement.

"We recommend exile and to bind his magic," Scott said, after conferring with the Sorrell coven for barely a minute.

Acting as the Copry coven leader, Rowan was left to make the decision for his family. The absence of any member of the coven beside him and his father was noted by every other coven, now aware that the demon horde had frightened them off or rendered them unconscious during the fight. For now, they were happy to believe that Ithen had infiltrated the coven and used his control of Cesa to manipulate them. Whether they'd been spelled, cursed or simply won over by Ithen was something they would only discover after the members had regained consciousness.

For now, Rowan had a decision to make, and they all waited with bated breath to hear what he had to say. "I say we stick to the old ways. Death for a coven traitor." He didn't glance at Storm, but he wasn't angry. He couldn't blame Rowan for feeling the way he did, because his father had suffered the worst under Ithen's curse.

"I support the motion." Florence Lasym was usually calm and poised, but she readily agreed with Rowan for once. "I don't believe someone who has committed the crimes that Ithen has can ever be considered redeemable. Balance should be restored with the spilling of his blood."

Storm nodded, though he'd hoped to avoid a death sentence if only to give him more time to find a cure for Cesa. "I'd like to recommend we strip Ithen of magic and wipe his memory. We can't undo what he's done or change his personality, but he wouldn't be any more dangerous than a regular human." He wanted a unanimous vote, but the least he could ask was that they rendered Ithen magically impotent; without magic or any memories related to magic, he could be confined in a prison or mental institution to suffer the way Cesa had for the last ten years and more.

Auden nodded with a cruel smile. "I agree." He was trying too hard to get on Storm's good side, but he made the vote equal.

Two counts for death, two for the elimination of magic. As the Sorrell suggestion of exile was accompanied by the idea of binding Ithen's magic, the vote became a majority for rendering Ithen human and left the how and when of that decision firmly in Storm's hands.

*

WITHIN TEN MINUTES, in which Storm cleansed his magic and accepted a rejuvenating drink and snack from Kyrie, chaos erupted amongst the covens. Irritated by the distraction, Storm left his secluded area of contemplation to find Gregory standing at the side of the bickering gathering, biting his thumb nail. "What the hell happened?"

"Mrs Sorrell got confused and had a flashback to when her father faced the council forty-five years ago. She was understandably upset," Gregory explained with genuine sympathy for her condition. "Florence made a snippy remark about how the Sorrell family were unstable and they shouldn't be allowed to remain in the circle. Scott shot back that Florence should get off her high horse because she's not even a *real* Lasym since she married in and...this happened."

The explanation was more than Storm required but let him know who was to blame. Putting fingers to his lips, he whistled loud enough to interrupt the shit-storm that Rowan stood in the middle of, trying but failing to diffuse the situation.

"Florence—keep your bitchy judgements to yourself," he demanded, refusing to apologise to Foley for telling off his mum because he looked embarrassed enough. "Mrs Sorrell has a legitimate medical condition that causes confusion, and in case you haven't noticed, my boyfriend's father is losing his mind. Attacking the mentally impaired—and being bloody tacky—might not be the best way to go."

He'd always hated her arrogance. Just because her family of

white witches dated to the beginning of magic, she thought she was better than most. One day he would dig into her family background to prove that *one* dark mage lurked in her line. For now, he had to yell at adults who behaved no better than kids.

He turned to the coven leader. "Scott, don't stoop to her level. She's just pissed that she didn't get her own way." Storm faced the gathered coven members to remind them of the facts. "In case you forgot, I didn't agree with Rowan either, but he's mature enough to accept my decision instead of pouting like a brat. Keep the bitching to zero or go somewhere I don't have to hear you. I have an important spell to work, and I now have to cleanse my energy again, thanks to you lot bickering." He didn't bother waiting for an apology or to hear the inevitable muttering.

Storm walked back to the quiet space he'd found to complete his cleansing and sank to his knees in the treeline to start over. Yael poured from a bottle of purified water into a bowl, blew their magic into the spell, and handed the bowl to Storm to drink.

Rowan lit the candle in the centre of the space they'd cleared amongst the fallen leaves, half white and half black to represent the two sides of Storm's magic. Blowing out the match he'd used to light the candle, he set the still smoking end into the side of the candle to represent north. He lit a second candle, then blew out the match to set in the place for south. Taking the box of matches, Yael lit the matches for east and west.

For a full minute, Storm sat on his knees, breathing deeply of the elements, connecting to the four corners of time and space, and using his magic to remove impurities. In a matter of minutes, he was ready to try the spell.

Approaching Ithen, Storm pushed back the sleeves of his jumper and stood a foot from where the mage hovered in the air. He brought Ithen to his feet but didn't remove the barrier keeping him immobile. While the script for this punishment was basic, he'd run a few ideas past Rowan.

"Ithen Deontay, you are judged by this coven, council, and circle to have committed crimes against magic, human nature and the Fates," Storm said, deciding to get a few things off his chest while he could. "You are hereby convicted of murder, treason, and betrayal and will face a sentence befitting your crimes."

Storm whispered his intent to his magic, which struggled because his innate powers were reluctant to let Ithen escape justice for the wrongs he'd committed against dark magic. The most important argument he could give his magic was the reminder that the only fitting punishment for a man who sought to become the only magic user left in the world should be to lose all knowledge and connection to magic.

Ithen's greatest fear was not being good enough or having enough power, unable to prove his worth with a flick of his wrist or bend the will of another with a whisper. They couldn't undo what he'd done and killing him would make them as bad as he'd become, so Storm thought they should turn Ithen into his worst nightmare: a regular, powerless human.

His magic calmed upon realising Storm wasn't prepared to

taint his magic with the murder of another human being. Gathering what magic he could into both hands, he lifted them to his mouth and blew. A black cloud of magic rushed toward Ithen, penetrating the confining barrier to wriggle into Ithen's ears and mouth in search of his magic.

Storm felt empty as his magic worked separately from him for the first time. The constructs of the spell were complex, so the distance was a necessary precaution; had he attempted to have contact with Ithen or be inside his head, Storm could risk losing his magic and taking Ithen's in exchange.

While he allowed his will and magic to flow through Ithen, seeking every last piece of magic within him, Storm turned his attention to the audience of coven members. "Through this journey to fulfil the prophecy, I've noticed disturbing truths amongst those of us with magic. It's made me question whether the prophecy truly means for me to become the 'owner' or 'leader' of those who have magic or if the Fates wanted me to *protect* magic, to ensure all magic is used properly, with guidance, logic and consideration," he confessed, looking at the coven members he had the most concerns about.

Florence was ruled by her stubborn, holier-than-thou attitude, while Auden's ignorance had led to the mistreatment of demons. Even Gregory had big shoes to fill, hopefully without becoming his grandmother and repeating her mistakes.

The few faces of dissent remained silent, unaware they were the focus of his words. "Whether magic or power, people can't help but feel threatened by someone with more ability. They convince themselves they've been persecuted or that a simple disagreement has become an attack or a fight to the death," he explained, making sure Florence noticed his stare. Her reaction to Mrs Sorrell's innocent outburst had been uncalled for and unprovoked. She needed to start acting like the goody-two-shoes she pretended to be.

"They even end up victimising those weaker than them," Rowan added, sending him a warm and supportive smile across the short distance between them. He glanced back at his father, who remained unconscious in Kyrie's care, his concern obvious.

"Yes." Storm wished he could comfort Rowan but knew better than to redirect his will from the spell. "Tonight, we've seen the devastating consequences of what happens when someone's will is forced and twisted. Cesa has been suffering for a decade, but even the witches and mages who fought with Ithen tonight have suffered moments of confusion. We don't know what will happen to those Ithen manipulated, but we'll do what we can to free them from his power. Those like Cesa Copry, under a curse for years, may never see justice or freedom," he said, sparing a glance for Cesa, his heart hurting to see the man helpless.

"I genuinely believe the world would be better off without magic, but that isn't my decision to make. The Fates gave us these gifts for a reason, and we've been selfishly misusing them. Myself included. From this moment on, I accept their prophecy, the path they've paved for me, and I will become the Protector of Magic. I will do all in my power to ensure anyone born with magic is taught and trained how to respect magic."

Reed Hadley had taught him so much, without living long enough to know his impact and the legacy he'd left behind. His nephews were never allowed to know the man who had become a teacher and mentor to Storm, but he would make sure his name was remembered. Though he had only read the man's words, he'd learned from his wisdom, through his mistakes, theories, and hopes for the future. He wanted the Hadley nephews to share in that knowledge.

"I also want to be abundantly clear that demons are our allies, not slaves or objects to be used for a purpose and discarded," Storm continued, sparing a smile for Yael, who stood nearby, leaning on their scythe. "Anyone who wants to bond with a demon will need the demon's permission. A contract will be required, sealed in the blood of both as a promise that any magic performed will be through free will. I won't watch any more demons being mistreated or kidnapped for their power."

Kyrie and Haven had suffered so much. Once this thing with Ithen was over, he would ask Kyrie to help him free any other demons held against their will by a bond only Storm could break. If he'd intended to add anything else, Storm forgot when an audible pop rippled the air, and his magic shot into his body with such force he stumbled.

The change in Ithen became clear instantly: he was now without magic. Storm's magic had escaped Ithen's body before the pop killed whatever traces of magic remained, then snapped home in panic at the last moment.

Pressing his heart, both to comfort his magic and in relief that the shock he'd suffered was nothing awful, Storm laughed out the excess energy.

Rowan was quick to join him, though Yael rolled their eyes.

Shaking off the nervous energy, Storm bent at the waist, hands to his knees, and took slow steady breaths. The panic of his magic and the subsequent shock of the pop had his heart racing and his palms sweating.

"Um...Storm," Gregory said, sounding oddly hesitant and someone gasped as bodies moved, pushing back to make room around the coven leader.

Storm looked up to find Ithen's hand around Gregory's throat. The man was seething, pale, and looked barely capable of doing more than holding himself up. With his hand around Gregory's throat, they couldn't be sure what he might manage before they could incapacitate him. Storm drew a blank on how to resolve this. If he used magic, Gregory could be hit or face a ricochet of the spell, but if he did nothing Gregory could die. A physical tackle was out of the question. Ithen was far superior in strength and physique to anyone gathered here, bar the demons.

"Ithen," Storm said, but stopped when he realised there was nothing he could say to diffuse the situation. He was the real target, but offering himself would be offering magic stronger than anything Gregory had.

Always one to overreact, Florence didn't hesitate to consider the situation. She wove white magic in her hands, whispering a spell that Storm deciphered at the last moment as a reverse healing spell—one to open any existing or healed wounds and make them bleed until Ithen inevitably died of blood loss.

Furious that she was ignoring the will of the council, Storm raised a hand the minute she let the spell loose and caught the ball of spite in his bare hand. The white magic burned his palm until his magic overpowered the spell and disintegrated the intent. "Don't be reckless with someone else's life! What did we just talk about?"

Florence truly had no regard for the rules, the council, or Storm's position as the Chosen One and the rightful leader of all covens. She blatantly ignored him and began reforming the spell, while Scott argued with Rowan about the wisest course of action.

Foley grabbed his mother's hand and winced as a spark of her magic singed him. They began bickering about responsibility, about listening to Storm, and Florence being so caught up in her emotions that she singed her own kid, something Foley took personally.

Before a single mage, white witch or human could notice, Storm felt the swell of Yael's magic, their anger, and the determination to protect him. Everyone else was focused on Florence being reckless and Foley reasoning with her.

Ithen froze as a crack resonated through the night, and blood spurted from between his lips. A black talon erupted through the hole punched through Ithen's chest...with Yael's hand curled around the mage's heart.

Chapter Thirty-Three

STORM NEVER THOUGHT he'd see the day when Yael acted on their impulses despite his warnings. Seeing their hand sticking through Ithen's chest forced the accusation from his lips, "Was that necessary?" Hadn't they spent what felt like an eternity arguing about whether to sentence him to death and about being better than the killer who had ruined so many lives?

"While your intentions are noble, removing his magic does not remove the evil deeply rooted in his heart," Yael replied, their hand still visible through the gaping hole in Ithen's chest, revealing the way they squeezed the heart in their hands.

Gregory gasped as Ithen's grip released in response, and he stumbled away, putting distance between himself and the threat. "I'm sorry, Storm," he said, rubbing his throat and eyeing Ithen nervously, "but I agree with the demon."

Looking at the other coven members—the Glades panicking over Gregory, and the Lasyms looking to Florence, who had the audacity to look so smug Storm wanted to smack the look off her face—he knew what had to be done. The attack against Gregory had united any naysayers into the same camp as those who had asked for Ithen's death, and it was out of his hands now.

"Fine." Storm retreated and let Yael have their way.

Putting their lips to Ithen's ear, they spoke clearly, their magic swirling through the contact of their hand around Ithen's heart. "As a higher demon, I have the right to dispense justice for the wrongs you have committed against magic," they said, throwing a proud look toward Storm that said they enjoyed surprising him with that news. "For the deaths of Asher and Veronica Tera, I condemn you to the pits of Torture. For the corruption of Cesa Copry, I condemn you to the court of Baelesh, Demon of Nightmares. For the betrayal of my mage—" They pushed at Ithen's shoulder to shove his body to the ground, while retaining their grip on his heart. "—I take your heart."

Ithen's body dropped with a sickening thud, and there was silence.

"Remind me not to piss off Storm's demon," Foley whispered to Denver, ineffective in the deafening silence that followed Ithen's sentence.

Storm answered honestly. "They're not my demon." He wasn't sure what was more amusing: the flicker of shock in Yael's eyes or the fact Foley backed away, as if a demon without a leash was a danger. To teach them both not to jump to conclusions, Storm clasped Yael's bloody hand in both of his. "You're my best friend, Yael. I hope we can be equal partners in any magic we choose to do. I'll be your champion, and you can be mine."

With a nod and a beaming grin, Yael tipped their head in acceptance. They shot a glance at Auden, who flinched under their gaze. "With your permission, I will give this heart to Kyrie in place of the one I truly wish to give."

Storm knew fine well they weren't joking. "Good demon," he teased with a quick pat on their head. "Give Kyrie the evil heart if you like." He stepped back with a smile, in no way jealous or angry that someone else would get Ithen's power. If Kyrie was handed the gift, he may well become a higher demon as Yael had become these last few weeks. He just hoped Yael understood the unspoken promise that came with giving another person a heart.

"Not the conventional way," Rowan whispered as he moved close enough to take Storm's hand, "but they're still giving Kyrie their heart. It's just unfortunate the heart once belonged to someone else."

Storm laughed in relief, realising this whole mess was over: Ithen was gone; Gladys had paid for her crimes; everyone who had betrayed him was gone or had been neutralised. His world was safe again.

"Storm!" Yael shouted.

Bodies jostled as he and Rowan were surrounded by a protective circle of witches. He didn't know what was happening, ducking then rising on his tiptoes to look through the crowd of bodies to see what could have caused such a stir. He managed to dart under an arm and spotted Yael standing at the treeline, watching Kyrie with a pleased smile as he ate Ithen's heart. He wished he hadn't seen that.

Sweeping his gaze across the expanse of the property, he saw the problem: Cesa Copry was running toward them at full speed.

As he opened his mouth to warn everyone to give them room—knowing in his heart that Cesa had been freed from Ithen's curse and had woken from his unconscious state terrified for his son's safety—he was too late.

An almighty roar erupted, followed by Yael's strong voice, commanding the witches and mages, "You will not touch Rowan Copry's father."

A moment of quiet encased the group as the coven members cleared a path toward Rowan. He looked so happy, like Christmas had come early, as he beamed at Foley. "We were kids together," he explained, looking overwhelmed but thrilled by Yael's dedication to helping his father.

Taking a step out of the circle, Rowan ran to his father and hugged him, instantly calming the man's panic. After they'd had a good two minutes of a reunion, Rowan stepped away to touch Yael's arm. "Without you, we would never have saved my father. Thank you," he said, then stood on his tiptoes to kiss their cheek.

While Yael blushed, Rowan returned to his father, talking quietly to reassure him that everything was okay. Whatever happened from now on, Cesa's mind was fragile and there was no telling if he'd fully regain his sanity or whether he would forever need Rowan to monitor his actions and behaviours for the sake of the family estate.

From the way Cesa fretted over Rowan, questioning his death and his resurrection, Storm knew Cesa would need time before he was comfortable with the world and the changes that had occurred while he was Ithen's prisoner. He'd missed so much of Rowan's life and was mostly unaware of the coven meetings and running of the estate, but they could help him catch up if he wanted to. If not, Storm would happily suggest Cesa retire from the coven and the estate, letting Rowan take over, to focus on his recovery.

The missing years, when he'd been too cursed to live a full life, were something they could never reclaim, but that wouldn't matter as long as Rowan had his father back for the rest of their remaining years.

Cesa eventually calmed down as Rowan helped him sit to rest his unsteady body. They should be inside by now, but there was no reason to rush. Cesa needed rest more than he needed the comfort of going into the house.

"I thought I'd lost you," Cesa said, staring at Rowan like he was a precious gift as tears welled in his tired eyes. "I couldn't bear to lose you the way I lost Asher." The pain in his voice was clear, and Storm wasn't sure how to help. When Cesa looked up and held his hand out, Storm willingly sank to his knees to sit with the broken family. "Your father is dead," he said, the quiver in his voice hinting that he still wasn't sure whether that was real.

Storm's heart hurt in the worst way. Cesa had grieved for Asher for years, but now that he was free of Ithen's curse, the hope and pain of not knowing if that nightmare was real must have been unbearable. Did he think Ithen had lied, cursing him to think Asher was dead just to put a wedge between them, when Asher had been alive the whole time?

Swallowing his emotions, he took Cesa's hand and nodded. "Yes, Cesa. My dad is gone, but he loved you deeply, well beyond his dying breath," he whispered, needing him to know, even if that left him as the villain who had to break the awful news that Cesa's nightmares were real.

Though he detected a few whispers and curious mutters from the coven members, he could have kissed Gregory for taking charge. "All right, this is a family moment. Let's give them privacy in this moment of grief," he said, physically pushing Florence away to give them space to breathe without the covens smothering them.

Once they had moved far enough away, Storm felt he could breathe better, could think clearer. He knew what he had to do and didn't ask Rowan for permission because his gaze was locked on his father, his eyes sad and full of grief Storm didn't want to add to.

Storm lifted a hand and called on his magic to draw a padlock in the air. The more details he added, from the keyhole to the intricate filigree handle, the more solid the padlock became. Once complete, he blew his intention into the magic, to unlock the door between this world and the next: an invitation for one man.

A ghostly door materialised in place of the padlock and Storm watched as the outline wavered between solid and transparent, a literal doorway between two worlds. There was no squeak or ray of light as the door opened, but Storm felt the rush of wind, happy to see his dad again as a sprinkle of rain drizzled through, eager to wash away Ithen's evil from this land.

When Asher Tera stepped through the door, Storm spared a smile for his dad, then turned to where Cesa sat, weeping against Rowan's shoulder.

"Help him." Storm pleaded.

Asher was the only one who could now. Whatever Ithen had done, or his death had unlocked, Asher was the only person living or dead who could undo the hands of time to heal the invisible scars and give Cesa peace of mind.

Asher's eyes welled as they raked over Cesa. He stepped forward and crouched in front of the man he loved, tenderly wiping his cheeks of the unrelenting tears. "Why do you cry, my love?"

Cesa looked up and stared at Asher for what felt like an eternity. When he reached for him and his hand passed through a ghostly body, Cesa descended into heartbreaking sobs and clung to Rowan.

Rowan held his father and met Storm's gaze over the top of Cesa's head, tears slipping over his cheeks from ice blue eyes full of sadness. "I know your mother is waiting, but...can you give my father this?"

He didn't have to ask what Rowan meant, just as Rowan understood what Storm was offering. This was the only way to make Cesa whole, to give Rowan's father peace, to heal his own dad, and to repair what had been ripped apart. "I can give you *both* this gift," Storm said, glancing up at his dad, who only needed to say that he was ready. Storm didn't know the extent of his powers yet, but he was starting to do complex magic with an instinct he'd never had.

Asher reached for him, but stopped inches from Storm's arm and nodded. "Your mother and I were different creatures at our core. She passed into the abyss a long time ago to begin a new existence," he confessed, turning his loving gaze toward Cesa. "I never could."

Storm smiled, taking those words as the agreement he needed. He gathered his magic, building the intent in his mind as he touched Cesa's arm. "Are you ready to die, Cesa Copry, of your own free will, aware of the consequences?" he asked, needing his explicit consent before he risked something so intricate.

Cesa lifted his head to stare at Rowan with an unspoken question. The moment Rowan nodded to give his permission, Cesa's chin trembled, and he faced Asher. The look that passed between them was the look of two men who hadn't truly seen each other in decades. Cesa's brief nod was the answer Storm and his magic needed to bind his will to the spell.

Storm didn't want to ask aloud but spared another look at Rowan to make sure he was prepared for what this would mean. Rowan was focused on his father, desperately drinking in every last detail of his father's face, clutching his hand tightly as if to remember the feeling in years to come. With everyone aware of what was about to happen, Storm grasped Cesa's hands in both of his. "It's my honour to say that you will now have eternity together," he said, feeling like this was an ending rather than the beginning, but these two men were never meant to live without each other.

Using his magic and his will, Storm allowed his consciousness to sink into Cesa's body. He could feel the fatigue, the aches and consequences of Ithen's curse, the instability that proved Cesa would forever be confused and suffer the loss of self that was crueller than the dementia taking Mrs Sorrell.

Once Storm reached Cesa's heart, he allowed his magic to encase, squeeze, and pulse as the heart struggled to focus on its task. Cesa's colour paled, and his chest stuttered, his lungs struggling to find the next breath. Storm made sure his magic mimicked the regular heartbeat rhythm, then gradually slowed so that Cesa didn't feel pain or the difficulty of breathing. He wanted this to be a calm, careful transition to ease him into his next life.

Asher waited impatiently, glancing between Storm and Cesa, no doubt frustrated at being unable to help.

When Cesa sagged against Rowan's shoulder, he helped his father lie on the grass to be more comfortable. "I love you," Rowan said, taking this last moment to make sure there were no regrets. "Thank you for raising me so well, for protecting me from Ithen, and for letting me become who I am and not caring that I'm half-demon and not whole witch." His tears dripped onto his father's chest as he bent over him, struggling with the decision to let his father go.

Storm eased off the pressure on Cesa's heart to give them more time to say goodbye.

Cesa touched Rowan's cheek. "Thank you for never hating me, my Rowan tree. I was a terrible father, but I was living as half a man and you should never have borne the burden of half a father," he confessed, the dart of his gaze toward Asher proof that he was fully aware of who he was and who he'd become. He wasn't half a man because of Ithen's curse but because a part of him had died along with Asher Tera.

"I understand. I have someone now," Rowan replied, gripping his father's hand tightly. He glanced at Storm and squeezed Cesa's hand. "I understand."

Realising there was nothing left to say, Storm repeated the rhythmic, slow process of allowing Cesa to die a natural death. His human body would be unable to cope with the pressures and presence of dark magic for long, but Cesa never took his eyes off Rowan and Rowan never stopped staring at his father.

In that final moment, Storm heard someone take their final breath for the second time; this time, Cesa made the choice. He died with a smile on his face, his eyes glued to his devoted son.

As Storm extracted his magic from Cesa's body and removed his hand from the man's face, Rowan descended into a flood of tears. Instinct said to comfort him, but Storm had a feeling Rowan wasn't ready to be comforted; he wanted to feel this, to experience the full gamut of emotion before he let go. With quiet sobs, Rowan clutched his father's hand and waited while Storm closed Cesa's eyes and prepared for the next step.

When Cesa managed to depart from his body, he was the spitting image of the bright young man Storm had seen in his dad's memories. He emerged from his body with stumbling steps and almost tripped over his body's outstretched arm.

Asher caught him and both men stared in bewilderment as they realised they could touch. Asher cradled Cesa's face in both hands. "Hello again, my love," he said, rushing in to kiss him.

Storm may one day be embarrassed to see his dad kissing someone he'd believed to be his arch-nemesis, but the joy they shared was too beautiful to allow negative thoughts to intrude. Even Rowan laughed and reached across his father's forgotten body to take Storm's hand, uniting them in this moment of joyous grief.

Their fathers celebrated their long-awaited reunion, then both men returned their attention to their children. "We will see you soon, little Storm," Asher promised, taking a step back, his hand clasped tightly in Cesa's. He gazed adoringly at Asher but paused long enough to graze a kiss across Rowan's forehead.

Storm was overcome with a sense of right, beautiful and

heart-warming, to see the relief in Rowan's eyes that his father was happy, whole, and sane as he walked away with the man he loved: two men, once separated by the Fates, finally reunited.

Chapter Thirty-Four

GREGORY WAS THE first to offer his condolences, long after Cesa and Asher had departed for the abyss. With his help, Yael, Kyrie, and the white witches gathered to create a burst of blooms around Cesa's body. Intricate work and intense concentration were required, as each bloom was created and called forth from the ground by the white witches who chose to honour the leader of a circle coven.

While they worked, Rowan leaned his head on Storm's shoulder. He watched the flowers bloom around his father's body in peace. "You saved my father, saved magic, fulfilled the prophecy, and I was with you every step of the way. And *still* you don't love me?" he teased, lifting his head to turn those twinkling eyes in his direction.

Storm laughed and brushed the tears from Rowan's cheeks.

460 | Elaine White

Some were drying but new ones appeared at the care and respect given to his father by the other covens. "Be grateful I'm a cold-hearted ass or you wouldn't be here for me to kiss," he confessed, loving the sound of Rowan's laughter right before Storm did as he'd promised and kissed him, "and learn to love."

Watching the ceremony Cesa's burial had become, they had a few minutes of grace to be together, breathe, and accept that their lives had changed. With Rowan beside him, Storm could handle whatever came next, but he hoped he wouldn't have to. If the Fates were kind, they'd have time together where they could just be—boyfriends, friends, partners—whatever they wanted to be. Unlike their fathers, they had the whole of their lives to spend figuring out what that might be.

The night was peaceful, the wind calm, barely more than a breeze through the trees. There were whispers of *peace, honour* and *comfort* in the air, no doubt the wind reading the emotions of the gathered witches and responding to the general mood. The light rain when his dad appeared had lasted just a few seconds, welcoming Asher Tera back to the land of the living and clearing the way for a new beginning.

Storm decided he would ask the wind and rain to create a storm tonight, once everyone was inside and sleeping off the after-effects of the long day. The land would rejoice at having something to clear away the lingering bad omens that dark magic left behind, something to give the Copry land back to white magic.

*

ONCE CESA'S BURIAL was complete, his body encased in flowers and earth, the covens gathered for a final conference. They'd come here because of the draw of Storm's magic and because the prophecy had demanded their participation.

With Rowan by his side, Storm faced the gathered covens. "The prophecy was clear—when the covens resort to chaos, I will bring you to heel—and I intend to," he confessed, his voice much softer than the words required. "In a few days, I want us to meet at my dad's house. The Tera manor will become a neutral area, where no one shall perform magic without my permission. Only demons who require magic to pass between here and the abyss will be granted blanket permission."

Storm ignored Yael's nod of thanks and Kyrie's wry smile, because he felt that he owed the demons that allegiance, even without their friendship to inspire the decision. "Meet me in five days and we will discuss how to go forward into a future where we are equal, where magic will be used for good and where we can have equal say in how we protect our legacies," he said, needing their cooperation and agreement to change how the covens functioned. Only together could they change how they treated demons, how they used magic, and reset the balance between Light and Dark magic.

"What about my grandmother?" Gregory asked with curiosity but no sign of anger.

Some looked shocked that he'd mentioned her, but Storm was glad Gregory wasn't shying away from the reality of the Glade coven's problems. "I can ask the demons to return her body, if you want?" he offered, but Gregory shook his head, and Storm realised the true meaning of his words. "I understand the threat, Gregory. I appreciate that you're willing to face the potential fallout head-on. Yael will work with you to explore the magic within your coven and determine those your grandmother may have corrupted or used magic against. Traitors will be dealt with according to their crimes." He was well aware that anyone who had worked with her would lie, but Yael would always find the truth, no matter how well hidden.

For the sake of the other covens, Storm clarified his meaning in the hope that no one would bother Gregory with questions. Gladys was still his grandmother, and he would still grieve her loss, even if she had brought him more trouble and responsibility than he'd been ready for. "Gladys has been using dark magic illegally. She may have taught others to do the same, so be kind to those who survive this night. They will need all the support they can get," he warned, letting them know they shouldn't judge anyone before Yael had made their assessment. Just as Cesa had been manipulated under their very noses, no one knew the extent of Ithen and Gladys's corruption.

Storm looked around those gathered, pleased they were on board, and wished them goodnight. He was mentally and physically exhausted, and he wanted to go home, sleep, and start a new life.

Rowan walked beside him, while Yael made sure the witches

and mages left peacefully. Kyrie paused by Cesa's graveside to touch a bare patch of soil, where a white rose rooted through the dirt and bloom into the moonlight.

Storm slipped his hand into Rowan's and led the way to the house, to their bed, and to sleep.

"If your house will be a no magic area," Rowan spoke with curiosity and a playful smile, "where will you live? Because I've noticed you sometimes use magic in your sleep." He flashed those flirty ice blue eyes at Storm, making his heart flutter at the teasing.

Resisting the urge to kiss him senseless—one that he would indulge in tomorrow—Storm gave a careless shrug. "After fulfilling a prophecy for you, saving your father, and resurrecting you, you won't let me live in your house?" He gasped in mock shock and disappointment. His heart sang when Rowan burst into a fit of tired chuckles and a snort that made his day.

Rowan stopped walking and dragged him by his jumper into a long and deep kiss. He melted into the contact, taking a firm grip of Rowan's hips to keep him close. When they broke away with matching smiles, Storm burst the bubble with rationality.

"While I love the idea of living with you, I think we have to find space for Yael. Once we bond, I doubt we'll get rid of them," he admitted, fully intending to bond within the next month. That would give them time to recover from recent events and time for Yael to adjust to being a higher demon, a revelation they would need to talk about tomorrow.

"Don't worry. The four of us have to stick together," Rowan

agreed and took his hand in a firm grip to resume their walk. "I thought we could shock the white witch world with a scandal?"

"Such as?"

Rowan looked up with a smile. "I thought I'd bond with Kyrie, if he'll have me." He positively skipped up the front steps of the house, pulling Storm along like a kid who had been given the greatest gift in the world.

"We'll have to be careful how we tell them. They might burst with excitement. Kyrie especially." The demon was the most excitable person he knew, second only to Denver during a movie marathon.

"That could be messy." Rowan laughed, carefree and unburdened despite all that had happened today. He'd lost his father, his life, and didn't seem to care about either because he'd gotten them both back. Leading the way up the main stairs, Rowan's pace suggested the last of his energy was waning. Storm offered magic through their connected hands to keep him moving long enough to get to their bed.

"We end the way we started, huh? The three of us together? With a new toy for Yael to obsess about?" he teased, the picture far sweeter than he'd imagined, and well beyond anything his lonely, bitter future self could have hoped for. Storm was no longer alone; he had Rowan and Yael back in his life, just as it should have been all these years and could be again. The addition of Kyrie, and he presumed Haven would be coming around more often, plus his rekindled and strengthened friendships with Foley and Denver, suggested the future was much brighter than he'd ever dreamed.

"Only, this time, we get our happily ever after."

Storm snorted and pushed open the bedroom door. "You forget Yael is a demon who just put a fist through someone's chest. Happily may be too much to ask, but I'm sure our lives will be interesting."

Rowan turned at the last moment and froze, quirking an eyebrow at the bed, where they found Midnight lazily sprawled across the covers.

As the least weird sight of the day, Storm wasn't surprised Rowan nudged the kitten aside and drew back the covers. He didn't have the mental energy to deal with the fact Midnight had coughed up the amulet, stayed long enough to fuss over Rowan, and slipped away without anyone noticing, despite being left in Kyrie's capable hands. How the cat got into a room and managed to shut the door behind her wasn't something he wanted to dissect.

"Just don't go dying on me again. I'm not sure I can resurrect you a second time," Storm cautioned as he pulled off his jumper and T-shirt to toss into the corner. He'd worry about washing later though he had a feeling both he and Rowan would want to burn their clothes. Rowan had died in them, and Storm never wanted to see them again.

Rowan huffed as he struggled out of his T-shirt, crinkled his nose at the potent smell, and threw the offending garment across the room. "Are you doubting yourself again?" he asked, slipping off his jeans and crawling into bed beside Storm.

"No." Storm turned onto his side and propped up with his elbow to stare at Rowan. "I just realised something terrifying," he admitted, getting lost to the thought of what Rowan might think. Rowan cocked his head, curious but not rushing him, as he clasped Storm's hand to his chest, his eyes drooping with fatigue. Storm bit his bottom lip and mentally processed the words. He wanted to be sure they were real this time, but he didn't have to worry; he felt more sure of this than anything he'd ever felt. "I already love you more now than I did. Maybe I'll love you more tomorrow than I do now. So...don't go dying, okay?"

There would be no bringing him back a second time. Dark One, Necromancer, Prophecy Child; nothing Storm was or was capable of could resurrect someone he loved with his whole heart.

Rowan's cheeks burned with a blush as he ducked his head to kiss Storm's knuckles. "I promise."

Epilogue

Ten Years Later

October 31, 2036

"DID YAEL MESS with the playlist again?" Storm asked as the thumping beat of MC Hammer's "Addams Groove" filled the living room.

Rowan's smile gave him away before he burst out laughing and started shaking his ass to the beat. "Nope. This one was all me."

If he wasn't so damned sexy, Storm would curse him with a binding spell for the next hour, to make sure he wasn't busting any of his horrendous moves all over the party.

Across the room, Foley dragged Denver onto the dance floor in the middle of the room while Gregory resisted his wife's attempts to get him to join in. He lasted until their five-year-old daughter begged her daddy to dance, because no one resisted Angela for long, not even the hardcore demons.

By far the cutest couple on the dance floor were their parents. Storm would have given a wave or a nod of greeting, but Asher and Cesa only had eyes for each other as they slow danced in the corner of the room. They'd decided not to cross-over because they wanted to enjoy a few decades regaining their lost time before they took the risk of their souls being reborn into a new body and potentially not finding each other again.

Storm doubted they could hear the ridiculous tune the kids were dancing to and gave the parents fond memories. He had a fair few of his own, but they had nothing to do with the song.

When Kyrie encouraged Rowan to dance, neither hesitated. They truly had become a family over the last ten years, as they said they would. Yael stood guard, as usual, crouched on top of the chaise by the window with their scythe as a fancy-dress prop rather than a weapon. Yael and Kyrie had spent the first few years after the prophecy was fulfilled hunting every demon trapped by a bond they had never consented to. Yael had killed a few of the evil mages and one white witch who tried to kill them, but they generally behaved themselves and allowed Kyrie to determine the punishments. When the information was gathered, Yael informed Storm through a mental link they'd formed when they bonded, and he would contact the nearest coven they could trust to handle the situation.

Yael was certain the human side of witches and mages made them believe they could subjugate demons, not the power or strength of their magic. Yael had remained convinced they would continue to discover demons being held captive by cursed bonds. After five years, people started getting the message and toeing the line to acknowledge what Storm would and wouldn't tolerate.

Storm let Yael believe whatever gave them purpose because they didn't need to protect him from much, and he didn't ever want to doubt their instincts about their kind. Yael was a higher demon now, more powerful than they'd ever been, and Storm trusted them with his life.

Haven had escaped mostly unscathed. He stood by the fireplace, always a wallflower during events because he hated being the centre of attention, only someone had cornered him. Storm smiled to find Haven blushing while a young dark mage peppered him with questions, happy to see the two young men talking and flirting. Haven had matured into a full-fledged adult just two years ago, and he should take the time to spread his metaphorical wings and figure out what he wanted from life.

"You okay?"

Storm accepted a glass of whiskey from Gregory. "Just nostalgia. I love having everyone together." It was nearly ten years to the day when his life changed forever. In two days, it would be exactly ten years since he travelled through time to fix his past, found a new love of his life, a new best friend, and succeeded in fulfilling the prophecy he'd failed to complete the first time around.

It didn't feel like ten years, but the proof was all around him; in how big Haven had grown, in Gregory's growing family, even in the amount of people who showed up to their holiday party.

"Scott says he's handing over leadership," Gregory said, surprising Storm with the unexpected segue. Mrs Sorrell had died just two years ago, on the sixth anniversary of when she'd gone into the nursing home Scott had been forced to put her into. He'd known Scott had been struggling since her death, but he hadn't expected him to step down. "He says he's starting to show signs of memory loss. He thinks the dementia might be hereditary, and he wants to pass on the mantle before he makes the same mistakes his mother did."

"Damn." Storm had suspected there was a reason Scott kept refusing to join them for councils and meetings, even declining the invitation for tonight. If he'd known why, Storm would have gone round to visit and talk with him in private. "The Sorrell's were stronger under his leadership," he confessed, absently wondering who may be ready to take over. His niece Claudia had the same strong talents Mrs Sorrell had, but the older boys Matthew or George had considerable potential to be more level-headed and share leadership between them.

Shaking his head at the sad news, he was about to ask Gregory if he had any hint of when the change might take place so he could be there, when Angela rushed over to hug his knees.

"Papa, come dance with me?" she asked, clearly refusing to let Gregory slip away.

With a wry smile of apology, Gregory took her hand and led her onto the dance floor.

Denver was nearby with the two-year-old little boy he and Foley had adopted last month. Both were trying to encourage Donnie to join in with the other kids. He was so shy that he hadn't danced to a single song all night, despite Rowan making sure to have lots of kid-friendly entertainment.

His parents had been the last of their coven and left a next-of-kin contact that named Storm as the boy's guardian and carer, if anything happened to them. When that happened—a spell gone wrong, he was told—Donnie was only a few weeks old. He'd been brought to Storm after undergoing tests to make sure he was well, and he and Rowan had taken custody of the sweet boy. That lasted for almost three weeks before Denver begged Storm to let them adopt. He and Foley had been married eight years now and he couldn't think of two better parents.

Kyrie had named him Donnie, in honour of Donald, the demon they'd fallen in love with, before they knew his real name was Haven. The name had stuck and once Denver knew the story, he refused to change his mind. Storm loved seeing them together, a happy family eager to embark on a new adventure together.

This room was full of love, old and new. Storm couldn't have asked for anything better to celebrate Halloween, his upcoming birthday and a celebration of ten years since the day he fulfilled the prophecy and took his place as the Dark One, to become the Champion of the Fates.

*

"DO WE HAVE to do this?"

Rowan glared and shuffled his tarot cards before laying the deck at the side of the table. "This is our Halloween tradition. We do it every year," he argued, ignoring Yael's snuff of amusement as they disappeared upstairs with Kyrie.

Choosing to ignore their early departure, Storm narrowed his gaze at his husband. "I had *other* plans for the night." Plans that involved going to bed early and not sleeping for a few hours.

A faint flush rose on Rowan's neck, even after all these years. "Reading your cards has never taken more than a few minutes. A few more to cleanse the room, then we can go to bed," he replied, his eyes slowly morphing from cornflower to ice blue, letting Storm know that his husband was in full agreement for how to spend the last of the night.

Storm dutifully pulled the top card of the deck to place, face up, on the left. Without pausing to look, he chose the second card for the centre of the table, adding the third on the right. "What do you see?" Storm asked, having never mastered the art of reading the cards. They usually always said something along the lines of *death, danger* and *rebirth*. Since all three were closely linked to necromancy, five times out of ten even Rowan, with his talent for the cards, couldn't get much sense from a reading.

Rowan touched his fingers to the cards and pouted in curiosity. "Your mother has left you a message," he said, pausing long enough to touch the centre card, turn it upside down and move on to touch the last. Whatever he did to the cards, he read them in a way Storm had never seen before, feeling their intentions and Storm, through his contact with the cards. A light laugh escaped those kissable lips as Rowan shot him a look of warning. "Seems she crossed over. This time she got her happy ending."

Storm didn't have to ask what that meant; Asher had told him the story enough times. Knowing Veronica could reunite with the man she'd loved with her whole heart, without anyone getting in the way, was the best gift Rowan could have given him.

"He waited for her," Rowan said, tapping the central card, with a glance through his dark eyelashes that set Storm's heart aflame. "Your family is notorious for lingering in the abyss for their dead lovers."

"You know death doesn't mean much to us," he confessed, having been willing to sacrifice his life to save Rowan's more than once over the years. Rowan had sworn to do the same more times than his heart could bear. Storm thanked the gods he'd never had to resurrect his husband again, because the riot of love between them would leave them trying the impossible...again. He'd break the abyss apart and stick a knife in the Fates, willing to do any-thing, including the downright deadly, to keep Rowan by his side.

Rowan rose to his feet, his eyes crinkling with happiness. "I know I said we'd be quick, but I forgot I asked the Hadley nephews to wait behind."

Because he genuinely regretted forgetting, Storm kept his mouth shut and followed his husband from the study to the main room. The two Hadley nephews sat on the sofa, listening to one of Asher's stories about his ascension while Midnight lay across their laps, fat, lazy, and content.

"Sorry to interrupt," Rowan apologised while Storm crossed to the bookcase to retrieve the Hadley grimoire. "We were going to turn in, but we have something for the boys."

Cesa and Asher said goodnight and disappeared into the abyss without complaint, leaving the Hadley boys staring in wonder.

Storm thought the whole night must have been a revelation for them, if two spirits could shock them. Clearing his throat, he crossed to where they sat and perched on the sofa opposite. Both boys were startlingly alike, almost twins, and each resembled Reed Hadley in different ways. Though they'd been kept from their dark mage uncle because their father thought him dangerous, they'd accepted Storm's invitation tonight, which gave him hope.

He and Yael had spent a lot of time studying the boys and their abilities over the years, making sure they only gave Reed's grimoire to witches or mages who could be trusted. Reed's brother had been oblivious and done more harm than good because Storm knew on first sight that both boys had an affinity for dark magic.

With the boys having recently turned twenty-one, Storm felt sure he could finally do what he'd always intended to without regret or worry. Holding the book in both hands, Storm smiled as Rowan sat beside him. They faced the boys together, needing to impart the seriousness of the gift they were about to receive.

"Your uncle is the reason I won the war, fulfilled the prophecy, and am sitting here today," Storm said, wanting them to understand how important their uncle was. "I found everything I ever needed to know about dark magic in here. He wrote in a way that speaks to how I use my magic, and he's been the only mentor I ever had who could help me control and bond with my abilities."

Rowan smiled, warm and supportive, as he lay a hand on Storm's knee. He understood better than anyone how true his words were. Until Rowan and Yael helped him find his way, he'd been floundering and lost, unable to connect with the magic inside him.

"This is your family grimoire, gifted to me by Reed's demon, who loved your uncle dearly and wanted his legacy and hard work to live on. I've tried to honour that wish, and now I hope you two will find the answers you need in its pages, the same way I did," Storm said, handing over the book that had saved his life on far too many occasions.

The boys stared in awe, both reaching for the book. Storm watched as they accepted joint responsibility for the tome and hoped they would honour their uncle the way he deserved.

"I'm starting a school," Rowan added, taking Storm's hand to show this was something they stood firm in. "We'll open to kids with dark magic who don't have access to proper teachers or guidance. Storm and I will be giving lessons in a summer school format—you practice magic and learn from the books we've found useful. You'll get the chance to speak to real demons and spirits about how to use dark magic the right way."

The Hadley boys didn't hesitate to express their thanks and ask to join the classes. They'd been kept from dark magic for too long, but Storm knew they would learn all they needed to know shortly. Between his knowledge, Rowan's books and Yael's love of bossing people about, they'd catch up. As they rose to leave, taking the grimoire with them, Storm breathed a sigh of relief to have finally accomplished what Reed would have wanted.

Rowan slid a hand over Storm's thigh. "Let's go to bed." The twinkle in his eye from earlier reappeared as though he couldn't have been happier to be alone. Rowan stood and left the room. Storm wasn't far behind, watching Rowan reach the stairs and start running, laughing as his jumper came floating down. Two more steps and his shoes tumbled behind. By the time Storm caught the distinctive clink of a belt, he was already running after his husband.

At the top of the stairs, he practically fell against Rowan, who was leaning against the bedroom door, waiting for him. "Happy anniversary, my precious demon."

Rowan melted with affection as he sank into Storm's arms and kissed him. He pulled away too soon and traced a thumb over Storm's lips. "Nine years," he said on a sigh. "I can't wait for the next nine hundred."

"Nine hundred?" Storm laughed, reaching past him to grab the door handle. "Do you have an immortality spell you never told me about?" he asked, easing the door open so Rowan could back into the bedroom.

"No." Rowan lay his arms over Storm's shoulders, the heady look threatening to take his breath away. "I have a necromancer husband who will never let me die. No matter what happens, I'll wait for you in the abyss, as you would wait for me. We'll have eternity together, which is better than immortality."

"Absolutely." Storm sealed the promise with a kiss...to love, to wait, to never let Rowan die. Each one was a promise he intended to keep. He hadn't failed Rowan yet, and he didn't intend to. As long as his soul still existed, he would never let them be torn apart and would spend the rest of his physical or spiritual life fighting to prevent the death of Rowan Copry.

Acknowledgements

First and foremost, thanks to my parents. I can't count the number of times I complained about this book, when I was working on the first, twelfth, and twentieth draft, then again when I began edits.

Thank you to everyone at NSP for taking the time and energy to talk plot with me. Thanks to my editor, BJ, for reining in my commas and other grammar nemeses.

Thanks to my friends on Facebook, who saw snippets of the first draft and told me to publish NOW, and tolerated the two-year wait while I battled edits.

And, as always, thanks to my readers, who continually take a chance on my work.

About the Author

Elaine White is the author of multi-genre MM romance, celebrating 'love is love' and offering diversity in both genre and character within her stories.

Growing up in a small town and fighting cancer in her early teens taught her that life is short and dreams should be pursued. She lives vicariously through her independent, and often hellion characters, exploring all possibilities within the romantic universe.

The Winner of two Watty Awards—Collector's Dream (*An Unpredictable Life*) and Hidden Gem (*Faithfully*)—and an Honourable Mention in 2016's Rainbow Awards (*A Royal Craving*), Elaine is a self-professed geek, reading addict, and a romantic at heart.

Other NineStar books by this author

Surviving Vihaan Series

A Recipe for Love

A Touch of Danger

Raised by Wolves

Bitten by the Bond

CONNECT WITH NINESTAR PRESS

Website: NineStarPress.com
Facebook: NineStarPress
X: @ninestarpress
Instagram: NineStarPress
BlueSky: NineStarPress
Threads: @ninestarpress

www.ingramcontent.com/pod-product-compliance
Lightning Source LLC
Chambersburg PA
CBHW060301100726
47907CB00002B/235